THE STRAY PRINCE

ELLA FIELDS

Copyright © 2021 by Ella Fields

All rights reserved.

ISBN: 9798581007105

No part of this book may be reproduced, copied, resold or distributed in any form, or by any electronic or mechanical means, without permission in writing from the author, except for brief quotations within a review.

This book is a work of fiction.

Names, characters, businesses, organizations, places, events and incidents are either the product of the author's imagination or used in a fictitious manner. Any resemblance to actual persons, living or dead is entirely coincidental.

Editor: Jenny Sims, Editing4Indies
Proofreading: Book Nerd Services
Formatting: Stacey Blake, Champagne Book Design
Cover design: Sarah Hansen, Okay Creations

For my children.
The most magical of all my creations.
You are the reason I keep going when I feel as though I can't.
Thank you for always finding me in the darkness and bringing me back to our beautiful life.
Also, if you ever see this, stop right here and put the damn book down.
I mean it.

A storm won't calm
until the damage is done

ONE

Audra

THE BLISTERING ICE UNFURLED BENEATH MY FEET, spreading toward the pink tinge upon the horizon. Stars began to wink out, the moon a fading ember in the lightening sky.

My breath shook from my lungs, clouding the air before me. My feet traversed the ice as though it were nothing but a cool slab of concrete. A slab of concrete that stretched farther toward the changing sky with every step taken. On either side of me, rolling waves lapped by, their salt-misted spray ricocheting off the frozen barrier.

Perhaps they were here, buried and veiled by the Gray Sea. Perhaps he would reveal himself to me, so I kept my gaze firmly upon the ice that grew inches at a time, seemingly out of nowhere.

But no, that wasn't right.

Or maybe it was. Maybe I was nowhere, and whatever path I was paving was leading me somewhere. Somewhere with creatures with bright red eyes, vibrant green hair, and long, slender hands. Soft, those hands. Softer than I'd have ever thought possible for a creature who could supposedly peel the flesh from the bones of men before using those bones to pry said flesh from their razor-sharp teeth.

I snorted, even as trepidation knocked at the base of my spine and dragged shadowed fingers over my vision. I told it to go away. For although we were all flesh and bone, I was no mortal.

I was a queen, and if they'd planned to make a meal out of

me, then surely they wouldn't have wrapped those strangely elegant hands around my slashed open limbs to preserve what little life I'd had left. To help me survive all those months ago.

So where were they, I wondered, pursing my lips against the gust of wind that howled before me.

A thud, and then a crack to the left of my feet. Slowing, I tilted my head and spied a long shadow beneath the frosted ice. It darted away before I could make out what it was.

And then it came.

Not a mermaid, but a male.

A male I knew all too well—a male whose face I'd recognize anywhere. Staring back at me through the glass, his expression blurred and shifted but those eyes... such unmistakable eyes.

Like burning gold, they were clear and easy to see but not so easy to read.

And wasn't that so often the case. Zadicus Allblood, the infamous lord of the east, my lover turned linked one, gave only what he wanted you to see, and one of his many skills was concealing that of which he did not.

Only now, his face might have been the same, as far as I could tell with half of it veiled in shifting shadow, but his hair was not. Bending low, I splayed my hand upon the ice. "Zad?" I asked, and then he was gone.

And darkness took hold.

The sun was melting the burning glass beneath my cheek. A gull's shriek pierced the wintry air, and I startled, pushing upright. My hands slapped at the patch of ice I'd been asleep on, my eyes protesting the harsh glow of early morning as I blinked, taking in my location.

Water. I was in the middle of the water, halfway to the looming mountains that gave entrance to the mass of sea beyond. Squinting, I absorbed the castle in the distance, the giant mountains at its rear—the entire city of Allureldin small enough to make my stomach churn.

Onlookers, tiny little pinpricks back ashore, were likely gawking, and then there was the male racing toward me. His hair was disheveled, shirt too, as though he'd woken and thrown himself out of bed, out of the castle.

A tremor raced through my stiff hands as I slowly forced myself to my feet to backtrack over the frosted path of my own making.

Zad met me in the middle. "Audra." Warm hands clasped my face. His breath as he said my name was a plume of welcoming heat. Frenzied golden eyes held a feral gleam, soaking me in. "What," he started, his throat bobbing before he tried again, his hold on my cheeks tightening. "What in the darkness are you doing out here?"

I didn't know. I did, but I didn't, and my heart became a thing with scales and weapons, trying to defend itself from the beating given by my flaring panic. "I... I don't know," I said, my voice hoarse. I repeated myself if only to be sure I was truly awake and that he was real this time. "I don't know."

Zad's brows hovered low over his eyes, his jaw flexing. Flicking a glance at the gently lapping water, he released a breath that seemed to carry too much weight, yet his shoulders were still taut, as was his voice. "Come, let's get you home."

With his arm around my waist, we crossed the melting, cracking ice, being mindful to watch our step.

"You're not wearing shoes," he said, so soft and almost as if to himself.

"I know, but I'm fine." My skin did not burn or stick or slide. If anything, it warmed, and he knew that.

A moment passed, and a sheet of ice cracked in two near the shore. More appeared with a jumbled thought, connecting the pieces, and we crossed to the sand with ease.

Mercifully, there weren't as many people gathered as one would think, likely thanks to the early hour. Still, I kept my head low, allowing Zad to answer the questions shot our way.

"What was her majesty doing out there?" a young child asked. "It's too cold to swim."

"Is she all right?" another asked.

"Is she fevered?"

"She is fine," Zad responded, tone curt enough to curb further questions.

When we reached the city streets, he bent down, and I didn't protest as he hefted me into his arms. I clung to him, exhausted and confused, as he trudged through alleyways and dodged puddles upon the cobblestone.

Low, he murmured, "Sleepwalking?"

No other explanation existed for how I'd wound up asleep on a path made of ice in the early hours of morning in the middle of the bay. Or the other two times I'd found myself in odd places.

"I suppose I did," I said, frowning at the collar of his shirt, which curled under the fabric as if he'd dressed with extreme haste.

The tension leaking from every facet of him was enough to make my eyes close and withhold the befuddling truth. That I couldn't understand it. It was as though another shadow had joined my own, and I struggled to make sense of what was happening. I loathed the idea of admitting so out loud.

A weakness. A queen easily tricked and lured.

I'd vowed to figure it out on my own before I gave voice to something that already held too much power. For the smothering feeling that still clung to me warned that to do such a thing without proper knowledge and a plan was to invite more trouble than we could afford.

Zad didn't allow me to remain silent for long, though. Ignoring Mintale's concern and barking at him to wait when he suggested he'd call for Truin, he stalked into my rooms and laid me upon the bed.

Listening to the sound of the bath being drawn, I peeled off my nightgown with unfeeling fingers.

Zad returned, but I was already walking to the bathing room, my hands hitting his chest. "It's okay."

"It's okay?" he repeated, as though I'd just lied through my teeth.

For I had, but I didn't care to allow myself the room to worry so much that I'd disappear inside it. "Plenty of people sleepwalk."

"Royals do not sleepwalk," he stated, rough and matter-of-fact. "Monarchs with powers such as yours *do not* sleepwalk."

I kept my eyes on his chest, watching the way it rose and fell, sharp and harsh with each breath. He stepped back, and my hands dropped.

Shaking my lavender-scented salts into the rising water, he gestured for me. I traipsed over the mosaic floor, not rebutting his touch as he reached out to make sure I was okay climbing in.

"You are too calm," he said, grabbing a cloth and dousing it in water. "Too quiet. This has happened before."

Steam rose into the air, the warm water doing little to thaw me. The ice inside my veins turned leaden, so heavy and still that for what might have been the first time, I felt cold—chilled to the marrow of my bones.

I swallowed, knowing I should've known better than to think I could keep that from him. And why I'd want to... I wasn't yet ready to dissect that. Perhaps I wanted to know why it was happening first. Perhaps the extreme lack of control mixed with the desire to find out what these dreams wanted was reason enough for me to hide it. To keep it to myself.

Of course, keeping anything to oneself when you had linked—formed a bond of both the heart and soul—with another was virtually impossible.

He could feel my unease as surely as I could feel his worry as if it were a second skin blanketing us.

Zad's silent fury filled the room as he washed me. "When?" A short, clipped word.

"Four nights ago," I admitted.

"And before then?"

I'd have rolled my eyes, but I couldn't muster the effort after spending too much energy creating ice strong enough to keep the sea at bay. I stared at the faucet, hardly feeling the rough fabric of the cloth as Zad gestured for me to sit forward and washed my back. "Two weeks ago."

He stilled, water dripping as he leaned away. "So it's becoming more frequent." Again, he'd seemed to mutter the words to himself. "Where did you wind up those times?" He began to wash me again, his gentle touch a stark contrast to the brittle anxiety darkening his eyes and tensing his limbs.

"In the kitchens. I was in the pantry," I said, almost smiling as I remembered the shock on Foelda's face when she'd opened the doors and the abrupt explosion of sunlight woke me.

After long breaths of silence, Zad wrung the cloth out, then offered it for me to clean my face. "I thought you'd risen before me. Yet you came to the dining room looking as though you'd just gotten out of bed."

I'd still been in my nightclothes. "The time before that, I was on the balcony at the end of the hall from my rooms." No one had found me then. Alone, I'd stumbled back inside and straight to my chambers to wash the fear and confusion away.

He cursed, vicious and violent, and I finally smiled, gazing up at him while he rose, turning in half circles over the damp floor while raking his fingers through his unkempt hair.

"Zad," I said, but he seemed to need a minute. Frowning, I gave it to him and climbed out.

He snapped out of his furious trance then and quickly unfolded a towel, wrapping it around me and then carrying me to bed.

"I can walk just fine."

"Quiet," he said, a loaded exhale coating the word.

I pinched my lips, rolling them between my teeth as he patted me dry. "Do you wish to brush my hair, too?" I offered with a snide tone. "Braid it, perhaps?"

Stopping, he looked around. "Where's the brush?"

I groaned. "Oh, for the love of darkness."

But the lord didn't seem to hear or pay any notice to me. He'd spied the brush upon my dressing table and swiftly collected it before taking a seat behind me on the bed to detangle my hair.

With gentle worry, he coaxed the bristles through the damp strands over and over, his silent thoughts overflowing and drowning the air with their intensity. Too cold, lost to my own concerns, I stared at the charred hearth, wondering if my soul was so much the same that I was beginning to lose myself.

I was almost too afraid to ask, but fear and I had never seen eye to eye, and I wasn't about to welcome it now. "Do you think I'm starting to..."

"No," Zad said, immediate and blunt.

My father had hundreds of years on me before his mind had begun to unravel, but I'd never known him to sleepwalk. I hadn't really known him at all. "But—"

"It's not that."

My teeth clacked as I snapped, "How would you know? What else could it be?"

Zad continued with the long strokes. The coarse hair of the brush trailing over my pebbling skin soothed, even if only a little. He set it down after a time, then turned me to pull my legs over his knees.

I was nearly naked, the towel falling open and draping over one breast, but he didn't seem to notice. His eyes, molten gold, were hard on mine as he gripped my face. "We'll fix this," he said, the words a promise I so desperately wanted to believe.

And I did believe him. For almost seven months, he'd scarcely left my side. He'd not only held to his oath of proving my stance when it came to males and love wrong, but he'd given me something other than myself to believe in.

Him.

My eyes fell closed, my hands lifting to cover his on my cheeks.

Warm, unyielding, and huge, I clung to them and drew in a lungful of his mint and winter morning scent. His touch, that scent, and his proximity... I settled deeper into his lap, my arms banding around his neck as the towel fell away.

He knew what I wanted, could scent the way it seeped through my pores and rolled off my skin. Heated breath rushed over my lips, his nostrils flaring. "What do you need?"

Smiling into his hungry eyes, I dragged my nose alongside his, my heart stalling when his eyelids fluttered. "You."

"You have me," he rasped, his hands sliding around my waist, squeezing. "Take what you want."

Freeing him from his pants, I watched his long lashes spread and felt the falter of his heart and the violent hitch of his exhale as I reached between us and impaled myself.

I needed this. Even without the horror of losing myself to dreams that dragged me from him, from the safety of my castle, I'd forever need *this*.

We were kindling who could only lay nestled close for so long without that spark igniting, the bond between us kerosene that would forever catch fire, no matter what ailed us.

His voice hoarse with desire, those eyes glinting, I seated myself fully and moaned, dragging my lips across his. "Love me."

A hand returned to my face, a calloused thumb rubbing over the puckered skin at the corner of my mouth, his own skimming mine. "For all eternity."

TWO

Audra

I woke to find Zad in the armchair with a book open on his lap, but his gaze fixed on the window across the bed. I knew from the absent glow in his eyes that he hadn't read a single word.

They dropped to me when I stretched my arms above my head, and asked, "Time?"

"Lunch," he said, closing the book and resting it upon the arm of the chair. "You should eat."

His hair was deliciously tousled, his shirt missing. My teeth dragged over my bottom lip as I eyed the broad planes of his chest, the muscle that rippled when he stood.

To my dismay, he plucked up his tunic and shouldered it on. "No more. I'll get you something to eat."

With a huff, I sat up and threw the bedding back, bypassing him to my dressing room. "I'm not a child."

"Believe me," he purred, behind me in an instant, his voice and breath a hot caress over my bare shoulder. "I'm well aware."

Selecting a burgundy gown with gold threading in the belled sleeves and over the chest, Zad waited for me to quit glaring, his patience unending.

Snarling, I lifted my arms, and once he'd pulled the dress over my body, I found his unreadable expression had changed into that of a semi-satisfied lord. Sinful lips curled, lighting those eyes with a fire that both maddened and endeared.

My annoyance slipped away like water over a cliff, and I

wrapped my arms around his waist, fluttering my lashes up at him. "You're so incredibly infuriating." The words were venom laced in sugar.

He brushed my hair back from my face, grinning like the arrogant predator he was. "You're so incredibly beautiful. Come," he said, stepping back and clasping my hand. "If you won't stay in bed and rest, then you'll at least head to the dining room to eat."

He waited while I slipped my feet into silken black slippers, then tucked my arm into his as we left my rooms. "All this isn't necessary," I said between my lips, nodding at Garris as he passed by. He dipped low, smiling, but it didn't touch his eyes as they roamed me quickly. Undoubtedly, he'd heard about what had happened. I was sure most of the guard and city had by now. That grated, and far more than I cared to admit.

I'd never been one to worry over the opinions of sheep until I'd come to realize that those loyal to me were so much more than that.

"Lord," I said when Zad didn't respond.

Tension still oozed from him like a hovering storm cloud, but his tone was casual, bored even. "Until we've nailed the reason for what is happening, if I deem it necessary, then it is."

His choice of words didn't go unnoticed, but before I could argue, he continued, "You are the heart of this kingdom, this continent, and more importantly..." He stopped outside the dining room a little way from the guards stationed at the doors. Cupping my cheeks, eyes boring into mine, he whispered, "You are my heart, and though I and many others know you're more than capable of taking care of yourself, darkness only knows what could've happened to you during any of these..." He halted, swallowing. "Instances."

Instances. The word tugged my brows low, and he smoothed them with his thumbs, then tilted my head back for a swift brush of his lips over mine before steering me into the dining room.

I wanted to scream at him, knowing he meant well, but not caring to be treated like some prized jewel when I could indeed fend for myself.

But I couldn't. I couldn't protest because that thing, that insidious crawling *thing* that haunted, reminded me I wasn't in control. This wasn't something I could control, not unless I planned to never sleep again.

My pesky lord was right. I couldn't threaten, torture, and kill something I could not see.

Zad froze in the doorway, that tension heightening tenfold when Truin turned from the far window. Steaming plates of fish stew, soups, and dishes laden with fruit sprawled across the table.

Across it, she curtsied, her milky brown eyes filled with concern as they beheld me. "My queen, I heard what happened."

Zad growled, releasing me to turn on Mintale as he entered the room behind us.

Mintale sputtered, his hands in the air, and skirted around the male who seemed ready to tear him limb from limb. "I didn't send for her, my lord. I-I swear."

The outburst, his anger, shocked me. "Zadicus," I hissed, regaining some much-needed ice. "Leave him be."

Mintale headed for my chair, but Zad beat him to it and flicked his hand to the door, dismissing him. Mintale wasn't his to dismiss, and he knew it, but he was angered to the point of not caring.

Mintale looked from the snarling male to me, and I sighed, nodding.

He left the room, and I took my seat, waiting until Zad had draped a napkin over my lap and taken his own before I said, "Truin, sit."

Zad snatched a piece of bread, tearing it in half with a savageness that caused most of it to fall into crumbs on his plate.

Truin seated herself beside me, her nerves evident in the way she kept her hands in her lap and her shoulders pulled right back.

With a calm I did not feel, I reached for the stew, but Zad grabbed it first. I lifted a brow. "What does it matter if Mintale called for Truin?"

So focused, so tense I wondered if his teeth might crack, he filled my bowl, then reached for more bread to butter.

"Zadicus," I said, my quiet tone giving away my waning patience.

He set the small plate before me, then steepled his hands beneath his chin. I could almost hear his teeth grinding. Finally, he exhaled, then muttered, "It matters for reasons I cannot yet disclose."

My brows jumped, and I tilted my head. "You dance around the truth."

He refused to look at me, and I noticed Truin eye him with a hefty amount of shock and skepticism. She opened her mouth to ask him something, by the looks of it, but the lord of the east rose swiftly, almost slamming his chair into the wall.

He righted it, dipping as he crossed to me to press his mouth to my forehead. "Apologies, my queen. I'll leave you to enjoy lunch with your friend." He was marching out of the room before I could even think to ask him what in the darkness had taken hold of him.

Truin watched the doors sway closed, then reached for some soup. "Is it just me, or does your lord seem to be getting more... territorial?"

"Like a beast you cannot train," I muttered, irritated by his actions and the many questions sailing through my mind.

Truin laughed, the sound tinkling like rain over a windowpane. Rolling some bread, she dipped it into the creamy broth. "He was indeed dancing around the truth."

I lifted the bowl to my lips, suddenly too starved to worry over decency. "I know."

We ate in silence for stretched minutes, the guards at the doors staring at the walls, the red and gray tapestry and drapes unmoving. Even the heat had quit rising from the food before us. A glance out the window showed clear skies, unmarred by snowflakes, drizzle, or wind.

Everything was too still, eerily so, as though one breath could cause a violent storm to roll in before we were ready for it.

Staring at them, I wondered if the guards questioned the same over the unnatural silence or if I was the only one who sensed it. Then, for what felt like the first time, I wondered what they thought about when they pretended to be a part of the furnishings.

"So the dreams." Truin snatched my attention back to the stone table. "You woke in the middle of the bay?"

I nodded, dragging a chunk of buttered bread through the dregs in my bowl. "I'd made a path of ice." Shadowed claws tickled my nape and feathered over my spine as I thought back to what I remembered. "A road, almost. Really, it would be rather impressive." I chewed and swallowed. "Of course, if it weren't for the absurdity and all."

She didn't smile. "You've done this before?"

"Not to that extreme."

"What do you remember?" she asked. "Of the dreams?"

"Not much, just..." Struggling to find the right words to describe it while wondering if I could, I settled on, "Just this sense of urgency. I had to hurry. To where"—I lifted my shoulders—"I've no idea."

"Sleepwalking," Truin said, thinking on it a moment. "It's quite common. But to wield magic while you sleep? Not so much. Especially of that magnitude. Magic wakes the mind too much. And that you've never been prone to such a thing before..."

"My father," I said, his dark eyes penetrating my thoughts, the malice ever-present within them. "Did he ever—"

"No," she said, reminiscent of Zadicus. "Not that I'm aware." Her hand reached for mine, and I lifted my eyes from my bowl to hers. They were smiling now. "Audra, you are not in danger of losing grip of yourself. Most certainly not at twenty-one summers of age."

I nodded. "Then when?" I pulled my hand free, my tone dripping with cold. "Do not placate me with riddles or lies. I am his blood, and he is mine. I am no fool. It's not a matter of if but *when*."

Undeterred by the hostility in my tone, Truin smiled in full and laid her head upon her hand. "You are his blood, but you are also your mother's blood." A blond brow rose. "Perhaps more so given the breaking of your father's curse upon Beldine."

The name of that place alone triggered something inside me. Sharp, blood-soaked, and loud, it shouted. But I didn't know what it was saying, and I didn't deign to give it much attention.

We'd heard nothing of the creatures who resided upon our neighboring continent, the one I'd almost died to reveal to the world once more. That fact was both unnerving and a relief. The former because it was not like the Fae to leave transgressions unpunished, especially one of that severity. And it was a relief because although no one had ever dared to war with the Fae—with Beldine—we still knew the result would not be favorable.

Meaning, every single one of us would likely die.

No. Thinking, dwelling on that day I'd lain bleeding out into the sea upon the soft sand to free the hidden realm, and of the consequences that had yet to come knocking, was of no use. I wouldn't agonize over what should happen. That would do none of us any good, and it might just bring those fears to fruition.

"What else could it be?" I said, feeling no ease, only a growing sense of foreboding. "Has someone hexed me?"

Truin sniffed the air as if she could scent such a thing. It would not surprise me if she could. Magic was easier sensed by those who wielded it. "No, or else I'd have surely known when I arrived. Besides, no one could ever get close enough to you to try."

That wasn't exactly true, and we both knew it. Even if it was a somewhat enjoyable and necessary pastime, I had no energy for needling the staff and sniffing out rats.

"Let me inquire about the matter with Gretelle. I'm sure she's bound to have heard of this before."

Gretelle, an aging witch, was the head of Truin's coven. If anyone knew something, it would be her. I longed to ask the crone myself to keep this locked up, but after this morning, I was beginning to see it was too late for that. In any case, I trusted

Truin. She was not only under my employ but also a friend who'd earned that trust.

So I nodded, images of that face, of Zad's face, shrouded in night and shadow, floated amongst words I did not wish to say. But perhaps, I had to. Perhaps, keeping the strange, impossible occurrence of the handful of times I'd seen that face when it couldn't have possibly been him to myself was not wise.

I opened my mouth, prepared to word my foggy experiences carefully, when a booming knock chased my courage away.

The doors opened a moment later, Mintale bowing as he entered. Eyes darting around the room in search of my bristly lord, his shoulders fell slightly when he found he was no longer here. "Excuse me, majesty," he said, hustling over to where we sat. "We've just received a letter from the king."

I eyed the offered letter as though it offended me, and it did. Greatly.

For although Raiden and myself had found some type of tenuous truce, I had no desire to cater to the alliance we'd formed, the unlikely friendship that'd blossomed since Inkerbine, right now.

Sighing, I snatched it, and Mintale stepped back.

Truin watched me tear it open, pretending to busy herself with some sliced melon.

I scanned it, and with a groan, I scrunched the letter into a ball and tossed it over my shoulder.

"He plans to visit then," Mintale guessed.

Truin contained a laugh, a snort escaping.

"Indeed," I drawled. "In a month." I'd seen the troublesome male more times than I'd have liked over the past seven months.

Every other month, he'd make his excuses to situate himself in my home and ruffle Zad's feathers. He never stayed longer than a week, and his presence was reassuring for the citizens, a reminder of our changing ways. We'd cover any business dealings we had during the first few days of his arrival, and I'd inevitably hope doing so would keep his visits brief. Yet it mattered not. Ever the entitled, spoiled prince turned king, he would forever do as he wished and outstay his welcome.

Mintale hovered, and I eventually wrested enough control of myself to declare, "Write him for me."

"Of course, your majesty." Making to leave, he paused. "Uh, should I say all is fine?"

I lifted my brows. "What else is there to say?"

His jowls swayed as he nodded emphatically and hurried away, pulling the doors closed behind him.

"You know," Truin said, licking melon from her fingers. "You could always visit him."

My upper lip peeled back, and she laughed.

Zad returned right after dinner, snow falling from his cloak and melting upon the furred rugs in my bedchamber. He removed it, slung the heavy velvet black over a hook outside the bathing room, and then kicked off his knee-high black boots.

I remained where I was, seated on the windowsill, the dying fire reflected in the glass.

"You've eaten?" he asked.

"I have." I fixed my gaze back upon the graying city streets outside as ice fluttered over them, and the bleak wintered mountains beyond. "Have you?" I supposed that was my way of asking him where he'd been, as we both knew I'd never design to appear the besotted female worrying over his whereabouts and demanding he tell me what he'd been up to.

"I'll get something in a little while," he said absently, striding to me. Cool fingers slid under my chin, tilting it up until our eyes locked. "I met with Kash." I waited for him to elaborate. "I wanted to see what he might know."

Tearing my chin free, I dropped my forehead to the glass.

"What would possess you to think the obnoxious faerie would care enough to know anything?"

I heard him sigh. Wrenched from my perch, I withheld a squeak. He stole it for himself and lowered me sideways over his lap. "He does not hate you."

I scoffed and attempted to wriggle free, but his arms tightened, and I didn't really want to be free. I liked the irritating male and his knowing eyes far too much. "I care not if he hates me. Such things have never bothered me before." And that was the brutal truth, regardless of the affair Kash'd had with my mother and what she'd felt for him before her demise.

"Audra," Zad said, so soft that I gave him my complete attention as if he hadn't already had it.

As he tucked tendrils of hair behind my ear, those amber eyes swam with a magic I'd never dared hope to attain before now. Affection. "Audra of the caged, beautifully fierce heart."

"Quiet," I said, but it was too low, too insincere, and his smile only grew.

Gently clasping the side of my face, he brought my forehead to his. "To think everyone despises you is not only a lie unworthy of your thoughts but it is also an insult to the many thousands who don't."

My eyes closed, and I sagged against him, my head falling to his shoulder.

Like a second skin, a much-needed blanket against the glacial chill nestled inside my bones, his arms folded around me and held me so close I could feel our hearts' synchronized beats. "I'm tired."

Zad was quiet for a long moment, his fingers running through my hair, tickling my back. "Sleep. I've no plans to leave you, and I will rest tomorrow."

I knew better than to argue. My eyelids drifted apart, snow dusting the frigid air outside. And then a figure moved into view, a black brimmed hat tipped low over his face, and looked up.

Feeling me tense, Zad did too. "What? What's wrong?"

But I couldn't answer. My tongue felt glued to the back of my teeth, and no matter how hard I tried, it wouldn't budge.

Zad stood, still holding me in his arms, and glanced out the window.

If he saw the same thing I did, if he saw the strange being that so closely resembled himself, he didn't say. Knowing that he hadn't seen a thing, a splash of disappointment curdled inside my chest.

That was impossible when it was but a figment of my unraveling mind.

I wondered if that was why I hadn't been able to tell him everything—who it was I saw. It was one thing to consider telling Truin. She would not have me under lock and guard for all eternity like the spooked, rigid male holding me.

Said male trudged to the bed, laid me down, then marched back to the window and pulled the drapes closed. He then moved to the other window and did the same.

I said nothing—couldn't—even though closing them was something I rarely allowed.

Sleep came for me, and for the first time in weeks, I welcomed it.

❧

Lying in the dark, I watched the lord of the east dress, the shadowed sinew of his shoulders and arms bunching as he pulled on his cream shirt followed by a charcoal buttoned vest.

He kept a small collection of clothing in my dressing room, and I'd taken some of my own to his estate the last time we'd visited. Sharing space with someone else in such a seemingly permanent way had taken some time to get used to, but not as long as I'd have thought.

It was as if he was always meant to hang his finest shirts and cloaks next to mine, to rest his sword and daggers next to and atop the bureau, and to leave his boots by the foot of my bed.

All those things were made easier to acclimate to when his body aligned itself with mine, for that was the part that had always come with an ease I'd ignored for too long. So much so that watching him prepare to leave filled me with something that alarmed more than it provoked fear.

Panic.

I detested it. In a way, I wanted to detest him for the existence of something I never thought I'd feel, that I never wanted to feel again, regarding a male.

But he was mine, and I was his, and with a coupling as bone-deep as ours, I knew that intensity was normal. That this entity inside, clutching at my heart and pulling it toward my stomach, was something I had to bear.

For as long as we both shall live.

"You should head to breakfast," Zad said, and I blinked, removing my eyes from his perfect, firm backside as he pulled his charcoal pants over it. Ever the royal, he never failed to dress the part unless in battle.

"You're not going to tell me to sleep?" I looked at the windows, but they'd been sealed.

He followed my gaze, but he did not move to open the drapes as he strapped on his weapons. The ting of his sword sliding inside its sheath a moment later caused my chest to quake, rattling my next breath.

"Ask me," he said, stomping into his boots.

I threw off the warmth of the bedding and walked past him instead.

He cornered me in my dressing room, and I turned, stark naked, willing myself to stand still.

His eyes shined with humor but soon darkened with lust as he took his time. One booted foot thumped to the floor, followed by another, and my breath hitched when they stopped.

Standing right before me, he seemed larger somehow, dressed and with his hair tied at his nape while I stood naked, my hair tangled from sleep. "Audra," he said, too gentle, dangerously so. "Ask me where I'm going."

"Why?" I said, pulling my shoulders back.

It served in lifting my breasts higher, and his gaze fell upon them momentarily, his chest rising and falling in a harsh wave. "Because you want to."

My lips curled slowly into a grin. "Do not flatter yourself, Lord."

Zad's eyes flicked up, a playful menace within, then I was in his arms, and his teeth were pinching my neck. He inhaled deep, his exhale a mixture of mirth and desire. "Do not lie to me, my queen."

"I do no such thing," I said, but I was nothing but heating flesh and shaking breath.

He reached between us, and my head fell back, angling to the side.

His tongue lapped at my carotid, his finger delving inside me, finding my need-drenched lies. My thighs clenched around his waist. He released a throaty groan, then rumbled, "I'm going to see my friends."

"Your…" I stopped, swallowing when his teeth grazed my skin, his finger rubbing now. "Your faerie friends."

He hummed in affirmation, and I heard the buckle of his pants come loose. "I will return by nightfall."

"Not if you do not leave now," I said, silently begging him not to by rocking my hips.

A wicked laugh climbed out of his throat, rough and coating my body in a wave of shivering excitement.

My back met the wall, and I bucked, my own teeth sinking into his shoulder. With one deliriously slow thrust, he was inside me, and I moaned, my legs tensing around him as I tried to adjust to the invasion. So thick, so long, but so achingly perfect.

I felt him throb, felt his next exhale tremble out of his mouth to wash over my neck, and then I felt the wall. Its cold, rock-roughened surface scratched into my lower back as he pulled out, then pushed in.

"Shit," I hissed, the pain of it crawling along my skin to meet with pleasure.

Unforgiving, he withdrew, then rammed back in again. "Do not," he grunted, repeating the torment with each demand. "Hide." My nails raked into the muscled mounds of his forearms, my thighs shaking already. "From me."

I couldn't respond, could only lose myself to the wild only he possessed and could coax from me.

But then Zad stilled, and I almost screamed, lifting my head to glare at him. I rocked onto him, breathing hard. "Don't you dare stop."

His nostrils flared, lashes hovering low over burning eyes. "Answer me."

"You did not ask a question," I panted, shoving my hair from my face. "You made a demand."

He merely lifted a perfect, dark russet brow.

I groaned, clenching around his length. That brought me a smirk but nothing else. "We might be linked, but I am still your queen."

He stared at me for a moment. A moment that made me feel so much more exposed than I already was, naked and filled with him, our sweat and breaths and insecurities mingling. "Exactly," he finally said. Something sparked in his eyes and in the slight croak of his deep voice. "You are mine. My Audra. My queen. My fucking heart."

I froze, my heartbeat slowing and my shoulders drooping.

Slowly, I leaned forward, my chest pressing into his, and sank my fingers into the thickness of his perfectly tied hair, happily ruining it. "Okay, my lord." I kissed him, the rough pads of his fingers sliding up my back and into my own hair. His eyes closed, his mouth softening beneath mine, and I repeated, "Okay."

THREE

Zadicus

THE SUN WAS CRAWLING TOWARD ITS HIGHEST destination in the sky when I reached the estate.
With no time to waste, I waved off the sentinels at the gates and dismounted, leaving Rivers at the foot of the stairs to the manor.

She was trying, of that I was certain. For months, she'd handed me pieces of herself that'd been locked away. I shook the dust from them, saw them shine, no matter how small they might be, and appreciated them for the gargantuan gift they were.

But this, the force across the sea that stole into her dreams and lured her from the safety of her bed, complicated things. *Complicated* was putting it fucking mildly. The intrusion, the uncertainty and fear, had her retreating into that dark cave where nothing and no one could hurt her so long as she didn't allow anyone inside.

To coax her out was akin to taking a blade to the chest, trailing it over the organ within, all the while hoping it did not puncture.

Audra was scared. She loathed to ever admit it, but if my queen adored one thing above almost anything else, it was control.

And something, *someone*, was robbing her of it.

For years now, all I'd wanted was for her to want me, to love me with the same savage need I harbored for her. I'd finally gotten all that I desired, and now, well...

She wasn't the only one afraid.

I hated leaving her. No matter how capable Audra was of

defending herself, there was naught to be done about who was currently knocking on the door of Rosinthe.

But we had to try. I had no idea what he wanted. It'd been hundreds of years, over half a millennia, since I'd last seen him smiling with grim satisfaction, my soul hanging from his hands before he'd swept himself into the breeze and disappeared.

Ever since, he'd been forbidden to come for me, to goad me into another fight he might not win, yet here he was, goading my heart instead.

Emmiline met me at the door, dusting flour from her hands onto a pale pink apron. Her golden brows lowered. "What's the matter?"

There was little point in hiding anything, not when everything was about to change. "He's here."

Her apron slipped from her fingers, her lips falling apart. Emmiline was my mother's sister, and at that moment, the fear filling her eyes brought back memories I'd long left behind. Memories I'd rather have wait for me to beckon into this wholly different life of mine than expose themselves before I was ready.

I was about to call into the void and demand to know where the assholes were when Kash and Landen swept in and hurried down the hall to the foyer. "We felt it again," Landen said.

Kash slipped a small knife into a hidden pocket inside his sleeve. "Dace is looking for Cross." Cross was a shifter, one of the giant wolves residing in the woods outside my estate.

I strode by my friends, marching to the study. They followed, Landen saying, "I fear it's time we meet with him to find out what he wants."

Pushing books aside, aging tomes with chipped gold filigree wrapped around each spine, I pulled forth a dust-layered box. Made of white Ashwood, it too was engraved with filigree, and it only opened at my touch. A low hum, barely detectable to most ears, preceded a click, and then I pushed open the lid.

The hinge creaked from years of disuse. Inside, resting upon a small green cushion, laid two onyx stones. I'd only need one, but I'd kept two just in case.

"Whoa, not like this," Kash said, walking up behind me. "You need to stop and think for a fucking minute." Reaching around, he slammed the lid closed.

My teeth snapped, and I whirled on him. "He toys with her while she sleeps. She woke in the middle of the bay, surrounded by ice and creatures that could easily have torn her flesh from bone."

Landen cursed.

Kash didn't move an inch, just stared at me with challenging dark eyes. "Have you considered that maybe this is what he wants?" His arms crossed over his chest. "That perhaps it is you he hopes to lure, not your queen? Remember," Kash warned unnecessarily, "how well playing his games has served you in the past."

My chest was rising and falling too fast, but I couldn't quell the tension, the anger that clenched my hands into fists. That ache, so old it was barely noticeable, pinched beneath the skin at my back. "I need to find out what he wants."

"Not on your own," Landen said with a bark of sharp laughter. "Treaty or not, you will land yourself in a trap."

I reopened the box, staring at the onyx inside. "He cannot harm me, but he can harm you."

Kash made a snorting sound, but he did not protest further.

To rise against the king of Beldine, no matter how strong, skilled, or powerful you were, was to die.

He was the soil. The trees. The blood. The heartbeat of a land older than life itself.

You couldn't best power of that magnitude. For it was not power, it was life, and it was death, and he chose how to wield it as he saw fit. Often in cruel, unforgiving, and unstoppable ways.

"Ry—"

I gnashed my teeth at Landen. "Do *not* speak his name."

"That is but a myth, surely."

Some said to speak the king's name brought yourself

unwanted space inside his mind while others said the wind would carry it to him. I didn't know if any of that was true, but I knew enough not to discredit anything. "Nothing is ever but a damned myth." Besides, after everything he'd done, and all he'd do if given a chance, he deserved no such recognition.

"The wind has ears," Kash murmured, then sighed. "Okay, so we'll all go on this merry little journey then."

"I'll go," I said. "I'll need you three to head to the castle and remain there."

Kash's brows rose, but Landen nodded.

"I need someone to watch Audra every moment even though she'll hate it, especially while she's asleep..." The box fell from my slackened hand, the rocks hitting the rug.

A shadow moved across my vision, and something tugged at my chest with enough force to shift my feet to the window.

"What is it?" Kash said.

No. The word howled through my mind, useless and empty. I could scarcely draw enough air in order to rasp, "We need to go now." I fumbled around the desk, disorientated with a wave of panic I wasn't entirely sure was my own, searching for the dried rose I kept in the top drawer.

"You can't," Landen said. "Someone will see you."

It was growing far too late to worry about hiding a damned thing. "Something is wrong," was all I managed to say, clutching the rose and urging the air to pull me into the void.

Wind howled inside the never-ending dark. Time and distance clashed together and wasted precious seconds as it swept me from my study and spun me to the original source of that dead flower.

I landed with a jolt and immediately broke into a run in the rear gardens of the castle.

Guards blinked and muttered curses as I leaped past them into the drawing room and raced down the hall. That feeling, the one that'd prompted me to take a risk I rarely took by sweeping into the castle grounds, was building inside me. A raging, barreling storm thundered in my ears as I hurried up the stairs and down the halls leading to Audra's rooms.

Azela, second in the queen's personal guard, stepped forward from the closed doors. "My lord?"

I knew what I'd find. Deep down, I'd known before I'd even swept from the study of my manor, but it still didn't prepare me enough for the sight of it.

And it could never make it any easier to bear.

The doors crashed open with a raged thought before I reached them, and I looked at the bed, its sheets rumpled, then at the windowsill. The bedchamber was empty.

Azela followed me inside, asking questions I couldn't hear so much as answer. The dressing room where I'd had her just hours ago was also empty, as was the sitting and bathing rooms.

"She's gone," I said, barely a sound, and reentered the bedchamber. "He's taken her."

Stunned, Azela opened and closed her mouth, her face paling as her eyes bobbed around the room. "Who?"

Ainx rushed in, followed by Mintale, who was huffing and puffing. The latter blinked, demanding, "What in the darkness is going on?"

"She's gone," I said it again, louder, and a searing panic strangled my vocal cords, warping the words, my breathing, the sluggish beat of my heart.

"What do you mean, *gone?*" Mintale asked, understanding I hadn't meant she'd slipped out for a stroll in the gardens, and looked at the bed. "I was just in here an hour ago."

"What was she doing?" Ainx asked, and I was thankful at least one of us had the mind to do so.

Mine was lost, reeling, swimming in darkness.

"She was, uh," Mintale started, then shook his head. "She was sitting on the bed."

"Did she fall asleep?" I finally managed to ground out.

When his furry white brows lowered in puzzlement, I stomped over to him and grabbed the lapels of his shirt. "Did she sleep after you left?"

"I-I-I do not know, m-my lord."

Of course, he wouldn't have known.

Grappling for some sense of rationality, I released him and raked my hand through my hair, causing some to escape its tie and fall into my eyes.

"Perhaps she is merely somewhere else in the castle," Ainx suggested.

Azela disputed that. "But she never even left her rooms. My lord"—she stepped forward, hesitantly—"what does it matter if she was asleep?"

Clutching at my hair, I ran my eyes over the bed, the bureau, and the armchair, then behind me to the sitting room, which gave a view of the glass case housing her crown. One of the windows was open, its drapes rocking on a faint breeze that gave away his scent. My nose followed, eyes snapping back to the bed, where, tucked underneath the pillow, a glimpse of white could be seen.

Snatching the parchment, I absorbed the words. His scent smothered it, and my blood pushed at the confines of my skin, boiling.

I have your queen.
If you wish to see her again, you know what you need to do...
Make haste, for I have tasted her dreams, and they are delectable indeed.
Sincerely, R.

I wanted to roar until the glass shattered from the windows, until it drowned out the ringing in my ears and the echo of my panicked heart, until I could fucking think.

I wanted to kill him, and it seemed that was exactly what I'd finally need to do.

"Lord Zadicus," Ainx said, sensing I now had some idea of what'd happened. "What is that?"

I scrunched the parchment, and his eyes popped as it turned to dust with my clipped words. "The king of Beldine has taken her."

"The king of Beldine?" Azela repeated, her brows knitting. "But... that's the faerie king."

Ainx licked his lips, trying to make sense of something that would make little sense to them at all. They did not know the true history of the royals. Of the Fae. They knew what had been forced upon them for over a millennium and, therefore, would find it hard to fathom why the creatures of Beldine held an interest in their queen.

"What does he want with her?" he finally said.

"I will handle it."

Mintale balked. "How?"

I crossed the room, allowing them what little they needed to know. "He does not want her. He wants me."

"My lord." Mintale scurried after me to the doors. "I am failing to understand. Why does he want you?"

I fingered the dried mint leaves from my pocket that'd once grown on the garden atop the roof of my manor and felt the admission leave me like a sigh of pained relief. "I am his brother."

Then I caught the sudden wind and swept back home.

FOUR

Audra

THAT SCENT. IT WAS BACK.

Only this time, it was everywhere, the air stained with the essence of it. My eyes fluttered open to find a spiraling tree-woven ceiling. It didn't seem to end, its branches wrapping and twining and overlapping higher than the eye could reach.

I'd never seen anything like it, but the scent of rainbows, of every delicacy and beauty one could dream of, was something I'd encountered before. It filled my nose, brushed soft hands over my skin, and clapped right next to my ears.

Wake up, it seemed to say. The trilling of birds, rushing water, and laughter enticed and shot arrows of fear into every slow-firing brain cell.

Beldine.

I'd fallen asleep.

I'd fallen asleep, and this time, I hadn't even left the confines of my room. He hadn't arrived. He'd already been there, and I'd followed like magnets had pulled us together, and then the world was empty, dreamless, and now I was gone.

"They say that to dream is to glimpse the ever," a sharp, rich voice danced through the shadows.

I scrambled to sit up, pieces of something beneath my fingers. Feathers, I realized, glancing down. The soft crush of boots stepping over them snapped my gaze forward to where the pointed tips of a burgundy pair appeared.

I forced myself to remain still, unsure if I was asleep or if this was real.

And then the shadows in the room retreated, slowly revealing him. He crouched down, a familiar smile upon a familiar face, only more serpentine. "To that, I say, why would anyone want to glimpse certain eternity when you could very well craft your own dreams instead?"

"You," I said, soaking in every feature—the perfectly straight nose, the dusting of faint freckles over paler cheeks, and the short midnight black hair that licked at intense cheekbones with its slight curl.

"Ah, indeed, we've met before." He lifted a long finger. "But not fully, so allow me to introduce myself." His golden eyes, the iris darker and larger than Zad's, sparkled with excitement. "I am Ryle, King of Beldine."

My lips parted, but that was all the shock I could muster because if I were being honest with myself, I knew that. I was certain that, deep down, I'd known who he was for some time now. Ever since I'd first glimpsed him through the window, down on the street outside of the castle one night while Zad had slept.

I just hadn't known what it had to do with Zadicus—why they looked alike. Honestly, I hadn't been sure that I wanted to know.

My failure to respond had him continuing. "I do believe you've mated to my brother."

That answered my question while also giving him the desired reaction he'd been waiting for. "*What?*"

"My brother," he said, toneless and as though I were daft. "Zadicus Allblood."

I sat with that for a moment, and seemingly amused, he let me, his eyes tracking my expression as though I were revealing buried treasure. I wasn't sure what he was searching for, but I did what I could to keep every rioting feeling from showing.

His brother.

The confusion cleared, the urge to refute his claim fading and making way for many unwanted truths to stumble forward. One after another, they flashed through my mind. The dreams and the king's resemblance to Zad. His stifling concern since he'd discovered I'd been sleepwalking. Kash and Landen and Dace...

My lord hadn't just befriended the creatures of the forest.

He was one of them.

Choking silently on every memory, I struggled to picture him as anything but what he was—mine.

He'd lied to me. And for what? I couldn't and did not have the strength to make sense of it. Closing my burning eyes, I swallowed and reminded myself that now was not the time to sink and fall into the cracks yawning open inside me.

Instead, I pulled back my shoulders and gazed around the circular room. It housed a bed made of feathers—some drifting to the floor around the branch-knotted frame—and worn books in towering piles on a desk and along the walls. Through a set of wooden doors with carvings of fruit and winged creatures etched upon them, I glimpsed what must have been a bathing chamber.

I could make out little else without standing, and although I desperately wanted to, my hands trembled, so I knew my feet would not hold me. Not until I'd steadied my breathing and shoved down the betrayal and fear that had twisted my chest and thoughts into something I could not undo.

"What do you want?" It seemed like the only logical thing to say, really, for he most definitely wanted something. Or else he wouldn't have haunted my dreams, stole and controlled them, and brought me here. Wherever here was, in Beldine, in *Faerie*.

The king tutted, as if disappointed, and rose to his full height. I kept my eyes on his boots, unwilling to crane my neck back to take in all that he was. "Have you no manners?"

Scowling, I failed to keep myself from saying, "Apologies, I must have left them in the room you stole me from."

Stepping back, he shot me a withering look, growing so still that my heart followed suit. And then... he laughed.

My heart boomed painfully, thudding slowly as the sound of his mirth cut through the air in a deep wave that did nothing to ease the anxiety growing within. "Apology accepted, *queen*. As for what I want," he mused, crushing lone feathers beneath him as he paced in a slow circle, a snake coiling to strike. "It is not so much what I *want* as it is what I *need*, you see."

"And what is that?" I asked, proud that I'd kept my tone bland.

"My brother, of course."

I tugged at my skirts, covering my legs and feet to quell the tremors vibrating in my fingertips—to smother the urge to kill and run. But I did not remove my eyes from him. It was instinct, an ancient sense of knowing, to make sure my back was not turned in the presence of this king.

"Not going to ask why?" he drawled, spinning, his eyes two hot coals burning into the top of my head.

"I'm not sure it's any of my concern," I threw back, daring to meet his eyes. It was a mistake, as were my words, judging by the way they flashed. "And if there was one thing my mother taught me before she was drained for loving one of your kind, it was to mind my own damned business. Something I really wish you'd have done and left me alone."

He was before me in an eye-widening instant, his teeth perfect like his brother's, and his lips peeled back over them as he snarled, "Your mother was a moronic whore, and your father nothing but a child playing with stolen fire." His nose wrinkled with distaste as his tongue dragged over one of his long canines. "And you are not worthy of a mating bond with one of *our kind*." I blinked, and his features smoothed into a shocking calm, his eyes smiling again. "But alas, it has served me well that this is how the fates have played us."

He stalked to a door I hadn't seen, for it wasn't visible until his hand touched it. It swung open, and I was tempted to ask him where he was going and what he planned to do with me.

But even feeling as though I knew nothing at all, I knew better.

Golden light, dancing not with dust motes but tiny glittering specks with translucent wings, crept downward through the spiraling ceiling. Silently, they dived and spun in repetitive loops.

I am your queen.

You may be a queen, but you are not mine.

Zadicus hadn't been lying. Calling me his queen had never seemed more potent before those dragging hours spent upon the feather-dusted tiled ground.

He hadn't called me his queen out of necessity or out of respect because he was one of my subjects. He wasn't one of my subjects at all. He was a stray prince who'd, for whatever reason, chosen to leave his kingdom.

What of Nova, I wondered. Had she been aware she'd married a faerie prince and not a royal? I wasn't sure they'd been married long enough for Zad to warrant spilling a truth he hadn't yet dared to admit to me. And what we had went beyond marriage, beyond traditional confinements, and even beyond death.

Yet he'd lied to me even though he could not lie.

I counted back to all the times he'd stumped me with his carefully crafted words, admissions that danced over his drugging lips like drops of wine. Puddles of truth had slowly gathered at my feet. His friends. The reluctance to overshare personal facets of himself. That intoxicating power that rippled from him like a second skin. The way he'd stare at the moon as though it were a friend waving from a faraway ship. How he'd cleaved the earth to save me.

Had he been waiting for me to dig deeper? To pry? To *want* to know him as much as he knew me?

A slime-infested feeling invaded my stomach as I realized that yes, that was exactly what he'd been doing. Why I hadn't, well... I didn't want to acknowledge and wasn't even sure if I could.

Not here, not in the shadowed corner of this foreign rainforest-scented room.

He should have confided in me. This was not a game. His past was not something he should've hidden, and now we were at the mercy of a king whose moods seemed to dance from dark to light within two beats of an erratic heart.

He should have told me, goaded me into asking in that infuriating way of his. Instead, he'd chosen to deceive me.

Now, he was just another male who was not what he'd promised.

Who was not who I'd thought he was.

But he was coming, of that I was sure, only what would happen when he arrived was anyone's guess besides the king's. He had his plans, and I was expected to sit here until they played out.

The king might have stolen into my dreams, my home, and disrupted our lives, but he failed to do his research. Otherwise, he'd know I was no one's pawn.

Pushing to my numb feet, I stepped over the drifting feathers and traipsed to the circular window on the other side of the bed. It was open, not a piece of glass in sight, and beyond it...

My breath froze in my throat as I beheld the glittering, crashing waterfall rushing out from below me. Trees, some fat and sagging, some towering into a night sky so dark and bright, and some curling into one another, skirted the rushing chaos of water in a semicircle of lush greenery.

Windows, much like the one I was staring out, were aglow in the trees. Lights flickered, shadows swayed, and laughter spilled out to dance across the water as though something wanted me to hear.

Something that whispered silent warmth across my wind-kissed cheeks.

Life. This place, this land, was teeming with life. As though the very creation of it stemmed from the soil and flowed into the unknowing world beyond.

I looked down at my hands, the wood of the curved windowsill warm beneath them, and then I noticed something else. The spires either side of me, twisting high into the sky to touch the fluffy white clouds, and the sentinels with their crossbows, who marched across the thatched and stone rooftops.

The rooftops of a castle that appeared to be made of stone and trees.

I stepped back, my heart fluttering through every limb as my magic stirred awake. It slithered beneath my skin in a way I'd never felt before. Crawling and humming, it twitched my fingers and filled the rushing beat of my heart, soothing it.

It was so startling that I pressed my hand to my chest against the thud as Kash's words came back to me.

Half breed.

Half Fae. Half mortal.

I'd known it as truth the moment he'd said it, but now, feeling where the source of that power of mine derived from, in the air, in my blood, unspooling from the light and shadows—it was forced upon me with sharp teeth, and it sank deep enough to reach my bones.

Everything we'd ever thought to be true was a lie.

I whirled for the space the king had touched, running my hands over the walls, frantic and suddenly claustrophobic in this place within the sky with its hidden doors and wide-open windows. To climb out of one was a death sentence I wouldn't dare entertain, and I didn't have to.

With a shudder, the wood shimmered, and the door with carved pictures appeared.

Apples and oranges and strawberries and grapes intermingled with leaves and what looked to be children with wings. But I had no time to study such things. I needed to find the king and get whatever plans he had over with—providing they not lead to my death—and get home.

It opened with a near-silent exhale of air, and I stood back, stunned, as I half-wondered if this could be a trick.

The hall was dark, but with each step I took, glass orbs in bronze sconces flickered to life. Peering behind me, I saw them wink out, and I felt that darkness at my back like a living creature.

Soil and something spiced floated upon the air, and I followed the scent, more lights coming awake to guide the way. I paused when a painting nestled inside an onyx frame inlaid with emerald jewels caught my eye.

A family, it seemed.

But the eyes of the young male, who I knew had to be Zad, had been scratched out. Above him, with a hand set upon each of his shoulders, stood his parents. Regal, with a swanlike neck, his mother gave a hint of a smile I'd recognize anywhere to whoever had created this portrait.

Her hair was a light brown woven with strands of gold. Her eyes blue, flat, and muddy like the sky before rainfall.

A cruel twist of the lips of which he'd bestowed upon his son, Zad's father stared with a darkness that shouldn't live in such vivid, golden eyes. His angular cheeks were harsh, the auburn fire of his hair falling around his shoulders in thick waves.

He was his son, and his son was him.

But where the other son was... I looked again at where Zad's eyes had been scratched out and reached up as though I'd touch his boyish features, the hands he'd curled into a ball before him.

"I made some adjustments." Ryle's voice slithered out of the dark.

My breath caught, and I lowered my hand, but I didn't dare hurry to turn to him. "I've not any siblings of my own," I said. "None that live anyway, but I cannot say I'd make the same... adjustments."

Ryle chuckled, the abrasive sound causing my shoulders to stiffen. "But they say you are truly wicked." Orbs fired to life in more sconces as he slowly approached, his hands behind his back. "Rumors are, of course, usually nothing more than muddled musings of the deliverer, but in this case, I had hoped them to be true."

"Oh, do not despair." Smiling, I angled my head, taking a

cautious step forward, and met those lupine eyes. "I merely prefer not to waste my time with"—I tossed a look back at the portrait—"such childish actions."

His expression wavered between glee and anger, and I found I rather liked that I could do that. It suggested an inkling of power, and if I'd need something to get home in one piece, it was that. "What did he do?" I pressed, the words more of a purr. "Steal your favorite lover? Best you in battle? Win the affection of Mother dearest?"

"She was never my mother." The cold, brash words cleared the dust and cobwebs from the ancient portrait behind me and told me all I needed to know.

Keeping my tone and expression neutral, I said, "A bastard, then." I felt it, the shift beneath my feet as though his ire, the bruising I was no doubt giving his ego, had awoken what he was.

The High King of Faerie.

I'd heard for the rulers of Beldine, the High King and his three queens, being a monarch was similar to those in Rosinthe—our powers tied to the land. But I'd also heard it ran deeper here, and that violent shift, the thickening of the air around us, gave truth to that.

That bone-deep, instinctual fear made itself known once more, urging me to tread with far more caution and to quit poking the beast.

Fine.

"You'd be wise to mind your tongue," he hissed.

My eyes sank into his; my spine taut even as my lungs squeezed. "A threat?" Again, I smiled. "Or a dare?" Inwardly, I winced. I had never been very good at doing what I was told.

Prepared for fight or flight, I waited for his wrath as it unfurled like a growing mid-winter night.

Then he laughed. It roared into the hall, echoing into others I'd not yet traversed—hoped I did not have to—rusted and sharp as though it'd been some time since he'd done so with no restraint.

"Winter queen," he said with a sigh that spoke of surprised satisfaction. "I do believe you and I will have more fun than I first thought."

I raised a brow as he stepped to the side. "I have to wonder if our definitions of *fun* might vary, King."

Another bout of laughter, low and edged. "Why wonder when we can find out?" He sketched a half-hearted bow, gesturing to the looming darkness. "After you."

The last thing I should've been doing was placing a creature such as himself at my back, but as we stared, our eyes locked, his amused and mine assessing, I knew I had little choice.

I walked ahead, and surprisingly, he fell into step beside me.

Within a few tense breaths, the shadowed hall revealed a set of ever-winding, circular stairs, and at the bottom down a short length of a pitch-black hall, we entered what appeared to be a throne room.

It was empty and mostly dark with only two sconces lit upon the far wall behind the throne. The sconces in here were larger, black with twisting, snake-like necks, and inside them were not orbs of flickering light but dancing flames.

The throne itself was a monstrosity of woven birch wood. In spindly, glittering pieces that reached for the tree-woven ceiling—which cleaved between what had to be the upper levels of the castle—the wood splintered into jagged, sharp spires in an arch behind a large velvet black cushion.

Little care had been taken for the armrests of thick whorls of birch, wrapped tight and punching straightforward. The legs curved outward, stabbing into the mosaic tile slabs like wooden blades and puncturing them.

Some would think it crafted with no thought for its king until they looked closer and saw the way it shined with ancient specks of onyx. And those legs, they hadn't punctured the tile at all, but rather, the tile had been laid around the throne, as though it could never be moved.

"A thing of callous beauty, isn't it?"

I struggled to find the words, but not because he was wrong. In fact, his description was quite possibly the best there was. But because of what was pinned to the wall behind the throne, trapped between the two burning sconces.

Wings. Giant black-feathered wings.

"Oh, yes, those," the king said, taking the three steps up and behind the throne with a prowling grace that anyone who didn't know better would call lazy.

As though he had all the time in the world, and I supposed he did, he rubbed his chin, staring up at the wall to admire what I was sure was his handiwork. "Has he said he misses them? I mean, it has been an *awfully* long time, but nevertheless, I've often wondered."

FIVE

Audra

It took one sharp lungful of air to gather exactly who this *he* was, and the shock was so heavy, so acidic in the way it rendered every limb useless, I couldn't keep it from showing even if I tried.

"Ah," Ryle said. "He did not tell you about them?"

I could feel his eyes searing into my profile, as my own refused to remove themselves from the brutality before me.

Those wings, their span so magnificent they took up almost half of the back wall, crumpled where they'd once joined and sank beneath Zad's skin—they'd been torn from him with such vicious savagery. Hatred glared in the warped sinew and muscle that'd been cleaved from his flesh.

The two long scars upon his back, scars I'd traced with my eyes and fingers, flashed before me. He hadn't reacted. He hadn't flinched or given any sign that a part of him was gone.

Ryle began to circle me, a hunter eyeing his prey.

The bitter sting of tears infiltrated, and I swallowed the urge to release all that howled inside. Zadicus hadn't just lied about where he was from. He'd always seemed more than us, more than anything I'd ever encountered. I'd stupidly perceived that splendor as part of our link, our eternal bond, the magnetic force that drew and caged me, instead of seeing him for what he truly was.

A different creature entirely.

"I'd have you lashed for lack of response," the king said, tutting. "The utter disrespect. But I'd be both blind *and* cruel then, wouldn't I?" he asked, not waiting for an answer that wasn't coming. "For it seems you are very... shaken."

I blinked then, my nails scoring into my palms. A faint wind curled tangled strands of my hair and cooled my flushed skin.

Ryle's footsteps ceased, his eyes narrowed, studying. "Am I right to assume you had absolutely no idea that your mate is not who you thought he was?" I kept my eyes trained on his and lifted my chin. I might have been looking at Ryle, but it wasn't him I was seeing. A wolfish grin blurred his features, but they were not his, and golden eyes, far brighter than that of the king before me, caught fire with his rich laughter.

My chest was too tight, the organ inside it pushing at its confines with every swelling beat.

Ryle's breathy laughter broke the spell, and I closed my eyes before gazing back at the hideously beautiful throne. "Interesting. How very interesting indeed."

"What is it you want?"

"We've already been over this, and all I want will be mine in no time at all."

I refrained from scoffing. "In no time at all?"

"Your beloved shall be here"—he pursed his lips, gazing around the room with feigned patience—"oh, any moment now." Then before I could react or ask him how he knew that, he clapped his hands, and suddenly, we were not alone.

Glamour.

A table with a feast fit for twenty monarchs stretched behind me, another cutting through its center. Glowing fruits overflowed from bowls, and fish and venison steamed the air. Baskets of bread and black goblets filled with wine were scattered between the plates.

And seated at the tables were hordes of people. All of them witnesses to the betrayal I'd just been subjected to.

Though not just any people. Fae, and royalty at that.

Now I knew the reason for the setup of the feast. Three

females wearing differing expressions of intrigue and small crowns sat at the heads of each table—the three queens.

Ryle seated himself at the tip of the giant cross the two tables made. Flicking a napkin into the air, he gingerly tucked it within the ruffles of his cream linen shirt. "Do have a seat, my half breed queen. We shall not bite." The wink that followed those words said otherwise.

A gruff voice seated down the table from him barked, "Speak for yourself, your highness."

Ryle tossed him a smirk that should have suggested comradery, but instead, the dark-haired male who'd spoken downed his wine with haste and kept his eyes trained on his food.

I wasn't sure where to look, what to do, or where to sit. All I knew was that I could not leave.

I caught the eye of a white-haired queen with eyes the color of burnt copper. She did not smile, and she did not snarl as she ripped into a leg of chicken with a preternatural slowness and chewed. At her right, a male watched her every move, his large, muscular frame oozing with a tension even I could feel. Linked, perhaps. He was wearing what seemed to be steel and leather. A warrior. Yet it would seem he'd linked to a Faerie queen.

Not that I could talk.

And supposedly, he'd be here soon. I wasn't foolish enough to believe I could escape Beldine and live to tell the tale. I'd done it once, barely, and had almost died. So I pulled my eyes away and gathered my crumpled skirts. Keeping my shoulders back, I made my way to the only empty seat available. Right next to the king.

It appeared each queen had brought some members of their courts with them, and their curiosity bled into the room as stalking eyes followed me to my seat.

"Can I eat?" I asked the king, knowing of the many tales regarding eating certain foods or wine in Beldine. Some said it would kill you, some said you'd lose yourself for hours on end, and others said it would entrap you, binding you to their lands forever.

He paused in chewing. "I find your sheer rudeness quite appalling."

Right. Said tales also spoke of ill-mannered humans finding their deaths prematurely. Even so, I was not human. I cocked my head. "That I asked if your food was safe?" My lips curled. "Or was it the manner in which I asked?"

His teeth flashed as did his eyes, and he reclined in his high-backed chair. "Both."

"At the risk of offending you further, how you choose to receive the question is no problem of mine."

Silence descended, thick and swift, and I glanced around at the stunned faces. One of the queens, her hair in braids that bounced over her curved, brown cheeks, grinned with obvious excitement. Others were staring down at their plates as if they couldn't bear to watch.

Frowning, I looked from them back to their High King, whose face was mottled red.

Shit.

It came out of nowhere—so quick I thought I'd been slapped, and I might have. Though it wasn't by his hand but his power. Thrown with unstoppable force to the side, I couldn't keep myself from toppling to the mosaic floor.

As I laid there, dazed with my cheek and jaw singing from the impact, I noticed the green and gold leaves and tiny fat cherubs in the cool tile.

"Get rid of her," I heard Ryle mutter.

Hauled from the room, I was dragged up the stairs, and I had little desire to protest.

After all that had happened, I found the sight, the solitude, of my feathered room with its circled windows a welcome relief.

"Wake up," a bland voice said from the door.

I knew I could've likely left the room at any time, but I hadn't. I hadn't slept either. Sifting through some books, I found nothing but a few worn journal entries and fictional tales of the Fae that looked to be stolen from Rosinthe. After stacking them as I'd found them, I'd then watched the sun dance down through the branches in the ceiling, listening to the water and squealing, squawking, and baying creatures outside as the castle quieted.

Now, with the stars glittering through the window, bouncing off the violent sprays of water beneath, it seemed everyone was wide-awake.

I'd heard shouts, laughter, and even some screaming. But I'd continued to gaze out the window, study the room I'd been thrust into, and wait.

I didn't deign to let the guard know I was also wide-awake.

Standing, I ignored the dress that'd appeared, a thin mixture of satin and ribbon that I knew would be vastly revealing, and marched to the stone-faced male at the door.

His slanted and darkly observant eyes tracked my every move. Tall and imposing in leather pants, he wore matching boots and a shirt with a metal breastplate, and I wondered what he was.

I wasn't left wondering for long.

Out in the hall, another guard stood waiting. With a nod to his friend, he walked ahead. A gray and black tail, tufted at the end, bobbed behind him.

A shifter. I was willing to wager the one behind me, whose eyes dug into my back, was also one.

Dragging my fingers through my hair, I wished I'd taken the time to search for a brush, but I soon lost all interest in vanity when I heard a feminine moan roll up the stairs we descended to the throne room.

The tables were gone. Inside were feathered mats, and upon each one, a pregnant female in various stages of undress.

When I halted, the guard behind me growled, pushing me forward. Turning, I hissed at him, but that only brought me a wolfish smile.

The king was not on the dais. The throne was empty, and as I let my eyes roam the room, I realized why.

He was fucking a female from behind, cupping her large stomach in his hand. Her eyes were closed as her ass gyrated with every violent thrust. Meeting my eyes over her shoulder, the king grinned, then threw his head back with a roar that shook the cavernous room and released himself inside her.

Rising, he didn't bother tucking his cock away. It hung between his legs, flaccid but already thickening as he strolled between the females toward me.

I tore my gaze from it and folded my hands before me, unwilling to appear ruffled.

"Winter queen," he said, a little breathless. With a swipe of his hand over his mouth, he licked his lips. "I do feel I should apologize for my... outburst last evening. Tense times and all that."

I cared nothing for whatever he meant by tense times, so I said nothing.

He smiled, wane and wicked, as if guessing that would be my response. "By all means, do take a seat."

He gestured to his throne, and a replica appeared beside it. "It has been a long while since a queen has ruled alongside a king here at the Onyx Court, so it might be a little dusty."

The thought of sitting there and watching all this had my empty stomach roiling, but I knew I had little choice. And walking to the dais, the king's burning eyes upon me, I then noticed the males.

Half veiled in shadow, they lined the walls, most of their expressions hidden or wrangled into indifference. Some wore warrior garb, others the glittering, ruffled, and colorful robes and tunics of nobility, and some wore labor-stained tunics and boots that'd seen far better nights.

All of them bled burning tension into the room.

The throne tightened around me as though molding to my frame. Inwardly, I coiled tight, but outwardly, I reclined, laying my arms upon the armrests.

Eyes danced upon me, the king standing in the middle of the

ginormous room with his stiff cock pointing straight at me. I knew I would likely pay for my snark, but I would much rather be returned to my rooms than stay here anyway. So I flicked my hand. "Proceed."

The king's brows jumped, and a few of the males upon the walls shifted.

One of the guards who'd delivered me, stationed at one side of the doors, laughed with his eyes.

I waited for King Ryle to explode—hoped for it even—but as if he knew I wanted that, he smiled. A cunning fox. The slight point to one of his ears revealed itself as he yawned and ran a hand through his sweat-misted hair. "My, my, this is harder than one would think."

I grinned even as my stomach turned. "I'm sure."

"Perhaps you could help me."

"I doubt I have the right… equipment for whatever it is"—my nose wrinkled, gaze jumping over the patiently waiting females—"you're doing." Some trembled, but whether it was in fear or excitement, I didn't know.

He mock-gasped. "How rude of me to forget how woefully uneducated you are of those whose power you stole."

I bristled but smiled.

His answering smile made some of the females weep.

Fear then, I decided. Most were trembling with fear.

"Allow me to explain," he said, dragging his long fingers down the spine of a female. All of them were on their hands and knees, heads bowed as though they could not stand to look up.

A glance at the walls told me why.

The males standing there were the babes' fathers, the female's spouses, and quite possibly, their linked ones.

Ryle paused behind an orange-haired mother, and she cried out. He hushed her, smoothing her hair down her back, then crouched down to grip one of her hanging breasts. "Just like you half breeds, we value our young and the creation of life above almost all other things."

She was quivering now, but her head snapped up, eyes locking on a male along the wall.

I didn't look. I didn't dare as Ryle stared at me across her back. "One out of three babes will survive infancy. Our power, our bloodlines, are just too much for their tiny bodies. But in recent years," he continued, voice roughening as his eyes fell away from mine, and he positioned himself behind the female, "we are lucky to see one in five babes survive."

"Dare I ask how this helps?" I said, surprisingly calm. Although I thought it all outrageously hideous and unnecessary, I was curious.

"A recent trial on my part," the king admitted, his fingers now between the sniffling female's legs. He frowned at what he no doubt did not find there, but he didn't care to prepare her before he moved forward and aligned himself. "Some five or six summers ago, I thought to fertilize the mothers just as my power, my very existence, does the land of Beldine. Twice a year, every expecting female in the realm is brought here for my blessing."

"Has it worked?" Perhaps a very dangerous question to ask the unpredictable king, and in a room filled with simmering, hostile tension, heartbreak, and fear.

He didn't answer, which was answer enough. He plowed forward, and the female screamed in various bouts of differing agonies.

I wanted to disappear inside myself. Of all the atrocities I'd experienced, of all the wicked things I'd done with my own two hands and magical abilities, not once had I ever felt like this.

Helpless, horrified, and disturbed right down to the dregs of my soul.

A low growl cleaved the stale air. The faerie's cries grew louder, her fingers bloodied, digging at the tile before her feathered mat as though she could pull herself away.

Bonds, almost translucent, had wrapped around her neck, an invisible leash the king pulled taut to keep her still as he fucked her without mercy. Within minutes, as though her pain or this entire ordeal excited him, his head rolled back and a sound akin to a purr climbed up his throat.

Another growl, louder and rumbling this time, and then the male she'd been staring at on the wall leaped forward. With a flash of night-bending shadows, he was no longer a male, but a formidable midnight black wolf.

My fingers curled into the sharp spikes of birch at the ends of my armrests.

Ryle didn't pause. He didn't even need to look at the guards.

He was everywhere he needed to be, everything he needed to be, without lifting a finger.

A chain of gold-coated iron looped around the wolf's throat before he could so much as lick his female's face. He was wrenched back by the guards, groaning and snarling and snapping, and Ryle only needed to glance at the wolf for him to yelp and land in a lifeless heap on the ground.

The female beneath the king screamed. "Quain!" she cried, long and loud as the guards dragged the shifter from the room.

I'd almost thought him dead until I saw the twitching of his back legs before he disappeared.

Ryle shuddered, spilling himself inside the crying female, who I was assuming was also a shifter, and as he moved onto the next, I felt myself drift away.

For the remainder of his so-called blessing, no one dared to disrupt him. No one dared to breathe louder than Ryle's barely contained grunts and groans.

For whatever reason they'd been here the previous day, his other guests were not in attendance. I studied the females who'd been abused but were still expected to wait in their positions of servitude until the blessing, rite, whatever form of torture it was, had ended.

Some had skin as white as the moon, others a rich honey, and some as dark as the hatred that wafted from the helpless males who'd been forced to watch. There were some with pale green skin, some with gills and webbed feet, others with hoofs and furred legs who I knew had to be lesser Fae or part of whatever they deemed as Unseelie.

The nobility stood out, not only due to their more human yet entirely unearthly traits but also for their wings. A deep blue rimmed with aqua, the insides speckled with black silken-looking splotches, butterfly wings sprouted from the back of a brown-skinned faerie. Her silver hair was short, giving view to those pointed ears, studded with countless tiny ruby red jewels. The female beside her, her skin almost translucent, also had wings, though hers were gray and feathered like a pigeon rather than the grand mass of what was pinned behind me.

Zadicus's wings.

Even facing away from them, I could not forget the sight. I doubted I could ever forget. Like that of an eagle, the midnight black feathers were long, luminous, and plenty.

I withheld the urge to shake the sight of them away. Not because it was hard to believe, but because it was not. I could feel him, his essence and scent, rolling off them. As though they watched me. As though they still lived. As though they waited to join their counterpart.

As though they were a piece of his soul, and darkness knew why, but he'd been forced to leave them behind.

A pair of forest-floor-brown eyes were staring at me, causing me to exit from my trance and soak in their strength as their owner waited patiently for the king's game of control to end.

An end I knew would stain the souls and relationships of those present for years to come.

I nodded, just a hint, and the female blinked, her lithe, milky-white fingers reaching up to brush over her chin.

Her stomach did not protrude as much as most of the others. I wasn't sure of the duration of pregnancy for the Fae, but I silently implored whoever might be listening, watching, that she would not have to endure this again.

She glanced back at the ground, and I folded my hands in my lap, my hunger, my own aches and pains, a backdrop to the misery taking place beneath the dais.

At long last, with the final faerie blessed, the king let out a satisfied huff, taking his time to rise and fasten his pants. He still had his boots on, and I wasn't sure why that pissed me off almost as much as his attitude toward his transgressions. But it did.

I wanted to kill him. To peel his skin from his flesh and study what laid beneath before pinning it to the walls of this room to drip endlessly forevermore.

"You seem to be having some violent thoughts, dear Audra."

My teeth were grinding. I relaxed my features, knocking some hair back over my shoulders by shaking them. "Whatever do you mean?" I said with sweet malice.

Another huff, and then he was stalking between a row of expectant mothers, indicating with a wave of his hand that they were free to leave.

He slowed as he approached, and though I kept my attention fixed firmly on him, I didn't miss the way the females raced off the floor and to their respective partners, or how a few of them seemed too broken to move, forcing the males to go to them.

"Let us not play games," he said, running his fingers through his hair, sweeping it back in a way that was far too pleasant for such a horrid being. "It would not be fair, being that you can lie, and I cannot."

I bit back a retort and smiled. "But of course."

Quick as lightning, he jumped up the steps to his throne, leaning heavily over its side to whisper with an excitement I wanted to murder. "So what was it? Did you daydream about killing me? Hurting me?" He gasped, chuckling low and deep. "Oh, please, did you wonder if I were to fuck you, too?"

It was then it truly struck me that no matter how many fables and tales were told, there would never be enough to adequately capture the color of darkness that resided inside Beldine's king.

Every instinct screamed at me to lean away, but I held still and tilted my head. "You wouldn't dare sully yourself with a mere half breed like me."

"You did unlock the doors for us," he said, dragging a fingernail over the wooden armrest. "You erased the curse. I'm not sure I've thanked you for that."

"Indeed, you have not," I said in an iced tone that warned him not to try.

His lips pursed, eyes falling to my mouth. "Some other time, maybe." As he reached out to touch it, I froze, his cool finger against my skin hardening my blood beneath it. "How in the mother of fates did you get these beautiful things?"

"Scars are coveted, I assume, by those who cannot scar?" Even as I voiced the question, Zad's back, the nicks upon his body, came to mind.

The king's eyes were transfixed as though he'd been taken someplace else. "Oh, we can scar, my pretty half-blood. Though it takes great lengths as I'm sure this did." He made to drag his fingers over my lips, but I pulled back. He grinned, canines gleaming and longer than my own, but not by much. "How?"

Pain. If I hadn't already been certain, I now was. He was a sadist, possibly the most fervid I'd ever met.

I saw little harm in telling him. "A heated poker and a magic-ridding rock."

His eyes came alive, the gold circling the black pupil growing thinner. "I've heard of these rocks. Tacky," he said with a cluck of his tongue. "But do tell, how a creature as beautiful and surely as vain as the rumors suggest, tortured the vermin?"

I lifted my lips, baring a hint of teeth. "I drained them in the market square."

He clapped, then rubbed his hands together, and I could've sworn if I looked that I'd find his pants tented, even after he'd fucked nearly twenty females. "This is fantastic, truly."

"Why?" I dared ask as he rose and stepped casually down the steps. A few lesser faeries had arrived, silent as stray cats, during our little chat, and were plucking up all the feathered mats.

"Our time together will be most enjoyable."

There were specks of blood on some of the mats, and darkness knew what else. My stomach filled with acid.

"Do make good use of the bathing chamber," Ryle called from the doorway. "Your presence will be required at dinner."

When he was gone, the scent of sex and ire lingering in his wake, I peered at the armrest he'd cut with his fingernail and found it cratered.

SIX

Audra

Had my mind not been so thoroughly spent, I might've screamed when the web-footed faerie entered.

I finished washing, then slowly pulled myself out of the tub, which had no faucet but had already been filled with creamy, petaled warm water by the time I'd returned to my rooms.

She curtsied, holding a sizeable cloth in her webbed hands. "Good evening, Lady Audra."

Lady. I supposed to her, I was no queen at all, and therefore I should be grateful she'd shown me at least that much respect. But I wasn't. It was just another thing that ripened the bone-deep hatred this place and its king had stoked to life.

I plucked the rough cloth from the faerie, drying myself as I watched her mop up splashes of water and drain the tub.

"Where does the water go?" I asked, thinking there was no plumbing. If they had any, then I had not seen it.

"Back into the land," she said.

I refrained from rolling my eyes. "Who are you?"

Her violet skin turned a shade darker, and she dipped again. "Apologies, I am not myself today. I am Temika, your lady-in-waiting, if you will." Straightening, she curled some inky black hair behind her elfin ears as her rose-pink lips lifted into an apologetic smile.

"The blessing," I said, handing her the cloth when I was done and then stalking into the bedchamber. My nightgown was gone, and I cursed beneath my breath at the arrangement laid out on the bed, which had now been dressed in velvet black. A few white feathers had escaped, sprinkling over the floor surrounding it.

"Our king is doing everything he can to ensure our survival."

That stilled my hands, which had been unfolding the scraps this faerie called a gown from the bed. "By raping females?"

She rushed around the bed, her long purple finger—her nails a natural-looking black—pressed to her lips. Green as deep as the tree foliage after a storm shone from her panicked, slanted eyes.

"Please. The wind has ears, my lady."

Of course. Exhaling so hard damp tendrils of hair blew from my face, I shoved my arms into the ivory lace concoction I was expected to wear.

The lesser Fae rubbed the wall closest to me, and a mirror appeared. Walking to my back, she fastened the ribbon ties, and when she was done, the black bow stood upright, as if I had my own set of small wings.

Brushing my hands down the jeweled chest, over the layers of soft silk that drooped from my half-exposed breasts to fall around my knees, I found I didn't hate it.

"Is it not to your liking?" she asked, a note of worry in the question.

"I'm just used to... far grander ensembles."

Temika fussed with the fluffy chiffon banding over my shoulders. "In your land, you are a queen, so I would assume so."

"Your queens do not wear this?"

"They wear whatever they so desire, and it shows." She hummed, a smile in her childlike voice. "You shall see for yourself at the feast."

True, and I suppose I hadn't the time nor the inclination the night before. "What are the other queens doing here? And why are there three and one king?"

Her pause and careful tone held some reluctance as she explained, "It has been this way for as long as anyone can remember, my lady. But it is not wise for me to educate you on things when the king might wish to do so himself."

I figured as much, and I knew what would likely happen to her should he catch wind she'd been supplying me with information. Still, I had to ask again, "Why are they here?"

"They await the act," she said, in a simple way that implied she would not elaborate any further.

"The act?" I repeated, wondering what type of ridiculousness that would be. Surely, I'd be involved.

She gestured for me to sit in a wicker chair and then began selecting pieces of my hair to braid. I watched her deft fingers in the mirror, unseeing, and then noticed the rouge and powders supplied on the bureau.

At my request, Temika handed me the rouge, continuing with my hair as I declared I'd paint my lips. I smiled as I opened the pot and dipped the slim brush in. It'd been mere days, but I missed it, as well as many other things I chose to shove to the back of my mind.

I had to if I were to endure and see this through.

"Is it true that you have found your mate in our prince?" she asked, her voice whisper-soft as though it were a juicy secret even though it wasn't.

"Indeed," I said, my hand trembling a little as the brush glided over my bottom lip.

Her lips pursed, then flattened, then pursed again as though she wished to ask more. I encouraged it. To indulge her might serve in her indulging me. "Ask."

She smiled at my hair, her voice even softer as she tied off the end of a tiny braid ghosting across my hairline and pinned it behind my ear. "It's just that I, well... I cannot believe he's here. The true heir, home at last."

The pot fell from my hands to the tiled floor, crashing into pieces.

Temika gasped and rushed to clean it up while I sat there, my lips smudged, my heart trying to evict itself from my chest to quit with this ever-evolving abuse already.

"I am so sorry, Lady Audra," she hurried out, her fingers stained from cleaning up the rouge. "I spoke out of turn."

"Stop it," I snapped, shooing her to her feet to pick up the brush.

She tossed the broken pot into a tiny brass cylinder upon the bureau, her hands shaking.

I fixed the mess I'd made of my lips. "I told you to say what was on your mind. I just..." I had to be honest, for maybe it might work in my favor, and if I were being honest with myself, I was desperate to fucking unload this disaster onto someone else. "I didn't know."

"That he is here?" She stood there a moment, her tiny, near non-existent nose scrunching, and then her eyes popped. "You did not know Prince Zadicus was the true heir to our realm?"

"Both." I rolled my eyes, handing her the brush as I stood. "I knew he was an heir, but I am no faerie. I do not know of your customs and whose right it is to rule." I straightened my dress. "Evidently."

"Of course," Temika muttered, disappearing into the bathing room with the lip brush.

She returned as I was tucking my feet into ivory slippers. Adorned with little bows at the pointed toes, they fit my feet like plush gloves.

"I'm sorry," she said again, and I almost growled at her for the repetitive use of the stupid word. "The shock of all this then..." She toed the ground with her bare foot, her eyes filled with sympathy. "It must be extremely difficult."

I nodded. Staring down at my slippers, I found the compassion I'd wanted to be more of an annoyance. Nevertheless, it infused my spine with much-needed steel, and I marched for the invisible door.

Before I could walk out, Temika murmured, soft as melting butter beneath the sun, "He will join us soon, and everything will be just as it should be once more."

I was beginning to fear just what that might mean.

The feast was held in the throne room again, and my chest grew tight with anticipation as I took each step down the winding stairs. With every sconce lit, the serpentine curls of wisteria that noosed around the railing were revealed, and as I laid my hand upon it, needing something to steady myself, it moved.

I withdrew my hand, blinking at the trembling plant. It shivered, as though my touch had awakened it, then stretched and stilled.

Temika left me at the foot of the stairs, and the sconces came to life in the soil-scented passageway dotted with guards. Light and laughter exploded from the throne room, throwing shadows across the walls to greet me. My steps slowed as my heart pounded hard.

He was here. For although the Fae could not lie, I hadn't known what Temika's version of *here* had meant. Now, though, I could sense it, *sense him*, as if a coil of slithering, sparking lightning had banded itself around my waist. It tugged, and it vibrated, the hum comforting even if I wanted to tear his stupidly handsome head from his shoulders for all his carefully hidden deception.

Only, when I reached the glowing doorway, the giant oak doors with carved wings thrown open against the walls, the feeling dissipated.

The revelry paused for all of a fractured heartbeat, eyes skittering from the returned tables to take me in. They soon bobbed away, uninterested, in search of entertainment with their own ilk.

"Ravishing," Ryle purred, shadow evaporating into smoky tendrils as he appeared before me.

Curious and wanting to hide and smother my thorn-stabbing disappointment, I eyed his black ensemble, taking note of his armored torso. The metal rippled beneath the dripping candle loaded chandeliers as though he'd tried to conceal the fact he wore protective clothing. Mahogany tufts erupted from the neck, matching that of the gauzy material fluttering down his arms. His pants were leather, tight, and his boots, black with giant silver buckles. "How did you do that?"

He cocked his head, taking a calculated step closer. I stared at his jaw, unwilling to crane my neck back to meet his eyes. It was clean-shaven, smooth and square but lacking the savage definition of his brother's. Was he older? Younger? I wasn't sure it mattered, or if he was who I should be asking. I tucked the curiosity away.

"Sweeping?" he said. My eyes lifted then, and I felt my brows pull. With a rough chuckle, he offered his hand. "With an object of importance in hand from the place of which you wish to be transported, you can sweep into the void and land there."

I was surprised he'd answered, and in such a way that I could understand—for the most part. That explained how he'd brought me here. The strange dreams, though... My guess was they were his attempt to lure me away from Zad or perhaps just another game. "No riddles or malice tonight?"

His hand waited. "Sit, eat. I have a few guests who'd like to see you." I ignored his proffered hand and reached for my skirts. Remembering too late there was little to hold, I shook my hair from my shoulders and made my way to my seat.

Chatter and eating continued, even as Ryle slumped into his seat. He did not reach for his food. He slouched, an arm bent upon the side of the oak chair, and his eyes on a steaming tray of what appeared to be salted jellyfish.

He held no interest in the disgusting-looking food, of that I was sure. Apples, large and red, sat nestled alongside the fat globes of purple grapes. I avoided the fruit, not wanting to chance that when I returned home, my own would taste like soot in comparison.

I decided on some chicken, withholding a moan as I sliced through a juicy breast, herbs dancing over my tongue.

"Wine?" Ryle said, still seeming every inch the bored king as he watched me.

"I'm no fool," I said, dabbing my mouth with the corner of a blood-red napkin.

He barked out a laugh. "You think I'd go to such lengths to bring you here, only to poison you?"

"It is not poison I'm concerned about." Not entirely, anyway.

He leaned forward, arms upon the thick oak of the table, hands clasping together around his empty plate. "Winter queen, please drink some wine."

I reached for it, not sure why I was even doing so. Then I blinked, and the compulsion faded, leaving a bitter whiff of smoke in its wake. "Asshole king," I said, sneering his way. "Water will do just fine."

Silence descended.

His grin morphed into something sinister, but after a moment of holding my gaze, mine daring him to send me back to my rooms, it fell, and everyone resumed conversation and eating once more.

A glass of water was poured by a female seated next to me. I thanked her, tried to catch a look at her face, but her gold hair spilled down the side of it, concealing whoever she might be.

A lover, I was guessing, if she sat this close to the king during a feast with other royal folk. She wore two thick golden cuffs around each wrist, but I couldn't make out what the engravings on them meant.

"Where is he?" I said, scenting and then draining the water with as much grace as possible. I was beyond parched, but I did not let on. There was something different about it, though nothing that caused alarm. If anything, it seemed cleaner or fresher than any water I'd drunk before.

"Your beloved?" Ryle plucked up his goblet of wine. He knew exactly who I was referring to, and so I merely waited. He rolled his eyes, annoyed at my reluctance to spar with him. "He is here, but you already know that."

"Where is *here*, exactly?" I pressed, growing frustrated with the games.

A clang of cutlery, and then a male across and a little ways down the table cleared his throat. Looking that way, I almost choked and set my goblet down with a thump. "Adran."

His white-blond hair had grown longer, his cheeks more gaunt, but his eyes still held that dancing humor he was always so fond of carrying. "Cousin."

I could feel Ryle's eyes bouncing back and forth between us—entertained at last.

"I thought you'd have been sea serpent bait many months ago."

"Oh, he was," Ryle interjected and gnashed his teeth when my eyes shot his way. "No being, *royal* or otherwise, sets foot on this sacred land without my knowledge, and when I learned just who this delicious morsel of tainted blood was..." He sat back, spreading his hands. "Well, a very helpful guest did he make."

"Helpful?" I said, looking back at my cousin.

He held my gaze with steely focus. No remorse, only cold-blooded survival in his eyes. I knew what he was saying without saying a word. There was no need to wonder nor ask why... *I did what I must, and you left me no other choice.*

I had tossed him out like rotten food, leaving him for the wild things to collect. But he'd betrayed me in a way that had almost resulted in my death, and now, he'd done so again. "You'll find I cannot be so lenient this time, *cousin*."

"Should we ever make it home," he said, voice low even though many could likely hear as their senses were far better than our own, "I'd expect nothing less."

I licked grease from my teeth, then rinsed my mouth with more water, saying to the king, "How helpful was he?"

"One cannot steal into someone's dreams without knowing, to some degree, who they are. Though I'd love to watch you torture the young lad." His tone was bland, and he waved the subject away with a flick of his ring-bedecked fingers. "It matters not right now. Let us dance."

I didn't have time to refuse.

My chair vanished, and strong arms captured my waist, twisting me away and then releasing. A smooth hand caught mine before I flew into the few standing guests, tugging me back to that armored chest.

My hands splayed against it. The violent trussing of fiddles and the wild beating of drums erupted, the strain of a lone flute trying to keep up. "Ryle," I started, but I was swung away from him again, and I spun, faster and faster than before. Faster than anyone with a beating heart should ever spin.

The world became a blur of music-entwined rainbows, and I was but dust bouncing across them, my arms not my own as they swam around me, desperately trying to keep me afloat.

I was brought back to the world with a violent crash—to that hard, cold chest. My heart galloped so hard that each beat physically hurt, and my eyes sang with tears. Not from fear, but from the whirlwind I was being forced upon.

"Stop," I said, clutching at the ruffled fabric of his collar as laughter entered my ringing ears. I didn't have the opportunity to see if the guests laughed at me. Like a toy, I was thrust back into the bright, stomach-snatching yet oddly addicting pirouette of sensation, the sound of the king's laughter the only tether to what was real.

I was sweating, panting, and unsure of how much time had passed when I collided with him again and felt the brush of cool lips upon my brow. I shook against him, not wanting to touch him, but knowing if I didn't hold on, I'd fall—drip into a puddle on the floor to be stomped on by all the dancing guests in the cavernous room.

Yet I knew I had to let go if I was to ever make it stop.

He pushed. I clung.

"Your royal greatness."

Ryle paused, his hand coiled tight around my waist, squeezing with the urge to continue playing with me.

Too dizzy, I struggled to make out who stood next to him, murmuring rough, urgent words.

His grip loosened, and then I was released, stumbling back and bumping into someone who growled and moved away. I met the stone wall, too hard, and winced. Panting and blinking into the dazzling blur of the room, faces eventually grew features, and colors separated themselves enough to form individuals and objects.

Ryle was entering a doorway near the back of the room. It was small, as though only used for dragging people in and out of.

Which is what happened next. Although he was not dragged.

Ryle was thrown across the room on a blast of invisible fury, dirt and dust spraying as he hit the opposite wall and slid down to his ass.

Zadicus.

Gold chains, looking as though they'd been snapped, trailed behind him upon the tile.

His chest was heaving, his long hair freed and hanging in sweaty strands around his face. Lips peeled back over his teeth, but he didn't advance on the king, who was shaking his head and rising to a sitting position against the wall.

Zad tore his fevered eyes from his brother and swung them to me.

SEVEN

Zadicus

"Never has there been a fury like that of a mated male," Ryle muttered, brushing his sleeves as he stood.

Fuck him. I'd deal with his pompous bullshit later.

Everyone moved aside, the clang of the chains they'd attempted to keep me contained with the only sound as I waded through familiar faces. I ignored them all, my only desire, my desperate wish, awaiting me behind the king's seat at the head of the table.

The sun was soon due to rise, and I was willing to wager he'd messed with her for hours, and that it was just dawning on her now.

As soon as I'd sensed it, that tinge in the air, the metallic essence of my lifeblood, I'd stiffened in my cell. And when I'd felt her panic only grow as if it were my own, higher and higher until I feared her heart might give out, I'd snapped. No longer would I be a pawn waiting to be moved. No longer would I play nice in hopes of getting us out of here safely.

He'd pushed me too far, and I'd killed two soldiers I hadn't recognized before tearing out of my cage, the chains snapping from the wall in my wake.

The gold embossed iron and the thorn barred door to my cell didn't stand a chance. I was too old and too tied to this land to be held captive by it.

"You're bleeding." Her first words to me. They were breathy but firm even though her chest was rising far too fast, her sapphire eyes murky with exhaustion.

Reaching her, I clasped her heated cheeks, my forehead meeting hers as I drew what felt like my first real breath in days. "My queen."

Her hands gripped mine, but though I was sure she'd intended to, she did not pull them away. I wouldn't have let her if she'd tried. Her eyes closed, her breasts lowering as she exhaled a harsh breath over my lips.

For two days and one night, I'd been locked in the bowels of my family's fortress. Two whole days of hearing all the ways this court had changed and all the ways it had not. Two days of sensing her spiked fear and heightened emotions, knowing she was here, alive and needing me, but biding my time.

Kash and Dace were still in their cells, and at my urging, Landen had stayed behind to let Audra's court know what was happening and what they should do. Nothing. A feat I knew so many of them would find difficult. I couldn't blame them, but they knew if they disobeyed Landen's orders and came here, it would not result in anything good.

Audra swallowed, the sound thick in my ears, in the silence of all the prying eyes. Words she could not say, would not dare to, shaped from her trembling lips. "Take me home."

I tilted up her chin and pressed my lips to hers, long and hard. That rock in my chest began to beat again, sluggish and slow and desperate for more.

She pulled back, her eyes opening, and in them, I saw the magnitude of all I'd kept from her.

There was no time to explain or apologize now.

"Love," Ryle drawled, clapping slowly. "Such delicious intensity. Why, I wish we could bottle it up and drink it, bask in its glow, for then perhaps we would not be so inclined to make such brash, foolish decisions."

With a reluctance that ate at my bones, I released my hold on Audra's jaw and cheeks, promising with my eyes to explain.

She lowered her lashes, and I gritted my teeth, turning to face my half brother. "You think to chain me like some mutt while you exert yourself and my queen with your immature games?" I took a step forward, purposely blocking Audra from the king, a move which he noticed. "You know better." I threw up my arms, the chains dangling. "You probably even expected as much."

"You never do disappoint with your predictability." Strolling toward the dais, to where I refused to let my eyes wander, he rubbed his head, granules of dust bouncing from his hair. "Almost six hundred years, and here you are, seemingly unchanged."

"Seemingly," I said through my teeth.

He nodded, lips pursed in mock thought as he stopped before his throne. He fell back into it, a granite crown encrusted with onyx berries and thorns appearing on his head. "Tell me, tell all of us," he said, gesturing to the still crowd, "how much you miss your home, what you miss the most, and I promise not to dance with your winter queen again."

The air grew drunk on anticipation. If I answered him, he won. If I did not, he won again. "You know the answer to that."

A short nod and the crown tilted back with his head as he gazed up at the wall behind his throne. "Again, predictable."

He snapped his fingers, and the iron chains fell away. Red, angry welts foamed around my wrists. I paid little mind to the pain for it would fade. The pain of what I'd given up, however, of what I'd exchanged for something I knew I possibly shouldn't have, never did.

Muscles in my back twitched, Audra's eyes probing the area as if she knew. She likely did. She likely knew an assortment of things I wished I'd been able to tell her myself.

But I was a damned coward, and there never seemed to be a good time to cough up a confession as huge as this.

"Rightful heir." The words were whispered amongst the gatherers surrounding us.

And it did not go unnoticed by the king, whose jaw flexed as he stood. "Come then," he said to me, standing and rounding his throne. "Come and say hello to them. I'm sure they've missed you, too."

My feet itched with the urge to move, but I couldn't. To do so would reveal another way in which he could control me, and that ache, that sense of missing a limb, a part of my very soul, flared and burned. I wasn't sure I'd survive nearing them, let alone getting close enough to touch them.

Stakes, onyx with rubies embedded in the hilts, held them to the wall, and I flinched. Searing agony crawled over me as though they were still attached, when Ryle pulled one of them down, ripping through muscle and bone and tissue and cleaving through feathers.

They floated to the ground, one resting over his boot, and he finally stopped.

My teeth were dust, I was sure. A steady hand on my back helped soften my breathing.

No longer was Audra behind me, but beside me, her touch an iced breeze to fight the inferno engulfing me.

Ryle noticed, of course, his hand falling to his side as he came forward and descended the dais. "Sweet," he said in a tone that conveyed he thought it was anything but. "He deceives you, mates with you, hides from you, and has you dragged into his treacherous past, yet you still dare to comfort him."

Audra wisely said nothing, and she did not remove her hand.

"Get rid of her," Ryle clipped, his darkening eyes on mine as the guards left the walls.

I snarled at them, keeping Audra at my back.

They hesitated, but their compulsion, their built-in inability to disobey an order, had them reaching for her.

I shoved one away. My magic wrapped around the mind of the other, ready to squeeze, but Audra stepped forward, and my jaw slackened as she walked to the doors.

The guards watched, then raced to keep up.

My eyes swung back from the dark that'd swallowed her when the king called, "Have her taken to my rooms." His gaze, more black now than gold, sank into mine. "Where she's less likely to misbehave, at least, with our *rightful heir.*"

Before I could lunge for him, he was gone, and I made for the doors only to have them close in my face. Growling, I tore at them, splintering the wood. He couldn't have her. I'd given him everything, but he would not get her. She wouldn't let him, I knew, but that would not stop him.

A crawling hush traveled over my skin, raising fine hairs, and I paused.

Turning back to my audience, I found them all bent at the knees, and when they straightened, one by one, they came forward.

"Prince." Dunn, a wolf who'd been in my family's service since I was growing into my power, was first to greet me. "We know this comes at a great cost, but my pack and I thank you for returning."

Scowling, I bunched my hands as he bowed and moved back, and more warriors and courtiers came forward to offer their gratitude and well wishes.

Immobile and hardly breathing, I stood there. I wouldn't disrespect them and all they'd likely endured while visiting the Onyx Court by tearing out of here like I so desperately wished to.

Finally, the queen of the Silver Court floated over, her hands bound together and hidden beneath shimmering silver sleeves. Her bright eyes were dim with what looked like defeat.

"Este," I said, my brows lowering.

"I feared because of your mate, you might not return."

"Why would I return?" I almost laughed. Surely, they knew of the bargain my brother and I had made all those years ago. "We had a deal."

She nodded as if understanding. Her voice was soft but thick. "Beldine is starving. The rain doesn't visit as frequently as it should, and the springs often grow cold. Many creatures in the forests grow ill and are losing their young, and so are we." Taking my hands, I felt hers tremble and saw her lips do the same. "It needs you, and the power only you, as its rightful ruler, possess."

"No," I said, now understanding the source of the sorrow in her eyes.

"We must feed it."

I swallowed, wrenching away from the queen, and ran a hand through my hair as all eyes pressed heavily on me. The expectation, the hope, and the responsibility... I wanted none of it.

"I won't," I said, gruff but firm. "Apologies, but fuck no."

"Surely, your half breed will understand, just as our loved ones must understand."

Audra would never understand, and I would never dare expect her to. Darkness, even I didn't fucking understand. Bastard or not, Ryle was my father's son, and it showed. So the idea of him not being able to feed our land and our people with his presence was something that had never so much as crossed my mind.

A warrior left the room via the entrance I'd stormed through, and Este backed up, her hand fluttering to her mouth. Her near-white hair fell to conceal her expression as she moved back toward the members of her court who were in attendance.

"What does she speak of?" asked a voice I'd have loved to have never heard again.

Adran. I sighed. Of course, the pest would live. "None of your concern." Marching toward the table, I grabbed a leg of chicken and tore the flesh from bone as people dispersed to their rooms.

"I'm sensing a sensitive subject, yes?" Adran poured a goblet of wine from a glass carafe. He passed it to me, but I refused. He lifted a shoulder, then drained it. Idiot.

"They were discussing why the king has stolen our prince's half breed *queen*," said Mortaine, queen of the Gold Court. She and her few court members were the only ones still seated at the table.

I glared, but she only smiled, sipping her berried wine—the shade similar to that of her eyes and shoulder-length curls. "Long ago, he made a deal with his bastard brother that forbade Ryle from ever troubling our dear prince again. So our High King, desperate as he must be to keep what he's taken, went and stole something else." Thin, plum-colored brows rose. "Or should I say someone? The only *thing* that would ever have our stray prince here skipping back across the Whispering Sea."

"Finished?" I said through my teeth.

Adran shifted.

"Well," Mortaine purred, pushing her breasts into the table as she leaned forward. "Being that it has been an awfully long time…"

Withholding a slew of curses, I wiped my bloodied hands down my soiled shirt and growled, "Enough," then waded away. I had to get Audra from the king's rooms or find the asshole and make some other bargain so he'd leave her alone.

"Interesting," Adran said in a dry tone. "But I'm dying to know, what exactly does his majesty need his brother for?"

"To feed the land," someone said as though he were daft.

"Gathered that already." Sarcasm dripped from Adran's voice. "Now, would you be so kind as to inform me how one does such a thing?" I was certain he already knew. The insufferable rodent merely wanted it confirmed.

"The act," Mortaine said, all venomous silk.

"The act?" Adran repeated.

I walked through the mercifully reopened doors as Mortaine explained, and Adran's laughter chased me up the stairs.

EIGHT

Audra

THAT SPECKLED, GLITTERING BLACK TOUCHED SLENDER fingers over everything. The more time I spent in this castle of doom, the more I came to see onyx interwoven among the moss, tiled floors, and the walls.

Though no place was as heavily occupied by the stone as the king's quarters.

I stood in the antechamber for long moments, studying the way the rock crawled between, or perhaps behind, the tree-woven walls. A dark green chest of drawers took up the space to my right, and atop them laid a collection of skulls that varied in size and shape too much to be anything other than real.

Human skulls, I mused, daring to approach and brush a finger over the brow of what had to have once been a woman.

Beneath my slippers, a burgundy rug inlaid with sharp black diamond patterns rolled into the adjacent room. His bedchamber. To my left, a door leading to the bathing chamber. It was cracked open, revealing a tub the size of a small pool inside.

A memory washed in, violent in the way it seized my heart and held it within its unforgiving fist. Of my lord in my own bathing pool, and myself on his lap with his adoring, hungry eyes staring up at me.

He was here, and besides looking as though he'd walked through a rose bush and was cut by each thorn, he was okay. I found solace in that—a relief heavy enough to loosen some of the weight in my chest, but only some.

He was both my ice and the burn.

"I thought you might like those."

I withheld the urge to startle, still trying to grow accustomed to his vanishing and appearing act. Though I doubted this king was something one could ever grow accustomed to.

Half a millennia.

They'd been under his rule for hundreds of years. The implications of that had hit me like a boulder to the head in the throne room, rendering me dizzy once more—most of all, what it meant for Zad.

For how old my lord truly was.

"I did not pick you to be the type for trophies," I said, keeping my tone clear of emotion. My finger paused on a skull missing the back of its head.

"He was bludgeoned to death," the king supplied with cool grace. "And I'd thought, given the rumors of your cold heart, that you'd have"—he paused—"what did you call them?"

"Trophies. Souvenirs, if you will," I said, taking a step forward, loathing that he was yet again at my back.

"Ah, yes. I'd thought you'd have many souvenirs of your own."

"Souvenirs are nothing but portable bruises." I reached the doors to his bedchamber, and they opened silently.

Unable to help it, I flinched when my hair was gathered from my back and wrapped in his hand. Warm breath fogged the skin of my bare shoulder, and he murmured, "Bruises. Bruises on what?"

"Your soul." I continued forward, and he mercifully released my hair.

A half-tester bed, the wood stained a rich brown, stood in the center of the room against the far wall. Two glassless windows sat on either side, a soft, springtime breeze flowing through.

The scent of jasmine, damp, and the sound of rushing water was everywhere, but not enough to smother Ryle's suffocating presence. Like oil, it dragged slick and slow over my skin. I longed to wash it off, but I knew trying to do so would take considerable effort.

The room was huge, circular, and I suspected if viewing from outside, it would be the highest point of the castle—if that was indeed what this place was.

I crossed to a long desk planted before one of the diamond-shaped windows, inkpots and parchment lined in tidy succession. "Has this always been your room?"

"Full of questions this eve." Noticing the fading stars outside, the pink and gold hues that had begun to erase the night, he corrected, "Morning," then chuckled to himself. "My, my. Time indeed flies when you're having fun." Hands tucked within his pant pockets, he rounded the bed, the emerald and black linens untucking themselves as he stripped.

"How long was I dancing for?" I was certain I already knew the answer, but the gravity of it was needed. A reminder, as unnecessary as it was, of where I was and who I dared to duel with.

"Not long. Five, maybe six hours." Shirtless, the skin of his chest lighter than his brother's, and his arms and torso far leaner, he shoved at his pants.

I leaned back against the desk. "Why not magic them away?"

"I like to watch you squirm," he said so plainly, eyes riddled with that cruel mirth twitching his lips.

They were thin, I realized, and a faint dimple appeared in his cheek.

"You sleep clothed?" he asked, running his gaze over my body in such a way that had me glaring when his eyes met mine again. He shrugged, grinning as he slumped over the bed.

"I'm not sleeping," I said. "Not in here."

"Scared?" he goaded with pouting lips.

A bang sounded, and I straightened.

The king didn't so much as remove his eyes from me and remained where he was as Zad's voice, faint, as though he were underwater, echoed from out in the hall.

More banging—like thunder striking a tree.

"Go to him," Ryle said, a careful caress. "I dare you."

I'd placed one foot in front of the other when my desperate heart made room for my brain to absorb the king's warning.

I closed my eyes. Reopening them, I marched to the king's bed and grabbed a black-furred pillow.

"Where do you think you're going?"

I hurried from the bedchamber and into the bathing room, my rage a fire climbing higher with each bang on the door outside. "To sleep." Then I locked myself inside, knowing it was futile. If the king sought entry, entry he would have.

Even so, the barrier gave a modicum of comfort inside the lair of a monster darkness-bent on giving me none.

※

Night pressed through the small oval window in the bathing room.

My back ached almost as much as the stupid thing in my chest, but I rose, stretching it out as a hummed tune from outside entered my sleep-addled brain.

I wasn't sure how long I'd slept for, but I was willing to wager, based on how awful I felt, that it wasn't very long. I'd lain there, curled up inside the large tub, the pillow beneath my cheek, as Zad's banging slowly abated. It seemed to take hours, and I loathed to think of what his hands looked like today.

Tonight, I mentally corrected, remembering a verse so often read from a book as a child. *They slept beneath the burning sun and awoke beneath the dancing stars.*

Other memories of Zadicus reading to me upon the roof of his manor, beside me in bed, and in the armchair near the fire came crashing in. All tales that hinted at his true self, nudging, avoiding... His hands would be fine, I reminded myself with my teeth gritting. For he was more than royal.

He was a stray faerie prince.

Using what appeared to be some type of brush made from

dried thistle, I scrubbed my teeth and drank some mint-flavored water that'd been sitting in a small decanter on the vanity.

Afterward, I stared at the pale cream of my skin, the sharper rise of my cheekbones, and the harsh set of my jaw in the gilded mirror. Rummaging through a basket beneath the vanity, I found a wide-toothed comb, the cool metal warming in my fingers as I dragged it through my tangled hair.

There was nothing to tie it back with, so I let it fall around my shoulders and steeled them, facing the door.

On the other side, the king ceased his humming. His hands were tucked in the velvet pockets of his green pants, a matching cloak thrown haphazardly over his shoulders. The warm spring evening meant he had no need for it, which was evident given his bare chest. And it made me hate him just that little bit more.

"Sleep well?"

"Indeed."

His brow rose as did the corner of his lips. "You know, I could force you to join me in my bed."

"You could try," I said, tone crisp. "But you would fail, and we both know you loathe failure."

He eyed me for a moment, then straightened, stepping far too close in half a breath.

It took considerable effort to keep my breathing normal. The last thing I wanted was to hint that he unnerved me in any way even though he knew he did. It was highly possible that he unnerved everyone in the same vicinity as him.

"I must admit I've been wondering." Touching a tendril of my hair, he watched the inky strand curl around his finger. "Why in the darkness my dear brother would ever mate with such a cruel beauty."

I ignored the urge to swallow, biting my tongue.

"Then while I lay awake in the late afternoon hours, I remembered something." A humorous huff stirred my hair as he lifted it to his nose and inhaled deeply. "Zadicus always did love his fruit.

Grapes, apples, lime, lemons..." His eyes sank into mine. "The bittersweet and the oh, so sour."

I offered a forced smile, my lips tight. Then I forced them apart to murmur, "How lovely. Now that he is here, shall we get to the reason as to why, so we can all move on with our lives?"

My hair slithered through his long, milk-white fingers, and at the last second, he caught the loose curl between them and pulled.

The loss tingled at my scalp for scalding moments. Strands of dark hair lay spilled over the floor, but he merely smiled before throwing open the door leading out into the hall.

In his absence, I stared at the hair for a beat, my chest rising with that ever-climbing fury. It longed to be unleashed, to howl through the halls and tear down his towering wood and onyx nightmare.

Not yet, I told myself.

Half breed. I'd seen only a measure of what the king was capable of, and my magic, as chaos-inducing as it could be, was no match.

The words thumped into the back of my clenched teeth. *Not yet.*

This hallway appeared different, lighter. Holes in the ceiling, thatched with what looked to be grass and glass, lit the sloping tile and the paintings on the wall. Inside the scratched and marred frames were images of beings I did not recognize. Small depictions of fluttering faeries upon a hillside and wild seas kept me company on the way to the stairs outside a smaller turret at the slopes end.

Where Zad had made off to, I didn't know.

Nowhere, I realized, when a hand grasped mine before I could place a foot upon the first step.

I was hauled into the shadows against the doorway to whatever lay inside the other turret behind the stairs, its etched wood beneath my palm as I steadied myself and pulled away.

Wild-eyed with mussed hair rocking against his jaw, he licked his lips. "Are you okay?"

"Did you sleep?"

He shook his head, his gaze surveying my body and the dress I was still wearing from last night. "Did he touch you?"

"Did you wait outside his rooms all day?"

"Of course, I did," he said as though there was nothing else he ought to have done instead, like rest, plan, and preserve his energy so we could get the fuck home.

I tried to contain it, tried to push it down and let it simmer rather than boil into a rage that sharpened every word. "Get your hand off me."

As he released me, Zad's eyes flashed with hurt, and he said again, "Did he touch you?"

"Let's just find out what he wants."

"Audra," he barked as I turned to walk away.

"Enough," I hissed, whirling on him. "It's because of you we are here. Because of your secret deceit. So whatever happens as a result of that is on you."

Jaw granite, he glared, tendrils of auburn hair snaking over his cheek and a gold eye. "Did he force you to do anything?"

That he was so concerned about whether his brother had me in his bed, more so than what he himself had done to me... "Let your imagination fill in the blanks. I care not."

He snatched my hand again upon the top step, his eyes wild once more. "You think you can attempt to stab me in the chest and then just walk away?"

I did something I hadn't dared to before, that I never thought myself capable of when it came to this male, and threw him back into the wall on a gust of snow-crusted wind.

I hadn't meant for him to hit it hard enough to shake, dust crumbling, or for him to curse in pain as he crumpled on the floor. But it had become too much. This insidious clenching inside my chest, the barbs that pressed and retreated repeatedly, and the rage that begged to be given an outlet—it was lucky I didn't accidentally kill him.

I swallowed knives before remembering that, of course, I couldn't do that.

He was a faerie prince, his uncovered deception revealing all the many ways I'd been a fool. Especially, looking back, as I'd once dared to protect him from Raiden's rage and the danger that could befall him should Raiden find out what the lord of the east, this prince in hiding, meant to me. That we'd linked.

My love for him had me willing to ache for what seemed an eternity until I found a way for us to safely be together.

I laughed, no humor to the croaked sound. "You..." I started, my voice hoarse. "I tried to protect *you*, someone I, and everyone else in my kingdom, should have been protected *from*."

He groaned, rising to his feet, his soiled tunic ripped and bloodied at the shoulder. "You never asked."

"You think I thought to wonder if you were some rogue faerie, hiding within my lands?" I scoffed, wading down the stairs. "Either help me get out of here or stay out of my way as I do it myself."

He said nothing else as I wound down the stairs and through the tunnel-like halls until I eventually came across a large dining room.

The king sat at a long, marble-topped table with a napkin tucked behind the tie of his cloak and covering little of his bare chest. The moon shrouded the top of the oval window behind his head, his dark hair unchanging beneath its light.

This was all a game, and I was but a chess piece, awaiting his next move.

Unless I decided to play.

Waving a silver spoon toward an empty place setting, Ryle grinned. "Do join me. You must be positively starved after all that dancing."

I was, but he needn't hear me admit it. He ate alone. No guards or advisors in sight. I had to wonder if the latter even existed in any of the royal courts of Beldine. Ryle lifted a spoonful of glazed berries to his mouth, chewing as he watched me approach the seat at the opposite end.

I made myself some tea, the gold liquid pouring out of a fat cream teapot inlaid with porcelain bows. The aroma was right and wrong at the same time. Black tea, but with pungent leaves that dissolved inside the small teacup. It was heady, that scent, and I knew I'd be ruined for all tea once I took a sip.

That did not stop me. I lifted it to my lips, ignoring the satisfied curl to Ryle's as I withheld a moan. Lowering the teacup, I reached for a muffin overloaded with raisins and frosted sugar.

The plate towered with them, and behind and to the right, a bowl of boiled eggs, larger than any I'd seen before, steamed the air. A giant bowl of whole fruit sat in the center of the table and on the other side, a fruit salad. Oatmeal with what smelled like cinnamon sat to my left, and I tugged it over, heaping a spoonful onto my plate. "All this food," I said. "And you eat alone."

"You are here, and that is plenty enough." He sipped some tea. "Besides, I don't like to share."

"So you'd rather people starve?"

"Not at all. I merely do not wish to always be in their presence while they eat."

I eyed his napkin, then his bare chest. "It is spring. What good is the cloak?"

"Rude. I should have your tongue," he drawled, teeth flashing, "around the tip of my cock."

I coughed, sending a piece of muffin flying onto the pressed white table linen.

He laughed so genuinely, his eyes watered. Swiping at them, he said, "Oh, you are just such good company. I knew I wouldn't mind dining with you. In fact, I think I might want to keep you a while."

"I would rather you didn't," I said. "I have a kingdom to rule, and we will likely run into some... issues should I not return home to do just that."

Ryle plucked up his fork and checked his teeth in the gleaming metal. "Ah, a continent now, is it not?" He lowered the fork, his eyes bright and dancing. "What is it like, being married to a fire-breathing brat while also having a prince of Faerie as your mate?" He clucked his tongue. "So delicious indeed. Why, I ought to have you in my bed to raise the stakes even higher."

Zadicus chose that moment to enter the room. "You touch her, and we will have more than a dying realm to deal with."

Ryle, with his sparkling black and gold eyes, stared at me as he said, "Brother dearest, I fear there's not enough room at the table for you. The kitchen staff will be happy to cater to your beastly appetite, though, I'm sure." At my raised brow, the High King slapped a hand upon the table, cutlery jangling. "You've not heard?"

In response, I shoveled oatmeal into my mouth, expecting to need to force it down. The cinnamon and oats exploded over my tongue, and I felt my eyes widen.

Ryle chuckled. "I hear the sex is better here, too. Just ask your lord."

Zad growled from behind me and then plucked me from the chair. "Enough."

"Why, he used to revel in our festivities. Females from all over would flock to our gatherings in hopes of landing upon his giant cock," Ryle said. "There were only so many he could service in one night, though."

"I said *enough*," Zad stated with a lethal calm that shook the table, food crumbling into dust before my eyes.

Swallowing, I moved out of Zad's hold.

Even Ryle looked as shocked as I felt, his narrowed eyes taking it in. They then lifted with a careful menace to his brother. "I was only taking the piss," he said with a smile that was less than pleasant. "No need for tantrums."

My head was trying to make sense of it. How just three words could contain enough power, enough ire to turn things into nothing.

"You know what," Ryle said, coming to his feet. "I am feeling rather generous. Take the evening to show your beloved our beautiful home."

Zad's suspicion mingled with my own. "I've no need for your kindness, and we both know it." His words hinted that he knew his brother needed him more than he needed Ryle's generosity.

"You understand what is to happen then." Ryle grinned. "Wonderful. We need not rattle the foundation of our fortress with unnecessary bloodshed."

Zad's voice was glacial. "Do not try to deceive Audra into believing it is not bloodshed you so often desire most."

"I daresay dear Audra already knows our kind love nothing more than to eat, fuck, play, and fight." Looking at me, Ryle tilted his head. "Show her around, take her to your favored places for trickery and slaughtering and dismembering. Let her see the flowers that have sprouted from all the creatures you've killed."

I was no stranger to the tales of this land, and I was beginning to think a lot of them held truth. But cruelty, savage brutality, was not something I was a stranger to either. "I'd love nothing more," I purred, silken with intrigue.

The king let out a roar of laughter, and Zad stiffened beside me, the heat of his ire enveloping as his arm brushed mine.

Stopping mere feet from us, Ryle stared at his brother. Though similar in towering height, Zad stood perhaps half an inch taller. Tension flooded the room, making it hard to draw a breath that wasn't loaded with their fizzing hatred. "Enjoy her, brother. But be warned, I'll be watching while I wait."

Zad lunged, but he caught only that thickened air and raked a hand through his filthy hair. So unkempt, so seemingly shaken to his core, I was struggling to keep hold of my reasons not to comfort him.

He'd betrayed me. He'd done so all the while promising he would not.

He'd sworn to stay by my side, and he had, but he'd also sworn he'd never deceive me as love had once done before, and he had. "I thought you couldn't lie."

As if remembering I was still there, his hand dropped, and his features softened. "I've never lied to you."

"Omitting the truth is the same thing. Do not deny it any longer."

He reached for me, but I backed up, then turned for the doors. He followed, clasping my hand in his when I was about to take the stairs back to what I hoped was my own rooms.

"We need to talk without prying ears and eyes."

"And if I do not wish to?" I said, petulant and uncaring.

We stopped at the bottom of another set of vine-wrapped stairs. His eyes darted left and right, and then he whispered, "As you said earlier, we need to get home, and we cannot figure that out here."

I pulled my hand free. "I'll figure it out on my own."

He shook his head, his eyes hardening. "Darkness' sake, Audra, do you not understand yet?" I blinked at him, and he sighed. "You, *we*, are in way over our heads. This is not something we can walk away from unscathed." He swallowed, lowering his voice as his evident fear got the better of him. "Please. I beg of you, just listen. You are upset, I know that, and I am deeply sorry, but I'm afraid all this may get worse before it has a chance to get better."

Staring into his eyes, noting the remorse, the way his entire frame swelled as though it took everything within him not to reach for me and swallow me within his arms, I nodded. "Fine, but I do not forgive you."

"I know," he said, gesturing to a dark hallway.

I walked on ahead, admitting quieter than a whisper, "I worry I never will."

Of course, he heard. His rough exhale stalked me. "I know."

We walked three halls, passing guest and sitting rooms littered with lesser faeries, and one teeming with those warriors, and finally, the dark gave way to crickets, rushing water, and the night sky.

We exited via a low arched door. It opened into a giant garden with overflowing vegetables and fruit-heavy trees, their branches sagging with bright apples, pears, and lemons.

The grass did not crunch beneath the soles of my slippers. It pressed softly like carpet and tickled like feathers brushing against my ankles.

The thought had me wondering over those giant wings in the throne room, my chest unbearably tight.

Willows and sycamores soared above us, higher than they had any right to be, their glistening, moonlit branches and leaves swaying with the invisible tide of the wind.

Quiet at my side, Zad allowed me to take everything in without interruption. To the right, behind more giant trees and rows of vegetation, loomed giant rocks and cliffs, the spray of the waterfall littering the air and foliage with glowing beads.

We pressed on through the greenery, veering left, deeper into a small forest, its floor shrouded in rocks blanketed in a deep green moss. I stepped over some, my eyesight adjusting to the vibrant colors, the echoing cry of birds, and the sway of the ferns, lulling and calling.

As though I were dazed, in a dream made from the imagination of a youngling wishing to enter a story, I pirouetted. Warm air glided over my skin as if in greeting. Moving to the giant, thick trunk of a tree, I gasped, spying a tiny moving hat in the grass.

"Little folk," Zad said with something in his voice that sounded like affection. "Don't touch."

I pulled my hand back, watching as one peered up at me, his little black hat tilted back, falling from his head. The female with him, wearing a blue dress, made a clucking sound that could've been mistaken for an insect, bending to retrieve it. She thumped it back on his head, and he turned on her, his voice unable to be understood, but I knew he was reprimanding her all the same.

They paused, gazed up at me again as if just remembering they had an audience, then saw who I was with. After a bow and a curtsey, the two scuttled inside the tree, a small piece of bark falling back into place to conceal them.

"Do they bite?"

Zad huffed. "No, but if you toy with them, they'll do much worse."

Observing their home, I pondered how many more might be inside, and if they had younglings, how tiny they must be. "What might that be?" They were small, but I didn't let that trick me into thinking they couldn't be dangerous.

"They will knot your hair while you sleep, and if there's not enough to do so, or if they just feel like it, they'll braid your eyebrows or nostril hair."

That didn't seem so bad, so I merely smiled.

Zad continued, "Should your hair be knotted or braided by the little folk, do not expect to untie the magic their hands have sowed."

"You need to cut it then?" I asked, and I couldn't keep my fingers from smoothing my brows.

"Indeed, and you would not think having no eyebrows as such a bad thing," he said. "Until it happens."

There was a wisdom to those words that spoke to experience. "When?"

He chuckled, walking on beneath the starlit canopy of trees. I followed, much preferring this to my rooms, even if I was reluctant to be around the source of what hurt me. "I was maybe ten summers old." Basically a babe in faerie years, I surmised. With a look over his shoulder at me and then at the castle at our backs, he said, "Ryle dared me."

"Of course, he did."

"He said he wanted to know if it were true and that I could have his strawberry pie after dinner until the next full moon."

"Did he stay true to his promise?"

"He did, but he did not say he wouldn't tamper with the

dessert." At my silence, he answered, "Boiled frog legs. I've never eaten a strawberry since."

I crinkled my nose, then sighed, giving voice to one of the many questions I'd been too stubborn to ask. "Who is the eldest?"

"I am, by four summers." We stopped at a small creek, and on the other side, a deer drank from its shimmering surface. At least, I thought it was a deer.

When it looked up, its slitted gray tongue was licking water from its purple lips. Silver and gray, it had the face of a deer but the body of a large mountain cat, its tail flicking while it studied us. "A spinder. Look away, and she'll be happy to ignore us." I did, and he continued, "My father loved my mother." He paused. "But he was obsessed. Some might say she felt the same until she stepped out on him during the gathering of stars and left us for a week to be with a warrior from the Gold Court."

We continued, the shrill chirping of crickets and birds, the scurrying of beetles beneath the grass, and the fading sound of racing water swallowing us within a cocoon.

"Why?" I had to ask.

"They'd been together for four hundred years, and not once had either of them taken another lover, which is not exactly heard of unless you are linked, and even then, some don't mind so long as they're present."

The mere thought of it curdled... I shook my head.

"Apparently, the affections of this female warrior had made her curious enough to test my father's wrath. I was but a babe, and they'd lost two daughters before I was born. Some used to say she was overcome by sudden bouts of grief."

"Did you notice?"

"No," he said. "I'd never truly known her all that well, and I was too young to remember the years before Ryle's arrival. She withdrew more after he was born and delivered to my father. The female who had hoped to earn a place in our court by giving him a healthy babe was eventually killed."

"Your father?"

"I suspect my brother."

I shuddered involuntarily. "What happened to your mother?"

"She poisoned herself. When that did not work, she stabbed herself in the chest with an iron arrow."

I struggled for words. "How old were you?"

"Sixteen summers. We are a species prone to dramatics, of that you can be sure." He'd said it in jest, but it fell flat upon the curling breeze. "And so my father did not take her grief too seriously until it was far too late."

"Ryle's mother…"

"When my father discovered my mother had not only lain with another but had also spent a week with them, regardless of their gender, he sought revenge and picked a female of low status to spend a week in his rooms."

My eyes widened, and Zad caught me before I tripped over a moss-blanketed rock.

"Your aunt," I said, understanding how they'd grown close enough for her to leave her home.

"My mother's sister. Emmiline does not care for Ryle, and when he killed my father…" I halted at that, and Zad offered a grim smile. "We both left. Ryle tricked him into drinking a sleeping tonic. He killed him while he slept after he'd made yet another remark about Ryle's less than pure blood, his blight on our family and its now tainted history."

"That is how the crown is inherited?"

"That." He tipped a broad shoulder. "Or a king can choose to step down, in which case he passes the title to his son."

His touch was so familiar, so comforting I'd forgotten I didn't want it and moved away. His eyes gleamed knowingly, and I said, "Not a daughter?"

"Not in the Onyx Court." He chuckled at my expression. "I know."

A veil of vines rippled up ahead, twitching more as we neared.

As Zad grew closer, I realized. This land… it wasn't just land. It was a living, breathing entity—that knowledge made more apparent by the male who'd stopped to inspect a grouping of toadstools. Red-capped with white spores, their heads were bigger than his large hand, and their legs as tall as his shins.

He crouched down, the air around his fingers growing visible if you peered close enough—akin to tendrils of faint smoke. "He had no power of his own. We waited, though. He even tried to have a witch spell him, everything and anything in hopes something would manifest, but nothing ever did."

I found that hard to believe after all I'd witnessed from the king so far. "None at all?" Moving over to Zad, I wondered what he was doing when I noticed the bases of the toadstools. Some were patchy brown. Others were bent and folding into the ground, their heads withering against dying blades of grass beneath.

"Other than paltry parlor tricks, he has nothing, which is why he wanted to be king"—he curled his fingers into his palm, the mushrooms changing, brightening in color—"to take it from the land."

"But it speaks to you," I said, my eyes fastened on the once limp toadstools.

"It is me," he said with so much resignation, it squeezed my chest. "Beldine might be under his rule, and he might be able to borrow from it as he sees fit, but he knows, everyone knows, whose lifeblood is knitted to it."

Zadicus rose just as a familiar roar rumbled above. Everything in the forest stilled, including my heart. Though I knew it couldn't be Vanamar, I still watched in silent awe as two furbanes swooped and tumbled around one another. Trees shook and branches groaned as the white beast's wings flapped like mini bouts of thunder before it gave chase to its partner, who appeared similar in color.

For long moments, we watched them soar over the castle, then circle back to dive to the river below. My stomach emptied as I imagined myself on Van and doing the same. Then it refilled with that aching heaviness when I turned to Zad, my gaze flicking to his back. Had he done that? Flown above the trees and rivers and met the clouds before the ability was stripped so callously from him? I couldn't even imagine...

"Why?" I heard myself finally ask. "Why didn't you tell me?"

He didn't hesitate. "Would you believe me if I said it never felt like the right time to admit something of this magnitude? That I was at war with myself over it because I never, not once, planned to return, so what did it matter, and why rush? Because you know I cannot lie, but that does not mean any of my excuses are good enough." Unable to meet his gaze, I watched his throat dip. "Audra." He clasped my fingers within his. "I won't lose you. I'd finally gotten everything I wanted. Can you blame me for wanting to enjoy it before I potentially ruined it by admitting all that I am?"

"Yes," I said, freeing my fingers, though the absence of his touch burned. "Yes, I can blame you." He watched me retreat. "There are some secrets too huge to keep, too important to hope to hide, especially from someone you'd all but pledged to commit your life to."

His voice roughened and took on that lethal edge. "I do not wish to stay here. I've lived in Rosinthe since your grandfather ruled, Audra. If I wanted to come back, I would have long ago."

"That's irrelevant."

"It's not."

"You said it yourself." I glowered at him. "That you are tied to this land. You give to it, and it gives to you in return." Staring into those fiery eyes, I felt my mind explode. "Wait, you..."

He waited, face tight with apprehension and his feet shifting.

"You would not need to drink blood after exerting your magic in extremes if you were here, would you?"

His lack of response answered that, as did the flattening of his lips.

"Zadicus," I groaned. My hands rose to my head, fingers

tunneling and pulling at my hair. "You are a king without a crown, do you not understand that?" Again, he did not answer. I marched over the grass, felt it protest at my abuse, and shoved at his hard chest. "You belong here, and you know it, and that's why you could not tell me, for you know I'll insist you stay and do what you need to."

Too quick for me to stop, he stole my wrists, lifting them to his mouth to kiss. "I belong with you."

"Liar," I rasped, knowing he wasn't and that he genuinely believed that. "You filthy fucking liar." He pulled me closer, and I sucked in long mouthfuls of rainbow-doused air and his scent. "What do you need to do? To help the young? To help the dying parts of this land?"

"Audra." His arms held me tight to him, his tone sharpened with warning.

"Just tell me," I said, sniffing and turning my head side to side against his chest. "Tell me because it's okay, because there's no way we can avoid this now, and because you can't leave them this way..." Even without bathing for darkness knows how many days, he still smelled like him. Heady with everything I wanted but could not forgive, could not have. Mint mingled with undertones of sweat. That sun-soaked winter morning scent that I now knew wasn't winter at all, but spring.

His entire frame seemed to wilt. "It's an ancient undertaking that has only been done a few times in the history of Beldine, and no one even remembers if it worked."

"What is it?" I seethed, gazing up at him, the moon residing in his eyes.

After a dragging moment of staring someplace behind me in that absent way that said he wasn't seeing anything, he released a hoarse exhale. "A coupling with the three queens and their High King. They call it the act."

I broke free of his body, though I knew he'd allowed it, and stumbled back. "What?"

"Ryle has tried." Zad licked his lips. "Nothing changed, so he wants me to—"

"No," I cut him off, now seeing the peeling bark upon the trees that sheltered us, scented the stench of rot in the many withering branches. As though the curtain had been pulled back by his gentle, low words, and what lay behind it, if you dared look closer, was not as beautiful as it first seemed. "I understand just fine," I said, not knowing my own voice or if I even spoke the words at all.

My senses flooded with the life around me and the shattering of my own, leaving me reeling, trembling on two feet.

Feeding the land. I almost laughed, remembering my visit—if one could call it that—to the Sun Kingdom and the ritual Raiden and his court thought to partake in, stolen from faerie lore. I'd thought it merely an absurd excuse to have sex with others and get drunk, and it likely was.

But it was also another faerie fable that might not be a fable at all.

Of course, it would be that. Of course, it had to be something that would revive just as surely as it killed. "You know," I said, out of breath even though I wasn't moving. "I'm beginning to wonder if this"—I gestured between us, at that hidden tether, the excruciating pull that only he and I could feel—"was some sick jest of your faerie fates."

"You know better than to so much as think that." Zad made to come closer until I tripped back. "I would lay down my life before I ever hurt you like that."

That was what I was afraid of—losing him, in any and every capacity.

And I was exhausted from that fear and the misery it brought with it. There had to be a way to end this torment, this sick torture we were forced to endure.

"You do it then," I said, growing numb to everything this male now seemed to be, for it was nothing I thought I wanted, and nothing I was so sure about anymore. Perhaps if he did what was expected of him, then it would murder me enough to be free of him—link be damned. "You feed the land with those queens, and then we can go."

"Audra," Zad growled, horror twisting his features. "Are you out of your fucking mind?"

No, but I was mad. So furious, I didn't know what I was asking for, and I no longer cared.

I whirled on him, whispering harshly up into his face, "You will do it, and you will do it with haste, for if I spend another unnecessary hour in this place, I cannot tell you what I might do." My chest was heaving, my eyes welling and burning. "Do not let our intolerable bond get in the way of what I need. What I need is to return to my people. What I need is to be away from you."

"Intolerable?" he said, a soft snarl that rustled the leaves.

I wouldn't be deterred or cowed by the sheer magnitude of him, the primal energy that radiated from him in dizzying currents. The way this place had taken everything he was—which was already far too much—and made it *more*. Or maybe, it had just revealed exactly who he'd always been. "You have much better hearing than I, so there's no need to repeat myself."

His arm coiled around my waist, the rise and fall of his chest mirroring the violent waves of mine. "I will give you the time you need, but do not think for one fucking second that I will ever let you stay away from me permanently."

"I don't want you anywhere near me."

"Your walls have returned," he said. Eyes flitting back and forth between mine, he gripped my chin with his fingers. "But I will shatter them again."

"I won't let you."

"You cannot stop me," he purred to my mouth, his fingers now brushing hair away from my face with a gentleness I feared might induce falling tears. "We both know it."

"I hate you."

Zad's lips parted, warm breath mixing with mine. "I love you."

He pressed whisper-soft kisses to my scars. "Now." His lips brushed the other side of my mouth. "Always." Then they moved to my nose. "For all eternity." His lips stopped on mine, and I lost myself to the desperate clawing of my heart, to the silken sliding tenderness.

A wolf howled in the distance, ridding the stupid from me. Growling, I pushed away and stumbled back, heading for the glowing towers through the trees.

"Audra, wait."

I didn't. I hurried back through the forest, tripping over vines but righting myself before I fell. He followed, but he did not chase.

NINE

Audra

I didn't see Zad again until dinner. I hid in my rooms, grateful to return to them and be left alone with my thoughts as I untangled them.

I wish I could have done the same with the knots inside my chest cavity.

A roar cut the silence in two, and my heart sank and soared as I scrambled off the bed to the window.

In the distance, a familiar white and blue horned beast with giant wings dipped low. Its feathers skirted the racing river as glittering water misted the air. Then another roar, so close it shook the foundation of the castle, as another entirely white beast gave chase.

I expected them to turn, to tumble through the air as their teeth snapped at one another. But they merely met above the water, and together, they flew toward the scythe-shaped moon.

More furbanes—or perhaps the same pair we'd seen earlier—flying free and without riders.

I watched as they disappeared around a sharp cliff and wondered how Vanamar was doing, locked up in his cage. I missed him. I missed my own court. I missed the people I hadn't known I'd miss until I'd been torn away from them for yet another male's schemes and treachery.

Temika arrived to dress me in a gown that reached my toes in soft, simple layers of ruby silk. Its bodice was two scraps that crossed over my breasts and gave view to my navel, cleavage, and more skin than what I'd grown up thinking was acceptable.

I swallowed down the impulse to demand decency and stood still as she dusted my curled hair with gold, and then did the same to my cheeks and my kohl-lined eyelids.

Everyone was already seated when I arrived in the throne room, including Zad, who watched me glide down the long table with unnerving focus. I couldn't read his eyes, his void and too-still features, so I attached my own to the king.

Ryle was lounging back in his chair, acting for all the world as though it were a miniature throne, his crown tipped haphazardly over his brow. "My winter queen," he said with a softness that grazed like the tip of a knife.

Zad cursed, but he was ignored. Gesturing to the chair beside him, Ryle's mouth curved. "You look dazzling." Without taking his eyes off my chest while I lowered into my seat, he asked his brother, "Doesn't she look good enough to eat, Zadicus?"

A screech sounded as Zad kicked his chair back, standing and heading our way.

Spreading my napkin over my lap, for something to concentrate on more than anything, I couldn't help but look as the king raised a hand. "Come any closer, and before you even reach us, I'll have given Audra another scar upon that sinful mouth of hers to match the others."

Indeed, a serrated knife appeared in his clenched fist, his smile unmoving as though he wanted Zad to test him, and he'd delight in doing as he had threatened. There wasn't any part of me that believed he wouldn't.

Zad stopped and glared, his entire frame trembling with the fury burning in his eyes.

"Do have a care, my lord," I said primly, reaching for what looked to be smoked fish cakes and depositing two on my plate. "We know how much I like my face."

Ryle's laughter poured out of him like an unexpected explosion, shocking everyone into complete silence.

Courtiers and warriors and even servants wore nervous smiles, and Ryle sniffed, wiping at his eyes before leaning close, his frothy blood-red shirt spilling onto the edge of the table. "It is a shame you are already married."

It was his airy tone that made me set the plate down and give him my full attention. "And why is that?" It seemed like a different life, the one I'd almost had with Raiden, who, for better or worse, was my husband, unless he eventually agreed out of it.

Which he'd made stubbornly apparent would never happen.

I wondered if he knew I was gone and was now in Beldine. I was sure word had been sent to him by now. What he'd do with it was anyone's guess—but likely nothing. I was no fool. I knew he held a deep affection for me, but I also knew that with me gone and possibly dead, the continent of Rosinthe would be his. And if he and I had always had one thing in common, it was greed.

"I have a feeling with you by my side, this long eternal life would never be dull." And if there was something the Fae loathed most, it was boredom.

His long, eternal life. For although I would outlive generations, I was not immortal.

It felt as though that knife in his fist had sunk into my stomach. Zad. He was already hundreds of years old, if not older, and… I couldn't look at him. Refused to remove my eyes from my plate. But I could feel him staring at me with an intensity that burned like knowing.

"Marriage is overrated," I finally said. "Do trust me on that."

Another laugh, this bout lower and huskier, but still capable of stalling conversation. Sitting back, Ryle dragged his thumb down the side of his knife, his eyes on his brother. "You were married once, I hear."

"Once," Zad grunted, sounding as though he were chewing with images of murder flashing in his mind.

"Did you ditch her for your mate?" Ryle dropped the knife. Reaching for a decanter of sour-scented wine, he poured some into his large goblet. "We really do have so much to catch up on."

Zad's nonanswer evoked a scowl, the decanter thumping back onto the table with enough force to knock the wine over its rim.

I stared at the dark red as it spread into the white table linen.

"Snow-haired one," Ryle said, lifting his wine to his lips. Upon every finger were jeweled rings in varying gemstones.

Seated farther down the table, my cousin ripped his attention away from a brunette female wearing a tiara. A princess, I realized, recognizing who had to be her mother, a queen, at the other end of the table. "Your greatness?"

I scoffed, and Ryle's fingers rubbed over his goblet, his eyes flitting my way with a gleam before he asked Adran, "This wife of Zadicus's, or once wife." He waved his free hand. "What is she like?"

"Ryle," Zad said, both a plea and a threat.

Their gazes locked, and the king sighed, looking at my cousin. "I suppose it *is* rude to gossip about someone when they can hear you." With a glance at my cousin that promised harm if he didn't give him what he wanted, he said, "Later then."

Adran nodded, reaching for his wine.

"Free them," Zad demanded, sudden and sharp.

Gasps bled into the air. Ryle's brows knitted in feigned confusion. "I do beg your pardon."

I cut into my food, eating quickly in case I lost the chance.

"You know exactly what I'm talking about. You've no need to imprison them, so set them free."

"Ah," Ryle said, "but I do. Are they not betrayers? You and I had an agreement. Your friends and I, however, most definitely did not."

That meant Kash, Dace, and Landen were here—and locked up.

"They did not betray you."

"They left, did they not?"

Zad didn't blink, his stare so cold, his imposing body so eerily still, I made myself blink twice to be sure it was him. "They were free to come and go as they so pleased, which, some years ago, is what we'd always done."

"If you believe I am to trust that half-truth, you and your *friends*," he spat the word, "will be more than sorry."

"Why are they here?" I dared to ask.

Eyes, down each table, fell upon me, including that of the king.

"Why are they here?" Ryle asked as though I were a child who'd inquired about the rotation of the sun and moon.

I said nothing else and sipped some water.

Ryle eyed me over his goblet, guzzling wine with a loud slurp. Lowering it to the table, he said, "You know nothing of our little bargain, do you?" With his brow arched, he chuckled at Zad. "You must have spent all your time together in other, much less informative ways."

"Audra," Zad cautioned.

I ignored him, waiting expectantly while still gazing at the king.

With a pointed look down the table to the wings behind the throne, Ryle sighed. "It was an exceedingly long time ago, so you'll have to forgive me if my memory is not quite up to the task of remembering."

Zad was silent, and I watched his brother watch him, noticed every twitch of his lips, the changing flecks in his eyes and the shifting clench of his jaw. Oh, how he so obviously loathed him with a vehemence that would have Zadicus dead with just a look if it were possible.

"Our father had passed, and as it so often happens, the person responsible for that, if they are of the same heart, inherits the crown."

I'd known he'd killed his father, knew why too, and tried not to allow any of it to trick me into giving a shit.

Silence permeated, everyone eager to hear a tale I was sure they all knew. Though I was certain they'd not heard it from the king himself and with his sibling, *the true heir*, in attendance.

"I wasn't sure it would work, of course," Ryle admitted. "Being I am the bastard child of a whore who gave me up as soon as she realized I'd be of no use in serving her desire for a better life." His eyes flickered, a humorous breath departing him. "She is dead now. I made sure of it the second she came knocking after news of our father's demise."

Cold-blooded to the point of believing he was just with every abominable action... I stared at my half-eaten food, recognizing that trait all too well.

"All at once, the land came to me," he said as though in a trance now. "Like a river trying to find a different home, it was both too much and too little. Powerful in a way I thought would surely kill me, and it very well almost did." I looked at Zad, who was staring at me, then I looked away. "But I survived." Ryle winked at me. "I'm far too stubborn to be defeated by that which I wanted most."

"And what you wanted most... power," I said as if piecing a puzzle together.

"Wrong." He gestured to me with his goblet. "Though it is a comfort I adore, what I wanted most was what no one thought I deserved."

"Status," I said. "Respect." *Fear.*

"Amongst other things," he muttered, his eyes darkening, the gold almost swallowed. I knew then he was done with me digging too close to his insecurities. "Anyway, so your beloved was in quite a state." He smiled, the memory clearly pleasing to him. "Tearing at the furniture and making all sorts of lovely threats."

"You did kill his father."

"*Our* father," he corrected, swallowing wine and setting down his goblet. "But you're right, yes. And as the true heir, I knew it was only a matter of time after my father's body was wholly absorbed by the land until Zadicus might make his move."

I did not look at the male being discussed, though I itched to. "You exiled him?"

A rich bark of laughter. "Nothing of the sort," he spewed. "No,

I challenged him, and like a mutt with his tail tucked between his legs, he fled."

Some warriors, the wolves, stiffened and glared down at their plates.

Deathly quiet, Zad's laughter rumbled like an incoming storm, growing louder until it suddenly broke with his lethal words. "You act as though my sparing your life was an insult."

"Oh, because it was." Ryle glowered. "Because you thought, if it came to it, that you would win." The echoing silence was rather telling, and judging by the way Ryle shifted in his seat, he was well aware of it. "You're a coward who thinks himself wiser than the fates, hiding amongst mortals and half breeds under the guise of protecting something that never needed, never asked, never so much as desired your protection."

My eyes shot to Zad, who was gazing at his brother with something that looked a lot like regret. Regret for what? Did he wish he'd killed him? I wished he had. For then, none of us would be in this predicament.

Zadicus was Ryle's greatest envy and threat, and Ryle was Zad's undeserved weakness. I tucked that information away.

Many things would have turned out a lot different if he'd not been such a coward and did what was necessary to secure his right to his land.

But he wasn't a coward.

He was a creature born of those with little morality and a lot of cruelty, yet somehow, he'd still found it within himself to walk away. Somehow, he'd held a scrap of love for an undeserving brother who'd never even think to pay him the same kindness.

And that love had cost him, their land and people, and myself dearly.

I wasn't sure if he was the stupidest son of a bitch alive or the strongest I'd ever known.

"So you took his wings," I said when the air grew too stale with barely leashed ire. "Why?"

Ryle stared at me, and for a moment, I thought he might backhand me again with that raw power emanating from him. "It is said that those with wings lose their soul if they are cleaved from their bodies." Looking back at Zad, Ryle said, "I wanted to see if that were nothing but fable, but most of all, I did not think he'd give them up."

People shifted in their seats, some daring to eat as the two brothers stared one another down from either end of the food-laden table.

"He did," Ryle said, followed by a harsh laugh. "Practically bent over and handed me the blade himself. I'd come looking for him, you see. The idea he'd run from me, that he thought I might be happy to let him live out his days in a continent we'd mocked, thinking I would not see him as a threat... well," he waved an indignant hand, "it was just all so preposterous that I had to pay him a little visit. And what should I find when I arrive, but a lord with land of his own. Tell us, brother..." Ryle grinned. "How did you end up a prince playing as a lord? I've often wondered."

Zad drank deep from a granite goblet, his eyes like fire as he dropped it to the table. "None of your business."

"No?" Ryle pouted, then looked at the guard behind him. "Fetch Dace Arrown and hang him from the rafters by his unglamoured ears."

Zad cursed, and Ryle halted the guard. With a remorse-filled glance my way, Zad then eyed his plate. "We were there only a month or two when some of King Henderson's men discovered our encampment in the woods. But instead of dragging us to the castle, the king came to me, and we brokered a deal."

Ryle rubbed his hands together. "This is Audra's grandfather, is it not?"

Zad nodded, and I sat still as stone, both in awe of what I was discovering and wrapped in a cold blanket of bitterness for how I'd had to find out. "He'd been having trouble with too many of our kind leaving Beldine after our father died. The young were going missing, mortals were being slaughtered or forced to partake in dancing and riddle contests until they perished, but he knew to kill us would mean making an example he could not afford to make."

"For I would have cut him down like the swine he and his son were," Ryle dragged out.

Zad looked as though he'd protest, but continued, "He gave me lands in the east, where most of the trouble took place, with the promise of more should things improve."

"And he knew what you were?" a queen, soft-spoken and unnamed, said with a look of astonishment. "What you are?"

"Indeed," Zad said, still focused on his plate. "Things improved. I accrued more land I did not want but knew better than to refuse, and unless Henderson needed help with other dire situations, I was left to live in peace."

"Perfect." Ryle dropped a clenched fist on the table with exuberant excitement. "Just perfect. Until I found you, of course."

Zad's jaw stiffened, but he nodded.

"I challenged him," the king said. "I said we were to end this now and get it over with, but he refused. He stated, rather emphatically, that he had no desire to kill me and become the High King of Beldine. So," Ryle said, sitting straighter now. "I decided I'd bargain with him to prove that were true."

"But you cannot lie," I blurted, hating that he'd taken something from him when it hadn't been necessary.

Ryle tutted, patting my hand with mock sympathy. "Foolish Audra, you should already know that those who cannot lie are the masters of deceit."

I withdrew my hand, Zad staring at where his brother's still laid over the table.

"His wings for his freedom, and I promised to never go in search of him in any way again if he never came in search of me." With a thundering smack of his hands on the table that bounced grapes and cheese from the trays, he declared, "Which is why, because we now find ourselves in need of his services, I had to lure him with bait upon a hook." His jewel-bedecked fingers crawled over the table toward me. "Here, fishy, fishy," he whispered.

I looked up at those monstrous wings, knowing Zad was watching me, and wondered what it might have felt like to have your limbs, a part of who you were, extracted from you with such brutality.

They were a sign, a message written in dried blood, brittle bone, and decaying muscle, to any who thought to usurp him.

"Sometimes," the king said, contemplative as he too gazed at them. "I give them a stroke, a tickle, a little nudge to say hello."

But I saw something else within those cleverly wrapped words, and I knew Zad already had to be aware. Ryle resented them. Yet another thing his pureblood brother had been born with, that many noble males had, and he had not.

I couldn't wrangle my horror quick enough, and Ryle chuckled. "We are nothing if not magic-enhanced monsters, else there'd be no tales to spin to your putrid ilk." He clapped his hands. "Thanks to your behavior and entertaining us so thoroughly, dear brother, you may have one of your friends released."

Zad's brows lowered. "One?"

"That's what I said, so choose."

He stood, violence rolling off him with such ease, such alarming speed, that even I stiffened in my seat. "Both, Ryle. Now."

Ryle only smiled, saying to his guard. "Release the one that fell in love with another half breed and show him to his own room. He can entertain us on the morrow."

Even I, who knew the male so little, knew Kash would never divulge something so personal, not even with a dagger pressed to his throat. He'd rather die, and perhaps, gladly.

The king stood, Zad too, but as the latter approached, the king clucked his tongue.

Then I was whisked away on a cloud of rapidly growing dust that threatened to heave the food I'd eaten.

I slumped to the floor inside my rooms, alone and disorientated as though I'd never left.

Later that evening, mere hours before the sun was due to rise, I listened to the sounds of debauchery. Screams, laughter, and music flowed inside the windows.

Now was as good a time as any, I thought, heading for the door. I had to figure out what room Kash was in and see if I could make him convince Zad to end this madness already.

But I almost tripped over a figure lying upon the floor outside my rooms.

He wasn't asleep. His hands were tucked behind his head, eyes steadfast on the ceiling, seeming deep in thought.

"Good to see you doing your best to get me home." I stepped over him.

He caught my ankle, then me around the waist as he stood and I teetered.

The rough pads of his fingers skated over the bare skin of my stomach and back. My body was pulled toward his by his hands and that needle-sharp need that resided inside me. Shivering, I pressed my palms upon the clean cotton shirt covering his chest. It was light, almost sheer, giving a glimpse at the muscled, tantalizing depths of him beneath. "I find myself wondering," he said, so delicate and hoarse, "if you can forgive me."

Foolishly, I met his eyes, felt my heart shake inside my chest, and clutched his shirt. "We both know I can't."

"You can." Panic danced within his golden orbs, his luscious lips parting. "One day."

I could do nothing but stare as I wondered if that were true.

"Kiss me then," he murmured, hands smoothing up my back to cup my nape. "Kiss me like you hate me, and I'll leave you be."

"You cannot be serious."

"What I am, Audra," he rasped, heat roughening the low words, "is starved." Then he kissed me, hungry, deep plunges of his lips on mine, pulling and tugging and melding.

I gripped his shirt, and then I bit him so hard I tasted copper.

He groaned, pressing me up against the wall. One hand framed my face and the other curled my thigh around his waist. Lifting me, he rolled his hips where I needed him, and I moaned, felt his teeth roam my neck, and tilted my head.

Searing heat ignited, my head spun, and though he'd said he had no need to feed in this way in Beldine, I still allowed it. I still wanted it.

I wanted the fire that crackled within my veins and the cooling rapture that pulsed and spread, rushing after it with waves of pleasure. But he didn't drink as he'd done before. No, he merely opened the skin and kissed and licked at the blood that escaped. Against him, I writhed, needing the friction of his tented pants, that bulging member inside them rubbing over me.

A wicked laugh washed over my skin, his tongue lapping at the puncture marks. "You might not forgive me, but you need me as much as I need you, and that will never fucking change."

Then I was cold, and he was leaving, adjusting himself in his pants as he strode down the hall.

I was going to scream, frustration coursing through me and throwing venomous words over my tongue. I trapped them, knowing he wanted that and was without shame in this new game he'd decided to play.

"I suppose I'll finish in my rooms," I said instead, smiling when he froze, and then ducking inside to do just that.

🌹

For three nights in a row, the same story played out with different endings and plot twists.

Kash refused to talk, as I'd predicted, and so instead, a mortal who'd been hidden away in the king's harem was brought to the throne room.

I could only guess his insistence on having every meal there had something to do with reminding Zad, his other guests, and himself of what he was and what he could do.

The woman was strung from the ceiling by her feet, the king whispering gentle murmurings into her ear that I couldn't hear as he rubbed her arms.

I wasn't sure how she'd gotten here, but she had to be over thirty summers by the looks of her. She screamed when the king stepped away. "No, please. I love you. I'll be better. I'll be the best. Please, please..."

I tilted my head as Ryle took his seat next to me, unfazed. "Kash," he called. "A gift for you."

I knew, everyone did, including the dark-eyed male seated away from Zad, that his refusal to play, to talk of his relationship with my mother, would not go without punishment.

For I wouldn't have let it either.

I sliced open some type of roasted bird, dipped it in a yellowed sauce, and sniffed it to detect for anything odd. Satisfied, I ate as the king continued only after he'd successfully garnered everyone's attention.

"Seeing as you're so fond of mortal women, I thought you might like one of mine."

Kash's jaw gritted, bitten words delivered through his teeth. "You are too kind, my king, but I fear I must decline."

Ryle dropped his cutlery with an echoing clang. "You decline?"

Kash nodded.

Pushing back his chair, Ryle stood, leering down the table at him. "You loved her, yes? Your half-blood queen."

Kash said nothing, but his eyes flared a little when the king moved behind me and gathered my loose hair to one side. "She bears a heavy resemblance to her mother, I've heard."

Again, Kash merely nodded.

We both knew where this was going, so I took another mouthful, outwardly unaffected as the king's mouth lowered to my shoulder while inside, every part of me grew molten with the urge to stab him in the eye with my fork.

"Hands off, Ryle," Zad barked.

"Come and stop me."

Zad rose, the air searing cold with power, but there was a scuffle, and I looked over as Kash shoved him back into his seat. Zad sat, eyes wild and tendrils of his hair escaping its tie.

The woman whimpered, and Ryle released me with a sharp intake of breath. "You marked her."

My eyes darted to Zad. Now, his outburst, the savage way he'd almost had me the other night in the hall made sense. Though he slept his days away outside my rooms, he hadn't tried since.

The gleam in his eyes and slight raise of his brow when I glared at him spoke of such unapologetic arrogance, I thought I might leap onto the table and lunge at him.

Anger shaking my hands, I set my cutlery down.

"She is mine," Zad said in such an offhanded way that I gnashed my teeth at him. His lips curved, and he looked at his approaching brother. "She is linked to me. My mate."

"Precisely," Ryle said, boots clicking over tile. "Precisely why I find it interesting, though not at all surprising, you'd try to deter me even more." His grin was shining knives. "Feeling a little… threatened, brother?"

Zad blinked, then laughed dryly, rubbing his hand over his bristle-heavy chin. "You do not want me to answer that."

After staring at him with such malice, such unchecked hatred, Ryle clamped his lips together. "Very well."

A dagger landed between Kash's fingers, embedding itself to the hilt in the table as though it were cleaving through warm butter.

"Kashen, if you won't speak of your half-human lover, then you must make good use of mine." Ryle drifted back to his seat. "For unlike my brother, I don't mind sharing my toys. Fuck her, force your cock inside her mouth, eat her fragrant juices, I care not." Seating himself on the arm of his chair, his velvet pants brushing my elbow, he stated, "So long as she's dead by the end."

The woman's desperate, pointless cries grew and fell onto unaffected ears.

Kash lifted his gaze from the blade to the king. "You cannot wish for me to kill one of your lovers."

"I've many more," Ryle said with ease. "She's been with me since she was eighteen summers, before we were trapped, and her breasts are already sagging." He wrinkled his nose. "It was fascinating at first, but now, I find I prefer her the way she was. Young."

The woman screamed his name, the rest of her pleas garbled as she cried, her face mottled as blood continued to rush to her head.

Kash stood.

Goblets of wine were drunk from as we watched him circle the tables to where the woman hung before the dais.

Zad wasn't looking, but then his shoulders stiffened. As though he knew he owed that much to the mortal, he shifted. As if he owed them anything at all.

Kash bent low, swiping tears from her bright green eyes, and the bitter scent of something infiltrated.

Magic, I surmised. For he had it as much as Zad, as much as most in this room, and he was using it to glamour her.

The woman smiled, sucking back tears. As though she were in a different place, away from this nightmare. She stayed that way, even as the dagger plunged inside her chest, ending her life in one quick thrust.

It clanged to the floor with ringing finality. Zad watched Kash as he glared at the king, blood pooling on the floor beneath the corpse behind him. Then Kash was dust, sweeping out of the throne room.

Unmoving, his head upon a fist, the king stared at his dead human lover for the remainder of our meal.

TEN

Audra

Z ADICUS WAS THERE, AS ALWAYS, THIS TIME SHARPENING a small blade.

He stood when he heard me enter the hall, tucking the blade inside a hidden sheath in his pants, the stone he'd used to sharpen it upon the floor. "Are you okay?"

In a nightgown made from gossamer and embroidered dried flowers, I walked to the railing and stared down into the dark abyss. The throne room was down there, veiled from prying eyes or those who wished to do something daring. "It was exactly what I would have done," I said. "So no, I am not disturbed. I am disturbed by the fact you will not end this charade already."

Zad reached for my hand, but I pulled it back and marched away.

"Where are you going?"

"To find the king and tell him you're done with dallying."

At the sound of raised yet hushed voices, I stopped at the end of the hall.

The female's was hushed, the male's rough and uncaring of who heard. A flash of white, the swaying of a thin gown, and that regal, soft voice. The queen of the Silver Court.

Zad tugged me back around the corner, pressing a finger to his lips as their conversation carried.

"...cannot expect me to," the male said, his voice rich and deep but caustic with emotion. "You allowed it once, but I refuse to allow it again."

"It is not up to me, and if it were, you know I would never so much as consider it."

"But you did it," he said, growling now. Zad's brows hovered over his eyes as he stood breathlessly still beside me. "You let him have you in front of thousands while I was made to stand by and endure it like it was some fucked-up honor."

"Because it is an honor to serve our king and to serve our people, to help our land." Though her words were strong, they lacked feeling and conviction.

"Do you hear yourself?" he barked, a wicked laugh following. "We barely survived that, and now you've dragged me here to do it all over again."

"I'd hoped it wouldn't—"

"That it wouldn't come to this, yes," he spat, exasperated. "But it has, and you knew it would. You knew it would, and you fed me your hope and your drugging kisses as though you could fool me into believing it would all be okay."

"Kole," she said, hushing him.

"No." The word was almost a wheeze. "No, I will not stand by while he makes a mockery of our bond and of this land you so wish to protect by whoring yourself out." Zad cursed under his breath. "Never again."

Footsteps echoed, a large shadow looming on the wall as the male came closer. "Do not walk away from me. You cannot mean to have me make an impossible choice. That is not love."

The shadow stilled, bobbing a little. "This," he hissed. "The fact you cannot refuse him and put me first, Este..." His voice grew choked. "*That* is not love."

Those words rocked me, and I wondered, from the other side of that very same anguish, if I'd react just as badly should Zad have decided not to refuse the king.

"Stop," she called. "That is an order."

He didn't. The walls quaked, and I melted back into the one beside me as the shadow changed from a long-haired male into a ginormous white wolf. Claws scraped against the tile, embedding as the beast skidded around a corner we could not see. Then a thundering crack, as though he'd found an exit and burst through it, and all was silent.

Este lingered. The residue in the air, their grief, and the magic the wolf had left in his wake suffocating. It dissipated with her hope for his return, a door down the end of the hall they'd been standing in closing.

"She is his queen," I whispered, shocked that her warrior, of whom she obviously loved, had seemingly abandoned her.

"They cannot control it when their emotions become too volatile. Especially the younger ones."

"He's young?"

Zad nodded, steering me with a gentle hand upon my back away from the now empty hall. "Not much older than you, I believe. I know his father, their alpha. Kash informed me that Kole is his youngest son."

"They've linked. Though she is far older than he."

"Yes, though age is never much of a concern to our kind. If they bleed or have matured into full male, then they are old enough to take a lover, or to be taken as one."

"To do so before then?" I asked.

"That is up to the youngling's parents to decide, but most decide to make an example of them."

Something I was familiar with. He squeezed my hip as if guessing my thoughts. "You've known, deep down at the very least, that I have been here a long time."

I swallowed, unsure if I could ask the question, being that he'd known my grandfather who'd died nearly five-hundred years ago. "How long?"

He caught my gaze with his. "Over six hundred summers."

My mind spun, and I blinked. "How much over?"

Those decadent lips shaped into a smirk that shone in his eyes. "Forty-three summers over."

I hated it, that just by staring at him I still felt so lost and found within my own skin. From one moment to the next, I was plagued with conflicting thoughts, endless questions, fathomless want, and murderous intent.

Six hundred and forty-three summers old. The reality should've stunned me, and I waited for it to, but instead, I found myself oddly at ease with the information. For it was true that I had known he was older than me by far.

Curiosity sparked. "What was my grandfather like? Henderson?"

"Much like your father had been before the years and his actions got the better of his mind," Zad said. "Arrogant and cunning, but also fair and a lover of family. So much so, he'd had himself killed on a hunting trip not long after the signs presented themselves."

That pulled my feet to a stop, and I frowned at Zad's back before he turned. "Signs? Before he lost parts of his mind?"

Zad dragged his teeth over his bottom lip. "Some say that caused the shift in your father to take hold earlier than most."

What he didn't say, the bright confirmation in his eyes, sank like stones inside me. "He killed his father?"

Zad, unable to say and locked into a promise he'd perhaps made long ago, just stared until I was certain that was what he'd meant. "Wow." Shaking my head, I started walking again, and he joined me. "So Henderson asked his own son to end his life."

"It appeared to be an unfortunate accident," Zad said blandly. "Of course."

All he'd said, and that he hadn't needed to say, crawled through my mind. I hadn't known my father well, hadn't wanted to, and any new information about him only seemed to further color him gray when I needed him to remain firmly in the dark.

For only monsters could breed monsters.

"Perhaps he'll return," Zad murmured, looking back. "Kole."

I knew better, and so did he. I also knew when he was trying to shake me from my thoughts, and my teeth gritted against the warm surge inside me.

Outside my rooms, I hesitated, my hand lingering over the hidden door.

"Zadicus." I fixed my eyes on his neck, the tense set of his strong shoulders, and suppressed the image of those queens touching them—*touching him*. Thinking about it, torturing myself, wouldn't get me home. I'd survived worse, I reminded myself. Yet I wasn't so sure about that. "There is only one way out, and even if there were another, would you really leave your people to rot with their dying land?"

We both knew he wouldn't, but he'd still try to find another way. He'd do everything he could to avoid a responsibility that ruined and renewed.

"I just need time." He clearly believed that, or else he wouldn't be able to say it. Shifting closer, he opened my hand and pressed the small blade he'd sharpened into my palm. He gently folded my fingers over it, his deep voice graveled. "I've been trying to figure it out, and I'll keep trying."

His expression was void as he stepped back, something of which I'd realized he'd had to train himself into doing, and therefore could not shake, not even with me, unless he reminded himself. But his eyes swam with a fear that had nothing to do with his brother.

And as I shut the door and readied myself to find some facet of sleep, I knew he was out there, at war with himself, especially after the conversation we'd heard.

He was not the only one being forced to make horrendous sacrifices.

※

I woke up in the air surrounded by a fluttering buzz, the wind on my face.

At first, I thought to close my eyes. For this was surely a dream I could escape by sinking into another.

Then I swung, falling into the side of a metal cage. The buzzing above me was drowned by cackles. Two faeries, cicada-shaped wings vibrating upon their backs, struggled to keep hold of the rope wound through the metal bars confining me.

I lurched, gripping the side of the flimsy cage as though it could keep me from tumbling into the crashing sea below. This was no dream.

I was being transported through the air.

With a jolt that clacked my teeth, the faeries dropped me upon a small flat expanse of crumbling rock, of which could soon become part of the Whispering Sea.

I wasn't alone. Beside my cage were two others, and inside them were Nova and Eline.

Nova screamed, grabbing at the long stick jutting at her through the bars. The faeries with long paper-thin faces, insectile legs, and clawed hands on rubbery-looking arms revealed sharp gray teeth as they laughed, trying to provoke Nova into climbing out.

I needed no provoking. As soon as they opened the side of the cubed enclosure, I crawled out. The breeze was strong enough to be cold, calling to the simmering rage within my veins. A small blessing in a land intent on giving me none, I flexed that rage, the coiled serpent within me awakening, all too happy to slither to the surface.

I let it, welcomed it, knowing I was about to need it.

Eline was silent as the faeries lifted her cage, tilted it, and she tumbled out.

I wasn't sure how the king had managed to capture them, but I had a feeling it was similar to how he'd lured me.

We'd been entangled in a spider's web, and we'd realized far too late.

"Audra," Eline said, the faeries fluttering away with our cages.

Waves roared below, surrounded and crashed past us as sea salt sprayed up into our faces. "Greetings, Little Lion. How does the king fare in my absence?"

She swung her head around, taking in the looming cliffs, the sea rushing between them and us, and swallowed. "This is real."

"I'd wondered the same thing," Nova said.

I sighed, gazing upon their finery and feeling that longing for home more fierce than ever.

"Raiden probably doesn't even know we're gone," Eline said, scrambling closer. We were the farthest thing from friends, but I supposed the enemy you knew was preferable to the enemy unseen. "He left yesterday for the Moon Kingdom."

It had been a month? "It's the full moon?"

"Almost," she said, eyeing me skeptically. "What is the meaning of this?"

"Time," I muttered, staring down at the violently frothing water below. "It must move differently here."

"Here?" Eline echoed, so confused she looked frustrated.

I was well-acquainted with the feeling.

Nova edged closer. "We're in Beldine, aren't we?" she asked. "Why?"

I didn't answer, mainly because I couldn't. I waited, looking for the king, for he was surely behind this, as they smacked questions at me and each other.

"How long have you been here?"

I decided to answer that. "A little over a week."

Nova wiped the blood from a cut on her arm. "I've heard their days and nights feel just like ours, but they are not. Time chugs like sluggish, thickened blood, and you do not realize it."

"So we might have been here for days?" Eline asked.

Nova threw her a scowl. "No, we just got here."

Eline seemed so perplexed, I was tempted to push her off the side of our little patch of rock to end her misery. "What do they want with us?" she asked.

"To play," I said, staring toward the horizon. It was blocked with other giant cliffs, a large shadow upon the center.

"Darkness," Nova whined. "Why aren't you dead then?"

I laughed, surprised at myself and the sound. "I suppose death doesn't want me. Not yet."

Nova stared at me, her hair whipping into her eyes. She didn't push it back as she asked, "Where's Zad? He's bound to know they've taken you."

"What makes you think they took me?" I said. "And that I did not enter their shores looking for some fun?"

"Because," she said, tone flat. "Not even the likes of you would wish to toy with an evil you cannot defeat."

She had a point. "He's here," I admitted. "A stray faerie prince, would you believe."

"A prince?" Eline gasped.

Nova's expression paled. I didn't know where she'd been or what she'd been doing with her life since she and Zad terminated their marriage some months ago, and I didn't care. Mainly because she knew. She needn't have asked what in the darkness I was talking about like Eline currently was.

She'd been married to him. Even if for only a brief time in his endless life, she knew him, and what she didn't know was beginning to make petrifying sense.

I smiled, but it fell fast. "I must have looked much like you do now, very unflattering."

Her lips parted, lashes fluttering. "So he's behind this." Her head shook. "He wouldn't..."

I looked at the marred horizon again, daylight leaking into night, and hushed her.

As quick as I could, I explained only what they needed to know, the wind doing its best to drown out my words.

"He won't let us leave," Nova said, stark resignation now etched upon her face.

"He has to," Eline said. "We've nothing to do with any of this. Especially me."

At that moment, a furbane, snowy white with silver-tipped wings, flew over our heads.

Nova screeched, and the king's laughter bounced off the rock and water.

Eline watched, wide-eyed, as the king of Beldine landed upon one of the two neighboring cliffs. It undulated at his back into a slow sloping hill, rock mingling with ever-growing grass, but no trees in sight.

"Fantastic," he said, leaping from his mount and landing with all the grace of the predator he was. "We're all here. You know each other, yes?" he asked, voice carrying over the wind. The wind carrying it as though it were its job. I supposed it was. "No need for introductions."

"What is this?" asked Nova.

The king looked at me expectantly.

I loathed to do his bidding, but there was little use in prolonging whatever it was he wanted with us. "A game."

"A game?" Eline snarled.

The king was grinning. I couldn't see his expression clearly, but I could see the flash of white teeth, his smug excitement fueling the new racing breeze.

I pushed my twirling hair back and began to braid it.

Nova eyed me, then wisely did the same, fingers moving swiftly through her honey-colored strands, as the king clapped his hands three times.

As though a curtain had been lifted, the cliffs surrounding and leading to the Whispering Sea were no longer empty. Hundreds, maybe thousands, stood in wait. Of what, we'd yet to find out. Did he expect us to fight one another to the death? To scale the cliffs and the water?

Eline's anger faded as she took in the swarm of faeries, the audience to what could very well be our deaths. Slowly, her hands released their brutal hold on her tattered pearl gown.

And then Zad roared, so loud, so violent that large rocks crumbled beneath the king's feet, and he leaped back just in time to avoid falling into the sea.

"Someone put a muzzle on my dear brother."

Warriors moved around another cage resembling the ones we'd been transported in. And I knew they were doing as the king requested, even as Zad cursed and shook his confines, the rattle loud enough for us to hear.

"Darkness save us," Nova whispered, tears in her hazel eyes when I snuck a glance at her. I wasn't sure if they were from the wind or fear or both.

"Now, my pretty things," the king said, and it seemed even Zad quit fighting. "Let us begin."

Eline squeaked. "Begin what?"

A scream, so intense I swore something trickled from my ear, came from behind.

I shoved Eline down, her cheek smacking into the rock as claws lunged for her back.

Neither eagle nor dragon, but something in-between with glowing red feathers and a scaled chest, the wide-beaked creature let out a howling scream again. Jagged teeth gnashed, its long black tongue flapping as its wings propelled it high into the air.

Then it swooped again.

Grabbing the dagger I'd kept strapped to my thigh—the one Zad had been sharpening before he'd given it to me outside my rooms—I rose to my knees.

"Does he want that thing to eat us?" Nova yelled with a glance at my blade.

"No," I said. "But if it does, it'll be a nice little bonus."

I struck, and the creature ebbed left, avoiding the glinting metal in my hand. Defense would only help us for so long. If we couldn't find a way off this tiny island that was no bigger than a large water well, it'd pluck us off one by one.

"What does he want?" Eline cried, desperate.

I watched the bird dragon turn, my heart sinking as another scream cleaved the air, cries sounding from our audience as a second beast arrived. "To entertain and to goad until he gets Zadicus to give him what he needs."

"Shit." Eline lowered into a crouch. "Why doesn't Zadicus just give him what he needs, then? Why bring us into this?"

Nova did the same but sank lower, as though she could make herself one with the rock. Being that she was a changer, I wouldn't be surprised if she could.

"I was his wife," Nova said, and my hand instantly burned with the urge to sink my blade into her splayed hand. "But you?" she said to Eline. "I've no idea what you're doing here."

"That should be obvious," I said, watching the creatures loop around one another, then dip low to the water. "Because he can." He could do all this and more, and if he needed to force Zad into action, why not push the stakes higher and have more fun in the meantime?

As if he'd heard me, the king's approval blew warm with the wind over my skin.

"Get back," I said, plucking Nova's torn blue skirts. She bounced back just as the birds, each one larger than all three of us combined, soared up the side of our island toward the sky.

Rock thundered into the sea, and Nova's chest rose and fell, the realization they'd almost taken her face as she'd peered over the side, making me wonder if she'd faint.

In half bloom, the moon watched from a nest of scattered stars.

We couldn't keep trying to dodge their taunting attacks. We were as much the creature's playthings as we were the king's.

And I was sick and tired of assholes believing they could get away with treating me as such.

"Change," I told Nova, then jumped and struck when one of the birds returned.

I missed, but I'd injured it enough to make it angry. It squawked, eliciting more excitement from the gathered crowds, then returned with a violent swoop.

We were done playing now.

Red feathers sprayed as I stood to meet it head-on and

released that rage. The bird monster stopped inches from my face, and I lifted the blade beneath its body, plunging it into what I hoped was its heart. My face, tendrils of hair whipping around it, reflected from giant dark green eyes.

The king tutted. "Whoever said you could use magic?"

"Nobody said I couldn't," I grunted, twisting the knife to ensure it'd reached the heart. Blood, so dark it was almost black, rushed down my arm, staining the flimsy material of my nightgown.

"Fair, but I must advise that you do not do so again."

I ignored his sugar-laced threat and tried to free my blade but gave up as my magic could no longer hold the dead weight in the air. The creature tumbled over itself, taking my weapon with it as it hit the waves with a splash so thorough, we were drenched.

The bird dragon's companion was far from happy.

So high, I shouldn't have even bothered to search for it amongst the stars, it raced into the sky.

Nova and Eline released loud breaths, slumping a little. But I knew this was not the time for a reprieve. It was time to prepare for a death-inducing strike.

"Up," I snapped at them. "Change, Nova."

She glared at me from the ground. "Into what?"

"Into that..." I waved a hand in the direction the bird creature had flown. "*Thing.*"

"I don't know what that is, let alone how to change into it."

"Then change into something else, just make sure it's formidable enough to be a threat." I retied my loose braid. "Or at the very least, a worthy adversary."

Through the clouds, the giant bird tunneled down like a shooting star.

The crowd tittered, undoubtedly holding their breath.

"Shit, shit, shit," Eline said, picking up a rock.

I raised a brow. "Do you not have any magic?"

"What?" Then she muttered, "Yes, of course. But he said—"

"Ignore what he said if you want to live." I kept my eyes on the creature. "Get up and use it."

Fire flew from her hand. Nothing like her beloved king, Raiden, possessed, but enough to startle the bird, who slowed, wings unfurling, and enough to have an arrow shot at her in warning.

She closed her hand, the fire vanishing, and her wide eyes on me.

I stared back at the king, who was standing on the edge of the cliff, legs set apart, hands clasped before him, looking as though he were merely waiting for a carriage to arrive instead of our demise.

"Stop," I heard Zadicus say and felt my heart pause in kind. "Stop right fucking now."

The king ignored him, acting as if he hadn't even heard him. The bird banked.

"Change," I gritted through my teeth to Nova.

Her mouth opened and closed, her eyes jumping from the beast to me. "I've never changed into an animal of any kind."

"You'd probably never changed into a human woman either," I snapped, "but lo and behold, you still managed to do that."

"I hit some kind of..." She threw her hands out, waving them frantically. "I don't know, *wall*. It felt like there was no other way out."

"So hit it again." Then I shoved her off the rock.

Nova screamed, the crowd releasing similar shocked noises as she plummeted toward the waves. I didn't have time to see if she'd sink or fly. The bird threw itself down.

"I'll do it," Zad shouted loud enough for the moon to tremble.

I harnessed that fury, lassoed it around the bird's neck, and pulled. Screeching, it crashed into the side of the island, claws cutting and scraping the stone as it tried to push away.

"Audra." Eline cursed, then proceeded to vomit onto the rock. "I'm... with babe."

Stunned, I jumped onto the creature's back, slipped, and tore at its wings as it thrashed, trying to buck me off. I could not afford to worry about what she'd admitted. I kept that lassoed band of ice wrapped tight around the creature's neck, to darkness with the king and his request for no magic. The bird stilled, and I patted its scaled neck, swallowing my fear as its large eye met mine. "Now, be a good little birdy."

Wrong thing to say.

It snarled, bucking again. "Big bird, then. Shit." An arrow whizzed by my head, and I glowered in the king's direction. "Get on," I told Eline, steering the creature into the air. We bobbed, but I held it there, ducking as another arrow almost took my ear. The king wouldn't kill me—not yet—I knew that much. But that didn't mean I fancied hanging around to be severely injured.

Eline didn't need to be told twice and rushed to the rock's edge. The bird clawed at the air, wanting to resist, and I grabbed Eline's arm, helping to swing her up behind me.

She struggled, but she'd have to hold on or fall off as more arrows flew.

I didn't believe the king cared to keep her alive. In fact, I was willing to wager he hadn't planned on allowing either female to return to Rosinthe at all. I'd have one incredibly pissed-off, estranged husband to deal with if Eline died. And... apparently, she was pregnant.

Ignoring that once more, I squeezed my thighs, and the bird dropped. We kissed the raging water below, and Eline's arms were so tight, I feared they might pull me off with her if she fell.

The wind was a howling storm in my ears, the creature's cries alerting the king's warriors to our whereabouts, but due to our low angle, they could not reach us.

Along the bottom of the long cliff on which they all stood to watch, we soared over the water and sharp rocks, and when we reached the open waves of the Whispering Sea, the arrows struggled to make the distance.

And then a furbane broke through the waves, shaking water

from its back, wings spreading and fumbling like that of a brand-new foal.

I supposed that was exactly what she was. Nova stumbled, her clawed feet sinking into the water as she did her best to keep herself in the air, and then she followed.

We headed northeast, and regardless of whether Nova knew how to fly well, I had to get rid of Eline. I whistled, and the bird beneath me squawked in response. I shuddered, my ears protesting and trickling again. Mercifully, the beast didn't buck. It seemed to have grown used to our weight upon its back or resigned to it perhaps.

Nova finally caught up, black as night and smaller than any furbane I'd seen, but a furbane all the same. I ignored that bite of anger in her large, deep-set eyes and flicked my own to Eline.

She blinked, understanding—I hoped.

"Jump," I told Eline when Nova moved in underneath us. The bird dragon tensed to lunge at the threat, but I pulled at the invisible reins.

"What?" she screamed.

"Jump. Nova will catch you." A dangerous risk for a female with a babe in her womb, but there was no other way to get her out alive. The king would kill them—of that, I was sure—if we all landed upon that cliff. He'd make use of them to entertain himself and his guests, and abuse his power in gruesome ways.

After wasted heartbeats, Eline shouted, "You mean to stay?"

In answer, I shoved her. With a shocked, cut-off scream, she fell into the air…

And right onto Nova's back. She slid, then caught the fuzz of Nova's mane and wrenched herself upright.

The king could punish me all he wanted, but he'd have to catch me first.

They rose, and I yelled across the wind, "Go home, and *do not* send anyone for me." Eline's green eyes scrunched. "Understood?"

With an unexpected reluctance, she nodded once.

"Now fly as if your fucking lives depend on it," I said. "For they do." Nova immediately took off, racing for the edge of the endless night sky.

Then I turned the beast back toward the scrambling king, who was shouting at his aerial fleet to give chase.

Smiling, I decided to prolong my punishment and give them something to chase.

"Rah." I dug my heels into the bird's sides, but instead of squawking at me in rage, its long neck ducked down, wings beating hard enough to lift the waves below.

We headed east, the roiling sea becoming less of a serpent and more of an open-mouthed shark. The water grew darker and calmer but no less violent. Land loomed up ahead, jutting cliffs similar to the ones we'd left behind.

The bird banked, sharp, and I cursed, sliding. Righting myself, I discovered why. At the darkest part of the sea, in the center of what I now understood were the four courts of Beldine, was a whirlpool.

A twisting midnight that absorbed the starlight and plunged deep into the unknown.

Stories of lost merchants, ships that'd veered off course, never to be seen again, echoed through my childhood memories. They needn't worry over a siege in these parts. For anyone who tried to sail through the Whispering Sea into the heart of Beldine would never even meet their shores.

I realized there were no shores to reach as soil soon replaced water and rock. As far as the eye could see, there were only towering cliffs and the land of each court that gently sloped toward the distant sea.

On the other side of that land were the shores with a glimmering sand I was all too familiar with. Clever, I thought, to know exactly where your visitors, unwanted or otherwise, would arrive at all times.

I leaned forward at the sight of a castle, its turrets, six of them, milky moonstone white against the dark curtain of night. I wasn't foolish enough to get too close, for although its queen was likely back in the Onyx Court, other warriors would remain.

Silver speckled trees with drooping branches swayed beneath us. We curved around a giant oak intent on curling itself around us. Greenery with splashes of forest circled a diamond of tiny villages and what looked to be a small city, all of it undulating beneath the castle, which sat a healthy distance from the base of the cliff.

Seeing enough, I encouraged the bird to turn back, knowing the king's warriors would soon be upon us.

In doing so, we loomed closer to the treetops, and as they untangled from one another in the brutal wind, I glimpsed the rot. Patches of darkened soil, deadened stumps, and blackened grass snaking between the trees in trails they appeared to try to bend away from.

An empty village resided near the base of the cliff with thatched rooftops overgrown by blackened vines. Charred earth zigzagged through homes, their sandstone exteriors marred with whatever ill health was spreading throughout the land.

Dead earth morphed into cracked, unstable rock, and I knew if not for the fact they couldn't survive off the dying land around them, then the residents of the village would've moved more so out of fear of the land eventually crumbling into the sea.

It seemed I was blessedly alone and unable to come to terms with what I was seeing.

I'd seen the beauty, the incomparable magic of this continent, but I'd now seen the damage caused by Zad's absence, too.

He hadn't known it would happen—I knew that—but it didn't change the fact that it had. And it wasn't only the soil that was dying; the ocean threatened to swallow not only the rotting corpses of the village homes but the people too.

I had enough of a heart to know it was wrong and that he should help, own up to a responsibility he'd never thought was his, even if the heartless part of me wanted to snatch him this instant and fly us home.

Across the sea we flew, and my breath caught. A manor, entirely made of bronze stone, sat in the middle of the next isle. A maze, rife with golden flowers, circled the glittering fortress.

Water, trickling underneath the night sky, laced itself around the queen's home before doing the same to the rock-built homes surrounding the maze.

Gliding as low as I dared, ferns and rose bushes came into view, the land dotted with an array of flowers and smaller shrubbery. To the east of the castle was a rainforest, and in the trees, glowing lights twinkled inside bamboo-constructed huts.

It all seemed so classically normal in a world where nothing was expected, and everything was possible for the right price.

I was nothing but an insect buzzing across this vast world. A world that belonged to a tyrant king by law, but to my linked male by heart.

Heading back over the sea, its spray licking at my bare, scratched-up feet, I found the king's fleet.

I smiled when they paused in the air, and we soared right past them, back to the isle of onyx and into its High King's clutches.

I had no idea what I'd do when we arrived. Perhaps the bird would eat me since I'd stolen it. Perhaps the king would shoot an arrow through my heart before we'd even neared the isle.

As expected, that didn't happen. The king's warriors stayed behind me, following me back to where the audience had now faded upon the precipice.

The bird creature was all too happy to land, though it didn't exactly know how to do so gently and refused to wait another moment to heed any instruction from me. Courtiers and warriors dove out of the way as we hit the ground with a jarring boom that knocked me off. Feathers careened into my face as I tumbled to the hard earth, and I did my best to roll to keep any bones from breaking.

The creature screamed high above, already flying away by the time I pushed my half-braided hair from my eyes and brushed rock and dirt from my arms.

My right arm throbbed, and I gingerly stretched it out. Not broken. A small mercy as the king's guards surrounded me.

The moon haloed his head, his hair swept back off the harsh planes of his face to reveal the full extent of his displeasure. Ryle's eyes appeared almost entirely black, his voice infused with malice as he asked, "You dare to escape from me?"

Now was not the time to be a smart-ass, but I'd never been adept at mincing words. "Well, I've been cooped up for so long that I felt like taking a bit of a wander around."

An unseen force pulled me up by my hair as the king's boots crunched over the ground, and he stopped before me.

"Ryle," Zad shouted, a biting threat.

The king's eyes flashed, the only warning I had before he buried his fist into my stomach.

I fell to the ground, everything turning darker than full night, my breath stolen from me.

Roaring and shouting entered my fogged thoughts, forcing open my eyes. Lying upon my side, I tried to breathe. Which was made harder thanks to Zad, who'd somehow escaped his scrap of a cage and was now upon the king on the ground.

"Zad," I said, but I had no voice.

Zad's fist smacked into Ryle's face, but his next attack hit the air as three guards hauled him off the king.

Face contorted with enough wrath to have the warriors holding him appear concerned, Zad's burning eyes fell upon me. Feral with unspent frustration and worry, they roamed over every part of me.

"I'm fine," I said, lying but glad to hear I had my voice back. It felt like my stomach had left my body, and in its place, something hollow and aching had taken root.

Zad's nostrils flared. He knew I was lying, but he could do nothing.

"Your little display of defiance will cost you dearly, Audra," the king said, brushing blood from his nose and dirt from his dark tweed jacket.

Rising to my feet, I withheld the urge to groan, my torso wanting me back on the ground. The cage Zad had been in was nothing but metal shards, and I blinked at it, slowly gaining control of my lungs.

"Touch her again," Zad said, grunting in the warriors' hold, his hair loose and falling into his face. The shifters had to be stronger than most creatures in this land to keep him contained. Then again, I was sure that was why they served the courts as they did. "And you'll not get what you need from me."

The king's perfectly groomed brows lifted. "You mean to say you're finally ready?" Stepping closer to his brother, a dangerous thing to do, king or no, when Zad was nothing but barely leashed anger, he murmured, "No tricks, no foul play, no begging for another way?"

Zad didn't look at me as he gritted, "I swear it. Let it be done."

Those words filled me with an even mixture of dread and relief. Yet I refused to allow myself the space to think of what he'd have to do. Of him with those three beautiful queens.

We were quickly escorted back, but I was no longer allowed free rein of the castle.

The invisible door became permanently so. Still damp from the bath Temika had run for me, I slid down the wall where it used to be, wiping some dried blood from my cheek that I'd missed in my haste to wash off the night's events. It'd come from my ear, I realized, remembering the trickle I'd felt, courtesy of the giant bird dragon's screech.

I must have fallen asleep because a series of knocks on the other side of the patterned wall had my eyes flicking open.

"Audra." Zad.

I turned as though I could see him. "I can't get out."

"I know," he said, and in his soft tone, I heard the pain of admitting he couldn't free me either.

In silence, we sat, the sun threatening to outshine the approaching moon through the windows, throwing its false golden promise across the floor.

"I love you," he eventually said. "That will never change, never cease."

I didn't hear that. Instead, I heard, "I'm sorry."

"I'm sorry, too," I whispered, for we both knew nothing would ever be the same once the full moon arrived.

ELEVEN

Audra

Forced to stay inside my rooms, I had a hollowing suspicion I was to remain here until the act was over.

The drums began with a slow beat, a call to the wild, to its creatures and the land, to something within the skin and bone that longed to dance and be set free.

I was no slave to it, locked within my rooms as I was, but that didn't negate its effects.

The soft strains of flutes were swallowed by the increasing violence of the drums, hypnotizing in an entirely unsuspecting way. I found myself at the window, my fingers curled over the round wood. Longing and fear and defiance made it impossible to sit still for too long.

The night grew, the full moon a glowing face over the rushing river below, its reflection eerily undisturbed.

Was my prince afraid? No, I knew better than to think that.

If I was hungry, locked high within the castle, he had to be starving wherever the gathering, the act, was to occur.

The drumbeats grew louder, faster, taking time with them. It would happen soon. Midnight, I'd guessed, being that the moon would then reach its highest point in the sky.

I couldn't do this.

I had to do this. *He* had to do this.

But was it really so much better to remain locked away? To ignore it? I decided no.

I had to see it. I had to desensitize myself to it. If I had any hope of ignoring the bond we'd forged, then I needed the reminder of what he'd done—of what he was doing. A scarring, unforgivable kind of betrayal.

I wanted to look him in the eyes as he took another female and shattered everything we were.

I wanted to support him in a way I never could again, knowing he had no choice and that this heartbreak was not only inevitable but necessary.

I wanted to see him. I *had* to see him.

Temika arrived a minute later with my supper, boiled quail eggs and cheese wrapped wild berries, as I'd requested earlier with little thought.

I waited. When she set it down, smiling as she curtsied, lips parting as she no doubt was about to ask if I needed anything else, I saw the dark flush in her cheeks.

She could feel it too. That energy in the air. The potent desire that felt as if it'd cleave you in two if you did not seek its source and let it unleash itself upon you.

Seeing it, the way her legs brushed together beneath a short ruffle of silver material, reminded me to stay on task. It made what I had to do easier.

Her hands clawed at her throat, her eyes flooded with fear, and I caught her as she fell, brushing some tendrils of hair off her face. I released my magic from her lungs once I knew she was out and grabbed the knife from the tray, tucking it within the flimsy elastic of my lace undergarments.

In a peach silken nightgown that only reached my thighs, I raced out into the dark hall and followed the noise.

Winding down and down, deeper into the castle until I wondered if I were underground, I tracked that beating heart all the way to a sealed round wooden door. Leaning forward, I exhaled over the hinges, and they iced, then cracked. Wincing at its weight, I did my best to remove the door and prop it against a dirt wall. It slipped from my fingers, and I stilled, waiting to see if someone heard the crunching of wood upon the soil. After a moment, it became painfully clear that there was likely no one inside the castle besides Temika.

The tunnel led to a grove, long spindly trees with branches so high you couldn't see them, towered above a large expanse of clover. Faeries were everywhere. In the clover, they laughed and mated, smaller goblin-type creatures dancing upon the backs of some couples.

My feet carried me forward, my hunger growing more desperate with the crazed sights before me. The deafening beat of the drums flooded my heartbeat, changing its rhythm to match.

A screech from high above in the trees, and I blinked and shook my head. Looking back, I realized my error. It was not a tunnel I'd walked through but a cave, and a little way around the bend was the giant mouth.

I ducked back inside, begging my eyesight to adjust to the dim, and tried to find a way to reach the back entrance to the cave. With it being beneath the castle, there had to be one.

Up a set of ten earthen stairs, I raced down a narrow passageway, my fingers trailing the packed dirt walls in search of something—anything. I stopped when something shifted underfoot and backed up to where tiny, almost imperceptible, flickers of light shone through the dirt.

Dropping to my hands and knees, I dug as fast as I could, needing him. Needing his skin sweating against mine and his hoarse breaths cocooned in the shell of my ear as he trembled beneath me.

They might need to have him, but I needed him first—just one last time. I had to.

It was a compulsion, a creaking whine within the marrow of my bones I could not ignore.

He needed me, and I needed him.

My nails protested as they hit wood, but my heart sang. I dug until I found a latch, about to open it when crumbs of rational thinking finally returned. I'd need to be quiet. I had no idea where the hole led, nor who I might find beneath it.

This was a bad idea.

I opened the latch, the hinges squeaking, but there was no way it could be heard above the music that stampeded inside this snake hole of a tunnel as I lifted the door open a crack.

Down below, shadows bounced off the walls from an unseen fire and floating bubbles that drifted through the air. Inside them were flickering bugs with giant glowing bulbs on their backs.

I bit my lip, unsure and unable to see anyone, then I opened the door all the way and jumped.

My teeth sang, one of my canines piercing my tongue. I swallowed the rush of blood, hurrying back to the wall. The bubbles floated by, most of them bouncing toward the mouth of the cave. Which, judging by the light flaying off the walls from the fire outside, was right around the corner.

A groan came from behind, catching and dragging my feet. I pressed back into the dark as two guards, armor glinting, rounded the darkest patch of the tunnel, carrying a bound Zadicus.

His eyes were downcast, lashes fluttering at the ground.

Focused on trying to maneuver Zad's near-dead weight to where he was needed, they didn't seem to notice me pushed up against a small crevice in the wall. Dirt sprinkled over my shoulders, but I didn't care. He was struggling, but only imperceptibly, as though he were asleep but would then wake, remembering where he was.

But his eyes had been open.

Something was wrong. But then the king's voice echoed through the tunnel, throughout the sprawling meadow and grove beyond. "It is time. Now remember, stay back, do not enter, or you shall forfeit your life." I crept forward, shimmying along the wall. "And we do not want such dramatics during this joyous, momentous occasion."

He said nothing else, and I had no clue where he might have

gone, but as I slid past the opening I'd jumped through—the above passageway thankfully too dark for the guards to notice the open door—I dared to keep going until I could peer around the corner.

A bed of furs, pelts of grays and cream tufted whites, were spread upon a low-lying dais. And upon the furs, his mouth gagged and his hands bound behind his back, hair dripping over his golden eyes and the sharp cliffs of his cheeks, was my lord.

The mouth of the cave, dressed with a translucent veil, was wide, but it was also low, giving Zadicus and his queens a modicum of privacy. Their lower bodies might have been visible, should anyone be close enough to watch, but unless the act took place lying down, the top halves of their bodies would not be seen.

A sense of sickening reality washed in, knocking me from the drugging haze.

About to dart forward and shake Zad, beg him to sweep us back home, consequences be damned, I almost growled when a wintry voice said, "What are you doing here?"

I spun back around the corner.

Este, dressed in nothing but a thin, white silken robe, gazed back at me with unnerving copper eyes. Her white-blond hair was unbound, curling over the rise of her breasts, sneaking inside her robe to rest over her creamy skin.

Those eyes, rimmed with kohl-lined lashes, as well as her height and that haunting stillness, were a reminder that she was not only a queen but a faerie queen at that. Regardless, I was tempted to shove her back to wherever she'd come from, but then someone ducked under the curtain, calling her name.

The drums grew louder, deafening, and those unreadable eyes gave a flash of what I thought might have been pity. "You cannot stop that which is inevitable, young queen."

I wanted to try. Gazing at her, her thin, towering body with barely a curve besides her breasts, I wanted to beg her to go back, to find her mate and forget this insanity.

But she'd already lost him, and I knew she would not let that be for naught.

Every limb turned to ice, heavy and painful to move, as I slunk back into the shadows.

Este stood there, the drums droning on, swaying us all on our feet, but not her.

I watched her pull her shoulders back, and with my dying heart clenching my fists, setting fire to each ragged breath, I watched her round the corner.

I was going to vomit. I swallowed the urge and closed my eyes.

There was little sound coming from the mouth of the cave, and I wondered if he was enjoying her even though he was bound and to be used. Surely, I'd feel it.

With a bond like ours, in life or death or extreme emotional situations, I could and should feel him—feel *something*.

But looking back on this eve, I'd felt nothing but my own anguish. Perhaps that was his too, the same kind of torture. Perhaps that was why I was here, for it was too much to bear. It was a horror I thought I could handle… until it was time for it to unfold.

My feet made no sound over the soil as I drifted back to find Este upon Zad's lap, trying to rouse him it seemed. Naked beneath her robe, her body rubbed over his, trying to get a reaction, but his head only flopped to the side.

"Rosesake," she murmured, as if to herself, and let out a low, strangled cry.

Those outside must have heard it and thought she'd made it in pleasure, as shouts and jeers plundered beneath the curtain.

"What's wrong?"

Este didn't startle. She'd likely sensed I was still there.

"They've poisoned him."

Uncaring of who might hear, I hissed, "They *what?*"

"He wouldn't do it," she said, tears in her voice as she gently slapped at his cheeks. "He thought he could, but when they took him to ensure he kept his promise, he apparently destroyed the room they locked him in, snapped the arm of one of Ryle's best warriors, and killed another before they could stop him."

I swallowed, my chest heaving with a shuddered breath. He'd killed. Such was his desire to keep from hurting me, to keep from ruining us even more. He'd murdered.

I felt my lips tremble and sucked them between my teeth. "So they poisoned him," I whispered, then frowned. He could not help the land if he was dying. "He will be okay?" I itched to rush over there, but I knew it would be a grave mistake. They'd see my legs, wonder who else was here with them, being that the queens were supposed to take turns.

"Yes, the effects should wear off soon, depending on when they last dosed him."

Relief kicked me in the gut. "What do you do until then?"

She stopped trying to sober him, her lithe form slumping, her head falling to his shoulder.

Zad groaned, trying to push her off.

He was in there. He just couldn't do anything. The horror of that... I couldn't even think it, but the queen gave voice to it.

"I suppose I'm to use the part of him that hopefully hardens, and his magic will awaken him more with the pleasure as it feeds the land."

"Over my decaying bones," I snapped, making to leap forward.

But I couldn't move.

The queen had stuck my feet to the ground, leaving my arms to pinwheel until I found purchase against the wall, more dirt embedding in my nails. The audacity. I threw all my might, all my anger toward her, only to find a wall of resistance.

I ducked just in time to avoid the ricochet of my own magic, narrowly avoiding a hit to the chest. "How—"

"I will unglue your feet if you leave," she said with a calm-filled authority. "I cannot imagine why you'd wish to stay. Are you some kind of masochist?"

She had no idea. "Unglue my feet, queen," I snarled, "and I'll show you exactly what I am."

A tinkling laugh left her, and she eyed me over her prim shoulder. "Cute."

Then after a moment of hovering in reluctance, her hands were trailing down his shoulders and arms. Zad muttered something behind his gag, which I noticed was a glittering black metal.

The queen hushed him, continuing her ministrations.

It felt like something was crawling over my own skin when his eyes slowly opened, blinking at where I was stuck. They struggled, desperate to remain open, and he shifted beneath the silver queen.

"That's it," she crooned to him, her hands smoothing back his hair. He shook her off. "Go," she said to me. "You are only making it more difficult for him."

We both knew I wasn't going anywhere. Staring down at my feet, I encased them in ice.

Ice that cracked.

The queen gasped as I launched forward and pulled her off the dais and into the shadows, but before she could react, I pressed my finger to her mouth. "I'll do it."

She squinted at me in the near dark, a low hum of incredulous laughter departing her rose petal pink lips. "You?" Her eyes narrowed. "You're not even full fae, let alone a fae queen. It will not work."

"This," I said, gesturing to where Zad was trying to watch us, but his head kept lolling, "isn't working either." I softened my voice, lowering it. "Leave while there's a slight chance your wolf might forgive you."

Her eyes widened at that, her lips quaking. She glanced over at Zad. Looking back at me, she nodded. "Pray to every deity you royal half breeds worship that this works, or we're all sea dragon bait."

Then Este was gone. In her wake, the scent of roses and morning dew lingered.

Zad's eyes were closed when I stripped out of my nightgown and undergarments, the dinner knife falling to shine in the dirt.

They opened when the makeshift dais shifted and gave away my presence. Meeting his clouded gaze, I sank onto his lap, intent on ridding the queen's touch from his chest.

My hands smoothed over it, over every inch of skin, and when they roamed up his chest to his neck, fingers tickling over his taut cheeks and jaw, the rough studs of hair erupting from his skin, I smiled. Almost entirely gold, a gold so deep it was closer to bronze, his eyes exploded.

He'd never looked more inhuman than at that moment, and though something nudged at me to run even though he was bound, that link of ours, my stupid heart, had my legs winding tight around him.

Muscles in his upper arms and shoulders bulged and pulled as metal clinked behind his back, and then his arms were around me, constricting and wonderful. His head lowered to my shoulder, my hands skimmed up the broad planes of his back. I felt him exhale as I rubbed my fingers over the scars, the scars I now knew were from his missing wings.

Gently lifting his head, I studied his overeager eyes, the drums outside the cave causing my blood to pound. His nostrils flared wide at my touch, and I dragged my lips over his cheek, nearing the mouthpiece that stunk of a magic I'd never dare try to best.

I did not have to.

Like the metal that'd bound his hands behind him, there was another click, and he reached between us, tearing it off.

It hit the dirt wall, and outside, the commotion climbed higher in answer.

With his hand behind my head, his chest a pounding storm beneath my palms, those eyes feverish upon my face, my breasts, and then my mouth, he grunted, "You shouldn't be here."

Slowly, I grinned. "But I am, so what happens now?"

His lips shifted with a hint of humor, and I pushed his hair back, inching forward until my chest touched his. "Now," he said, gruff and low, fingers bunched in my hair, tilting my head back. His eyes left mine as he ducked, his breath heating my throat. "I devour you until you beg me to stop, but Audra," he said, sounding breathless, rocking beneath me as if he could no longer wait but was forcing himself to with every breath he shakily drew. "Audra." My name dragged from deep in his throat as though it were the cure and the curse.

"What?" I said, nothing but melting wool in his arms as he bent and sculpted me as he saw fit.

The threadbare cloth that'd covered his manhood slipped over my thigh, the rough feel of it evoking a moan. His tongue lapped at my skidding pulse, his free arm lifting me onto his hard length. I slid down with a silent cry, and he huffed with wicked intent against my flushed skin. "Even if you beg, I will not be able to."

I needed him, needed this like nothing I'd ever needed before.

I gripped his hair in kind, and he smiled in response, but it was all predator—nothing sweet in sight. My mouth dropped to his, his cock twitching inside me. I rolled my hips, my lips rubbing his. "Then it's a good thing I've never been one to beg."

Something unfurled on the wall behind him, the entire mouth of the cave now shrouded in shadow.

Wings, I realized, my lips parting in awe, and then Zad's teeth stole my bottom lip and tugged. "No one sees you but me."

I stared at them in wonder, marveled at the way the shadow wings moved with him while not even attached to his body. Phantom and unexplainable, they'd appeared at his urging to wrap around us like a feathered breeze I could see but not feel—as though he'd hidden his true shadow from me, from all of us, all this time.

He'd glamoured his true self.

The realization, that heady intensity that'd melted every layer of ice inside me, sank deep, and I pushed strands of auburn hair back from his ears—hair that seemed to catch and absorb every ounce of light in the cave. I'd known for days what I'd find there, known what else he'd hidden from me, yet my heart still stuttered as I beheld the soft curves at the tips of his ears.

A low purr, his lashes bobbing, as my fingers traced the lobes. They were just like mine, the cartilage only changing the higher my fingers rose. They were not pointed but curved in a harsh bend by the side of his head.

Zad's lashes rose as my fingers drifted down his neck, my hands splayed across the clenching muscles of his shoulders. My eyes were wet, not with hurt or fear but with wonder. Large hands clasped my face. We stared for unending moments, though it had to be costing him to remain still. Desire, this bone-deep lust, warred with love and longing.

And then they clashed.

It was harsh, and it wasn't anything I'd grown used to. It was pure hunger unleashed. His hands bruised every place they touched, and my nails scratched, pleading with my urgent breaths for more. He moved me over him as though I were nothing but air, so thorough in his aim, and so hard, I could barely see straight, but I didn't care.

I wanted it, all of it, anything that was him and nothing that wasn't.

He said nothing, and I doubted he even could. He'd plunged so deep, a scream tore from me, and he held me back just far enough to squeeze and suck my breasts before hauling me against him. Hard and unrelenting, he used me until I blew into a thousand pieces over him.

As though we'd forged a bond all over again, we both shuddered so violently, the earth trembled around us. In awe, I watched dirt sprinkle from above, shaking and clawing for more as he laid me down and covered my entire body with his and his winged shadow so that only he could see it. He licked at my mouth, my neck, my heaving breasts, and grew hard inside me once more.

Pushing one of my legs up and over his shoulder, he groaned into my neck, licking the curve of my throat over and over as he slowly moved in and out of my body.

There was no pain, no quick mask of pleasure to relieve it, for it was nothing but a toe-curling pleasure to have his teeth pierce the flesh he'd so gently softened for himself to feed on.

My eyelids fluttered as my hand clenched tight in his hair, holding him to me. Above us, the soil came alive, the roots of the tree-laden castle shifting and slithering, dirt raining and glittering. As though he'd summoned them all, those bubbled bugs floated above the cocoon of concealment Zad's shadow had provided, so that even in the dark, I could see him.

Zad's magic had always been more. More than me, more than Raiden, more than any royal I'd ever encountered. I'd always thought it was the air of primal authority he'd carried with him that made it so, and although that was largely why I'd found myself so attracted to him, I'd never guessed how deep that energy of his, the feral way it sang to me like a wolf calling to the moon, had run.

His magic, this force of unimaginable power that dizzied and drew, it was more than even him. It was the air, the earth, the mists, our blood, the beating of our thundering hearts, and the changing skies.

It was Beldine.

The guards eventually arrived with Queen Hydrah, but we didn't stop. I couldn't ask him, and I didn't want to, and I knew there was no way he would.

A wall, naked to the eye, stopped the guards from nearing us. They rushed outside, and Zad removed his teeth from my neck.

My lips sought his, licking the blood from them, smiling against them at his soft growl of approval.

"Leave them," the king said.

"But he's..."

"It's working, so I care not. Out."

I was too far gone, too much of nothing but everything Zad needed, to care.

He kissed me in time with the movement of his powerful body, muttering words to me I was too dazed to understand. Filthy approval, I guessed, for when I tightened around him, he hummed into my ear, picking up his pace.

Zad roared when I fell apart, joining me. The muscles in his neck corded as his head tipped back, his powerful arms holding him up while his hips made fine work of rendering me useless, and he finished emptying himself inside me.

Within seconds, his head lowered for his soft lips to drag over my chest to my chin. My mouth opened, welcoming his tongue even as my lungs struggled to keep up. A violent groan evoked a full-body shiver, and he pressed himself as deep as he could go before leaving my body.

But only for one panicked heartbeat.

I was picked up and placed onto all fours, my back arching when he entered me from behind.

The sun was leaking inside our own little world when I opened my eyes to find Zad's body curled around mine. One arm was tucked beneath me, holding my head to his warm chest and his hand half covering my ass, the other upon the small of my back. His fingers were tracing the indent of my spine, our legs entwined.

"I love you," he said, voice strained and roughened with sleep, his breath stirring the top of my hair. He kissed it, holding me tighter, however that was possible with all of me touching all of him. "My perfect storm, my entire fucking heart."

Something leaked from my eye, my arm slithering from between us to wind around his toned waist. The scent of sex laid heavy on the floral, smoke-infused air. As it should, considering how much of it we'd had. The act, if that was what we'd done, was a muddled blur of ecstasy-ridden waves.

I said nothing back, not because I didn't want to, but because he knew. He knew it as surely as he knew his own love for me, that I returned his feelings, no matter how furious I was with him. For that hurt, his betrayal and deception were still there. It had faded in the wake of the reminder of us. It'd been too intense for it not to, but it hadn't been erased.

And I wouldn't have done what I did, risked both of our lives, if I didn't still love him. It was madness, sheer insanity, to risk myself and him in that way, but love, I'd come to learn, did not care for rules or risk. Love was untamable, a force of magic no one could escape should it befall them.

I was trapped, and as much as it terrified me to know that, it terrified me far more to be without him.

"Did it work?" I finally asked, the king's voice, how he'd known I was here, muddled inside my memories.

Zad kissed my head again, then groaned as he untangled himself from me. "Come and see for yourself."

The gleam in his eyes told me all I needed to know. It had. We'd done it. Him and me, no other pureblood, royal females necessary. Still, I humored him and gingerly shifted to dress in the clothing lying crumpled upon the dirt floor.

Zad caught me before I could step down and, instead, picked me up.

"I can walk," I needlessly said.

"Then perhaps I need to carry you back to those furs and wrap your legs around my neck once more." He set me down, and I scowled at him, eliciting a husky chuckle as he fetched my clothes.

Painfully aware of the mess between my legs, I tried to kill the unfurling shiver and failed, unsure how I could possibly want more.

With a gentleness so like him, he pulled the frothy nightgown over me, forgoing the undergarments. I pushed my arms through the straps, then dragged my fingers through my knotted, tangled hair.

Abdominal muscles gathered and released as he bent to retrieve the beige cloth he'd worn the previous night and hastily looped it around his waist. He was staring at me, face unreadable but for that smile in his eyes, and I couldn't help it. I smiled back.

My animalistic lover, my gentle prince, and my territorial lord.

Indeed, it probably would've been nice to have been carried.

With just a few steps toward the sheer gauzy curtain strung over the cave entrance, I was doing my best to keep from wincing.

Zad huffed, the glint in his eyes as he clasped my hand within his full of that maddening arrogance.

"Don't be too pleased with yourself."

"Oh, but I am." He pushed the curtain aside, bending and tugging me through. "Thoroughly," he said to my ear, then nipped at my lobe.

I made to shove him away but laughed as he pulled me into his side, his large hand upon my hip as we took in the destruction of the night.

But there was none to be found.

New flowers were unfurling, the spray of the river through the trees leaving droplets that glittered over each gold and green leaf. I'd already discovered the treacherous beauty of this land, but I was beginning to think I'd only glimpsed it.

Through the trees, we walked in silence, both of us seeming to draw new breath as we absorbed new life. Tittering laughter came from a creature swinging high above in the canopy of giant trees. In the bright light of day, the bark was no longer a mottled brown but gray with black stripes and patches running through the trunks.

Slowing, Zad waited as I dragged my fingers down it. It shivered, and I snatched my hand back, blinking.

He chuckled, pulling me along. "They like to be touched."

I said nothing, still feeling the coarse velvet of its bark upon the tingling pads of my fingers.

We veered left, skirting the edge of the waterfall, its salty mist rising to dampen the dried sweat upon our skin. Alongside it, the castle at our backs, was a path lined with what I'd once thought were white pebbles.

They were beetles.

I stopped, as did Zad, and stared down at them. Tiny black legs poked out from ivory shells, differing in size, but none bigger than my hand.

"Sugargems," Zad said. "You cannot harm them. Their shells are harder than steel."

We walked on, and I wondered if I was missing countless hidden secrets. I had to be, but I didn't ask him to stop. Though he seemed content to amble, taking in this place he'd once called home.

"It's alive," I murmured. "All of it."

Zad's jaw flexed, his chest lowering with a loaded exhale. "I hadn't known he'd lack the power to keep it so." Ruefully, he smiled. "He is my father's every dark mood. So much like him that I never once thought to ask or to check."

We skirted a marching group of large insects, their long legs jostling their thin, golden bodies from side to side. "Kash, all of them, they didn't know?"

Zad shook his head, making to shift a large fern from the path for me to pass, but stopped to rub his fingers over it. The green, so light it was almost yellow, darkened to a deep emerald. My hand tightened around his as the color spread through the fern and down into the soil.

"I think it's safe to assume that Ryle did not wish for anyone to know he was lacking."

"Until he stood to lose not only his title but also the land of which granted him as much."

Zad squeezed my hand. "We're going home."

Home. Just that one word was enough to infuse more energy into my spent body. "Do you truly think he'll just let us leave?" I might not have known Ryle as well as Zad, but I knew enough not to expect anything.

"We did what he desperately needed me to," Zad said, and the path veered down a steep hill, lined with toadstools and glowing green shrubbery. Now behind us, the falls could still be heard, but the crashing mingled with the rush of the river beside us, racing below the cliff.

To our left and up ahead, nestled deeper among the trees,

were homes. Some a glittering black stone, cottages with fat chimneys puffing breaths of smoke toward the sky.

The homes in the trees appeared small from where I'd glimpsed them in my rooms, looking out the window. Being closer, I now saw they were huge. More oak and strips of bamboo were used to create pathways in the air between the tree houses.

A hole in a giant granite rock soon greeted us, and we stepped into the dark.

Rushing water morphed into trickling the farther we descended.

Zad whistled, and within seconds, those creatures, the tiny bulbous glowing insects, appeared. Now, they were free to bob about without bubbles. Clicking noises tickled my ears when they bounced by my head, lighting our way down the slope.

The dark tunnel opened into an impossibly deep chamber, and the bugs disappeared. They were no longer needed.

Flaying light streaked over the damp walls, rainbows arcing over the glistening, bubbling pool of water. It stretched to either side of the rock-hewn walls and flowed between two cracks at either end to rejoin the river.

Zad released my hand. "Rainbow Springs." Noticing I'd not moved, he gently gripped my nightgown, then pulled it over my head. "I came here almost every day when I was a youngling." Crouching, he removed his cloth and laid my nightgown atop it, then rose.

I tore my eyes from the storybook imagery surrounding me and stared at my mate.

My linked love. The match to my soul. The male capable of changing the beat of my heart. Naked, painfully beautiful, irrevocably mine, and in this strange land of his, a stranger.

Feather soft, his fingers dusted down my cheek. "You have not forgiven me?"

Staring at his chest, the scratches from my nails already healing, most gone as if they'd never happened, I felt my body sway closer to his heat. A heat I now knew was more than I'd ever thought it was. That drugging pull was my need for him, but it was also just him.

I loathed to think of the effect it had on others.

My cheeks filled with air as I inhaled and slowly released it, staring up at him. "I love you." It was all I could think to say, all I could give him.

I could lie. But just because I loved a male to the point of self-ruination did not mean I'd lose that shard of ice I was born with.

He'd hurt me, and no, I had not yet forgiven him. I wondered if I even could when I was still trying to accept all he'd hidden from me.

I heard him swallow. Talented fingers crawled under my chin, tipping it, his eyes demanding mine. I gave them to him, let him see what lingered inside, and watched him begrudgingly accept it with a jerk of his head and a roll of his lips.

He kissed me, a quick brush of his lips upon the scars residing next to my mouth, and then he led me to the water. So thick, it felt as though I'd plunged breast-deep into a pool of milk as it enveloped us.

Zad didn't release me. He set me upon a rock beneath the water, its bubbles tickling my chin.

I sat still, even as I longed to dive to the bottom to see what creatures lurked below, and allowed him to do as he wished. His hands caressed every part of me. Beneath my arms, over them, fingers gentle while still cleansing, his eyes fastened on every place he touched, every part visible to him.

Tilting my head back, he carefully massaged and rid the tangles from my hair, his breath feathering over my lips. "We will make plans to leave. But first, I must ensure Dace is released."

I'd almost forgotten the quiet male still lingered within the bowels of Ryle's keep. "What are they doing to him?"

"Nothing," he said. "I've been checking and taking him food."

"They won't feed him?"

Focused on his task, he muttered absently, "Sometimes, if his majesty feels so inclined to allow it."

I watched him as he washed my hair, my fingers weaving through the thick water. "You do not wish to stay? Your presence is likely still needed."

He propped my head up, and his lips flattened. "We've done enough."

With his eyes shifting to mine, he dragged his roughened palms down my sides, and my legs opened on instinct. He reached between, mouth curving while he gently rubbed. "You're still filled with my seed."

Those words made me remember what Eline had said. That a month had passed in my absence. "I've not taken a tonic in a few weeks, perhaps longer given how time passes here."

"You cannot conceive unless I fuck you with the intention of putting a babe in your womb." Factual words, yet my breaths grew louder, and my nipples, already pebbled in the warm water, became painfully erect.

His smile grew to his eyes, teeth scraping his bottom lip. "You're sore."

"Incredibly, but if you stop, I will mount you anyway."

He picked me up, then turned to sit on the rock with me in his lap, his fingers returning between my thighs. Leaning forward, I pressed my lips to his, moaning when his length bobbed against me.

My knees scraped against the mossy stone, but he pushed me back. His voice gave away his desperation as did the harsh rise and fall of his chest as he said, "No, but I will cleanse you." Those eyes flashed. "Though it pains me to do so."

I wanted to ignore him, but I knew he was refusing for my own good. Within seconds, I was too hypnotized by the brushstrokes of his fingers against me, by his thick shaft against my stomach, to care if he entered me or not.

Lazily, he kissed me, his eyes open every time I opened my own. "To watch you break over me," he said, his mouth ghosting across mine and down my chin. His tongue lapped at the bruising bite marks he'd left on my neck, his groan dizzying in my ear. "Is an honor that will never fail to undo me in kind."

A throaty curse accompanied the milky liquid in washing over my skin when my fingers dragged over him, then clenched when I indeed broke.

Unmoving, except for our slowing hearts, I dozed with my nose against his throat, his arms a cage I'd rejoice to stay trapped within.

He must have slept too, for when I traced the scars upon his back, he shuddered then stiffened. The memory of his shadow, the monstrous feathered wingspan crawling around me, made me bold when typically, I'd wait for him to give himself to me.

That tactic had obviously failed us—my stubborn desire to withhold how much I wanted him, how much I hungered to know all of him, even though it was futile. If I'd swallowed such useless pride, that echoing fear from past betrayals, then perhaps I'd not be seated in a faerie spring beneath a kaleidoscope of rainbows.

So I didn't remove my hands, and he didn't ask me to, the puckered skin smooth beneath my gently pressing fingertips. "What was it like?" I said, running my lips over his shoulder. Muscle rippled, arms clenching around my body. "To have them." I wouldn't make him speak of losing them. Not when he was so close to them. The pain was apparent enough in his voice.

"I'd known no different, never thought to, until they were gone." I heard his throat constrict. "They were another set of limbs, I suppose you could say. Vital and rarely thought of but magical and life-changing all the same."

Thick muscle, bulges that would not exist in most male backs, shifted beneath my touch. "You could fly."

His voice turned wistful. "From my room to the kitchens, over the battlements and through the swaying arches of trees." I could feel and hear his smile, and I feared that I might cry like a fucking babe if I saw it. "I raced the waterfall and often banked too late, and would need to wait a few days for my bones to heal before trying again and again."

My arms squeezed. "What did Ryle make of them? Of your ability to fly when he could not."

"What do you think?" Zad huffed. His tone lost its warmth. "His resentment stained the air so thick with ire that I actually pitied him, and so after some time spent tormenting him for being the brat he was, I then made sure to fly out of his sight. For a time, I thought my father might have pitied him, too, before realizing he'd merely lost his love for the gift he'd been given with my mother's death. All High Kings are blessed with the ability to fly. Are given wings. It is the sign of a true heir."

"Of which he obviously does not bear."

Zad hummed, then shifted me off his lap and propped me up onto the ledge above, out of the water. Dripping and swiping droplets from his face, he walked up the curving path. Without an ounce of shame, I studied every inch of his glistening body, my eyes tracking his long wet hair that spilled water over his shoulder blades and down the vast planes of his back to his perfect ass.

When he turned, two folded cloths were perched on his upturned palm, bearing the sigil of the Onyx Court—black wings with glittering stones beneath. Gray horns morphed from behind the stones and curled into roots that wound into the air in spirals of thorns and leaves alongside each wing.

"You are stronger than him," I said. "Can't you get them back?" For the king had not only kept them to remind his court of what he was capable of but also for further bribery should he ever need to.

Zad helped me up, and I dried myself as I waited for him to answer.

"We have an agreement," he said with no inflection and shucked on his threadbare cloth while tossing me a glance that said he wished to discuss this no further. "It is as good as law to our kind, and to break it would ignite grave consequences."

I bit the inside of my lip and got dressed.

He waited at the cave's opening, and my thoughts ran together in cruel, unidentified loops. One thing was clear, and I had to ask, "Could you kill him now?"

Zad's brows dipped, but I waited. Finally, he scrubbed his hand over his mouth. "I do not know." Gesturing to the entrance, drenched in warm afternoon rays, he continued, "I think, if I had to, then yes." But it would stain his soul as surely as mine was already stained.

"One of your friends then?" I suggested, far too eager judging by the twitching curl of his lips.

He took my hand, thumb brushing my damp skin. "To kill a High King is no easy feat. It can only be done by someone of the same heart," he said. "Of the same bloodline."

I pondered that, frustrated, but smiled when Zad caught a passing, tiny bird with rabbit ears and whiskers. "A curdle." He dragged his finger down its fluffy blue mane of fuzz before giving the creature to me.

Tucked in the cup of my hands, it peered at me with little red eyes, then bit me and darted back into the air.

Zad's howling laughter chased away my scowl.

TWELVE

Zadicus

WITH AUDRA SAFELY RETURNED TO HER ROOMS, I went in search of Kash to make plans for the journey home.

He was meeting with a rogue wolf in the market near the seldom-used trade entrance to arrange a small ship. I'd sweep Audra back to Allureldin in a heartbeat, but neither of us had anything from there, besides clothes and weapons that had long disappeared, in order to do so.

It was nearing dinner when I finally made it to the dungeon.

Dace was seated against the wall, his soiled hands between his legs. It was too dark, the foliage of his cell too thick, to make out his expression. "It is breathing," he said by way of greeting. A rough laugh mingled with his next words. "I had not thought to check if it was until it was not. Even with the brief visits I dared to take back here, I never thought to notice it was perishing, dying a death slow enough to forewarn."

I nodded to a guard, who jerked his head in response. His loyalty was to my brother, but I'd known Melron long enough that he'd not turn me away, nor would he repeat conversations had in his presence.

In a land rife with trickery and deceit born from the inability to lie, the wolves were the most loyal creatures in it. Which was another reason, aside from their immense strength and brutality if wronged, they were so highly respected and held high in rank and importance amongst the courts.

For their innate sense of right and wrong, but also because out of all the creatures in this land, they would be the only kind able to usurp faerie nobility.

Keep your enemies close, they said. Though I did not think most of their ilk would so much as consider such political atrocity. Again, too loyal.

"It's healing," I said. "We are done here."

Melron shifted on his feet but did not stop me when I laid my hand upon the impenetrable vines.

Perhaps he was too stunned, or his loyalty to my brother only ran so deep. Regardless, he didn't utter a word as the vines slithered and curled away, falling into the mortar and dirt like wilting curtains.

Dace stepped out, and the vines slowly rejoined, stitching and weaving back together.

He waited until we'd hit the stairs. The guards there were not so willing to oblige us, but at the look upon my face, they chose to keep their complaints to themselves while we moved up the dirt-clotted steps to the throne room.

Before we reached it, Dace touched my arm. "She will not forgive you."

He knew, as well as I did, that no matter how much my cold queen felt for me, she would ignore those feelings if I betrayed her in irreparable ways. It was already proving difficult, as it should be, to melt what my deception had iced.

"She might not, but it was not the queens I laid with."

Dace's hand lowered, his expression puzzled.

I felt my lips twitch and something else as the wild echo of the previous night trampled through my mind. I forced it away, else I'd storm through the halls in search of reprieve, in search of my queen, and she needed rest.

"Audra," he said, awe coloring his quiet voice.

I nodded. He wanted to ask how—how it had worked, how she'd made our coupling even take place—I knew. But he knew the answers already.

"I thought I scented vermin." The door to the throne room opened, lighting the dark, the king standing on the other side. "How nice of you to finally join us."

My spine pulled taut at the sheen in his eyes. The arrogant posture that spoke of inevitable plans already underway. That reeked of shit already being thrown.

About to ask where she was, instead, I shut my mouth and shouldered by him into the room.

To find Audra seated upon the smaller throne beside the High King's.

Her eyes did not meet mine, but those of the gathered courts pressed heavily on me.

They'd evidently been waiting for me, and had I not have taken the outside entrance to the dungeon, I'd have known that.

But then I might not have gotten Dace out before whatever was happening unfolded.

Dressed in a blue that differed beneath the dripping candles in the chandeliers above, hair pulled back into a loose chignon with a midnight blue rose, her posture speaking of a confidence I knew she did not truly feel, Audra was every inch the faerie queen.

Though she was only half faerie, her father had more of our blood in his veins than he knew what to do with, and so she was well-practiced in the art of playing games to keep one's life.

My heart throbbed with both adoration and fear.

"You two," Ryle said, throwing his legs out to stroll casually to his throne. "Honestly, I should have you whip one another until I see bone for the trickery you bestowed upon us all." Ryle scowled when some of the gathered guests dared to murmur.

They quieted when I said, "Had we not, you might find yourself appearing far too desperate once again."

His eyes darkened, hands balling, but Audra cleared her throat.

My gaze swung to her, and still, she did not look at me.

She stared at my brother in a way that said they'd spoken

in-depth during my absence, and I would not like what they'd discussed.

Disbelief cut like a knife through the throbbing organ in my chest. Whatever she'd done, it would not be worth it. It would only cause trouble when we'd finally almost gotten ourselves out of it.

Ryle's smile simmered with smugness, and he sighed, loud and forlorn. "But alas, your young queen and I have reached an agreement I think you'll rather like."

I feared the clanging inside my chest could be heard, the silence so thick. "Audra," I said, tried to, but words failed me when two warriors stepped out from behind me and walked to the back wall.

My back spasmed, pain so sharp and sudden wracking me, I folded over.

When I straightened, the stakes that'd been imbedded in my wings were free, and they were being carried, with not a little amount of difficulty, to the king.

I wanted them. I wanted to leap forward and snatch them away from him before he could dispose of them, of the long-lost piece of my soul, before my very eyes.

But Ryle didn't touch them. His eyes drank in the slowing of my violent breathing, my every reaction, with a satisfaction I longed to break from his face.

He jerked his head to his sentinels, and I shoved them off when they reached me. "What have you done?" I said, although I was beginning to understand.

"Isn't that obvious?" Ryle said. "After all this time, I've decided to give you your precious wings back." Pursing his lips, he then smiled. "Apologies, brother, they might be a little dusty."

"We had an agreement."

He waggled a jeweled finger, still grinning. "I do not forget, nor will I fail to hold up my end of it. I'm offering you a gift," he said. "Will you take it?"

"At what cost?" I gritted.

Ryle's grin turned serpentine, and at that moment, I knew. At that moment, I regretted never taking all the chances I'd had to end him.

But if I had, I would not be here. If I had, I might've grown more like my father—miserable and unfeeling. Feared and adored but unloved.

I would not know her, and not to know my queen was a thought I could not bear.

"A piece of your soul is returned in exchange for another piece of your soul," he said. "It's all so very simple, really." My teeth ground as my heart raced, roaring so loud in my ears, I could scarcely hear him talk. "Audra has agreed to extend her stay in Beldine. A year and a day in exchange for the safe return of your wings."

My eyes sought hers, my heart sought an explanation, and my body swelled with the urge to run to her to both shake and kiss her senseless.

That was the issue with loving someone. By making yourself vulnerable and allowing them to see who you truly were, they'd not only use it against you, but they'd use it to try to help you.

But if Audra thought I needed my fucking wings more than I needed her, then did she really know me at all?

And whose fault was that? My own. I only had to look inwardly to find who was responsible for this situation. I'd been raised similarly to her. To conceal and to dodge, to only fight when necessary, and to value the things that mattered least.

For years, I'd fought the link to her, and when I'd given in, it'd taken over a year to have her lay her soul down for me to inspect, to let me in. And when she had, I'd been so consumed by her, so petrified she'd shut me out over the slightest slight, that I'd failed to let her know all of me in kind.

I'd failed us.

And what Ryle would do with her during such a short yet insurmountable length of time... I did not plan to find out. "No." The word was a bark that jumped off the walls, startling everyone.

"No?" Ryle said, his eyes dancing as he took a torturous step closer to Audra, up onto the dais. "I would not think I need to inform you of an agreement forged in blood, brother, but nevertheless"—he waved a flippant hand, jewels flinging light upon the shadowed walls—"a blood bond can only be undone in death or when the promise has been fulfilled. So it is with little regret I must inform that until a year and a day has passed, you will have no say in what happens to your queen."

My stomach lurched and sank, dragging my heart with it as I glanced at Audra's wrist, where he had extracted blood. A white bandage was wrapped around it, dotted with droplets of blood.

My blood.

She'd let someone else take that which she'd only ever offered me. She'd given someone else something that was never again supposed to belong to anyone else.

I stepped back, tripping on nothing but anger as my brother rubbed his cheek. Purposely done to give view to his own wrist, which bore no bandage but ribbons of dried blood.

She'd drunk some of his blood, sealing a bargain I could not break.

For me. She'd done it for me even though I did not and would *never* want her to.

"You can't do this," I snarled.

Ryle slumped onto his throne, kicking a leg over its armrest, and pointed at the crookedly perched crown upon his head. "I can, and I have, and I am so fucking pleased I can hardly breathe."

Gazing at my queen, he ran a finger over her bare arm. I snarled again, tensing, shaking with the urge to rip his hand from her and his body. "You see, I've come to realize that I rather like her company, frosty as she might be." As he looked back at me, his voice carried his desire. "I feel she's a good fit for me."

"Audra," I said again, rasped, choked, uncaring who heard.

This time, she looked at me, and in her eyes was nothing but that ice-cold vehemence.

She'd made her choice, and she would never apologize for such a betrayal. As I walked closer, my every breath burned as I scented her, scented her stoic acceptance, but underneath, unable to be veiled no matter how she tried, not from me, were the undertones of fear. "Is this vengeance?"

"Zad," Dace warned.

I ignored him, my peripheral catching him being escorted to one of the two overlapping banquet tables.

Audra did not move, did not seem to breathe. She just held my gaze, no emotion in those blue eyes, then shifted them ahead to our audience.

"Fear not, brother," Ryle said with forced cheer. "You've got your wings, and in a year and a day, unless she chooses to stay, you will also have your lovely half-mortal queen back." He chuckled, appearing good-natured, though he was most assuredly not. "Although I cannot promise she will be the same queen once I am done with her."

Before I could lunge, he clicked his fingers, and I was cuffed from behind. I'd been too shocked, too lost to the flames of betrayal to realize the guards behind me had been prepared and waiting. Growling and gnashing my teeth, I shoved and thrust my power at them to no avail.

The scent of that power-sucking rock—Vadella—infiltrated, burning around my wrists. How like Ryle to seek something that could slowly kill us if kept too close. Like the animal I probably appeared to be, I was dragged in chains, cussing and twisting and head-butting and kicking, to the floor below the dais.

There, I was held down as more rock inlaid cuffs were strapped to my ankles, then I was spun to my stomach, my chin smashing into the floor. Blood filled my mouth, but I couldn't tell whether it was from my snapping teeth or the warriors, and I didn't give a shit.

As I looked across the tiled floor, every muscle strained with the urge to fight, to make every spectator to this torture bleed out. But I could do nothing.

"Alahn," Ryle called.

I flinched, not realizing the ancient healer was still alive and in Ryle's service until now.

"Do affix these ghastly things to my dear brother's back, and make it snappy. I find myself tiring of the sight of them."

"Yes, my king," came the reed-thin voice of the male faerie who used to tend to every wound of mine growing up and who tried with every strength and spell he possessed to save my dying mother while I'd stood paralyzed behind him.

His hand pressed gentle yet firm upon my lower back, soothing even as I wished he'd fuck right off. "Easy," he cautioned. "This will hurt, you know that, but it will hurt a lot less if you don't fight it."

A wave of cooling air swallowed me, rendering me wholly still. It felt as if I were floating rather than trussed up on the floor beneath my mate's and brother's traitorous feet.

I didn't have it in me to feel embarrassed. No. I was far too angry for that.

I was rage personified, whether the healer held me within his spell or not, and once I was unleashed, I would kill my bastard brother of whom I never should've held an iota of love for. I would snatch him around the throat and tear his ears from his head with my teeth, I would—

A cleaving of bone stole my breath and my every murderous thought, seizing my lungs and mind in a vise intent on wringing nothing but unadulterated agony from every pore.

Perhaps I roared. Perhaps I moaned like a dying beast.

I didn't know. I passed out. Then I came back to, but the pain was so complete that I sank in and out of consciousness over and over.

And when I finally woke from it all, I was no longer in the throne room.

Snow fell outside the familiar stained glass window. Sunlight was snuffed behind the fog, but it was daytime, perhaps late afternoon. It was an illusion, surely, and I had no knowledge of where Ryle had stolen the power to create it, but I was done.

We were leaving.

A silent curse dragged from my throat, my teeth meeting and clenching, as I rolled and my wings twitched, feeling returning and rivers of pain accompanying.

Fuck.

I'd already left.

I was in Audra's bed, her scent wrapped around me like a fragrant blanket I longed to smother my face in while tearing it to shreds.

I sat up, every breath gritted and whistling through my teeth, and stared over at the crackling fire. I swallowed, my throat raw as though I'd been screaming for hours on end.

The bone and muscle in my back howled, twitching without prompt, adjusting to old muscle what had to be only hours later—even as I tried to gather much-needed breath.

The doors opened.

"My lord," Mintale said, bowing deep with a bowl of something within his hands and every line of his face creased with concern. Bandages were draped over Truin's arm, who stood behind him, peeking around his shoulder with the same sentiment in her brown eyes.

Kash entered behind them, prompting them to hurry into the room. He stalked to the armchair by the fireplace, where Dace slept, still in the putrid clothes he'd worn in the dungeon.

"What happened," I said, my voice so hoarse it was barely detectable. I tried again, wincing as I cleared my sore throat. "What did she do?"

"You already know what she agreed to do," Kash said, toneless, as he stripped back the bloodied bedding. He stopped when he realized I wasn't going to be able to stand. Not yet. "The king, however, left us little choice. We had to sweep you back here before you regained consciousness."

"And you did," I said the obvious. "Knowing I would want to kill you for it."

Kash stared down at the pearl button in his hand, then tucked it back inside his pocket. Audra's mother, his former lover, had given the button to Kash so he could sweep in and out of their meeting places within the castle grounds. I withheld a slew of violent curses.

We could have used it days ago.

"You needed to heal the land," he said without a hint of remorse, knowing exactly what I was thinking. "Besides, she's been..." He stopped, eyes downcast. "It's been so long, and it's so worn. I wasn't sure it would work."

I still glared at him.

When he looked up, his eyes flashed. "Kill me later and thank me now."

I bit back a groan, my tense muscles fueling the burn in my back. "Why?" I gritted.

Awake now, Dace sat forward and cracked his neck. "The king could not kill you, but he thought to make one of his queens try for failing to mate with you."

"Audra protested," Kash said, looking as though he wanted to roll his eyes. "Of course, she had not thought of his adept skill at trickery while making such a brash decision. Disappointing, really, as he truly makes it his first priority. She reminded him it would be a mistake to end you, being that they might again need your assistance. So I said we'd leave with you right that very second and that we would not return until her time with the king was up."

"A gamble." My eyes flicked to where the button lay inside his pocket.

"It paid off," Kash said, watching Mintale scurry forward to set the bowl of ointment upon the nightstand. Tipping his shoulder, he added, "Maybe. Before the king could neither agree nor disagree, we were close enough to you to leave, and so we entered the void."

She would not stay there. No matter how furious with her I was, no matter what bargain she'd made, I was going to kill the king and break it, and bring her home.

Dace nodded, understanding when I looked at him. Kash merely stared, and I wondered if he'd stay behind this time.

With nothing to do for it now, now that she'd rendered me useless for the time being, I beckoned Truin and Mintale to begin the torturing task of changing the sopping bandages wrapped around my torso.

Truin's voice was soft, as though she feared me when she never had before, but she asked anyway. "She is okay?"

I grunted, my eyes upon the snow-dusted window. "She is fine." I saw nothing but the bandage upon Audra's delicate wrist and the unflinching resoluteness to her eyes.

Landen entered. "Welcome home."

I was home, but my home was not here. She'd tossed me out as if she'd done me a favor, but I knew it was more than that.

Audra rarely forgave.

She retaliated.

THIRTEEN

Audra

RYLE HAD BEEN WAITING IN MY ROOMS, SPRAWLED across my bed as though he had every right to be there.

He was the king, so perhaps he had.

I didn't regret it, especially when I remembered the longing, the flinching, his shadow. There was little chance Ryle would ever agree to give his brother's wings back, and although Zad's reluctance to kill his brother might have been understandable, it was also foolish.

For as long as he had a piece of him, he could control him, and if he'd destroyed them, of which he'd hinted at... I loathed to think of what might happen, of the effects of murdering such a vital part of my faerie prince.

"I fear I'm not quite ready to have you leave, winter queen," he'd drawled, twisting the gems around his long fingers.

I'd stopped at the foot of the bed, and said, "I have my own kingdom to rule."

"Continent, it would seem." His eyes lifted from his fingers to mine. "You have your king to take care of such tedious matters. Why not stay a while longer? Why, you've only just begun to discover the wonder of Beldine."

I'd discovered more than I'd ever dreamed, and as mesmerizing, alluring, and beautiful as it was, I was content with leaving. "Tempting though it is, I must return home." I'd then turned for the window. A dangerous thing, putting my back to that malevolent force while secluded in such a confined space, but also necessary.

Proven so when he'd said with dragging boredom, "Perhaps I can tempt you some more."

A year and a day.

I circled my wrist, then plucked off the bandage, tossing it to the floor with not a small amount of disgust. For the king. For myself. For what I must do. For what I'd done.

An extended stay was all too easy to agree to when I hadn't been ready to face what we'd become when it would be just the two of us once again.

Now, I had a year to either make peace with all Zadicus was or move on, and I'd managed to give him a piece of himself that'd been missing for far too long. Now, all I had was the memory of his agonizing roars, his powerful thrashing body engulfed by warriors and pain, and those gold eyes, burning with betrayal, to keep me company.

As well as his brother.

We'd been fools to think this would end after the act.

I'd been naïve in thinking he'd leave me be. "Come," he said now, standing in the doorway to my rooms in a purple velvet cloak that matched his pants and a ruffled black shirt. Somehow, he managed to look utterly ridiculous while looking entirely too good.

An illusion. A trick of the eyes to comfort when you should run.

Walking over, I ignored his offered arm and headed out into the hall.

Streams of starlight slanted over the floor, the paintings scattered amongst the walls, from the holes cut into the ceiling.

"Not going to ask where we're going?"

I tucked my hands inside the gray woven sleeves of my gown. "I'm assuming it's nowhere I wish to go, so no."

He said nothing as we took the stairs down to the throne room. Save for some of his guards and heaping trays of steaming food upon one banquet table, it was empty.

They'd all gone.

The members of the three other courts and their queens had left the following evening after Zad's departure. The only one remaining was Adran, though I didn't know where he'd scuttled off to. Presumably someone's bed or a tavern.

"Eat," said the king when I stared at my empty plate. "We've places to be."

I didn't ask, but I did eat. Stuffed crab legs larger than my hand were piled onto my plate by a server, followed by green beans soaked in a white sauce, and a mound of some sort of meat.

"Roasted sea serpent," the king supplied, cutting into his own. "A delicacy."

In silence, we ate, the throne room seeming larger than ever before in the aftermath of all that'd transpired. My skin began to itch with my growing discomfort. With the reason I was still seated here, next to the silent king, who ate his food with careful slowness, his eyes upon me.

To accept the link to Zadicus all those months ago had been a mistake. I'd known it at the time, but it was unavoidable. Rarely ever did someone refuse to accept a link—that invisible, inescapable pull they felt toward another being—and go on to live a happy life.

I'd have been miserable either way, and so I may as well be miserable while giving Zad something he missed, something he cherished dearly when I could not yet come to terms with giving him myself.

Hope, often useless, and so often precarious, was all that remained. And I hated it. Hated how I'd given myself but a feeling that could unfold into dark nothing that slipped through the fingers like time.

Finally giving in, I sipped the wine poured for me. He'd have to release me after my time here was up, whether I'd drunk the wine or not.

Supposedly, it could only bind you to Faerie for months at a time anyway. Besides, I cared not if I wound up within the Whispering Sea or lost inside a forest, unable to escape Beldine's clutches. After all this mess, I dared this land to try to keep me. I'd be ready.

So I drank, the king looking on with keen eyes as my mouth tingled, my own eyes flaring wide. "I daresay you'll never enjoy your finest wines again."

"We'll see," I said, blinking away shadows that grew over the table. My limbs loosened, the throbbing in my chest lessened, and my eyesight worsened.

And then it adjusted. As though I'd been seeing the world through muck-splashed spectacles that'd now been wiped clean, the world exploded.

The king's skin glimmered with a light sheen of perspiration, his scent becoming more apparent—Elderberry and something spiced.

His hair was no longer dark but differing shades of porous brown, the ends struck through with gold. It was his eyes, though, that truly unnerved. They were unchanged, save for the growing flecks of onyx within the gold that rimmed the pupil. His lashes lifted up and down, longer than I'd noticed before.

For I hadn't noticed, and somehow, I was aware that the wine had enhanced my senses while being aware of nothing at all.

I was seeing him, the vivid colors and shapes of the room, as he saw them.

As a full-blooded faerie.

"Marvelous," he crowed, chair scraping as he stood. "This is going splendidly."

I hadn't the desire to ask him what he meant. Not when his hand folded over mine, and the sensation of his smooth skin evoked mini rippling shivers.

Such atrocities he'd caused with that hand, free of bloodstains yet forever marred.

I lifted my other hand as he pulled me out the doors and into the hall. Mine were exactly the same. Smooth yet roughened with every harsh act of my own.

A carriage, dark with a white-rimmed door and window trim, waited outside what had to be the front entrance to the castle.

I was tugged down four steps, furbanes and other creatures carved into the glittering stone, across the warrior-strewn forked bridge and carpet of dew-crusted grass, and with his hands around my waist, thrust inside the grand interior of the carriage.

Filigree patterns jumped out at me from the cushioned seats, and the king ushered me to sit before doing the same.

Within seconds, we were airborne, and I gasped, allowing his hand to take mine once more as we lurched into the air.

"You did not see the furbanes, I take it."

There was laughter in his voice, humor that dragged my eyes to his. "No, and I didn't know..."

"To use them in such a way?" he asked, his thumb stroking my hand. I had enough sense of self to pull it away. He smirked. "They are free to roam wherever they wish, but in my stables, I keep two, and the stable hands will change them out every few weeks."

I was surprised he cared enough to do such a thing, and he must have read the shock upon my face, in the words I refused to say.

"Darling queen," he purred, that dimple appearing. "You've only to look at yourself if you seek to understand me."

Yet... even if I was of rational mind, without faerie wine swimming through my bloodstream, I wasn't sure I could do that.

"Look," he said, gesturing to the window.

I leaned over, shifting the frilled white curtain aside to find the stars. The winking and twinkling expanse was broken up by the occasional flying insect or bird-like creature. "What was that thing called?"

He'd heard its screech, but even if he hadn't, I suspected he knew exactly what I was referring to. "A glondolin. Ferocious, especially during breeding season."

I'd thought it was eternally spring here. Still, I asked, "When is that?"

"All the time," he said, nonchalant. After some moments, he broke my focus on the tree-speckled land and its midnight waters. "You shocked me senseless, I must admit."

"With the glondolin?"

He hummed, and I felt his fingers skim the ends of my hair at my lower back. I stiffened. "I was torn between the need to whip you myself and the desire to fuck you for days." My breath froze, his voice lowered. "I wanted to do both."

In my addled state, I tried to gain some wits. "That is too much pain for me to consider pleasure."

"Really?" he said, his touch gone, yet I did not look at him. I kept my eyes fixed out the window, thankful for the crisp night breeze. "You'd rather inflict it than accept it?"

"Wouldn't anyone?" I challenged, turning to face forward.

His eyes burned into my cheek. "No, there are those who relish in being hurt before their afflictions are soothed."

The memory of Zad's teeth scoring into the softest part of my neck singed. "With the right partner, I daresay you might be right."

The king goaded me no further, as the carriage dipped and took my stomach with it.

He laughed, raucous and beguiling, as I gripped the window, and we jostled before hitting the earth with an unexpected smoothness.

"You're too much fun," he said, wiping beneath his eyes. Then he stepped out and, to my surprise, held out his hand to help me do the same.

My slippers sank into deep green grass, the breeze rustling dandelions and, to the east, a field of wheat in the distance.

Accompanied by two shifter wolves at our backs, we crossed the soft blades until our feet met cobblestone. Rising high into the hillside nestled amongst a dense line of woods that rolled toward the sea, sandstone, onyx, and wooden shops sprawled into a serpentine city.

It was small, but it was bustling with faeries. Many paused, dropping into a deep bow at the sight of their king. Eyes—some feline and others beady, huge, or glowing—stared openly at my presence beside him.

"Welcome to Onyx City," the king said with a laziness that spoke of indifference. Too much of it for such a vibrant, humming hub of activity.

Perfumed desserts carried on the breeze, and I waited for the putrid stench that always came with crowded quarters to make itself apparent, but it didn't arrive. Steam rose from little carts between alleyways, horned venders with swishing tails bowing to their king as they flipped some type of meat upon a portable stovetop.

In the distance to the left, above the water falling into the river, loomed the castle.

Moss shrouded with squared turrets, it pressed between the hillsides on either side of the flowing water that burst into the deadly drop below. It was bound to the earth with tree roots, vegetation growing thick around the onyx stone. A tree trunk, I realized, almost as large as the city we were walking through, bridged across the water and supported the castle's lower levels. The stone reinforced it on both sides, reappearing through the vines in a checkered fashion. The higher levels were as I thought, wood and branches bent to the maker's will.

I didn't know who that was, but I found myself wanting to. "Who was the first ruler of the Onyx Court? Of Beldine?"

The king gazed around at the shopfronts, garlands with glowing beetles were strung above doorways and windows, lanterns and candles sat in and outside of others. "Olynda Allblood. Our fate dealer, alongside her daughters."

"A female?" I asked, pleasantly surprised.

"Indeed," he said. "It's rumored even she did not know of how she came to be, let alone how she'd been named queen of a land rife with monsters. Some say she schemed so much in her human life for coin and status that not even the darkness would take her, and that if it were riches and power she coveted, then that is what she'd receive."

"Be careful what you long for," I muttered dryly, skirting a puddle of something fluorescent yellow, tiny white flowers sprouting around it through cracks in the cobblestone.

"Too right, you are," he concurred smoothly, and with what sounded like a dose of experience. "Some say we are descendants of the darkness, of the Unseen himself. Others say we are the cursed, thrust into the in-between, welcome in neither the darkness or the ever."

Peering around, I tried to stomach that, but it was taking longer than I'd have liked to clear the fog in my head. One could argue that being cursed to live in such a place was no curse at all, but I knew all too well that the beautiful were not always what they seemed.

"Olynda failed to birth a healthy daughter. She tried, and to numerous males, but all that granted her was five surviving sons and two dead daughters. The last male she was with married her, becoming the first king, and then murdered her when she lost her mind to grief."

Ryle sneered at a passing insect, swatting it with force at a water well. It splattered, staining the dark stone a vibrant green. "A kindness, they say, for she was no longer of this world in spirit. Her husband, Jahne, then declared himself High King, spreading his lovers and their babes over our vast land to help govern it."

"Rosinthe," I said. "What court did it belong to before it was cleaved from Beldine?"

"No one knows for certain," Ryle said, seemingly annoyed by this fact. "It is thought that, due to the harsher climes of your land, that it once belonged to the Silver Court and the Bronze Court."

"It's not winter in the Silver Court."

"You would know after your little display of defiance." He snorted. "No, it's not, but it grows cooler than any other court, and gold is warmer. I daresay that many years of separation from its true home has caused your continent to fall into the extreme of what it once was, for there is no longer enough magic to help keep the balance."

We continued uphill, past boutiques with finery that shimmered and a shoe shop with slippers dancing in the arched window, but we did not need to walk far.

Amongst a crowd of waiting citizens, a dais taller than my head emerged from the ground, shaking it. I almost grabbed for the king's hand but planted my feet and waited until it'd finished its rumbling ascent.

"Are you to kill someone?" I asked, looking away from a young green-skinned girl with reptile eyes and orange braids.

The king laughed, gesturing for me to move first up the steps.

I did and slowed halfway. They were made of dirt. The entire platform we crossed to the center made of soil.

All the better to absorb the blood.

"No, my dear Audra," Ryle said, the words caressing my ear. Removing a blade from his sleeve, its hilt embedded with three blood-red rubies, he said, "You are."

Unmoving, hardly breathing, I stared at the two bound faeries that appeared. They stared back, their silver eyes shining with fear, and their golden hair braided with tiny leaves.

"What are their crimes?" I asked.

"Does it matter?" The king circled behind me. "It only matters that they are guilty, or they would not be here."

I studied their faces, the thin slant of their chins and the translucent, papery wings upon their backs. "They hail from the Silver Court?" Ryle's footsteps ceased. I turned away from the prisoners, facing him. "I am not your executioner."

He shrugged. "You are my pet, a year and a day, and had you no penchant for bloodshed, perhaps I'd not ask this of you." His expression hardened, as did his tone. "But because you do, and because their deaths will be worse at my own hands, you will kill them. A small mercy for those who deserve none."

He wasn't compelling me, but he was reaching the end of his patience, which I knew did not extend very far.

I knew because even though I did not know him, I knew myself.

You've only to look at yourself.

"I do not kill for sport." I curled my lips, uncaring if he snapped. "I find it rather... dull."

"Well," he said. "You do kill, and you do it so well." Gesturing to the faeries behind me, he tilted his head. "So go ahead, gut them like the filthy swine they are."

My eyes flicked over our audience, small in size, everyone going about their business as though attending an execution was not mandatory, nor was it something of interest.

They'd seen too many of them for it to be anything other than normal.

"If I don't?"

"I will make them suffer, and it is your face I will press upon their minds to carry with them into the darkness."

I licked my drying lips, the blade within my palm heavier than it ought to be. Turning back, I did not wait, and I did not hesitate any longer.

I struck, the dagger embedding itself in the faerie's chest. Before the dead faerie's partner could make a sound, I lunged across the dirt. With her dying accomplice's blood covering the blade, I sank it between bone, cleaving flesh, and felt her last breath stain my cheek.

When I finally let myself meet their eyes, I found them staring up at the night sky. The dagger slipped from my bloodied hand, falling soft onto the dirt, as the faeries dissolved, no longer flesh and blood but glittering red air that rained over the soil and our skin.

"A blessing," the king said. "To have the dead wash over us."

I couldn't look at him. I couldn't talk. I snatched my hand away when he reached for it to help me down the stairs and walked a healthy distance ahead of him.

The audacity. To keep me and have the hide to call me a pet.

I might have been a half-blood, but I was still a queen, regardless of whatever deal I'd brokered with the black-and-gold-eyed demon.

And I did no one's bidding.

My anger was searing enough to break the magic of the wine I'd drunk at dinner, and it was apparently evident enough for the king to say, once we'd climbed back inside the carriage, "They were spies."

The door had just closed, and my neck cricked as I tried to keep myself straight while being jostled into the air. I needn't have asked for whom they were spying. "Queen Este," I said instead, forgetting my rage long enough for curiosity to seep in.

Ryle nodded, staring at the window behind me. His legs were spread, jeweled fingers between them, hanging. Draping his other arm across the back of the seat, he expelled a breath, rubbing his sharp chin. "It would seem she's not very impressed with me."

Remembering the argument she'd had with her wolf, the flash of white fur, and the look in her eyes when I'd wrested Zad from her, I couldn't imagine she would be.

Apparently, I wasn't the only linked creature incapable of forgiveness. "She lost her mate over the act."

"They're mates. They're *destined* to get over it." Ryle spat the words and rolled his eyes as if he actually knew anything about the life-altering bond. "I fucked her brains out many moons ago. If there was a time for being petty, it was then." Narrowing his eyes on me, he smirked. "You interrupted before she laid with Zad, correct?"

I nodded.

He waved his fingers. "Well, there you go. There ought to be nothing to act foolish over then."

He hadn't loved.

He hadn't known love at all. The only person to ever show him an iota of it was gone, his wings returned. He was also his biggest rival. A threat. "Matters of the heart are far more complicated than you could ever guess at."

"My king," he said, lips twitching.

I raised a brow, and he continued, "While in my company, while you are a guest in my lands, I am your rightful king." Eyes slithering over my frame, he sneered, "Act as such."

I said nothing, and neither did he, but I could feel him watching me as I looked out the window to the stars. In my lap, my hands clasped, the blood of Queen Este's spies already dry. "So she sent her spies, but what for?"

"Revenge. Perhaps they were assassins." He sighed, slumping back against the seat. "I care not."

"You did not question them?" My chest squeezed, a time that seemed so long ago infiltrating. Of my uncle Rind asking me the same thing. For a fleeting heartbeat, I pondered what he'd make of this whole mess—the strategies he would've used to right it—and if my own methods of survival would shame him. "They might have had something useful to say."

"What is there to question?" Ryle said, impatient. His eyes closed, his crown tipping forward over his forehead. "They are traitors, so they die."

I decided it didn't matter what Rind would think.

There was no room for shame in games of life and death.

FOURTEEN

Zadicus

EMMILINE GASPED, HER HANDS SPLAYING OVER HER mouth. "He gave them back."

She'd known I'd returned. I'd sent word but not the details. I flexed my wings, new and old muscle folding as I walked up the steps of my manor.

"He didn't give them back," I said, bitter cold but unable to help it.

Kash took the horses to the stables, Landen kissing Emmiline on both cheeks, and Dace followed before leaving us alone in the foyer.

Moving forward, she reached out as if she'd touch them. I hadn't regained enough strength to glamour, so we'd left under the cover of full dark, a large cloak thrown over them, which was rather pointless given their size.

Not that it would matter should anyone see them, but with Rosinthe's queen missing, the city of Allureldin was in shambles and Mintale was struggling to contain it. So it was best not to further the flames of their fear and create new rumors by showing off.

Seeing my expression, Emmiline pulled back and, instead, walked around me, inspecting them. "Alahn does splendid work. How is he?"

I withheld the urge to snap at her for the stupid question. "I wouldn't know, on account of these"—I jerked my head at my back—"being forced upon me while I was bound to the floor." It was strange to feel both offense and annoyance for something that was essentially *me*—for the wings I'd spent decades missing and dreaming of after they'd been ripped from my body.

But it was impossible to feel grateful for something I had learned to live without, when their return stole something I could not.

"Forced?" Emmiline said, rounding to meet my eyes. It seemed to dawn that I was here without Audra, and that I was far from fucking happy about it. "I'll put on some tea."

Kash joined us in the study in time to fill in Emmiline on what'd happened.

"What does he want with her?"

Leaning against the wall, I didn't answer her. I couldn't, so I stared at my full cup of tea, trying to keep my hands from breaking the delicate porcelain.

Kash did. "I'd wondered the same thing." I shot him a look, no patience remaining. He sighed. "To entertain himself, of course. It must grow lonely, being despised."

Emmiline's plum dress shifted as she brushed apple cookie crumbs from her lap. "You ought to have killed him." Meeting my eyes, she lifted her chin. "Do not fail next time."

Landen snatched a cookie from the desk. "It's his brother."

Her eyes remained on me. "He has proved himself unworthy of your mercy time and time again." At that moment, she reminded me so much of my mother I felt my wings twitch with memory. But then her expression softened. "You managed to keep your soul by leaving, but to ensure it stays, you must return and do what should have been done hundreds of years ago."

I knew exactly what must be done, and I'd do it, but... "I have no desire to rule Beldine."

"We know," Landen said, with not a small amount of arrogance. "You poor thing." I raised a brow, and he smirked. "Don't worry, you can stay with your queen while we rule it for you."

I snorted. Though as I stared at him, the humor leaving his face, and then looked at Kash, his dark gaze upon the full tea in my hands, I saw he was serious. They would. Setting the tea down on the desk, I rolled my shoulders. "We can figure out the bullshit later. Right now, we need to move."

"You're strong enough to return?" Emmiline asked, observing me from where she sat in the armchair.

I could do with more time to adjust, but the pain had faded enough that I could ignore the lingering aches and spasms. "I'll be fine."

"Don't you think we should wait?" Landen said, surprising me. Out of all my friends, he was the one who seemed to care about Audra, and not out of some sense of duty toward me. Or past lovers, like Kash.

"For what?"

"A better plan," Kash said. "An army, perhaps."

"They don't just appear, and we have little time for preparations. We act, and we act now." For every minute I was here, Audra was left to rot in my brother's presence.

I strode to the door when I heard Dace storm down the hall to the study. "The sun king requests a meeting," he said. "Immediately."

I scowled. "How?"

"Cross sent word."

Of course. For reasons I might never understand, one of the wolves hidden here liked the spoiled brat. From what I'd heard, the king had been journeying to Allureldin, as planned with Audra before she'd been stolen, when he'd received news of his lover, Eline, being taken.

He'd returned home, where she now was, thanks to Audra.

"He can wait," I said and entered the room. I winced, taking a seat behind my desk, my wings crumpling against the chair.

Dace smirked in the doorway, crossing his arms. "We will need to have new chairs fashioned for you."

"I've no intention of staying here," I muttered, standing. When Audra returned, we would spend most of our time at the castle.

Black feathers floated to the floor. Dace eyed them. "You really believe we can best him?"

"We need an army," said Landen. "Kash is right."

I pinched the bridge of my nose, staring down at documents that blurred and seemed from another life. A life I'd crafted of my own away from the treachery and backstabbing antics of Beldine. I could return and try to rally enough supporters. Darkness knew there'd be enough to move against my brother. But to even step foot upon the sand of his shores was to invite ourselves to his dungeon.

Which was precisely where I'd rather, and where I needed, to be.

We could fight, and I could destroy him. The act had not granted me the power to do that. I'd always had it. I'd merely left it unused for far too long. But he would be sure to take my heart with him and use her to his advantage, proving that almost impossible.

Through my teeth, I conceded, "Then I suppose we'd better humor the king."

❦

King Raiden arrived a day later, bringing with him a golden-haired female.

And Nova.

"I owe her a debt," she said by way of greeting, stepping into the foyer of what had once been her home. "And I always pay my debts."

Indeed, Audra had done the unthinkable by helping them escape both the glondolin and the king.

I ignored the temptation to rub at my tight chest and met Nova's eyes. In them, I found nothing but stark determination, and I looked away before I found anything deeper.

I was a selfish bastard. I knew that, but I had no fucking room for any guilt.

Not when I was being eaten alive from it already.

My linkage to the queen had not only wiped out the remaining love I'd had for Nova but it had also spun my attraction to her into dust. Even so, a fondness remained. It was impossible for it not to after the time we'd shared together. I cared enough that I did not wish to see her harmed or dead, which was exactly what Ryle had counted on by bringing her to Beldine.

Emmiline directed everyone to the drawing room, all too happy to have guests for a change, as she took tea orders.

Raiden, his expression void and his jaw set, lingered behind his blond female seated in the wingback chair.

Just the sight of him curdled my blood with the desire to snap his neck and rip it from his arrogant shoulders.

Nova, gazing at me from where she'd claimed the divan, said, "I'd always wondered what those scars on your back were from." She was not staring at me, but my wings.

They shifted in response, lifting higher when I entered the room and leaned a shoulder against the wall beside a picture of the creatures I'd left behind.

"A long-lost faerie prince," the king said, green eyes glittering with satisfaction. "How did our queen handle that?"

"She's not your anything," I snarled, ignoring the look Landen flung at me from across the room where he reclined over the window seat, arms crossed, appearing effortlessly relaxed.

An illusion. His fingers danced close to his side, where his dagger laid strapped, hidden beneath his tunic.

The king looked as if he wanted to argue—a common desire of his—but he seemed to remember himself when the female beneath him shifted in the chair, her eyes downcast. She was dressed in some type of shift, a vibrant purple with gold tassels dancing along the hemlines and chest, her cleavage on display but half-hidden with a golden, gauzy shawl.

I angled my head when her gaze lifted. "What did the king want with you?"

Her lips parted, eyes darting over my face as though she wasn't sure she should answer. "I don't know, my lord."

"He's a Beldine prince and no lord of ours," Raiden said.

I smirked. "Keep telling yourself that."

His nose jerked, as did his shoulders, pulling back as he dragged a hand over his cropped dark hair. "It matters little, and her name is Eline. *Lady* Eline."

Dace, leaning against the bookshelves, coughed to hide a snort.

Raiden glared.

Eline spoke up, confident but soft. "I've no idea what he wanted with me. All I can deduce is that the king knew of my…" She halted, licked her lips. "Ties to King Raiden, and of Raiden's obvious ties to Queen Audra."

Tension simmered between Raiden and his lover.

Emmiline entered with a silver tray of tea, setting it upon the stone table in the center of the furred rug.

Only Kash pressed forward to prepare himself a cup, indifferent to the eyes watching him as he tossed three sugar cubes into the porcelain.

"Are all of your ears pointed?"

Adding a dash of milk to his tea, Kash said, "Why don't you come closer and see for yourself, king?"

Raiden grinned, even as his eyes lit with ire. "I can admit you're not hard on the eyes, but I've long discovered I prefer females."

Kash paused, then slowly straightened, the saucer rattling in his clenched fingers.

Shit. I scrubbed my chin, wincing at the thickening stubble. "Let us get to the point of this visit."

Nova nodded, resituating the light blue skirts of her dress.

Kash stepped back, then dropped into an armchair, his attention fixed on Raiden as he stirred his tea.

Raiden flicked at nothing on his shoulder. "I've come to discuss what is to be done in Audra's absence."

Landen's mouth shifted side to side, laughter glowing in his eyes.

I dragged in a fortifying breath. To finally kill him would be almost as satisfying as the first time I'd fucked his wife, but alas, the repercussions were not worth dealing with. "We must march on Beldine."

The females exchanged troubled glances.

"We must?" Raiden said, a brow raised. "Look, I came here out of respect for Audra. When really," he drawled, "I've no need to consult with anyone. We could assume she's lost to Beldine and move forward without her, but due to our... history." He smirked my way, and my teeth gnashed. "I thought I'd give her more time."

Dace shifted to face the window, his hands fisted at his sides.

My words were clipped, my anger growing by the second. "She is trapped under the king's thumb. Do you not worry about what will become of her?"

"If it were anyone else, most certainly." Raiden shrugged. "It's Audra. I'm positive she'll fare just fine."

Every muscle clenched, my bones groaning with the need to send him flying through the window.

Emmiline moved beside me to lay her hand upon my arm. Waves of warmth drifted over my skin, as they so often had when I was a youngling coming into a power I could barely control.

"You're a real piece of shit," Kash said.

Everyone's attention shot to him, but not mine.

Raiden's face drained of humor. "I'd beg your pardon, but I think I'll just have you strung up in the gallows by your faerie ears instead."

Teeth grinding, my voice became almost unrecognizable. "Enough. If you won't help, then *leave*." My nostrils flared, my entire body now aching with the urge to destroy him. "And I'd do so quickly."

I heard Nova swallow as Eline stared up at Raiden with beseeching eyes.

After a broiling half minute, Raiden sighed and rolled his neck. "What would you have me do? Beldine's king is a creature with power beyond anything of our kind."

"Give us some of your best warriors," Landen said, lifting a knee and leaning forward to rest his arm over it. "Rally Audra's too, being they are momentarily under your command."

I was tempted to punch him for reminding the king of what he stood to gain from Audra's absence.

Raiden looked at me, lips twitching before curling back to show a glimpse of teeth. "I'm failing to see what is in this little quest for me."

Fury burned every gritted word. "The female you supposedly love returned home safely."

A sly smirk brightened his eyes, his fingers curling over his cheek. "But then she would be reunited with you." His lips pursed. "I don't find myself enjoying the idea of that."

Kash cursed, and I lunged, grabbing the king by his pretty ruffled peacock shirt. "Listen, you entitled fucking—"

Dace yanked me back by my almost healed wings.

I hissed, pain flooding and ricocheting through every healing bone and muscle, and shoved him hard enough to send him sailing out of the room to the hall.

"Goodness me." Raiden chuckled, and I spun back. "Settle down, faerie prince. No need for dramatics." The mirth faded, his expression turned solemn as the temperature in the room settled, and his tone earnest. "Indeed, I will accompany you, and I will bring my best warriors." Looking at Eline, he said, "Because yes, I do care for our queen, and because she rescued the mother of my unborn babe."

I looked at his lover, who was staring vacantly at the tea setting, quiet yet evidently tense. Then back at Raiden.

Dace brushed the sleeves of his black tunic. "Congratulations, asshole."

Emmiline dipped her head, smiling. "How long?"

"It has been nearly five moons," Raiden answered for Eline.

Nova was quiet, her fingers winding in her lap.

With any pregnancy, whether it be royal or Fae, there would be mixed feelings. Joy, so much joy that the accompanying fear could become debilitating. As there was too high a chance that babe would not survive infancy if he or she was born.

It slithered into the room now, and I unfurled my aching wings, stretching them. "Are you to stay behind, Eline?" I wouldn't suggest it. The choice was hers. But I had to know so I could prepare.

She nodded, eyes lifting to watch the feathers at my back as they slowly quit rustling.

"Of course, she is staying," Raiden said.

Howls cleaved the air, the sentinels—wolves in the forest beyond the estate—whistling to signal someone's arrival.

Emmiline made a gesture, and I waited with the rest of our silent guests as she soon delivered two more inside.

Ainx and Azela.

They dipped low upon entering the drawing room, dressed in their uniforms, hair windswept as though they'd raced against time to get here.

"You're going back?" Ainx said, his jaw taut. Then he added, "My lord."

I nodded, gazing at Azela, who tucked her hands before her and pulled her shoulders back. "We wish to come with you."

Beneath my breath, I groaned, "Fuck." Audra would lose her damned mind for allowing such a thing, but then again, she was the one who'd struck a bargain with the descendant of the darkness.

Kash bit his lips, and Landen stared at Audra's head guards as though weighing how long they'd survive.

"This is not a war," I said.

"Did you not ask for warriors?" Raiden asked.

But all I heard was, *Why haven't you punched me in the face?*

It took extreme willpower not to indulge the imaginary

request. "We take them as backup to distract and also make the king think twice before acting."

Raiden grinned down at Eline's braided hair. "Smells like an unavoidable battle to me."

"You would wage war against your own people?" Azela asked before I could make the king's head explode out of his fucking nostrils, and I didn't miss the way she now stared at me.

With a healthy dose of fear and wavering uncertainty.

I didn't hesitate, barely drew half a breath, before looking at her and saying, "For her, I'd wage war against anything that stood between us."

Azela's eyes swam, her throat bobbed, and I glanced at Kash.

He slurped loudly from his floral teacup, and I nodded. "Let us prepare then."

FIFTEEN

Audra

Beldine was an intoxicating elixir.

It was no wonder humans had once been drawn to this place. The danger, the deadly traps planted throughout the land, were all too easy to ignore when starlight washed over your skin, bathing you in a warm glow that reached the marrow of your bones.

It sang to the darkest recesses of the heart and bade them to swim to the surface. Here, living eternally beneath the bright night sky, it didn't just seem like anything was possible.

Everything was possible.

And the wine. Darkness save me, the wine was incredible. A drug I couldn't get enough of, and after days of being careful, only allowing myself one daring glass, I surrendered.

During every meal, it was served, and I happily drank my fill. The time between was spent with the king, outside on the grassy rooftops and battlements, along the hillsides that rolled with the misty river, or dancing through markets, snatching anything my heart desired.

The king laughed again, rich and volatile, and I found myself staring over at his cheekbones, reminiscing of a pair so similar, a pair I missed so dearly. If I'd forced myself to be away from him, away from the rest of my people, for a year, then I was to do anything that lightened the heaviness their absence pressed upon my chest.

The last thing I'd expected was for the king to grant me such a thing, but with every passing day, the time he spent with me only increased.

"And then what did you do?" I rolled to my side, picking at the array of four-leaf clovers.

Ryle stared up at the dark sky, his laughter ebbing, hands clasped over his chest. "I hit her over the temple with the candelabrum. I intended to do it just the once, but she fought back, her nails scratching at my cheek." He was referring to a past human lover who'd exploded into a jealous rage after Ryle had been with another from his harem.

"You lost your temper," I said, smiling.

"Yes, and after two blows to the head, she was dead."

I sucked my bottom lip. "You kept striking her anyway, didn't you?"

His head turned, eyes narrowing on my face. "You know me far too well."

My smile remained.

He sighed, fingers reaching out to caress my cheek. "I do not find myself regretting many of my actions, but that is one I often wonder about."

His cool touch was barely there, yet I couldn't keep myself from growing tense. "Why?"

Eyes upon his fingers as they slowly crawled down my cheek to my hairline, he murmured, "I've yet to find anyone who can suck my cock as well as she did."

I laughed, and his fingers fell away as he watched, smiling.

"Did you enjoy putting your mouth on my brother?"

The question stopped my heart, my laughter, and I blinked at him. Steel and curiosity stared back at me, waiting. "I did," I admitted.

A minor twitch of his lips was the only reaction. "I wonder what he's scheming right now."

I did not wish to wonder. I had hope he was furious enough to stay away and wait until I returned to bestow that fury on me. "I daresay he's busy healing."

"You do not think he'll come for you?"

I picked at some clover, rubbing the velvet pads between my fingers. "I hope not."

The king hummed, giving his attention back to the sky. "Because we are having such fun?"

I hummed in return, rolling to my back as well.

A smattering of bat-like creatures—elhorns, the king had called them—fluttered above, squeaking with each flap of their membranous wings.

"Zadicus used to have all the fun," the king said once they'd flown past. "Always plotting with his stupid friends, taking everything I wanted for granted as though to inherit the title of High King was nothing..." He trailed off, and I feared my breathing was suddenly too loud. "They called me the bastard prince, his friends." I felt his eyes on me a fractured heartbeat later. "Did he tell you that?"

"He didn't tell me anything about you, about any of this," I said, flinging my hand wide, clover flying and snatched by the breeze. "You know that."

His tone sharpened. "Of course, and tell me, how does that betrayal feel?"

I couldn't resist answering, not when his power vibrated over my skin, a current calling to the storm inside me. "Like I'm a fool who'd been too enamored to open her eyes as wide as they should've been. Who'd been stupid enough to trust in something I'd already learned not to trust."

His hold on me disappeared, the cool spring air blowing grass and clover against my bare legs and arms once more. "In the end, he was the fool."

I was determined to end this conversation, but I found myself saying first, "Did Zad call you a bastard?"

Ryle chuckled. "No, his heart is far too mortal for such things, but he did not have to. Even when I was a youngling, it was a wide-known fact." He sat up. "But take no pity, for I showed them exactly what a bastard-born heir is capable of."

We trekked back to the keep, the silence loaded but not uncomfortable. The path that led the way was worn by feet, only willowy trees and ferns and the many glowing insects buzzing within them to guide us.

The keep was a fortress tucked within the land, but also the land itself.

Its doors towered high, almost kissing the tops of the windows of the second floor, two-headed sea dragons and furbanes carved into the arching wood.

Two rows of sentinels, seven on either side of the bridge that crossed and met over the rushing water, stood eerily still. Silver helmets with black feathers sprouting from the top hid every part of their faces save for their eyes. Etchings in the metal portrayed what the warriors beneath were—whiskers and snouts and snarling metal teeth.

Their armor was a shining dark silver, the night sky reflected in the unscathed metal. I was tempted to ask when they'd last needed to wear it in earnest, due to its pristine condition, when the king said, "In the forge below the city, we have an arsenal of weapons constantly being crafted, as well as armor. If it is dented, it is replaced."

I scowled at him in question, and he felt it, for he added, "No, I do not possess the power to enter your mind, even if I compel you." I wanted to know who did. One of the three queens, perhaps. In the many stories I'd been told, that power had been mentioned countless times. I asked nothing and said nothing as he said, "Sometimes when you let that titanium wall of yours down, it is quite easy to tell what you're thinking." He tilted a shoulder. "Or perhaps it is merely the wine that makes you easier to read."

My stomach filled with ice, sobering me substantially.

Inside, he led me through the halls, and I soon discovered I would not be returning to my rooms tonight. I'd wondered when he'd drag me to his own and force me to do things I could not do.

With air growing stale in my lungs and my eyes stinging, I

glanced around the fire-lit walls, searching for an excuse, an exit—a weapon.

But he took a sharp turn up a steep, curling flight of stairs I hadn't yet seen. They spiraled to a large room. A curtained poster bed draped with stained sheets was set into the far wall. Upon the right side sat a long chaise, similar to the emerald one in his rooms, and on the other side, three easels, two of them empty.

My eyes swung back to the bed, my uneasy stomach settling somewhat. Not blood, but paint.

The king pushed up the frilled long sleeves of his shirt, exposing milky muscled arms, and crossed to the easels. "Remove your dress and undergarments."

Having spent what had to be weeks here now, I knew a compulsion when I heard it, felt the odd vibration traveling with his voice. Yet after drinking the wine with dinner and lunch, I couldn't so much as try to refuse it.

The white gossamer slipped from my shoulders, Ryle's gaze kissing my bare back as he instructed, "Lay upon the chaise."

"You paint?" I asked the obvious, unable to stop myself from doing as he'd requested.

The chaise wasn't velvet as it appeared, but a dark green moss. Rigid, I laid over it, but gradually relaxed when the king explained, "I do, though I must admit, I am not very good."

A canvas had been set upon the easel, and with a rhythm that spoke of more joy than I'd ever seen upon the barbarian before, the king began to paint.

After a time, the sun gilding the long rectangle window behind him, splashing ribbons of light upon the paint spotted floor and highlighting the concentration that chased shadows from Ryle's face, I felt my eyes drift close.

He did not demand I open them, and so I let myself go.

A featherlight touch wrapped around my ankle, tugging me from sleep. The sun was burning in the sky, igniting the golden flecks in the king's hair and eyes as he lay slouched at the end of the chaise I'd curled up on. Paint covered his hands and his shirt, still wet by the way it glistened in the rays of sunshine. "Come here."

I did, my limbs protesting from the lack of sleep and the way I'd been lying. Scooting close enough for his clothes to graze my skin, I waited as he studied me with tired eyes. "Hold still."

Again, that brush of his power, as if he knew he could only get away with pushing me so far without its influence. Like snow flurries melting into my skin, his eyes held mine trapped as his wet fingers painted my arms with circles, swirls, and what felt like flowers.

I wanted to look, but I couldn't. I didn't dare look away from the tempest in his eyes.

I couldn't deny that although I despised him, I was also drawn to him. The compulsion, the wine, only unearthed that deceptive, curious part of me. What I could not understand was *why*.

Why, when he leaned forward, his fingers reaching for my hand and turning it over to circle my palm, and his mouth brushed my cheek, I could not pull away.

His hold on my body eased.

He was giving me the impossible choice. Kiss him, let him have me, or walk away and face the consequences. I was already living a consequence and uninterested in facing any more.

His lips tasted like the berried wine we'd shared with our last meal of peanut-soaked asparagus and roasted hog. They were softer than I'd have liked, more gentle than I could bear, and warmer than what they should be. His fingers danced over my palm, and my stomach stuttered, my body betraying me in ways I'd probably forever regret.

"We could rule the world," he said to my parted lips before encasing the bottom one within his. "You and I... we could rule this continent, and yours, we could reunite them." His breath washed over my mouth, inside it, my tongue tingling. "And we'd be too powerful for anyone to stop us."

You cannot stop me.

His voice, his very breath, morphed into another's.

Do not think for one fucking second that I will ever let you stay away from me.

I reared back, but Ryle grabbed me by the hand, his other gripping the back of my head. His eyes, lightning flashed within them, his voice hoarse. "We can talk of that another time." As if he'd thought that was why I'd retreated, his mouth fused itself to mine once more.

I pressed my hands against his chest and pried my lips from his. His hold loosened, his breathing ragged, and his eyes... so dangerous. I swallowed, licked my lips, and ignored the urge to wipe them until they bled. "I'm afraid I'm still tired."

Ryle's touch fell away, and he was slow to nod once. "Return here when you wake."

"You're staying?" I wasn't sure why I'd asked or why I cared to know.

He looked at the empty bed, dressed in all white, decorated with specks and smears of paint. "I'll be busy a long while."

The tone of his voice hinted at activities I would rather escape from. I'd never set foot in the south wing where his lovers, both human and faerie, were rumored to spend most of their days. Though I had seen some at dinner or breakfast if he chose to let them out. Pets, and I was but another.

I stood, refraining from racing out the door and, instead, inclined my head.

His eyes simmered with approval and lust. His lean form draped over the chaise as though he were the one waiting to have his portrait painted. "Go, my frosty queen. Run before I change my mind."

I did, the heat of his stare burning my naked skin as I collected my gown and undergarments.

The door shut behind me, but I didn't stop, didn't dress until I'd taken the stairs down to my rooms.

The sun had barely set when Temika entered.

She stood in the doorway, her webbed hands clenching together, and her expression grave. "The king requests your company in his art studio. Immediately."

I set the hairbrush down, rubbed a red rouge over my lips, and rose from the dressing table. "He is still there then."

She nodded, looking as though she wanted to say more.

Eyeing her on my way to the door, I wrapped my purple robe around my undergarments. "Can he wait until I dress?"

"I fear not, my lady." Her tone, her demeanor, reeked of impatience born from fear.

There'd be no feast anytime soon, I guessed, and I had a sinking feeling I was about to lose my appetite anyway.

Sighing, I slung my shields up and waded by her, heading out into the starlit halls.

The king's stronghold was silent, yet I could feel the hum of activity travel through the soil and mortar-rendered walls.

During one of the many tours the king had given me, I'd discovered the kitchens held an influx of pale pink-skinned, paper-winged pixies, and the dungeon was like nothing I'd ever seen before. It was more of an enchanted, living garden, caging anyone behind writhing wreaths of copious vines, its leaves and thorns fed by the blood and excrement of prisoners.

Still, even with the tours and having been there mere hours before, I took two wrong turns before finally finding that curling set of stairs to the tucked away room. Reaching the hall, the walls bare of portraits but reeking of flowers, the air jasmine and berry scented, I had to wonder if behind them were the rooms of his lovers.

A shriek that rolled into a long moan slithered out the cracked open door and down the stairs, raising the hair on my covered arms.

Of course, he'd invite me while still deep inside another female, and of course, that was why Temika had looked as though she wanted to warn me.

I climbed the stairs and opened the door, leaning against the rough wall in the doorway. I yawned, notifying him I'd arrived, and tried to look anywhere but at the two paint-covered naked bodies upon the poster bed.

The king groaned. "Look at me."

My eyes snapped to his, even as my teeth gritted in protest.

He writhed over the blue-haired vixen beneath him, her breasts bouncing with every purpose-driven thrust, and her legs in the air. He was holding them, gaze on mine as he licked her ankle. "Audra…" With a silent roar, his body shook, and he fell over her, but his eyes remained on me. "Fucking finally," he muttered, shoving away from the female on the bed.

She rolled over, assessing me from head to toe. With a wink of her blue eyes, eyes unnervingly similar to my own, she stood from the bed.

The king smacked her ass hard enough to make her flinch. But she laughed, and I felt his hold on me fall away as he said to her, "Leave us."

Naked, save for the paint marring her slim, tall body, she skipped past me.

"She has nice eyes," I remarked.

The king huffed, slipping his legs into the same pants he'd worn last night. "Observant, aren't we?"

"I was trained to be."

"I think you meant to say *raised*, but I understand." He walked closer, his chest gleaming with sweat and paint, and murmured, "I was raised with similar cruelty, after all."

I ignored that and feigned another yawn. "Having erectile issues?"

His jaw hardened, and he swung his feet toward me, lazily but with an eye-catching menace. "For your information, my half-blood queen, I've never suffered any such thing." He glanced down at his pants, which I assumed were tented. "More so, the issue lies within my insatiable appetite." His gaze lifted to me. "But is that truly an issue?"

Choosing to ignore that, I kept my eyes on his, knowing how stupid the words were before they ran from my mouth. "You could force me."

"Oh, I know, and it's so fucking tempting I can hardly breathe around you." His words unraveled into a rasp, and he cleared his throat. It didn't chase the lack of sleep from his voice. "But creatures like us"—his finger looped around a thick ribbon of hair over my breast—"we deserve to be earned."

At that, another female sauntered by me and entered the room, this one with inky black hair and green eyes. Thick, sky gray wings, like that of a moth, sprinkled a fine layer of dust from her back, bobbing with every soft step.

"So," Ryle said. "Allow me to tempt you in kind."

Darkness be damned, he truly thought he could sway me with such antics.

Of course, he did. While he and I were similar in ways that disturbed and fascinated me, he was the fucking High King of Faerie. He might've passed for a royal, but a royal he was not. And as I'd once loathed to discover, we had something he and his kind lacked.

A trace of humanity.

"I'm hungry," I lied when he spread the female's legs, his fingers reaching between.

"I care not. Have a seat, and by all means, feel free to touch yourself." I didn't move, and after a moment, realized I couldn't, as he muttered, "Suit yourself."

My feet had been locked in place, as had my eyes.

For untold minutes, I watched them feast on one another, watched his gaze never stray from me as he came, and then bent her over.

Before he could reach orgasm again, a clanging sounded outside.

I felt my bones creak as I tried to look behind me, but then two sentries rushed up the stairs to the room, right as the female came, her cries muffled as the king snarled and shoved her head into the white linen.

"Majesty," one said, moving beside me. Standing this close to one of the werewolves, I had to wonder if they were as tall as Zad or even taller. Well over six foot five, at least.

He glanced at me, frowning, then removed his helmet, his voice clearer, and his silver hair glistening in messy tufts. "Majesty," he said again, louder.

Ryle finally paused, and snapped, "*What?*"

"A runner just arrived with news of a fleet bearing moons and suns upon the horizon."

Panic warred with excitement.

Ryle's eyes flicked to me, and I realized in his shock, he'd released me. The female rolled away as he rebuttoned his pants.

Sweat dotted his hairline. He swiped at it, nostrils flaring in my direction as if trying to scent what I was feeling. "Send every pack. No, send the entire regime."

The guard behind me balked. "Your highness—"

"Every warrior, in training or not," Ryle demanded with cold authority, crossing to me. "Send them," he barked. "I want them all, and I want them alive, so we will give them no choice but to surrender."

Both warriors bowed, but before they could leave, the king ordered, "Breen, take Rosinthe's queen to my rooms." He stalked by me, the scent of sex and bergamot and some spice I couldn't name steaming the air. "Ensure that is where she stays."

Breen jerked his head to the stairs, his eyes beseeching, pleading for no trouble. A male who did not wish to mishandle a female.

But I was too shocked, too fucking terrified—and not for myself—to argue, let alone make plans to flee.

Sixteen

Audra

RYLE'S FURY SOAKED INTO THE WALLS OF HIS stronghold, the tension in the quiet air palpable. Even the fall of water outside seemed louder, more violent.

Or perhaps, it was just that everyone had quieted. That ever-present hum now nothing but dead silence in the absence of nearly every wolf in the Onyx Court.

Temika brought me tea and little rock cakes loaded with fruit, the tray rattling in her trembling hands as she laid it upon the desk in Ryle's bedchamber. "Can I get you anything else, Lady Audra?"

Yes. My lord, I felt like saying. I wanted him brought safely to me so I could kill him myself.

Out of all the stupid things to do... I squeezed my eyes closed against the gathering wet. Torn between wanting to kill him and kiss him stupid and fearing for his life and the lives of those he'd brought with him, I was too rattled to remember how much time had passed since everyone had headed to the eastern shores where the ships had been spotted upon the horizon.

"No," I finally managed. "I'm fine."

I turned for the desk, tightening my robe, and heard the doors close. The sound echoed, and I waited, the steam rising from the tiny teapot slowly abating.

The doors opened again, and I did my best to snuff my emotions so the king couldn't scent them. Zad was here—he had to be unless his anger was such that it could be felt over miles of land.

After all, it was his land, tied to him in ways I could never dream to understand.

It wasn't the king who entered, but Zad.

Clad in the same armor the kings' wolves wore, he removed his helmet to reveal burning gold eyes. Alight with relief, they flickered over every part of me, roaming, absorbing, and unblinking.

Mine did the same, hungry to feast upon every beautiful angle of his face, the auburn hair pulled taut to his nape, likely to make sure it stayed concealed beneath the helmet.

His lips were parted, and I watched as they thinned. He took a step closer, his thick, perfect brows hovering low, then seemed to shake himself out of some type of stupor.

"Where are your wings?" I said, rasped, my stomach tight.

He blinked, and there they were, black-feathered beauty arching high above his shoulders. They stole the light from the room and swallowed it, reflecting it back with a gloss that made my tongue grow thick. They were different from the wings I'd first seen in the throne room, brutally staked to the wall.

They were alive. They were him.

"Do they seem worth all this?" His upper lip curled back, and in his voice was none of the relief I'd seen burning in his eyes.

I stepped forward, wanting to touch them, marveling at the way they kicked out with the flare of his nostrils, long feathers tickling the rug on the floor.

But then his words registered, and I remembered what I'd done and why he should not be here. "You need to go." I threw my eyes to the windows, then to the almost closed doors behind him. "You shouldn't be here."

"I shouldn't be here?" he said with a bark of humorless laughter. His stare grew colder, as did his tone. "There's no time for this." Gesturing to the doors, he said, "Let's go. I can sweep you back to the estate, and then I'll return."

I smiled, a sad flash of teeth, then sighed. "We both know that fixes nothing. You're wasting your time, and you're about to get yourself and many others killed." I lowered my voice, hissing, "Leave, and hurry, you giant idiot."

His eyes widened, his finger jabbing at the metal over his chest. "Me?" He snarled. "Fuck, enough, we need to—"

Footsteps pounded outside, and Zad lunged for me.

I stepped back, narrowly avoiding his touch as he began to fade, and heard him growl as he swept himself out of the room.

Guards rushed in, two of the remaining handful the king had left behind. They searched every chamber and even went as far as to open and close the bureau and desk drawers, as if someone could hide in there.

"Will you do me the courtesy of telling me what is going on here?" I asked, crossing my arms. "This is rather rude, I must say."

They finally acknowledged my presence—well, one of them did. The other was peering behind the doors, heading into the bathing room again.

"We heard something, and now we've scented..." He gazed around. "Something."

I lifted a brow. "Something?"

The soldier removed his helmet, and I recognized him as Breen, who had been put in charge of watching me. "Yes, my lady. We've scented the prince."

"Oh, right. Well, you won't find him"—I poured myself some cold tea—"being that he left with your loud arrival."

He blinked, then frowned. "So he was here?"

"You know as well as I do that he was, wolf," I said, sipping from the teacup. "But as I've already stated, you won't find him now."

After staring at me a long moment, as if wondering what I was playing at and if I'd tell him anything else, he resumed his search. It didn't last long, and they soon left, leaving the doors to the antechamber wide open.

Midnight darkened the sky, and I eventually bathed before dressing in a lavender gown that gathered around my feet in gentle pleats. The shoulders were beaded with gold spheres, and Temika dusted my eyelids in the same shade.

She'd just finished pulling my hair back into a loose braid that curled over my right shoulder when the castle came alive, doors opening and footsteps marching, orders bleated from outside, sharp enough to carry through the windows.

I refrained from rushing to see what had happened and nodded at Temika in the mirror. "That will be all."

"They return," she said as if I hadn't heard. "I'll go see where the king wants you."

I couldn't avoid bristling at that if I'd tried, the manner it was spoken. As though I were his toy and he'd do with me as he so wished.

It might have been true, for now, but that did not mean I couldn't detest it quietly.

My mind was a riot of mismatched thoughts. Where was Zad? Had he made it back to whatever group he'd journeyed here with? Was he okay?

Temika returned with Breen and another guard, and I was escorted to the throne room. Relief at being able to discover my people's fate, my heart's fate, blurred with dread, each step too fast and too fucking slow.

Except for the king and his typical line of warriors upon the two long walls, the throne room was empty.

Temika curtsied at the door, and Breen took post outside it.

I stared at the king, who stared at me from his throne as a lone, long finger massaged his temple. He was wearing the same pants he'd donned in his studio with a long-sleeved armored shirt. "Audra," he said as though I was giving him a headache. I hoped I was. "Do come here."

Walking forward, I noticed the banquet tables were piled high with food, goblets gleaming under the candle-strewn chandeliers above.

Reaching the dais, I curtsied, slowly lifting my eyes to his. He clicked his fingers beside him, and I lifted my chin, stepping up to take my seat on the smaller throne.

"No," he snapped before I could lower myself to the twisting wood. "Here."

His lap. Darkness engulf me, he wanted me to sit on his lap like a good little pet.

Smiling a little to ward off any display of my hesitance, I did, his leg hard beneath my ass as he shifted me where he wanted me. I knew better than to ask him anything when he was in a mood that could flick between crazed lust to violence in a heartbeat. It leaked from his every pore and stiff limb, simmered in the gold and black of his eyes.

Cupping my chin with the ends of his fingers, he directed my gaze to his. "Tell me," he said, that oily feeling entering my mind, pulsing over my skin. "Did you know your beloved would come for you?"

"I did not know, but I had hoped he would not," I said because I'd been compelled to, and also because it was the truth.

The king's attention dropped to my mouth, fingers dragging down my neck to circle the tops of my breasts. "Well, he has. But," he said, "we've reached yet another agreement."

He read the eagerness in my eyes, and his lips curved. "Zadicus, along with his accomplices, handed themselves over in exchange for their fleet's safe passage home." His fingers trailed back up, tracing my lips, pausing upon the scars. "You owe me."

"Indeed," I said, my relief and gratitude all too real as I relaxed a little in his lap. I curled my legs up higher, draped myself over him like a fur-lined cloak, my arm crawling behind his neck to his shoulders. "You let my people go."

His mouth twisted, some of the darkness leaving his eyes. "Most of them, yes."

"What do you plan to do with the others?"

He stiffened beneath me at that, but I still splayed my hand over his taut stomach. "Why, I plan to torment them as any good king would." He looked to the side, to where the door leading to the dungeon was. My heart kicked and screamed as at least ten guards opened it and disappeared.

A small table loaded with herbed chicken legs appeared next to his throne with a click of his fingers. He plucked one up, tearing into it with vigor, while I fought with everything I had to remain somewhat relaxed.

There were no other visitors, no courtiers arrived, only the prisoners.

I kept my eyes from roaming over them all. I kept my expression bland as they were herded in like sheep. I kept my heart from breaking when I saw who they were.

Zadicus, Azela, Kash, Dace, Berron, and Raiden.

The latter shoved a guard off, one eye swelling. "I must say." Raiden tilted his head to me. "It does not seem as though you are in need of rescue, my queen."

The king chuckled, then pointed at Raiden, demanding, "Let this one eat. I like his spirit."

Not one to argue with a good deal, Raiden didn't protest as he was dragged to the back of the room and pushed into a seat. He stared at his bound hands expectantly.

The shifter merely grinned, then retreated to the wall as Raiden stared at all the food he could not touch.

"Use that snide mouth of yours," Ryle said.

Raiden stilled, knowing a dare and a threat when he heard one.

Hot and probing, Zad's gaze was a building inferno. I paid him no mind and looked at Azela. She lifted a shoulder, chains rattling as it dropped.

Kash just stood there, appearing petulantly bored.

"Do you have no care for the male who went to such lengths to retrieve you?" Ryle purred, his hand at my back, fingers upon my exposed skin.

"He's a fool," I said, meaning it.

The king grinned. "Poor, dear brother." Then he said, "Give them all a seat. They must be tired after their daring journey."

Shuffling and clanging ensued, and Zad entered my line of vision. His lip pulled back, his eyes flashing, and the words, "Careful, now," shaped silently by his lips.

In response, I fluttered my lashes.

A sharp sting snapped my spine taut, accompanying the sound of a rip.

My dress. The king had ripped my gown, and his nails had scratched my back while doing so. A reminder, a warning to his brother, and to be sure he'd garnered my full attention.

I peered into his face, questioning.

He beckoned me closer, so close he could drag his teeth over my cheek. "I will make him regret the day he mated to you, far more than he ever could." He heard me swallow and smiled. "You seem torn," he whispered to my ear.

"Because I fear I am," I said, barely a sound, and when his lips moved for mine, I stayed breathlessly still, allowing them to meet.

Gone was the delicate way he'd tried to convince me to bend just hours ago. It had been replaced with a savage display of what could only be construed as ownership.

His lips pried mine apart instantly, his tongue dragging over their edges with deliberate slowness.

Zad roared. Flecks of mortar and dirt drizzled, the entire keep trembling. I broke away from the king in time to see a thin crack race up the floor toward the throne, waves of heat rippling out from deep within.

Ryle stared at it, and it ceased, then he lifted his eyes to Zad, who had snapped the chains that'd bound his hands.

He stood between the two crossed tables, smoke curling from his wings, from his entire being, in sharp tendrils toward the ceiling. His chest heaved, his nostrils flared wide, and his brows sank low over his rage-heavy glower.

He took a menacing step forward.

Before I could draw breath, my ears ringing, the king's warriors charged, and he was taken to the ground.

Five warriors wrestled him, two falling away with blood running from their noses and mouths. I stood as an invisible force flung the wolves off him, one hitting the wall with a violent crack.

Again, Zadicus strode forward while the king remained seated behind me.

I tried to move, tried to tell him to stop, but I could only gape as he rolled his shoulders and swiped the back of his hand over his bloodied lip. His eyes were on mine, shifting briefly to the king behind me, his fury so suffocating he didn't realize, or perhaps did not care, that more warriors had advanced on him.

He stared at me as they did, defeat and a myriad of hostile emotions smoldering from him as a cloth was stuffed near his flaring nose, and his eyes fluttered shut.

It took four warriors to drag him to the side door by the arms and legs, and then through it. Its clang reverberated, and still, I watched, waiting for him to release more of that thundering rage again and put up a fight.

But he didn't.

Whatever they'd made him inhale had knocked him out.

Silence rained over the throne room, and the king let out a long-suffering sigh. "Return the rest to their cages, and have our meals brought to my rooms."

I went with him, of course, being sure to keep my attention fixed forward, away from the eyes of the prisoners being hauled to the bowels of the king's lair. Shaking, I excused myself to the bathing room, where I splashed water from the marble bowl upon the vanity onto my too-white cheeks.

He should've left. He should've done as I'd said and returned home.

Now, we were both to be subjected to the king's whims.

Fucking fool, I thought. Stupid, arrogant, insufferable, perfect fool.

"Your marriage to the king," Ryle said when I joined him, the word *king* said as though it shouldn't exist. "You wish to end it, do you not?" He was sprawled over the bed, eating a leg of chicken, eyes on my ripped dress and the skin visible.

I was both surprised and relieved by the subject. Relieved he wasn't going to goad me into tormenting Zad further. At least, for now.

I folded onto the puffed, furred stool at his desk and helped myself to some chicken and spiced dipping cream. "I do."

Ryle made a noise of consideration. "Perhaps I can help you with that."

But at what cost? I did not ask. Instead, I poured myself a few sips of wine, and said, "How?"

"Never you mind." He tossed the chicken bones to the floor, reaching for his wine. Standing, he drained the goblet, prowling slowly toward me. With his fingers curling around the end of my braid, he said, "I'll need you free of such ties if we intend to rejoin Beldine with its cleaved sister, Rosinthe."

I could think of nothing worse than our two continents rejoining—the horror and bloodshed it would cause.

So I drank more wine and tried not to.

I woke on the chaise at the end of the king's bed.

A few sips of wine had turned into three goblets at the king's encouragement.

I hadn't needed much in the way of encouraging, though, not when I could feel Zad's presence, that unwavering lethal rage, deep below. Not when I remembered how he'd looked at me in the throne room, as though he could murder the king and me in one single move before he'd been taken down.

I could not blame him, but I could not stand to remember either.

Coward. I was a fucking coward, and I was painfully aware of it.

The king had me dance myself stupid while he'd remained upon the bed with his winged lover. They'd both laughed, clapping and kissing and clapping some more, and when things got heated, his compulsion over me broke, and I excused myself to the bathing room.

Locked inside, I'd stared at the fading moon through the window until the sound of their fucking had ceased. Then knowing I'd need a somewhat decent rest that wouldn't be achieved in the bathing tub, I'd snatched a silver embroidered cloak from the king's wardrobe. Padding softly over the floor, I'd spied their naked bodies entangled upon the ginormous bed but paid them no mind as I'd succumbed to sleep the moment my own had slumped over the cushioned chaise.

The king was gone when I woke. It was late, well past breakfast judging by the slant of the moon and the bowl of some type of meaty smelling broth that'd grown cold on the desk.

I ate, the rich flavor barely arousing my taste buds, and then I dressed in a simple black gown that, appearing leather at first glance, had been slung over the armchair. Its stretchy fabric clung to every curve, but I was thankful it showed little cleavage for Ryle to dare touch. I wasn't sure whether to be disturbed over my growing affection for the Fae's unusual finery and fashions, half wondering if I'd miss them.

I removed my braid, dragged my fingers through the waves of my hair, and other than dabbing a little rouge to my lips, I chose to forgo makeup. In slippers that molded to my feet, I opened the doors, nodding to the sentinels standing outside. "The king?"

Breen answered, "In a meeting with his war council."

"The queens are here?" I asked.

A jerked shake of his head was all the response I'd receive.

No, then. Of course, he'd fail to include them in whatever outrageous plans he had. To him, the three queens of this realm were probably nothing more than decorations he'd been forced to keep.

I wasn't sure if I was allowed out, so I didn't bother asking. I walked by them as though I had every right to, and neither of the werewolves stopped me.

As though I were merely heading out for one of my leisurely strolls, I took the private entrance Zad had once taken me through to the gardens.

And then I hunted.

Thorns broke the skin of my fingers, and I swatted away countless insects, rummaging through shrubbery under the guise of inspecting the beautiful roses.

After some minutes, a tinny whistle sounded, but I ignored it, pressing on and rounding the corner to where the waterfall's spray bounced up into the air, bathing the earth and the exterior of the castle.

It sounded again, closer this time, pulling my eyes from the bushes, stone, and woodwork to the grassy expanse to my left. A sentinel stood a little ways from me, facing forward, his armor glittering from the light mist of the water.

I walked over when he flicked his gloved fingers.

He said nothing as I neared, but I saw the door on the other side of him. "My partner is relieving himself," he said, a quiet invitation when I hesitated.

I wasn't sure who he was and who his loyalties belonged to, but I wasn't about to argue.

I accepted the invite, heading inside, where I took two sets of stairs and turn after turn, ignoring the prying eyes from behind leafy cells until I finally found him tucked well away from the others and in impenetrable confinement.

In the deepest, darkest, dampest part of the dungeon, he sat in a cell with nothing but a rusted pail. Unlike the others, he'd been caged in iron, the towering thick metal embedded deep within the earth and ceiling.

It wouldn't kill him, not for a long time if at all, but it would weaken him considerably the longer he spent trapped down here.

I tried not to think about how long that could be or how I was supposed to bargain his way out of this. The king had no intention of letting him leave, and I was of sound enough mind to know a form of bribery when I saw one.

He would keep him to ensure I played nice and went along with whatever schemes he was dreaming up.

I'd need to worry about that later. Right now, my every desire and fear was caged like an animal, and after his outburst the previous evening, I had to wonder if perhaps he was. If I'd been too adept at ignoring signs I didn't want to see, the obvious details and lack thereof before me, somehow knowing it might lead to disaster.

He wasn't human. He wasn't royal. He wasn't anything I could contend with.

He was a beast, a creature that until recently, I'd only ever heard about in storybooks.

But he was mine, and I was his, and I couldn't deny that I wanted him no matter who or what he was.

I wanted him even if I could not find a way to co-exist with everything he made me feel, the constant threat he presented to my heart, and the way he'd so calculatedly hidden huge parts of himself from me.

"Has he had you yet?" His first words to me.

I ignored the sting and how he did not even design to look at me. His eyes were on the damp soil, his back against the earthen wall.

"I've missed you, too."

A humorless laugh left the shadows. "Tell me, Audra. Was it more power you wanted? Revenge? I could have given all those things to you, and gladly," he said, tone scathing, "without you whoring yourself out to another male."

I flinched, stepping back.

"Nothing to say?" he goaded.

"I did it for you," I said, softer than I'd intended.

Another bout of cold laughter. "Please," he said, sobering quickly. "That is what you might wish for everyone to believe, but we all know you do nothing if it does not benefit you."

A killing blow, and he knew me well enough to know exactly where to strike. "If that is what you think, then perhaps you don't know me at all."

"I do think you're right." He looked over at me then, but the shadows that clouded his cell were too dense for me to read his full expression. His eyes, though, were alive with enough ire to be seen in my dreams for many nights ahead. "I'm beginning to think I never really did."

I'd had enough. "Stop this," I hissed, crouching, the gown bending with my body. "I am here because of you, and I remain here out of my love for you."

"Love," he said as if tasting the word. "You do not understand it, Audra. You've no idea what it is or what to do with it."

"I understand what not to do," I said before I could stop myself.

He grinned, the white of his teeth flashing. "You were smothering him like an unnecessary blanket. Is that what you do when you love someone?"

"Zad, you lied to me," I reminded him. "And furthermore, you know I'm not—"

"No," he said, soaked in disdain. "I care not what reason you might have had. Not when I have watched you give yourself to another male once before, and it almost killed me. You weren't to know, you weren't ready, and so I never blamed you, but this..." My heart plummeted as his voice deepened, lowered. "I fear I cannot forgive you for this."

I tried to keep the panic, the pain, from my voice. As airy as I could manage, I murmured, "Then it would seem we've encountered a stalemate." We both stared, a thousand broken promises within our eyes. "Very well, my lord."

I gripped the bars to stand, feeling the hum within them, a warning to the heritage within my blood. I felt it balk, curling away from the metal in a way I'd never experienced around iron before.

Lifting my chin, I waded through the dark.

"Do not return," he said.

I stopped, licking my lips. "Excuse me?"

"I said, do not fucking return."

A heated retort swelled over my tongue, iced my teeth. I swallowed it, pushed it back, but it came out anyway, scathing enough to make my eyes close. "We both know I won't, for I've far more important things to do."

"There she is," he said. I said nothing, remaining so still I wasn't sure I breathed, and he bit out, "The queen I once knew and adored."

Once.

Hollow and echoing, the word banged around in my brain, my heart refusing to accept it.

Out of his line of sight, I pressed a hand against the damp wall, wondering if he could scent the roiling turmoil.

On the way out, a hand grasped mine. I made to yank it back, but their grip was unrelenting, steel wrapped in flesh.

The guard pried my fingers open, a dagger placed within my palm.

My fingers curled around the faded, silver whorls etched into the worn black hilt. Gazing up from it, I met cloudy green eyes.

"From Kash," is all the warrior wolf said before staring above my head to the opposite wall.

Nodding once, I tucked it within my sleeve. I'd have to head back to my rooms to hide it.

Knowing I could not do that, I slipped out the way I'd come and circled the outer castle walls, offering a tight-lipped smile to a fluttering kitchen hand in the vegetable gardens.

Her pale pink lips did not move, but her eyes, the blue so light they were almost white, trailed me.

Moments later, I walked the halls, stopping at a framed portrait, looking for all the world as though I were admiring it to anyone who happened by.

No one did. Any sound came from below in the throne room.

Shifting the heavy silver frame forward, I found what I'd hoped the picture hid, a crack in the stone behind it. I wedged the blade in-between, dropping the frame back in place as footsteps clanged up the stairs at the end of the hall.

"My Lady," a guard said, dipping slightly. "We've been looking for you everywhere."

Indeed, he still wore his helmet, but his eyes held a sheen of desperation. I folded my hands before me and stepped back from the portrait. "Why?"

"The king has been waiting for you. He requires your presence in the throne room immediately."

I gestured for him to lead the way and made sure to check my hands for any dirt.

Raiden and Berron sat halfway down the table with their hands chained in their laps and no sign of Zad or the others.

I claimed my seat beside the king, offering a wan smile. "I hear you've been searching for me."

Ryle looked up from a document he'd been perusing, fingers dragging around the lip of his goblet. Through me, over me, and roaming, he surveyed every inch of my body, his nostrils flaring slightly. "You went to see my brother."

I'd been an idiot to forget his sense of smell was far stronger than my own.

So there was little point in lying. "I did, yes." Forcing a sigh, I plucked a sparrow heart, still dripping blood and covered in roasted nuts, and deposited it on my plate. "He is none too pleased with me."

Ryle stared at my goblet, and it filled with wine. "I could imagine he wouldn't be."

I added a large baked potato to my plate. "So," I said. "What is the point of their presence?" I gestured with a flick of my eyes to the quiet males seated down the table from us.

Ryle was looking at me when I lifted my head. "I thought you'd like to see them, being that it's been some time, no?" Without removing his eyes from mine, he stabbed his fork into a sparrow heart, his teeth pulling it from the metal with deliberate slowness. "Both were lovers of yours, after all."

"Some time ago, yes." I sent a sly smile their way, knowing it did not reach my eyes.

Their own darted to me, unreadable beneath the few candles lit from above.

I gave my attention to my food as the king said, "In light of your relationship with the king, I thought it best he and I reach an agreement."

"Oh?" I looked at the document before him that he'd been reading, unable to make out the woven gray writing from my vantage point.

Ryle tapped the table, and the document, as well as an inkpot and a peacock feathered quill, appeared before Raiden, his empty plate crawling to the side on a slight wind.

"Go ahead and sign, king," Ryle said, a spark in his eyes as he willed my husband to do as he said. "Sign it, and you may leave without harm."

My lungs shook with my next failed breath. He was leaving and on his own.

Raiden stared at the parchment, his dark brows furrowing, then looked at the king. "How am I to bring the gold to you?"

Gold? My eyes swung to Raiden, but I felt an invisible current pulling at my chin, forcing them to my plate. My mind whirled as I succumbed, dizzy from the effort to fight it.

The Fae hoarded gold and traded in silver. In treasures and trinkets, they kept their gold in their fortresses, keepsakes, frames, carriages, dinnerware, and a myriad of other items. To do so was to trap it forever, by scattering it for safekeeping.

The king would take Raiden's gold as well as his life, and no signature would stop him.

I needed to turn my head, to lift my eyes, to scream at my idiot husband to stop this before he was tricked, but it was like walking against a wind intent on pushing me over.

It was all I could do to keep my chin from hitting my chest under such force.

Ryle waved a hand, his voice deepening, the energy in the room shifting. "Do not worry yourself over such trivial tidbits. Let it be done."

The chains on Raiden's wrists fell with a clang, freeing his hands. The scratch of the quill meeting parchment sounded too loud for such a small thing. But I knew, deep down, that what he was doing was no small thing at all.

He'd been compelled.

The king clapped, his laughter rich and rough. "Oh, how splendid."

Free of his grip, I looked at Raiden, whose eyes widened farther by the second. They snapped to the king as he stared at the document, then to me, outrage darkening the green orbs.

I said nothing, but I felt my lips part as Raiden snarled, "Termination of marriage."

Shit. My stomach clenched with both relief and horror. I'd wanted nothing more than to be free of him in that way, but what that would mean for Allureldin… "Raiden," I started.

The king cut in. "Dear Audra, are you not pleased? You did say you wanted the marriage dissolved."

I shook my head, gaping at Ryle. "Not like this. Not—"

A chair screeched over the tiles. "You tricked me, king." Raiden's shoulders rose then dropped, his teeth bared. "You deceived—"

"Enough," Ryle said as Raiden kept talking, yet no sound escaped.

He frowned, realizing, his face twisting with rage as he came toward us. But two guards grabbed him by his biceps and hauled him back to the door leading to the dungeon.

He quit fighting once they'd rounded the banquet tables, his shoulders slumping with heaving breaths.

I wasn't sure he'd forgive me for this. It wasn't my doing, but it also was, and for as much as I no longer wished to be his wife, I still cared. I cared enough for it to bother me if he hated me. I cared enough about him for this to feel nothing less than wrong.

Ryle snapped his fingers, gaining my attention. "Eat," he said. "We've a ball to plan."

I looked at Berron, who was still staring at the table.

"I heard that one likes males, so I'm giving him to my guard who also enjoys males." Ryle said it so plainly as though to hand a creature to another to do as they wished was a regular, everyday occurrence. Spearing another sparrow heart, he spoke around the delicate meat, "I thought I'd do right by you and let him eat first." He winked. "Eat up, and perhaps put some thought to showing me your gratitude later."

One of his favored guards, Nerro, arrived minutes later, and though I tried, Berron wouldn't look at me.

"Ryle," I said, adding, "my king," when his eyes narrowed. "Berron is one of my best warriors, loyal to a fault, and I fear what something like this might do to his mind after all he's already done for me."

The king leaned forward, his breath blowing warm over my lips when he clasped my chin. "What shall you do for me?" His eyes bored into mine, but there was no force there. He was letting me decide.

Knowing that, knowing he wanted me to go to him of my own volition, I said, "I will sleep in your bed if I am the only one in it with you."

Berron cursed. I ignored him.

"Sleep," Ryle said as though the word puzzled him. I could

see the defiance growing in his eyes, felt it within his firming fingertips, and braced myself for his resounding refusal.

But then he sat back, his lips pursed, and rubbed at his chin. Sparrow blood stained his lips, and he licked them. "You know what," he said as if confused. "I am so intrigued by the simplicity of this, I am going to agree."

SEVENTEEN

Audra

THE KING'S ARM WAS TIGHT AROUND MY WAIST WHEN I opened my eyes.

Berron had been brought to the king's rooms. As though he were a new pet, the king had told him to sleep on the floor before joining me where I'd laid on my back in his giant bed.

A ball was to take place within hours, invitations already long sent to the other courts of Beldine.

"A celebration," the king had said when it was just us in the throne room, accompanied by his silent and eerily still sentinels. "Of our upcoming nuptials."

The words had sliced me in two where I'd sat beside him, fear racing through me too fast to mask. If he'd noticed, he hadn't let on. He'd merely gone over the lists of dishes he'd like the kitchen staff to prepare while I'd struggled to nod and smile in acquiescence.

I didn't know when he'd decided to touch me, for I'd fallen asleep much quicker than I'd predicted. In fact, I'd expected not to sleep at all. I suspected that I'd been lulled into a dreamless landscape by the male gripping my hip, a low groan leaving him as something hard dug into my ass.

He might have wanted me, but by no means did he trust me.

I bit my lips, my eyes closing, but before I could stave off the panic long enough to think of a way out of this bed and this room, the king rolled to his back. "I do believe it's been a long time since I've slept so thoroughly."

A thump sounded on the floor. I sat up to find Berron

pulling himself, his limbs still bound, toward the wall. His hair was mussed, red lines marred his cheek, likely from resting over the rug.

He met my eyes, and I willed him to tell me if he was okay, but he only looked at the rising king and then at the floor.

"Come," Ryle said, clapping his hands as he stalked naked from the bedchamber. "You need to bathe."

Berron's stare rose when the king disappeared.

I shook my head. No, I hadn't slept with him, and no, I didn't know what his plans were.

He shook his own, chains rattling as he rubbed his cheek.

With nothing else to do, I slipped from the bed and into the bathing chamber, finding it blessedly empty.

Steam spun toward the open window, the glow of late afternoon snatching it from the room.

Pulling off the lavender camisole I'd donned before bed, I climbed into the full tub and laid back against the rim.

"I've had a new dress made for you," the king said, startling me.

He stood at the vanity, dipping his fingers inside a small pot of cream he used to lather his lower jaw and cheeks. I waited for a blade to arrive, but he never retrieved one.

He leaned forward, splashing water from the bowl onto his face, washing the cream off. Wiping his damp, clean-shaven skin with a cloth, he frowned over at me.

I blinked, thankful the citrus-scented soap bubbles covered most of my chest, even though he'd seen more than I'd have liked him to already. "Thank you."

I fixed my attention on the water, my fingers weaving through it, as he strolled closer.

He fingered a curl of my hair, then traced my bare shoulder. "I do not know how much longer I can wait."

I wasn't sure what to say, but I needn't have worried. A knock thundered. Ryle stepped away, walking out, and I heard, "They're arriving, your majesty."

"Show them to their quarters," he said. "And take this mongrel thing with you."

I heard them drag Berron outside into the hall, the king returning a moment later. "I must welcome our queens." He shifted, the act such an oddity that I frowned up at him. "They do not know of my plans, so I expect not all will be pleased."

I tilted my head, asking when I already knew the answer. "And why would that be?"

He licked his canine, then turned to push his arms into a bright yellow tunic, ruffles spilling from the neck. "Because although you are wickedly lovely, you are not of full blood."

I couldn't quell the urge, nor the winter steel behind the words. "And poor genetics have already created enough issues for you."

Swift and glaring, he entered the bathing chamber, tucking his tunic inside his leather pants. "You dare to insult me?"

"It is no insult, but merely the truth." Slowly, I dragged bubbles over my arm and fluttered my lashes at his iced expression. "The truth isn't always worth knowing, but ignoring it achieves nothing."

He knew what I'd meant. That we could rule this continent and any others, but it wouldn't change the fact that he hadn't the power to give this world what it needed. We knew that was why Zadicus still drew breath.

Ryle's rule was archaic and spineless, but although everyone knew he was lacking, he was still the king.

The vicious, tyrannical king of Faerie.

Oh, he knew exactly what I meant, his eyes sparking with the need to punish, but the carriages outside were undoubtedly nearing the road leading to the bridge.

With a growl, he spun and exited his rooms.

I slumped beneath the water, and for just a moment, allowed myself to believe I was in my own bathing room. That I was home.

Now dressed in a long velvet black jacket, white roses embroidered into the lapels, and white pants that clung to every muscle of his thighs and legs, the king was waiting for me outside the doors to the throne room.

His black boots were silent as he came forward and offered his arm. "You look good enough to eat."

Approaching slowly, Temika at my back, I smiled hard enough to feel it crinkle my eyes.

The dress he'd had made fit like a glove, tight around the chest and stomach and falling into a gradual avalanche of eye-catching pearls. Its pearlescent gold satin rubbed over my skin with a softness that resembled that of the milky water of Rainbow Springs.

I shoved the memory away, the gold eyes that flashed through my mind, and looped my gloved arm, made of the same material, through his.

Temika released the train of my gown, and it slithered silently behind me as we neared the doors, flanked by six warriors.

"A gift," the king murmured, stunning me. "From the creatures of the sea."

I felt my breath grow cold in my throat upon entering the overflowing throne room. Fae, of all statures, lingered and talked, royals and nobles seated at the banquet tables, accompanied by courtiers and lovers.

And at two smaller tables on either side of the dais were mermaids.

Legs, unnatural looking and draped to the side of their chairs, were bare. Wraps of differing greens around breasts and waists were the only clothing the unnaturally still males and females wore. They did not drink, and they did not eat. Some, the rare few who weren't staring at us, eyed the food with muddled looks of disdain and curiosity.

I asked the question as quietly as I could, hoping it was heard over the sound of the musicians in the far corner of the throne room. "What are they doing here?"

Ryle chuckled, saying between barely parted lips, "Why, they are from the Emerald Court." At my silence, he asked, "Have I failed to inform you?"

He had, and he knew it, but I kept my mouth shut.

"While they do not deign to humor many of my invitations, every court, as well as guests of their choosing, are always in attendance during celebrations such as this."

Gold and black vines draped from the ceiling, rolling in soft looping currents, crossing and intersecting throughout the room. Glittering bronze beetles buzzed around them, their wings shining bright enough to aid the chandeliers in lighting the crowded space.

A whiskered faerie threw his head back and laughed at something his thin-chinned companion said, catching himself and sobering as we passed.

With each step we took toward the dais, the strains of violins and harps grew in volume, as more and more chatter and merriment ceased.

I dared a look at the banquet tables to my right. Berron and Raiden were there, and I was shocked to see them unchained and drinking wine. Of course, the wine. They were laughing, Raiden smacking a hand upon the table as the horned female beside him watched in amusement.

I couldn't see Azela and Kash, and I knew better than to think Zad could be trusted to enjoy the festivities. In the dungeon, I told myself. They had to still be in the dungeon.

Ryle stopped to murmur something to one of the guards, and then we took our respective seats.

Heads dipped low, some eyes glancing our way, and we waited until the music died.

"Good friends," the king said, standing and taking me with him. "I thank you for joining us on such a momentous occasion, a time of righting all our ancestral wrongs."

Some brows furrowed, but otherwise, most everyone seemed bored.

Raising my hand into the air with his, he continued, "Audra, queen of Rosinthe, our long-lost piece of land, cleaved away from us and given to half breeds and humans alike, has agreed to help us gain back what we've lost."

I surveyed the slow-growing confusion, realizing it was not confusion at all. It was annoyance and distaste. As I'd thought, they did not want to be reunited with a slice of land filled with ilk they'd rather not sully themselves with.

Yet they could do nothing but sit in silence as the king went on, "We will achieve this by welcoming Audra into our home and into our hearts, as my bride," his voice carried, "as my queen."

Gasps cut through the air, blinking eyes and twisting heads, causing the king's hand to clench around mine as he lowered it. Knowing he would be fighting an uphill battle by trying to sway them with more speeches, he waved to a guard by the door leading to the dungeon.

To our guests, he then boomed with a broad smile, "Drink, eat, dance, and enjoy yourselves stupid."

A heavy pause stifled, and then a fiddle started up in fast succession, followed by a flute. Slowly, everyone returned to their conversations and dancing, many filling goblets to the brim with wine.

I expected we'd sit, but instead, we remained standing before the thrones as two warriors brought Kash through the side door. The merfolk tilted their heads, one gnawing on a bone, as he was dragged by them and trussed before the dais.

Golden vines floated down with a look at the ceiling from the king, latching and twining around Kash's wrists, then lifting.

He made no protest and didn't so much as flinch as his soiled feet swayed just above the ground. His eyes were shut—swollen shut—bruises blooming dark upon them and around his cheeks.

Darkness save me.

I knew what he'd request before the words even left the king's mouth and looked at the food-and-wine-littered floor, tracing the patterns there, preparing myself.

So casually, as though he were merely asking I fetch him a drink, Ryle said, "Audra, would you be so kind as to show our people just how much they can trust and adore you?"

Releasing my hand, he retreated to his throne, lounging over it. I looked from his expectant yet relaxed expression to Kash, whose head had flopped forward, dark hair standing in dirtied tufts.

Licking my lips, I ignored the tittering and whispers from the crowd, and asked the king, "What exactly would you have me do?"

He flicked a hand, his lips curling into a smirk. "You are adept at torture, are you not? I should think you'd already know what we do with traitors."

A guard came forward and opened a shiny silver box. Upon a glossy black pillow inside lay a serrated blade, its sharp edges darkening in color.

"Iron infused steel," exclaimed the king. "To make sure he does not heal too fast."

My lashes lowered with a controlled, bracing exhale. There was no other way, I reminded myself. And so I steadied my hand, my mind emptying of every reason not to grab the gray hilt and do what was necessary.

Ice crept inside every vein, wrapped tight around my racing heart, slowing and soothing and numbing.

He was no longer my departed mother's true love. He was no longer the male who'd attempted to warn me of Beldine before any other. He was no longer the surly dear friend to Zad. He was no longer someone who hadn't wanted to yet ultimately had still attempted to help me.

He was a means to an end.

The guard stepped back, closing the box, and the merriment barely paused as I struck Kash's bare chest and dragged the dagger down.

He groaned, his eyes slits behind mounds of bruising, staring at me as though he'd expected differently.

He shouldn't have. For although many things had changed, I was still and would always be the daughter of a monster.

And the only way to best a monster was to become one yourself.

Clapping and shouts echoed, the king declaring, "*More.*"

I glanced around the room, to the guards by the walls, and then I looked at the gushing wound upon the chest before me. Blood washed his soiled skin, from beneath his pectoral to his hip. It wasn't enough. You couldn't see the ribs, couldn't see his entrails.

So I struck again and again and again, the metal so slick with blood, it caked around the hilt, made it too slippery in my numb hand.

"Come here, my queen," Ryle purred, and I could practically taste the excitement and arousal in the air, the latter growing thicker as I took a step back toward the dais.

Before I could near the king, the blade vanished from my gloved, bloodstained hand.

The king clasped it, tugging me over his lap. Eyes fever bright on mine, he brought my hand to his mouth, lips wrapping around each bloodied finger.

Despite everything, I couldn't help but shiver at the eroticism of the act, the dark sensuality of it.

Like calls to like, and for a heartbeat, it would seem that I'd forgotten myself, fraying and slumping over him, feeling his arousal against my core as I made to move closer. "Turn around," he said, releasing my wrist, his other hand upon my lower back.

Blinking harshly, I did.

And felt that numbness, everything inside me, collapse into decaying dust.

It wasn't Kash who hung from the ceiling. It wasn't Kash's chest and torso that was so bloodied it was a wonder he was still gasping for air.

It wasn't Kash struggling to stare at me through bruised eyes, slivers of gold suffering peeking through.

It was Zadicus.

I coughed, choking on my next breath, on my heart, which tried to climb out of my body and splatter itself at its mate's feet. The pain of it was so complete, I half-wondered if the king had cut open my chest to pierce the dying organ beneath, ensuring it stayed exactly where it was.

His fingers clasped my chin, turning my attention back to him. "You were marvelous."

The attendees continued with their evening, as though it were a small thing to have a would-be queen almost murder her mate.

He'd used glamour. He'd made me believe it was Kash when, all along, I had been the only one in the room never knowing who it really was.

The arm around my back tightened, pushing my core into his length over his pants. "I want you right now."

Rage held me so still and roughened my voice to a barely audible hiss. "You tricked me."

Ryle was too entranced to notice or perhaps did not care. "It matters not," he said, ragged, bunching my dress higher to reveal my legs. "Kiss me." He hadn't compelled me, but I wouldn't put it past him to when I could feel how much he wanted more than just a kiss.

So with my soul dying a slow death behind me, I lowered my head, my mouth to Ryle's, and pried his lips apart with mine.

His groan was so deep, he didn't hear it. My tongue stroked so slowly, he jerked beneath me. His breath shuddered into my mouth, my fingers toying with the pearl buttons of his blood-stained white shirt.

Hairless and smooth, as I'd come to assume most Fae male chests were, my fingers splayed over his skin. I moaned, shifting over him. Our teeth scraped, my own tugging at his bottom lip as I pulled away and laid my forehead on his, breathing heavily.

My wet fingers wrapped around the hilt of the dagger at my thigh, plucking it from its holster between one heartbeat and the next. The king's eyes were hooded, nearly closed, as my nose brushed his, and I dragged my fingertips over the sharp edge.

I barely noticed the sting, but Ryle felt the energy of my awakening magic leak into the air and frowned.

Too late.

The dagger plunged with sickening ease through flesh and bone, sinking into his heart.

For a moment, just a moment that felt as though it would last all eternity, he simply stared.

Shock mingled with luminous wrath, but then he smirked, the hand behind my head slipping, struggling to keep purchase as he brought my lips to his. "Fellow heart of ice, you really should have thought twice..."

My brow crinkled, stomach quaking with dread.

Then in flurries of ash that rose slowly into black butterflies, the High King of Beldine dissolved beneath me and exploded on a plume of ear-shredding silence.

My knees fell against the still warm seat of his throne, a black mist raining clear over my skin like lava, sinking inside my every pore.

Pain, unending and electrifying, buckled each limb, threw my head back, and blinded me. It worsened when, through the fraying cracks of life and death, I realized that I couldn't and might not ever see Zad again—his last memory of me enough to reduce all we'd been to cinders.

No.

Nails I couldn't feel clawed at dark nothing as my defiance howled deep enough to form fissures in this never-ending void.

Screams tore up my throat, but I couldn't hear as I vaguely registered the sensation of falling. Then my spine arched, my very bones groaned and cracked as my body writhed on the floor beneath the empty throne.

EIGHTEEN

Audra

A GARBLED STRING OF GROANS CAME FROM BEHIND, AND then voices, hushed and confused.

"Did she...?"

Someone sang, "The king is dead!"

"Only of the same heart," someone mused. "She ought not to be trusted then, really."

Another hollered, "Oh, shut it up and be glad the brat is dead."

I closed my eyes, and when they reopened, I was still on that harsh, blood-marred floor, shaking. Guards surrounded me. Two removed their helmets, one I recognized from the dungeon, crouching and leaning forward.

My breathing was too loud, the pounding heartbeats around me flooding my ears, and that groaning sound arrived again. "My lady..." The shifter stopped, frowning. "I mean, my queen, can you hear me?"

I blinked, swallowing hard, nothing but ice in my veins, attempting to soothe all that had been ravaged, all that still burned.

The guard nodded, seeming at a loss for what to do, and then Kash appeared. "Take these fucking things off, Melron."

Melron rose and fumbled with the chains, and then Kash bent before me, unscathed save for the grime on his face. "Audra," he said, yet his voice sounded different. It was richer as though color had been added to the dark.

And his eyes... they were not black but a glittering onyx.

Onyx.

I'd killed the onyx king. "He's dead," I rasped.

Kash smirked, shifting strands of hair from my face. "You got my present." Still swamped in fading agony, I failed to acknowledge the rare show of affection from him. Before I could respond, he turned back to Melron, murmuring, "Get Zad to the healer. I'll take her upstairs."

"What of the guests?" another guard asked.

Kash cursed. Indeed, there was a loaded silence in the overcrowded room. "Dismiss them, I care not."

"We have a new ruler," said Melron. "And a *female* at that. They'll hardly leave until they've fact-checked this entire unprecedented situation."

"Then they can do so on the morrow." A spiced citrus scent enfolded me when his arms did, lifting me from the floor, carrying me through the throng.

"What's happened?" I said once we were climbing the stairs. "To me."

Kash's arms tightened, and I flung mine around his neck, my head dizzy, the dark halls suddenly far too bright. "You had to know that if you killed him, you'd either die or ascend to the throne."

The king's final words became clear. He'd expected me to follow him into the darkness. And I'd thought I would.

I'd thought I'd die, and I'd been prepared to, was prepared to face the wrath of the faerie queens when I'd stolen their leader from them all, leaving them with a half-dead heir.

"The land has opened itself to you," Kash whispered. "It runs through you as it does Zad."

Such emptiness inside life-changing words.

We reached my rooms, and Kash set me upon the bed. "Zad," I said, scrambling to climb off even while every muscle protested. Everything was ringed with fog, but I had to see him. "I need to—"

"He's being tended to," Kash said. "Stay here, and I'll have someone send word of his well-being."

"No," I snapped, irritated. "I almost killed him…"

"Indeed." Reaching for the pitcher and goblet Temika hurried in with, he poured water inside it. "Tell me, who was it you saw? For I know it was not him."

He passed me the water, and it trembled within my unsteady hand. I sipped, refusing his offer to help. "You."

Kash whistled, sharp with a bark of laughter. "You didn't hesitate."

"You know I could not." I met his eyes, knowing he'd understand.

He stared for a breathless beat, those glittering eyes studying, and took the goblet from me. "Rest," he said, then gave my shoulder a gentle shove so I fell back over the feathered mattress.

I was about to tell him he was crazy for thinking I could do such a thing when Zad was darkness knows where, and the Onyx Court was likely in shambles.

But before I could open my mouth, my eyelids fluttered, and everything turned dark.

❦

Raiden, Azela, and Berron were in my bedchamber when I emerged from the bathing room some hours later.

Waking to find myself covered in blood, in both Zad's and the dead king's, stole my breath. I'd hurtled from the bed so fast that I'd teetered and fell into the wall.

The room had been empty, but I'd known there would be someone outside. It hadn't mattered. I had to be rid of it—of the shame and the fear and the sickening memories clinging to my skin.

I squeezed water from my hair with a small cloth, a cherry red robe adorning my damp body that I'd found hung behind the bathing room door.

"Many may question it, but I think you're suited just fine for the role of faerie queen," Raiden said, no mirth to be found. "You played the king's game better than he ever could have. The victor." He crossed one leg over the other in the twig ensconced armchair by the bed, his smile insincere. "Beldine's new High Queen."

I dropped the cloth to the bureau. "I hadn't thought that last part would actually happen."

His raised brow said he thought differently.

So be it. I looked at Azela as she approached. Without her usual garb of leather and training pants and dressed in a soft cream wrap dress with peacock feathers, it took me a moment to drink her in.

Her blond hair was tied at her nape, as per usual, but a few pieces had escaped to curl around her cheeks, softening her hard gray eyes, making the pert curve of her nose and lips more prominent. "My queen," she said, quiet as she curtsied.

My eyes felt too dry, stinging, and then her arms came around me in a hug so tight, I thought I might unravel at the seams. Slowly, I wrapped mine around her back, my eyes closing.

Pulling back, she gripped my biceps. "You've been sorely missed."

I snorted, directing my eyes to the ground. "I'm sure."

"You have," Berron chimed in from the bed, laying over the end on his side.

I smiled his way, and he returned it. "Mintale?"

"He might need to retire when you return," he said with a slight wince.

I was inclined to agree, imagining the frantic demeanor of the old royal as he tried to keep Allureldin from falling to its knees.

"Ainx and Landen are helping him," Azela said, snatching a grape from the tray of fresh fruit that'd been delivered. Either with them or when I was in the bathing room.

"I'll bet Ainx was none too pleased to have been told to stay behind," I murmured, and plucked some grapes from the gleaming tray upon the small dressing table.

Azela laughed, then said diplomatically, "He's honored to

serve you in any way he can, but Zad made him see to the fleet's safe return."

I looked over the people in the room, friends, I supposed, though the jury was out on Raiden.

Indeed, he gazed at me with a mixture of what could only be described as both contempt and affection. The combination did not allude to good things. "I'm sorry," I said, and watched him stiffen.

"My, my." He straightened in the chair, tilting his head. "A rarity and I don't believe you. You knew what he was doing."

"No," I said. "Believe it or not, for as much as I tried to keep up, I so often found myself just as surprised by Ryle's decisions as everyone else."

"How easily you speak his name now that you've taken his place," Raiden drawled.

"I didn't want this," I said, hoping he'd believe it. "But there was no other way out. I was biding my time, waiting, but you all forced my hand before I could discover what the ramifications might be." When Raiden only glared, I asked, "Why didn't you leave?" He'd been granted permission, had unknowingly ended our marriage—possibly our alliance—to do so.

Licking his teeth, he released a quiet laugh. "I'd planned to, but I couldn't when I thought you might be in way over your head." I narrowed my eyes at him when he clipped, "I thought wrong."

"What did you hope to achieve, Audra?" Berron said. "If you did not plan to kill him."

I twisted to him. "Oh, I'd always planned to kill him." His lips twitched at that. "But I needed to know what would happen first, what would happen after I did, and if there was another way to achieve what was thought by many to be nearly impossible." He caught what I didn't say. I needed to know if I could succeed in killing him and if I would die.

"So you made a bargain with the High King of Faerie," Raiden said, wearing a crooked smile. "Just to find a way to kill him. Darkness, you truly are a bold creature, indeed."

"And to get Zad and his friends out," I shot back, scowling. "He wasn't going to allow him to leave, nor his friends for siding with him. Ryle might have agreed not to kill him, and he discovered he couldn't because he'd risk killing the land, but mark my words, he'd have found some other way to keep him enslaved."

Silence arrived at that, Berron nodding his head. "It's kind of a mess down there," he said. "I suggest wine."

"Duly noted. And Zad?"

Berron shrugged. "Last I heard, he was awake and grumbling, I mean healing."

Relief flooded, drowning some of the guilt. "He glamoured me," I said. "The king. I didn't know..."

Raiden scrubbed at his cheeks.

Azela cleared her throat. "We figured all was not what it seemed."

"It never is," I said, releasing a sodden breath. I swallowed a grape and headed for the wardrobe.

The lower halls were teeming with faeries, the shifters doing their best to control the chaos.

Questions were thrown at me by the dozen, but I could answer nothing. I could do nothing but blink slowly and offer a forced smile. The noise grew deafening, the harsh brightness of it all too much.

I refused to do anything until I'd seen him.

Tension mixed with every ache, making my movements stiff and clunky. It felt as though another layer of skin, softer and harder, had encompassed me. I wasn't sure I'd grow accustomed to it, to all this new strangeness, but I had no choice, and after many weeks of uncertainty, I knew better than to sulk about still being alive.

I would adapt.

Save for Melron and another guard I did not recognize, the

hall outside the room I knew Zad was residing in was empty, though the chatter and excitement could still be heard from every corner of the castle.

Melron stepped aside when I reached the door, blocking it. "I'm sorry, my queen, but he has requested solitude for now."

I stopped and exhaled a shocked laugh. "That's a load of bullshit if I've ever heard it." His eyes widened, the other male beside me coughing to mask his own laughter. "Move." When his eyes narrowed, I gritted out, "Please."

His lips thinned, eyes softening. "I'm afraid I cannot do that."

I looked between the two sentinels, my stomach caving, and reluctantly nodded. "Has he requested no visitors, or has he simply requested that I do not visit?"

The pitying gaze told me it was the latter. I backed up, nodding again. I could force my way in. I was now their High Queen, darkness save me, and so I outranked Zad. "Do tell him I came by anyway."

Wrapping my arms around myself, the scratchy material of the cotton ankle-length gown I'd donned irritating my heating skin, I made my way to the throne room.

Kash was already there, standing before the dais with his feet braced and his arms crossed over his chest as courtiers and the remaining guests mingled and approached him.

He was fielding questions then. Good. The last thing I felt like doing was giving answers to things I knew so little about.

I'd taken two steps into the room, the remnants from earlier in the evening scattered across the tables and floor when howls rent the air.

I froze, my eyes darting to every being who dropped into a deep bow. The shifters were first, their howling loud enough to make the walls creak. Then the guests. All of them, even Kash, with a sly smile upon his face.

When silence drenched the wine and blood tainted space, I motioned with my hands. "Rise."

They did, some looking uncertain as they eyed my journey to the dais, and others grinning; some even had tears in their eyes.

Standing beside Kash, I nodded to him and then found a ginormous male before me.

"Elkin," he said, bowing his head. "Pack leader of the onyx wolves, your majesty." His hair was sandy, a dirtied blond, and his cheekbones high like that of a mischievous aristocratic male.

His eyes, though, the moss green held eons of memories, wisdom, and horror, that hinted at knowledge only a creature of his status would have. "Elkin," I said, struggling not to crane my neck back to hold his gaze. "I apologize for the bloodshed caused by my visit."

Not only was he tall but he was also broader than any male I'd seen before, and I had to wonder if most high-ranked wolves would be the same. Remembering the flash of incredible white from the huge wolf bounding down the hall those weeks ago, I shook my head.

Elkin's thick brows furrowed. "No apologies necessary, my queen. In fact," he said, his smile roguish, "had we known of your intentions, we would've gladly assisted you."

I'd assumed there was little loyalty, but I hadn't the time nor was I willing to take the risk in counting too heavily on that.

"You disliked your king."

He barked a laugh. "That's putting it mildly. We detested him since the day he was dropped upon the castle's doorstep, bringing with him enough misfortune to slowly murder our people and our lands."

I did not care if I offended him. "Yet you did nothing to be rid of him."

His eyes widened then twitched with annoyance, but he could not deny it. "Though the shifters of Beldine had little loyalty to him, we are just that," he reminded me. "Creatures of Beldine, and we would not see our realm suffer from lack of a ruling heir."

I nodded. "Very well."

Eyeing me a moment, he added, "We had no knowledge that a High King could be usurped in this way, it's..." he exhaled a rough breath. "Well, it's unprecedented, frankly."

"I would not recommend trying," I warned, cold but with a smile.

He grinned in kind and then bowed deeply. "Quite the opposite, my queen. We are in your debt and all too happy to be of service."

I wished the rest of the meet and greets could've gone as smoothly, but I was a half breed, and the queens made no secret of their disapproval. That I was to rule above them. Though it was also implied that it was past time a High Queen retook the throne of Beldine.

I did not suspect trouble, but I didn't not expect it either. Time would tell.

Especially when the Silver Court's queen was not even in attendance.

"Was she here during the ball?" I asked Kash.

He stared at her representatives, who were retreating toward the doors. A male had merely offered well wishes from Queen Este before saying he must take his leave.

We hadn't the chance to fully understand who he was, let alone ask him where she was.

"No," Kash said. "I did not see her."

"That does not bode well," I said, remembering the spies from her court. I was halfway through telling him about it when, in a manner that could only be described as floating instead of walking, two merfolk came forward.

Red eyes that had haunted my dreams and waking hours for months after I'd almost drained into the Whispering Sea glimmered with knowing.

Bowing, her dark green hair, almost black, fell in long spiraling curls around her slender golden shoulders and chest. Hair that I knew would turn a brighter green when kissed by water, for I'd seen so myself.

"Adayla," she said, her voice wind chimes and whispers all at once.

I refrained from wincing at yet another foreign sound.

She gestured to her companion, hair a bright orange and eyes the color of wet soil, who dipped low. "Rayne," she said, her long fingers around hers. "My mate, or as you call it in the stained realm, linked one."

Rayne's freckle dusted nose scrunched with her smile, a smile that was not to be trusted.

Neither of the two females standing before me could be trusted—that I knew for certain—but the same could be said for most of Beldine's inhabitants.

The merfolk had helped me, and doing so had helped them, else they would not have come to my aid.

Kash was tense, wariness rolling off him like a looming thundercloud.

I could scent it, as I could the honeyed and salted water from the females before me, my nose twitching at the intensity.

I was all too familiar with having a heightened sense of smell, but I was beginning to think the bone-crunching pain that had crippled me when the king died, the black dust my skin had absorbed with burning greed, was to thank for the increased awareness of all my senses.

The land has opened itself to you.

To say I'd need time to adjust was an understatement, but I could not afford to show any discomfort or anxiety here. Not now.

Right now, I needed to do what was necessary to get out of this mess, back to my own life and my wounded prince.

A life with a male I'd never take for granted ever again.

"Thank you," I said.

Adayla's long-lashed eyes closed briefly in acknowledgment of what I was thanking her for. My life, and that they were here now, rather than racing back to their ilk to make plans to be rid of me.

That could happen, and it undoubtedly might be in certain

lands, but I had only enough energy to focus on what was currently unfolding.

"We knew you would be the one," Adayla said, so still, I wondered if she was breathing. I dared to let my eyes wander, and indeed, there appeared to be gills at her neck, half-hidden by her hair. "We tasted so in your blood, Queen, when it flowed into the sea, and that is why we helped."

Swallowing, I looked between them both, my hands folded before me, and gave them a genuine smile. "And that is also why you attended?"

Rayne lifted a shoulder, her orange braided hair rolling from it. "We cannot miss the changes in history's tides. We will take our leave now." Eyeing me, she said, "Keep eyes at your back, for there are some who might think to test your half-blood abilities."

With that, they bowed again before retreating to the awaiting merfolk by the throne room doors.

Sooner than I'd anticipated, the cavernous room was nearly empty, the few creatures remaining either drunk or guards.

"What's next, my queen?" Kash asked, and I could hear the amusement in his voice.

I bristled, exhaling loud enough to have some of the guards turning our way. "I have no fucking idea."

NINETEEN

Audra

The following evening, I finally drew what felt like my first real breath in the aftermath.

Kitchen staff and servants presented themselves to me, more shifters, and even some who'd chosen to keep clear of the court theatrics visited.

I did what I could, making no promises and ensuring everyone was fed and as comforted by my half breed presence as possible.

I gave little worry to my icy demeanor, being that no one else seemed to mind. But after hours of forcing pleasantries and hearing horror stories from strangers' lips about their late king, I could feel myself fraying.

Kash excused us and had Berron take me back to my rooms. I'd protested, wanting to try my luck with my angry lord, but I'd stopped when Berron said, "Audra, you tried to kill him. You played him. Even if it was for his own good, you played him far too well to expect forgiveness now that your plans have unfolded as you'd hoped."

He was right. He was right, but he was also wrong. "I don't expect forgiveness, but he is my mate, and he will need me, whether he wants to or not."

The use of the faerie term had raised his brows, then he sighed. "Right now," Berron said, clasping my hand in his gentle grip and steering me back to my rooms. "He needs his emotions not to get the better of him while he heals."

He'd left me in my rooms minutes later, demanding I get some rest too, and I had half a mind to walk right back out and see to my lord's well-being. My broken stray prince.

But I'd stopped at the invisible door, my head upon the carved wood, feeling the hum of its essence over my skin, and then I'd readied myself for bed instead.

After tossing and turning for hours, sleep finally took me, but it was stolen by the midday sun. I dragged my fingers through my hair and guzzled some water, staring out the window to the drop of violent waters below.

Before I could talk myself out of it, and before I allowed anyone else to, I soon found myself outside the prince's rooms.

To love him, to love anything, was to suffer. Though I'd learned it was a torment I'd rather live with than without, and that he'd do everything—he had done everything—he could to keep that from happening.

Melron was there, but the other sentinel was not. "I will see him now." My tone brooked no room for argument, and though the wolf's lips whitened with displeasure at disobeying his prince's orders, he did not stop me. He couldn't stop me.

It turned out to be a single room—dark, no bathing or dressing chamber, just a large expanse of black patterned bedding and matching drapes. They were drawn, keeping out the afternoon light, but shifted with the sway of the breeze.

"You took your time." His voice rode along the shadows of the room, of my soul, crisp and dry.

Melron closed the door behind me, and I took two cautious steps forward. "I wasn't allowed entry the first time."

"You're a queen. No," he said, his laughter hoarse as he shifted to his back. "The *High Queen*, and regardless, we both know you do whatever your heart desires."

To that, I could find nothing to say. Nothing that might make all that'd transpired seem less gruesome, wrong, and soul-staining.

Still, I had to try. So I drifted closer to the bed, my eyes roaming his bandaged torso, the wings that took up the entire width of the ginormous bed. I glanced around, noting the desk and the strangely shaped armchair by the window. It had all been designed with a pair of monstrous wings in mind. "This was your room."

He didn't respond, his attention fixed on the ceiling, hands clasped over his healing abdomen. "Zad," I said, and heard my voice hitch, moving closer.

"Stop," he said, the command raw.

As if his needs were all my body wanted to tend to, I did, biting my lip so hard I tasted blood in an instant. "I did not know it was you." He had to know that by now.

Reaching out, I tried to hear his heartbeat, to scent him, but all I could smell was dried blood mingled with mint. And though I tried harder, the sound of my own heart pounding in my ears was all I could hear for stretched, agonized moments.

Then the violent, fast-paced thud of his overpowered it. He murmured, "Leave."

"Zadicus," I tried again. "He'd used glamour, he—"

He jerked to a sitting position. His eyes flared as he snapped, his voice so guttural, I tripped back into the desk. "You think I don't know that? You think I didn't guess what he'd do when he dragged me from the bowels of this darkness damned place and before the waiting eyes of every court? You're a fucking fool, Audra, and it is not because you almost killed me, but because you think that is the issue here when we both know otherwise."

"I did what I had to," I said, my voice too gentle. "I didn't want to be here, remember? I did what was necessary to get us..."

His humorless laughter raised the hair upon my nape and wrung my heart so tight, I couldn't breathe. "How many times are you going to use what I hadn't yet shared with you against me?" He barked, startling me. "Huh?" Shaking his head, he lowered himself to the bed with a pained groan. "It doesn't matter. This was never going to work anyway, not when you constantly find every reason for it not to, so just get the fuck out."

"You cannot—"

"Go." Slithering heat curled around my arms, invisible and squirming, hauling me to the door. Melron opened it as I was pushed by an unseen force from the room, and he caught my arm, steadying me as Zad's growl slipped through the closing door. "Do not come back."

TWENTY

Audra

"Take it bloody easy," Kash snapped, wiping at the scratch on his cheek.

"You said try harder"—I spread my hands—"so it's your own fault."

"I said to send it *farther*, not smack me in the fucking face."

"Don't mumble next time."

"Your improved hearing knows I did no such thing." Still grumbling, he tossed the large twig back at me with nothing but a thought, and I winced, squinting until it stopped right before my nose and fell to the grass.

"Better. No ice this time."

Indeed, it was more difficult than I'd thought to force my magic to stay down while trying out these new abilities. My head was beginning to hurt.

"You're an ass." The wind washed over my face, taking my focus and turning it toward the keep. "With a bad temper."

"Says you." Kash's voice came from far away, low notes of sound, like that of a faraway song, as another reached me. He stopped beside me. "What is it?"

I shook my head, allowing my eyes to skip over the fading night sky beyond the castle. "Raiden's leaving."

We headed back. "You must keep learning, Audra."

"I'll be fine." And that was something I finally believed to be true after these past few months. The land spoke to me, and I listened. It touched me, and I touched back. I needn't and wouldn't stress over trivial tricks. I'd learn whatever else I needed to when necessary. Though I was sure the annoying male would insist on cornering me for more of these practice sessions anyway.

"There are more important things to worry about." Like the lord of the east who still laid holed up in his room most nights. When he appeared, it was to eat and talk quietly with Dace and Kash, never once looking my way.

Save for the darkness that pillowed his now often dull eyes and a slow gait that had improved after a couple of days, he seemed to be healing well.

A little more than a week had passed since he'd forced me from his room, and I hadn't spoken to him since. Instead, I'd busied myself with the menial tasks of getting to know our new court, the ins and outs of how it was run, all the while wondering and trying to discover how self-sufficient it could be without my prince and me.

I wanted to go home.

Kash could stay, and I knew he would if and when I finally asked.

Passing the sentinels on the bridge, I nodded when they bowed and hurried to where I could hear a conversation coming to an end in the hall above.

"Silk," Raiden said, and I halted atop the stairwell, watching the hard planes of his face slowly soften as we both seemed to marvel at what time had bestowed on us—where it'd taken us. "I wish I could say it's been fun, but I know your kind do not appreciate lies, no matter how beautifully told."

"I'll be returning home soon." I took a couple of steps closer, failing to think of something else to say as grass green eyes gazed down at me, absorbing my every feature in a way he'd once done long ago.

Dace and Azela stood behind Raiden, Azela clearing her throat and walking to me. Pausing for only a moment, she then threw her arms around my shoulders. "Please do."

Shocked, I just stood there with my breath freezing inside my mouth. Before she pulled away, I patted her back, evoking a watery laugh.

"Home," Raiden said, scratching at his chin. "Do you know where that is anymore?" His question, though bothersome in tone, didn't anger.

For I knew the answer. I knew home was wherever my heart was.

I now knew home needed not be a place.

If it was, then perhaps all this madness would seem easier to navigate. So, for now, I'd follow my gut instead of my heart and go where I was needed—the next best thing.

A slow ache spread from my chest to my head, bouncing hard enough into every crevice that it was almost blinding. "Goodbye."

Raiden didn't look back as Azela smiled.

Dace nodded at Kash and me, and saw them to the antechamber, where I knew he'd sweep them into the void and back to Rosinthe.

No sooner had they disappeared than a muffled shout sounded from somewhere deep in the castle.

"Adran?"

Kash sighed. "He's being kept in the staff quarters under guard in a small bedchamber and making a lot of noise about it."

"If he continues to bother them, have him sent to the dungeon."

"You plan to kill him?"

I rubbed my temples and made my way to the stairs. "Believe it or not, I've had enough death. Now, if you'll excuse me, I've got a rotten headache."

The headache soon became a full-body ache, and if I didn't know any better, I'd think I'd succumbed to some type of human illness.

Impossible, yet two days after Raiden's departure, I could barely stand to look at the stars.

Without knocking, Kash entered my chambers at dusk and halted when he saw me leaning against the wall by the bed. "Did you sleep?"

"I need you to do something for me." I traipsed to the desk, to the document I'd had Temika arrange for me, and tapped it. "I want you to..." My jaw sang and I snapped my mouth closed, rotating it and drawing a slow breath. "Take the title of regent," I managed to get out. "I need to leave."

"Audra," Kash started, something strange changing the dark notes in his voice. Concern, maybe, but I cared not. "Audra," he said again, and turned me to face him. "You're pale as fuck."

"Did you hear me?" I pressed, unable to focus on his dark eyes.

His face swam, fractured with diamonds of light that bubbled and burst. My eyes absorbed it all, causing the splitting inside my skull to become near unbearable.

Kash directed me to the armchair. "Close your eyes." A cool goblet was placed in my hand, his own gentle as he helped lift it to my mouth. "Sip."

After a few moments, my heartbeat dragging as though it couldn't keep up, I peeled open my eyes and slumped in the chair. The burning slowly mellowed to a steady simmer. "Shit." I rubbed my head and set the goblet in his palm, a tremor in my hand I couldn't hide.

"You've not released enough of yourself into the land."

"I don't know what that is supposed to mean, nor do I care." I swallowed and tried to straighten, Kash kneeling before me now. "I name you regent. You will rule this damned place in my stead."

"You cannot leave," he said. "Especially not like this."

"Do you accept or not?"

"Why?" A question harsh enough to cut through flesh.

I'd have rolled my eyes if I could've. "Not to torture you if that's what you think, and not just because it'll give you something to do other than wander around in endless gloom until you meet my mother in the ever, but because you are what these people need." I swallowed once more, my voice cooling. "You and Zad are the kind of leaders they need in my absence, they trust you, but I will not give him to them." *Not without me*, I didn't say.

Watching me for a heavy half minute, Kash then stated, "They might not trust you yet, but they have welcomed you. They prefer you."

"Over the creature who ruled before me, of course, but nevertheless"—I looked down at my hands, watched the tremors twitch each finger—"I cannot remain here."

He understood what I hadn't decided yet, placing the goblet upon the dressing table. "You will split your time then."

"Perhaps," I offered as the outrageous, unique situation I'd found myself in reared its head again.

Unblinking and arms crossed, Kash nodded once. "As you wish." He strode out of the room a breath later, and I flopped over the arms of the chair, closing my eyes.

They reopened when I felt *him* moving up the hall toward my rooms, a dark, inescapable storm.

With that fluidity that made my every sense wake up and pay attention, he walked right in and closed the door behind him. I watched as though in a dream as he crossed my bedchamber and stopped mere inches from my bare feet.

Eyeing my nightgown as though it offended him, he sneered, "Too good to join your new court for dinner?"

"I'm unwell," I stated blandly, too bland for the enormity of whatever it was that ailed me.

Zad said nothing as he stepped forward and took my hands, pulling me from the chair to my feet. Without any warning, he kissed me.

It wasn't soft and loving—it was raw and unbridled determination.

Shock rendered me immobile, but only for a failed heartbeat, then I kissed him back with that same amount of savagery, wanting even while I had him.

Copper welled over my tongue from his teeth, his groan a rumble I greedily swallowed. "You wicked fucking creature. How vile your soul must be." Rough and sweltering, his hands roamed everywhere. They fisted the material, then tore my nightgown from my body.

After a bruising squeeze of my hips, the rustle of his clothing hitting the floor, he turned me, pressing his naked form to my naked back. Strong arms wrapped around me from behind, his teeth at my neck, velvet tongue lapping.

Breathless and disorientated and uncaring I could fall if he weren't holding me, I laughed softly. "Are we talking about me or yourself?"

He didn't laugh. He bit me, and I withheld the scream, trapping it inside my throat. He didn't numb the pain. He did nothing to soothe it. He gripped my breasts in his large hands and squeezed. "Did he touch these?"

"No."

"Liar," he hissed.

"He didn't," I said, needing him to believe—*just needing him.*

Twisting us, he lifted me to the desk and pried my legs apart. Fevered gaze holding mine, he dragged a hand down the center of my chest, over my stomach, and stopped where I needed him most.

He pushed a finger inside, eyes hooding when my back arched, and I moaned, rocking forward. "This?"

"No," I said.

He huffed, withdrawing.

I gaped, trying to loop my legs around his smooth, toned waist when he fisted his cock. He pumped the long, thick member, eyes on mine, and then they drifted down—down between my legs, his teeth scraping his bottom lip.

His arousal was so extreme, I could smell it—the barely leashed desire to take and own and claim and erase.

He just needed the truth. To be reminded I was, and always had been, his.

If only he'd believe someone capable of lying.

With a cruel calm, he asked, "Did he see you?"

I wanted to scream, but I didn't. I couldn't. "Yes."

He froze, the head of his cock touching my entrance. Enraged eyes lifted, and I did everything I could not to cower. "*How?*"

"Zad," I pleaded.

Gripping my thighs, he pulled me onto his waiting cock, and I moaned so loud I did almost scream from the size of him, from the absence of him.

"Fucking *how*, Audra," he gritted.

Panting, I tried to adjust to the delicious burn. "He..." Zad picked me up off the desk, and I could hear his teeth grind, see every muscle flex with the urge to kill a male who was already dead. Oh, he was furious, and I couldn't resist trailing my fingers up his arms, marveling at the sight, at the primal menace rolling off him. "He painted a portrait of me, but he did not see much."

He snarled, ducking to sink his teeth into my neck. "Darkness, Audra. I fucking loathe you."

My nails sank into his biceps. "I love you."

"You don't, you like the way I make you feel, the way my cock fills you like nothing else ever has. You're infatuated, attracted to me in agonizing ways because we are linked, but it is painfully clear you do not love me."

He was wrong. So unbearably wrong. "I do."

A large hand smothered my mouth, then retreated as he growled and flipped me around to take me from behind.

"I will talk regardless of if you can see me."

"Talk all you want. I've become adept at ignoring lies."

"Why are you here then," I said, a whimper escaping when he left me only to slowly crawl back inside.

"Because this"—he reached around, smacking my clit, and I trembled, my breath stuttering as lightning coursed through me—"is mine, and though I wish otherwise, I cannot control the need to remind you that."

"You're an asshole," I said.

He yanked my head up by my hair, then wrapped his hand around my neck, pushing my chin to his mouth. His tongue licked at my jaw, a long, slow swipe, the arm around my stomach, banded to my hip, kept me trapped. "I want to destroy you," he said, his voice hoarse. "I want to fuck you until you can't breathe, can't see, can't feel anything but the shape of me every time you move."

I tried to talk, but then his teeth scraped my neck, and all I could do was tremble and moan.

"I want you so blind with need, so fucking ruined for me, that you feel even a scrap of what it's like to burn when I torture you with another female."

This wasn't him, or maybe it was. Maybe his time in Allureldin—his terminated marriage and his quiet life away from the treachery and debauchery of Beldine—had only blanketed those base desires. The instinctual reflex so many of his kind had—hurt them, deceive them, and be hurt tenfold in kind, should you live to be tormented in such devious ways.

Still, I pleaded to him, to the male I'd fallen in love with, had linked with, for that was who I needed. Now and always. "We both know you cannot do that to me."

He rotated his hips, and I mewled, about to detonate, even with the widening fissures inside my chest. "We'll see," he growled into my neck when he pumped and then grinded his hips, and I fell apart. He held me up, teeth pulling at my skin and his fingers now between my legs, rubbing. "That's it," he purred. "Drench my cock like a good little half-blood queen."

I couldn't stop him, could only lose myself in his arms as my vision blackened before returning with so much color, I grew dizzy once more.

His laughter was wicked and low as he worked me slowly, taking his time to finish with me.

I was a liquified mess, and he made sure of it. My breathing labored, I wheezed when he picked up the pace. His hand moved to my breasts, squeezing, rubbing, then slapping.

I jolted at the sting, and he hummed. "Again."

I'd already fallen to pieces over him, and I had no desire to give him anything else.

He pinched my nipple, and I squirmed, sweat gathering at my back from the heat of him. "Again," he ordered, a guttural demand that forced my body to betray my mind. "Such a lovely, toxic royal brat."

That hand tightened around my throat, oxygen leaving me in harsh pants. His hair hung in tendrils around his cheeks, his teeth gnashing when he grinned. But his eyes... those golden eyes were all I knew and nothing I recognized. They were everything he truly was.

A faerie prince. A creature of immense power.

A predator.

I was both entranced, coming undone at the seams, and petrified, my heart galloping.

Lowering his lips to mine, he snarled, "Come on my cock hard enough to deserve my seed, or I'll find someone who does."

"You wouldn't—"

"You've no idea what I'm capable of, and you know it."

I snarled in kind, but it only served to make his eyes widen with lust addled humor. He dove, lips snatching mine, teeth cutting as he tugged before plundering with his tongue.

It felt as if he were trying to invade every inch of me, and I was so stupidly obsessed with him that I felt myself soar and begin to fight back.

He growled approvingly and didn't stop me from reaching up to hold his face to mine.

The sound of our skin meeting, his grunted curses and breaths as he filled me with his seed, and the taste of his velvet mint tongue had me crumbling.

Before I could completely finish, before I could unleash what he'd built, he removed himself from my body and released me.

With a shocked shout, I fell over the desk, shaking, my orgasm-clouded brain needing a moment to realize what he'd just done.

His clothes remained, but his naked form was gone.

❦

Despite being left alone to finish, I woke feeling better than I had in months. Hours crawled by while I stared at the swelling night outside my bedchamber windows, listening to the water sail beneath the castle to throw itself off the cliff into the rocky depths below.

Creatures, beast and bird, called to one another, and I discovered that when I hummed a tune similar to that of the night birds, they paused and sang back.

Another lifelong bond I never once saw myself making.

Kash. Zad.

It didn't take me long to realize the prince hadn't come because he had to have me. He came to me because I'd needed him. I needed the release, to rid some of what I'd absorbed, and he'd hated it.

He'd hated it, but he'd still done it.

I took a shred of solace in that.

At dinner, I watched Zad as he ate faster than I'd ever seen before, then excused himself. His scent lingered long after he'd left the throne room, and I stared at his chair at the head of the long table. A place I wouldn't dare sit. The original chair, the one Ryle had used—unnecessary and a reminder of all that'd transpired in this room—had been replaced.

"The dining room," I said without removing my eyes from Zad's almost finished meal. "Could we eat there next?"

Kash exchanged a glance with Dace, and one of the warriors

on the wall shifted. "We could," Kash said carefully. "Though Ryle has been the only one to use it since he took to the throne."

"So?" I said, cutting into my bloodied slice of venison. "I used it with him once." The memory should've filled me with that familiar sense of unease I'd only just recently begun to shake. Instead, I felt nothing but a minor twinge of sorrow for what could have been.

It wasn't as though the king hadn't been given chances to do better, to stop with the horror and fear-mongering.

I froze then, my fork bending in my hand when it dawned on me that Zad might also hold that against me. The death of his brother.

I'd saved his realm, and in doing so, I'd destroyed his heart.

Setting down my cutlery, I rose and excused myself, hurrying from the room and down the halls, racing past watching warriors and into the final hours of night.

The breeze rid the damp from my eyes, washed over my exposed arms, and danced through the sheer fabrics of my green and blue gown.

I took the same path I'd taken months ago. A different lifetime, it seemed, that Zad had stolen me from his brother and shown me the forest nestled alongside the castle.

I'd visited countless times since, each time finding it more vibrant. Life and color so rich it made my chest warm and called to the blood that rushed faster within my veins. Just like those times, I let my fingers glide over the moss shrouded rocks. Some rose higher than me, kissing their brethren, glowing brighter as I passed by.

I ventured deeper into the woods than I'd dared before until I came upon a tree that stretched so high into the sky, I wouldn't be surprised if it knew the stars. At the base of its impossibly large trunk with a circumference that rivaled the castle's spires, I sat upon a flat stone. It hummed beneath me, warming the grass under my bare feet, and I reclined into the bark, feeling it shift at my back.

Magic. True, awe-inspiring magic.

That awe I'd felt while exploring the land from the sky weeks ago hadn't dulled any. It'd only multiplied in varying ways—ways that spoke of a reluctance to leave.

For the land wasn't just Zad now.

It was me, and I feared my presence here, although helpful, might also harm.

Twisting my hand in my lap, I stared at my fingertips and watched the breeze roll into an iced wind. I would freeze it, surely. A heart like mine might not have been as dark as it once was, as what it could have become, but it was still cold nonetheless.

Beldine—Faerie—must remain as it was before my arrival. In eternal spring. Though perhaps it wouldn't change. Either way, I knew to remain here for too long was not in anyone's best interests.

I was still pondering the great vastness and confusion of it all when a pair of gold eyes drew my attention to the brush up ahead.

You've no idea what I'm capable of, and you know it.

Indeed, he was right.

What would become of us now? A queen of two realms and a runaway faerie prince without a throne. A lord from a different land.

My linked one. My mate.

I couldn't give him up. I wouldn't. I just didn't know how to keep something that refused to come back to me.

A silent alarm snapped my eyes to the brush again, the hair at my nape standing as I rose from the stone and watched a large snake slither closer through the long grass up ahead.

It was no snake. Though its long, black and silver scaled body resembled one, its head was like that of a wolf. A forked tongue flicked out once, twice...

And then that wolven face came into clearer view as I wondered where that instinct to flee had gone. For I definitely should've run for my miserable life by now.

Unable to move, I stood my ground, my shoulders and spine

taut, and my hands hanging calmly at my sides as the snake beast stopped, and I studied its face. Half of it was covered in black fur, whiskers sprouting from its long, gnarled nose. The other half was matted, chunks of fur missing, and where it should've been, a bloodied rot festered, nose swollen and cracked, and its mouth too.

Long-forgotten instinct finally returned, and I reached for a blade that wasn't there, courtesy of being so thoroughly distracted by Zadicus.

"Stand still," came his voice now, and although shocked, I didn't take my eyes off the snake wolf. "Breathe and take a step forward."

He'd followed me. That, or he'd sensed the danger or my unease. I didn't know and hadn't the time to care. I was about to ask if he was truly insane when the beast whined, the sound similar to that of a wolf with the sizzle of a hissing serpent accompanying it.

He or she came closer, its enormous body dragging over a patch of fading starlight, bringing that face into better view.

The stench… "Darkness damn me." My nose scrunched. "What happened to it?"

"It is not just us and the land that suffered," Zad said, aloof. Yet I knew he was on high alert. "She's called a vipane. They nest in burrows by the creeks where some of the starvation in the soil has hit hardest."

Still staring at that blackened skin, the exposed rotting flesh and bone, I watched her maw open as she released another pain cracked whine.

His voice, so calm, so like the lord I recognized, came closer, his heat and scent suddenly everywhere. "She aches, and though she will heal with time, as the rest of the land does, you can help her. She wants you to."

As if the sight of the beast's face, the milky hue of her remaining eye, was a current, a sharp twinge stalled my next breath. "How?"

"Introduce yourself." He made the request so simply that I wanted to turn and scowl at him.

"What?" The beast huffed, grass swishing with the impatient flick of its tail, and I sighed. "Oh, fine. I'm Audra." I waded a little closer. "Your queen, apparently, but if you bite me, you die."

Zad released a near-silent laugh as if he were reluctant to allow me to hear it.

Ignoring the ever-present sting he'd left me with, I took another step forward, giving the beast a look that said this was as far as I'd come, and she'd need to close the gap herself.

Without pause, she did, and my heart jumped and froze. In a flash of movement, she was before me, muzzle pressing into my outstretched hand as though she'd been holding back before, not wanting to frighten me away.

Wincing, not just from the stench—and due to the fact I had to touch the wounds upon her face—but because of the zap that vibrated through me, I did my best to stay still as the beast closed its eyes.

"What should I do?" I asked of Zad, taking in the rot that I realized also spread down the right side of her scaled body.

"Exactly what you're doing." His voice was closer as though he'd moved with me. "She'll take what she needs and then leave."

The vipane's tongue flicked out, her eyes opening, no longer gold but a deep orange. Slit pupils dilated as she gazed at me, and I felt my limbs grow loose with the comforting swell of magic that coursed through us both.

Her nose wriggled as skin re-stitched itself, and her wounds began to close over.

"That's enough," Zad said in a steel tone that made the beast take notice of him, seemingly reluctant as she pulled away.

Between one heartbeat and the next, she was gone, and the music of the forest returned.

Turning my hand over, I inspected it, but there was no blood, no ooze, nothing save for specks of stardust and a lingering vibration that slowly leaked away through each fingertip. "Wow."

Zad made a grunting sound, and then the soft crunch of his boots over the grass registered, and I scrambled to follow.

"Wait," I said when we'd reached the edge of the forest, and it seemed he was doing his best to talk himself out of staying anywhere near me.

He stopped, and my heart soared as I rounded on him and gazed up into his shadowed face, my eyes absorbing each hardened and rugged feature with an urgency that likely reeked of desperation. I didn't care.

"Look at me," I said, taking his hand.

He allowed it for all of a breath, and without laying eyes upon me once, then growled and circled me, heading for the keep. "Keep out of the forest, and go to bed."

"You'll join me?" I purred, trailing him.

He scoffed. "You know I won't."

"Why not?" I demanded, knowing he wanted to, tasting it on the air he left in his fiery wake.

"I've better things to do."

"Close the door," I called to the warriors awaiting our return, who hurried to do as I said.

Zad laughed, feathers stirring behind him. "A brat indeed."

"How many times do I need to say I'm sorry?"

"Interesting," he said, a brow quirked as he finally looked at me. "That you think you've once apologized when I've not heard you do so at all."

"I'm sorry," I rushed out, "for so many things. That I killed him, but I couldn't see another way out. I hadn't realized he meant so much to you..."

His low laughter, the hand he scrubbed down his face as he turned to the forest we'd not long vacated, choked off my words. "You think this is about you killing him?" Unable to answer, I didn't, and he gazed back at me, seething, "Audra, I'd kill him for every time he so much as looked at you if given the chance." Eyes roaming me, he shook his head and looked away. "You'll never understand, and I'm tired of trying to make you. Leave it be. I'll leave on the morrow, and you can have your new kingdom."

My heart plummeted. "You cannot leave."

Wings twitching above his shoulders, he stared right through me, his beautiful face utterly blank. "Is that an order?" He tacked on, loaded with sarcasm, "My High Queen?"

I didn't answer, found I couldn't as I nodded to the guards to let him inside because yes, I would order him to stay if I opened my mouth, and we both knew it.

And we both knew it wasn't him who had to leave.

He didn't want me here any more than I'd wanted to be here when I'd first arrived.

He didn't want me here at all.

"Melron," I said once Zad had disappeared. "Have someone tell Berron and Kash to meet me in the throne room."

With a dip, he gave a grim smile. "Of course, my queen."

🌹

"Dare I ask what new adventure we are to embark on now, my queen?"

Despite the sorrow and anxiety weighing heavily inside me, I couldn't keep my lips from curling.

"You look like you've killed a king." Berron dragged his knuckles down my cheek. "And had your heart broken. Again."

Inhaling a burning breath, I held my hand over his. "I never do learn."

Eyes full of understanding, he nodded. "There's no fun in that, though, is there?"

"Life would be an absolute bore," I said, laughing a little. "Ready to go home?"

Berron grinned.

"No," Kash said as soon as he saw us, and I stepped back, hands tucked behind my back as I gazed at the wall where Zad's wings had once been displayed. "This is insanity, Audra."

How he knew what I'd ask of him, I didn't care to wonder. "All you need to do is take us there." Turning to him, I softened my voice. "I'll return when I'm ready, but I must go back."

Kash flicked some hair out of his eyes and exhaled roughly. "Because of Zad?"

"Because I've been gone far too long," I said, my words growing thick. "Because it's time I go home."

Berron looked between us, silent.

"Besides," I said. "I trust you."

Kash's glare melted, and I looked at the floor, where blood had pooled and flowed like small rivers.

Retrieving something from his pocket, Kash stared down at it for a moment. "He won't like you leaving."

I didn't bother arguing, didn't bother telling him that not only would his friend like it but he'd also probably be relieved by my absence. Urgency tightened my voice and spasmed inside my chest. "Please, just take me home."

TWENTY-ONE

Zadicus

I'D NEVER FORGIVEN MY FATHER FOR WHAT HE'D PUT MY mother through.
 She'd made a mistake—a gigantic, unforgivable mistake. Yet, I hadn't understood why he'd retaliated in kind. Why they hadn't merely parted ways or worked through it.
 Until now.
 The problem with having your soul tied to another, although paralyzing, wasn't always the fear of losing them. It was the unnamable violence that ignited when that love was tampered with—scarred and sullied and changed into something you never wanted it to be.
 Imperfect.
 And though I longed for vengeance, if only so she could understand the magnitude of her actions, Audra was right. I couldn't fucking do it.
 All ten of Ryle's lovers, human and faerie alike, stared back at me from chaises, beds, and a small table setting in the gargantuan parlor they'd been given as living quarters.
 A boulder of regret for so much as walking here and sending the doors crashing open lodged in my throat.
 "Prince Zadicus," many of them greeted, lowering heads and bodies in a sign of unnecessary respect.
 And still, I stood there, unable to move into the room, unable to move at all.
 A female with dazzling, narrowed blue eyes stepped forward.

"May we help you?" Her question was cautious, curious, for she knew—everyone in this darkness forsaken land knew—that the new High Queen was my mate.

"Leave," I heard myself say, tearing my gaze from hers and turning back into the hall.

"What?"

"Leave," I repeated. "Or stay. The choice is yours, but your services are no longer required."

I was followed down the hall, but I didn't slow, didn't turn back. "My prince," she called. "Some of us have no homes to return to."

I paused at that, pinching the bridge of my nose.

Of course. Of course, some of them would be without living relatives or friends outside of this castle. This was not my job. It was not my place to tell them what to do.

But I took some bitter satisfaction in doing so anyway. "You will be given new tasks if you choose to stay. Tell those who wish to leave that they are free to do so whenever they are ready."

I walked away before she could ask anything else of me and headed to the throne room.

Kash swept in as I entered, charging straight for the decanter of water and a goblet upon the banquet table. "You smell of your brother's lovers."

"How would you know?"

He sipped and shrugged. "Never you mind."

"I released them. Though some will probably remain and will therefore need to find other roles." I glanced around the empty room. No guards. No Audra.

"Don't worry," Kash said, his goblet thumping to the table. "She won't be able to scent them back in Allureldin."

He'd reached the doors before what he'd said sank in with cold clarity. "She's gone?"

"For now," he said, disappearing.

I wasn't sure how long I remained frozen there, gazing at the shadows swirling in the doorway, hearing nothing but the slow whine of my heart in my ears.

Then a silent, humorless laugh broke from me, and I reached for the decanter. I didn't drink from it. No, it crashed into the empty throne, bouncing off it into thousands of tiny shards as I forced my breathing to settle.

It didn't. Not as I exited the throne room and passed questioning warriors, taking to the stairs, following them as high as they'd take me. Harder and harder, my heart pounded, my breath a long-forgotten idea inside my crumpling lungs, and I burst through the door of the tower to the battlements.

Air, crisp and sweet and nothing I needed, engulfed me, my wings unfurling and spreading. I leaped to the stone and vine-wrapped ledge...

And then, for the first time in hundreds of years, I jumped.

Muscles jerked and protested, my heart sank for a new reason as the ground rose to greet me. Then mere feet from the water, I caught the tide of the breeze and banked.

Laughter, shocked and choked and all too real, alerted the guards to my presence above them, my wings flapping faster and faster as I soared toward the moon.

Since getting them back, I'd been too busy resenting them to entertain the idea of using them.

As a youngling, I'd fly until I'd need to keep my eyelids peeled back with tiny twigs—forever thinking I could one day reach the stars. I never did. I never would.

But it didn't matter.

Not when my breathing slowed and some of the ice inside my chest thawed. Not when I could do something I never thought I'd be able to do again.

Not when I could fucking fly.

TWENTY-TWO

Audra

Snow flurries danced outside, and I left my robe on the windowsill and crossed the room to the bathing chamber.

Inside the water, tendrils of steam floating toward the same ceiling I'd stared at more times than I could remember, I half-wished it was a different bathing pool—a different chamber.

But that was selfish.

It wasn't that I wasn't glad to be home, the welcome I'd received—Mintale going so far as to dare hug me—warming the iced cracks in my heart.

But it wasn't enough to repair them.

Truin's pattering footsteps outside in the hall, coupled with her scent, gave her away before her voice did. "If it isn't the first High Queen of Faerie."

"Second, and I warned you not to tease," I made to snarl, but it came out as more of an exhausted puff of air.

The witch, noticing this, gathered her skirts to seat herself upon the edge of the bathing pool. "I do not tease, my queen. In fact," she said, her voice lowering, "I find it all so very fascinating."

My first day home had consisted of meetings with my court, but yesterday, I'd chosen to lie in bed. Unaccustomed to sleeping at night, Truin had caught me as I'd woken up from a long nap. I'd told her everything, feeling little relief from doing so but finding myself grateful to unload, nonetheless.

"Not to mention," she went on, unnecessarily, "incredibly brave."

"I'm glad someone seems to think so," I griped, knowing that I didn't think myself brave. Cunning and determined, most certainly, but never brave.

"You've wounded him," Truin said, tone cautious. "Gravely, and more than once."

"You need not tell me." I sank deeper into the water until it kissed my chin.

Silence permeated, Truin tucking a strand of yellow hair back into her braided knot.

I knew what she was doing, yet I still played right into her hand, needing to more than I'd realized. "I've tried," I said, rising to sit and run the cloth over my skin.

Truin hummed. "I can only imagine what your version of trying might be." I shot her a warning glare of which she did not heed. "You cannot expect forgiveness without acknowledging wrongdoing, my queen."

The cloth hit the side of the giant tub with a splat, and I climbed out, wrapping a towel around my body and padding into my bedchamber.

Truin followed. "It seems hard, but it's worth it."

"And how would you know?" I snapped before I could bite my tongue.

Accustomed to it, Truin just offered a small smile when a knock sounded upon the doors. "I might not know much about romance." Her hand fluttered before her face as she searched for the right words. "But I do know hurt. Some hurts cannot be fixed, no matter how sincere the remorse. Others," she said as I pulled on my emerald robe, "they can be fixed if you're willing to try."

After staring at her milky brown eyes for a moment that loosened the tension in my jaw, I looked at the doors. "Enter."

Truin's cheeks pinkened as the Fae male entered and bowed. "Majesty." With a nod to Truin, he smirked in a way that spoke of familiarity. "Lady Truin."

Lady? Stopping before my dressing table, I widened my eyes at Truin, but the witch ducked her head, excusing herself.

Landen's gaze followed her exit, then swung to me and hardened. "The snow melts."

Watching the doors close, I pulled the comb through my damp hair. "And?"

Landen's low urgency collected my attention. "It is too early, my queen."

Two weeks passed with little speed and a growing current of anxiety.

Atop the second tallest mountain, leaning against Van, I watched the stars begin to wink into place in the sky, the breeze growing cooler with the absence of the sun.

Plucking another wildflower, I handed it to Vanamar, who accepted it with a grunt, a warm huff from his large nostrils dampening my skin. He stilled, and I patted his leg. "Relax, it's only Berron."

"Does he seem to care that you reek of Beldine and whatever otherworldly powers you now possess?"

I picked another wildflower, joining it with one in my lap. "If by swishing his tail so violently with excitement when he saw me that he put a hole in his stall wall, then yes, he cares very much."

Berron chuckled, and I glanced over at him while he let Van sniff his hair. "You look good." And he did, his dark hair held that familiar sheen, as did his eyes, and he'd gained back the weight and muscle tone he'd lost—not from his short stay in Beldine but from the horrors wrought to him by the Sun Kingdom many months ago.

A different lifetime, it seemed, and one I didn't know if I still belonged to.

"You always look ravishing, but… something is missing," Berron said, gazing at me now.

And the way his eyes dulled as he studied me grated. "That's fairly obvious, isn't it?" Though my voice was a lot softer than I'd intended for it to be.

"Audra," Berron said. "Swallow your damned pride already and go get it back."

"It is not about pride," I snapped, and Vanamar tensed.

"The realms then? Because you can stay or go or do both if you please, and Raiden will just have to deal—"

"It's not any of that," I cut him off, my chest squeezing with that pesky ache. "I do not wish to talk about it."

"Okay." Berron gave Vanamar a flower, cursing when the furbane nearly took his finger. "So what will you do then?"

"The winter melts." I gazed at the sprawling city, my eyes chasing the cobblestoned streets that wound downhill to meet the river and valleys below. The salt from the sea flavored the frigid air, and I inhaled deeply. *Home.*

"I've noticed," Berron murmured. "Many have." For this eternally cold kingdom, who knew what the consequences might be if the season shifted after thousands of years.

"I've brought Beldine with me."

"You carry it with you. For now, it is you."

Allureldin, the Moon Kingdom, had always been my home. It always would be.

But I could live without a place, and though I'd thought differently and fought it at every available opportunity, I couldn't be without him.

"I know," I finally conceded. "I need to go back."

My friend took my hand and held it without words until the moon had climbed high above the castle.

TWENTY-THREE

Zadicus

HER LIPS ON HIS, HIS OPENING HERS, HANDS TOUCHING *her...*
I drank some more from the goblet and slammed it down on the table.

It was instinctual, ingrained, and archaic—this need to destroy something that'd laid hands on what hadn't belonged to him.

But he wasn't here, and so I was left to rot and wither with a hatred that had no outlet. A hatred that kept jamming up my every thought and true desire.

A hatred that kept me from what I needed most.

I'd always known my queen, my perfect fucking storm, would cut me open and leave me to bleed out. What I never expected was to be forced to stomach it as though it was forgivable all because she'd said so.

Because it was all part of yet another dark plan of hers. A plan that could've very well wound up with her being killed.

I'd had no plan, no way out of the mess Ryle had pulled us into, other than taking each harrowing night as it came. I'd had nothing except a past that wanted me dead and a future continuously threatened.

I did nothing.

"You should have seen his face," Moyra said, a female warrior in the queen's guard. "Purple and blue, the fates damned idiot."

I didn't care but offered a brief smile before draining what remained of my wine. She'd helped herself to a seat beside me in the throne room, halfway down the table. The seat at the head of the table empty.

Wanting to drink and ensure no trouble broke out in Audra's absence, I didn't have the heart, or enough fucks to give, to move nor tell Moyra to go away. Rarely did anyone sit near me unless they wanted to discuss politics while skirting the subject of my missing queen.

Moyra leaned closer, her berry and sweat-misted scent clouding me. "As he lay there, blood dripping from his butchered nose, I told him that just because I'm a warrior does not mean he gets to treat me as though I'm not a lady."

Her words had begun to slur. I nodded, looking down into my empty goblet. "I daresay he'll give you no more trouble."

"He asked me to dinner," she said then, evoking a shocked laugh from me. "Yep," she said, drinking her ale and thumping it down onto the table. "And I said yes."

Darkness be damned. I didn't know whether to laugh or groan.

"The queen." A pixie ran in, his dark blue hair sailing behind him. "The queen has arrived."

A moment later, there was a boom high above, hard enough to shake the walls of the throne room, a roar thundering through every open space.

No one moved, and then they all did at once, rushing to tidy up some of the mess upon the long tables and the floor, and returning to their stations.

Kash entered, saw me, and crossed the room. "You coming?"

In answer, I poured myself some more wine and sat back in my seat.

He glowered and turned on his heel, heading to the stairs outside. No doubt to show Audra where to park her beast.

She'd flown here. I shook my head, then sipped. Of course, she had. At least it was safer than coming via boat, even if other creatures in the sky might make a dive for her and Van before realizing who she was.

My eyes closed at the thought, and I downed more wine, forgetting Moyra was there until she said, "She's your mate."

I cupped the goblet between my palms, staring down into it once more. "We linked, yes."

"Same fucking thing," she said, then remembered who she was talking to, "my prince."

"She is my mate," I said, the ache within my chest overpowering the wine's numbing effect.

"I'm confused." Moyra swiped the back of her hand across her mouth. "Why not go and greet her, then?"

The doors at the back of the room opened, and I could scent her, could hear the racing beat of her heart before she neared my line of vision. "It would appear I'm too slow," I drawled.

Moyra gaped at the queen, who was storming our way.

Over the rim of my goblet, I eyed every inch of her. Her midnight dark hair, tugged back into two braids, gave every asshole in the room full view of the art that was her face. Sapphire eyes, lit with winter's rage, leveled on me and then my unwanted companion.

Looking back at me with pinched red lips, Audra slid her hands over the black velvet of her gown, the matching cloak still flecked with tiny specks of snow. "You look comfortable."

I refrained from snorting. "Someone had to do the job you ran away from." I swirled my wine, gazing up at her beneath my lashes. "You left this court, almost the entire realm, in a state of confusion and panic."

Moyra jumped to her feet, belatedly bowing. "Welcome home, my queen."

Audra paid her no mind, her simmering eyes steadfast on me. "I need to speak with you."

I smirked at the formality but set the goblet down and rose from the chair, defiance and anger keeping my limbs from doing as they wished, keeping them from curling around her until all I could taste was her creamy lavender scent and all I could feel was her heart beating in tandem with mine.

"I'm afraid I'm busy," I said, nodding at both females. "Do excuse me."

I made haste to the exit before Audra could respond, Kash's disapproving stare causing my teeth to grind.

Painting was never my first love, but it was one I'd long left behind.

In fact, it'd been so long, I was afraid I wouldn't remember what to do. But I needed *something*.

I had to get it out. All of it. As much as I could. I feared I'd scream at the moon each night if I didn't find a way to release it.

After Audra had fled back to Rosinthe, I'd found myself roaming the halls, avoiding ghosts at every turn, trying to ignore the pain I could almost feel across an ocean, and discovered the set of stairs I'd forgotten about.

I'd climbed them, opening the door to a room filled with smears of paint, canvases both full and empty, and the enormous window with curtained vines.

The last time I'd set foot in this room was after my mother had died, and after pouring my rage and grief onto anything and everything that could be painted, I'd stormed out and never returned.

Darkness only knew where all those paintings were now—not that they'd have been any good.

Likely destroyed, I knew, as well as my other belongings that I'd failed to find while forced to stay and heal in my old chamber.

For the first few nights of Audra's absence, I'd lost myself among the starlight-splashed textures, the moon shrouding every brushstroke like a much-needed drug to numb the pain.

And then I'd found it. The picture my brother had shown me while I'd been caged like an animal in the dungeon. It'd been tucked against the wall behind two other half-finished paintings as though someone had seen it and thought it was best to hide it a little.

The canvas housing Audra's naked form.

Rage, unlike any I'd felt before, had the painting incinerated, the colors falling like ash onto the paint-smeared bed within seconds.

Had he had her there, too? I'd been so desperate to know, I'd tried to recapture the image that'd singed itself into my mind by painting it anew to search for clues.

And that was where she found me, staring at my re-creation once more, her heartbeat slowing and her breaths shaking behind me. "We were never on that bed," she said as though she'd seen the way my attention had been dragged to it before I'd known she'd been watching. "The chaise, but other than sitting together and a kiss before I pulled away and left, nothing happened."

My fists shook at my sides, the paintbrush falling to the floor.

Soft steps neared, the sound of her picking it up struggling to reach me while I gazed at the green chaise. "He fucked his lovers on the bed, and once or twice, he forced me to watch."

Fuck. "Audra."

"You need to know," she said. "I know you do because while it might hurt, it hurts less than wondering." Her voice grew stronger, steadier. "Your brother stained this land, almost beyond repair, and I refuse to allow him to do the same to us."

I swallowed, dipping the brush back into the paint pot.

"Your paintings. Upon the walls at the manor."

"Some," I said. "They're old." Taken with me from a life I longed to forget.

She guessed at what I didn't say, and if she was frustrated by my unwillingness to provide more, she didn't let it show. "You painted growing up. Did Ryle?"

"He tried," I said before I could help myself. "I had no idea he'd continued until I found my beloved's nakedness staring back at me through the bars of my cage when I returned." I stopped, remembering the smug look upon Ryle's wretched face. "He seemed rather proud of it, though I wasn't sure if it was the painting or the way he'd gotten you to undress for him."

"You knew," she said, a broken whisper. "Yet you made me tell you in my rooms." I said nothing, refused to, and she watched my every move, then sighed. "Zad, I did what I had to."

I let the silence stretch and my annoyance fade a little before responding. "Games. You two had that in common. Everything is but a game to be won."

"Zadicus," she started.

"It infuriated him to no end," I decided to go on. "That I held some skill with a brush and paints. A mortal talent for a mortal heart, he'd say."

"Your heart is anything but mortal, though it is far better than anything I've encountered before."

The brush stilled, as did my every thought.

"And I should think myself stupidly fortunate to call it mine."

My throat swelled, eyes closing briefly before I reopened them to paint the stars out the window in the hillside.

It grew so quiet, nothing but the sound of our hearts, our breaths, and the near-silent squelch of the brush meeting canvas. It took everything in me to keep my back to her and continue painting something I no longer gave a shit about.

She was right there. She was trying.

And I was stuck in purgatory, unsure how to fucking leave to take back everything I wanted.

"I should have told you," she finally said, so soft yet so sure. "I should have, but I was scared and hurt. Although the plan might not have worked if you were aware, if others were, I know I still should've talked to you, and I'm sorry. I'm sorry I let him touch me, and I'm sorry you thought the worst, and I'm sorry I thought I had to let you."

The brush skidded over the page, ruining it. I didn't care. Dropping it, I turned around.

Her eyes, wet and pleading, watched me, her hands twisting in her gown with her desperation and discomfort. I could scent it in the air charging through the windows, see it in the small pinching of her lips and in the corners of her eyes.

She hated this, having to do this, but she would do it. She would admit wrong for acts that had saved us all—for something she shouldn't have to apologize for—and she'd do it for me.

For she thought that was what I needed.

And I did, darkness strangle me, I fucking did. But I was being a bastard. In my self-loathing and disappointment, I'd wanted to blame her—wanted her to show me she wanted me as much as I wanted her. Even though I knew she did. Even though she was the one to keep a level head and see us out of certain disaster.

I'd known, and I'd always been grateful for all she felt for me but wouldn't readily show. That was, until we'd arrived here, and I'd lost my damned mind through fear and jealousy.

I couldn't talk, didn't know what to say, how to make her stop when my hungry heart wanted to hear more, all the while knowing I was torturing her.

"I cannot remain here," she rasped. "And I cannot go back. I will not be in any realm where I have no home." Stepping forward, she stopped before me and took my slackened hand in hers, a lone tear falling down her cheek while I lost myself in her eyes. "You are my home, Zadicus Allblood, so it is my turn to beg of you to stop locking me out."

Removing my hand from hers, I watched as dismay crept into her eyes, and then shock when I grasped her cheek within it, my thumb brushing away the wet. "You murder me while trying to save me, but you are blind, or else you'd know I'd sooner watch these"—I tugged at a wing, feathers spraying—"fucking things burn before losing you. I'd watch them turn to ash, and I'd do so with a smile and not an ounce of regret."

"Zadicus."

"Quiet." I searched those ice-cold, watery eyes. "You still don't get it, do you? I was dishonest, yes, but being honest can sometimes take time, Audra. Especially regarding something I've had to hide since before your father was even crowned king. I'll admit it took me longer than it should have, and for that, I am sorry. But to wound me purely because I hurt you?" A low laugh left me. "When all along, my only wish, my every desire was to keep you. My every decision and hidden truth an effort to do exactly that..." My head shook. "That is not love."

"You know it as well as I do, my stray prince." I could hear her heart scream, cooling her words. "Love is war, and if you strike, I strike back twice as hard."

I staggered back a step, her eyes drenching me with bright disbelief. "Then I surrender, and I must take my leave."

"Don't," she said, but I headed for the door. "Don't leave."

I heard her swallow. "I've never left because I desire to, but because it is always you who pushes."

"So push back," she croaked, stalling my steps, chasing away my next breath. "Fight."

But I didn't turn around. I couldn't. I'd fold like wet parchment, and I wanted to fold. I wanted to melt at her fucking feet, but nothing of the sort left my mouth. "I'm tired of fighting. Perhaps you can let me know when you are, too."

"I said I was sorry," she yelled, knowing many could likely hear but perhaps uncaring. I turned as she continued, "I'm sorry I touched him. I'm sorry for all I thought I must do and do alone, but know this, my lord," she whispered with a hiss, her eyes a burning blue, "I would do it over and over if it meant waking up next to you for the rest of my existence."

Blinking, unbreathing, I felt my lips part as everything inside me grew violently still.

Tears dampened her cheeks. I was such an insufferable, stubborn asshole. Darkness, what the fuck was I—

A horn blared, traveling into every window of the castle and stirring the brushes in their pots.

Audra's eyes widened as it stopped, then sounded again.

"Twice," she said, her brows furrowing as she tried to remember what Kash had likely informed her. What I should have informed her.

"The war horn." I took her by the hand, leading her from the room.

TWENTY-FOUR

Audra

WARRIORS AND FAERIES RACED EVERYWHERE, into one another, and toppled down the stairs, clearly unaccustomed to the idea of war.

Zad's hand in mine felt hot, tight, and oh, so perfect, but I had little time to adjust to the sensations before Nerro and Dace found us. "It's Este, my prince and queen," the warrior said, sounding out of breath. "She rides toward the castle."

"How many accompany her?" Zad asked.

"We cannot be sure with our scouts still returning, but she travels with her army."

I held back a curse, knowing I should've paid more mind to the Queen of the Silver Court's absence and lack of welcome.

Zad led us down the hall and up another flight of stairs that never seemed to end until we entered a circular chamber filled with armor and maps. We crossed the room to the arched doorway and stepped out onto the battlements that gave a view of the sweeping cliffs either side of the castle and the rushing river beneath.

"Quickly," Zad said, tugging me back inside the room before I could see what he'd checked and handing me a sword.

Briefly inspecting the worn yet fine metal, the leather pommel molding to my grip, I watched Zad select his own and then hand me a breastplate. "I have my own armor in my rooms." A gift from Elkin and his pack that I'd found waiting for me upon returning.

"We've no time," he said, walking over to strap the plate to my chest when I didn't move fast enough. "I have no idea what she wants, but that her army journeys with her means we're in deep shit."

"We will speak with her."

Zad released a dry huff, his smile grim as he tightened the straps and then reached for his sword. "We rarely seek to negotiate. If we bear arms with an army, we mean to either capture or kill." He met my eyes, his own hard and swirling with worry. "Usually both. Stay with me."

I didn't argue, knowing it was prudent I listen to him. Remembering who was more adept with faerie warfare, I followed him out the other door behind the stairs.

Zad stopped atop the battlement and looked down at the forked bridge as warriors converged over it and took up their stations along each side and the paths leading to it. Others ran farther, meeting with many who emerged from the trees.

And when I looked at the west toward the city, more wolves were running in groups, weapons bared, strapping on fighting gear, yelling and howling to one another.

"Where did they all come from?" I'd known the king had a considerable army, but I hadn't known the numbers nor what would happen when called upon. I'd thought most would live in the barracks of the castle or nearby.

"Their homes," Zad said before meeting with an archer some feet away.

The warrior he was talking with threw his eyes at me twice until Zad snapped, "She stays with me."

Warmth encompassed me, and I offered a smile. "You couldn't lock me away if you tried."

The wolf blinked, then nodded and looked at the horizon.

I did too, in time to see a furbane scream across it, a female on its back, her white-blond hair making her recognizable to nearly anyone.

Este.

"Down," Zad ordered, and I obeyed as an archer farther down the battlement was plucked from his station.

The furbane dropped him into the falls behind the castle, then did a loop with the queen on its back whistling to the army that'd invaded the valleys and forests, racing toward us with a speed I knew would have them arriving in minutes.

"Back," Zad said to me. "Stay low," he told the archers, who didn't seem to need telling at all, already crouching and on guard.

I reversed closer to the tower we'd just left, my sword still at my side but ready to swing if need be.

Some of the Silver Court arrived on horseback—mostly the Fae—and the others in wolf form. In blacks, silvers, grays, whites, and fawn, mixed and varying in size, the beasts closed in.

Many of our own warriors were still racing in from all sides, and I realized with not a small amount of alarm that they would just meet the enemy on time and fight until the death without any hesitation at all.

An enemy that should not be, for if I was right, and Kole had not returned to Este's bed, then the queen wanted one thing and one thing only.

A cure for her broken heart.

Impossible, yet I could relate. So I ran.

"Audra," Zad bellowed, his footsteps on the stairs behind me as I raced down, down, down, into the stomach of the keep a comfort but unnecessary. "Audra, stop."

"You stay here," I shot behind me. Snatching a helmet that'd been hanging from the spear of a chipped wolven statue, I dropped it upon my head as I turned the corner, then another, moonlight spraying over me as I pushed through warriors at the entrance.

Shocked murmurings and pleads came from behind me, generals and even their youngling warriors beseeching that I get back inside.

I didn't listen.

"Stop her!" Zad roared. "Fates be damned, fucking stop her."

They didn't listen.

I was their queen, and like it or not, I would do as I wished—even at the expense of my own life.

A violent growl sent shivers down my spine, and then Zad landed before me in the center of the bridge, hard enough to quake the stone and shake the dust.

He'd flown. I hadn't the time to absorb that, to marvel as I longed to. He glared. "Turn around."

"You turn around." The enormous expanse of those wings blocked my view. "Or at least move before you get us both killed."

He stared at me.

I stared back.

Finally, he grumbled something that sounded like, "Forever the death of me," and tucked his wings behind his back.

We turned right at the fork, and together we hurried to the end of the bridge, warriors at our backs, sides, and our fronts. They parted when we met them, but I knew we weren't moving fast enough before growling and screaming cleaved the air.

I grabbed Zad's hand. "You need to get her attention."

"I told you, we do not negotiate."

"Your brother did," I needlessly reminded him. "We can help her. We know what she wants."

A bloodcurdling howl cut across the river, pain-wracked with fury and despair.

"Zad," I urged. "We need to buy time. Distract her at the very least."

Knowing I was right, he clenched his jaw.

Then the queen plummeted toward us, and I was in his arms, airborne. My heart lurched and stopped, and we soared into a tree as the queen, atop her furbane, laughed and did a loop in the air before swooping upon a group of warriors near the bridge.

Zad turned, absorbing the impact with a crunch that had to have broken something.

We wobbled to the ground, and he winced, cursing as his

wings banked, giving us a softer landing than I'd anticipated. "You need to see the healer."

"I'll heal within the hour."

"We don't have an hour," I said, my eyes darting everywhere, searching for the sword I'd lost.

A warrior, seeming no older than I was, crouched down into the dirt, his teeth bared and his sword raised as the queen dipped again.

My eyes narrowed, fingers unfurling, and although it pained me to do it, I stole the air from the queen's furbane.

Screeching and stumbling, the creature narrowly missed the young warrior as it slammed into the ground and took out half the bridge with its wing. Warriors cursed and leaped. Some fell into the river while others tried to fish them out, the furbane in a heap on the bank.

The queen, sword in hand, jumped off and rounded the beast's side, taking in the damage—wholly unaware or perhaps not caring that more than twenty warriors had now surrounded her.

"Rinny," she cried, the beast twitching as I released my hold on its airways and walked over.

The queen sagged with relief when the furbane tried to get to its feet. Unblinking, I kept my eyes upon it, willing it to stay down.

"Remove your hold on my furbane, *queen*," Este sneered, leaping to her feet with a preternatural grace.

"We both know I won't be doing that." I inspected my nails, battle cries and growls clouding the air, the scent of blood and sweat and fear reminding me to hurry and put a damned stop to this. "Your wolf is not here, and we are not the answer," I said. "Go home."

"An order?" She tilted her head. "Cute, but I think I'll take what I came for first, if you don't mind."

Pursing my lips, I lowered my hand. "Well, I suppose it depends on what that might be."

"The king stole my heart, but being that he is no longer with us, I'll be taking my revenge out on you." Her eyes flicked to Zad, who moved from my back to my side.

"Este," Zad said, his voice soft, masking the danger lurking in his eyes and fluid steps. "Audra had nothing to do with Kole leaving you."

Este hissed at that, her eyes slitting and her features icing. "I've no reason to slay my High Queen," she said. "I'm here for *you*." She lunged before she'd finished talking, Zad's magic blocking hers just in time and right before his chest.

Half-hypnotized, I watched the invisible forces clash and push, and in doing so, I lost my concentration on the furbane, who rose to her feet with a deep wound in her side.

The queen pulled back abruptly and ran, but Zad was ready, gently throwing his defense into the dirt. A crater appeared, grass exploding and wind howling, as the queen struck again from atop her furbane, and they rose above us.

"Este!" someone shouted.

She ignored them, tossing an iron star at a nearing warrior. He bounded to the side, and it skimmed his arm, taking skin and flesh with it.

"Este!" More urgent this time, stealing her attention away from every threat that'd encircled her.

And there were too many.

An iron-crafted arrow struck her from behind, and the silver queen tumbled from her beast.

Zad ran and leaped into the air, and her furbane screeched, shaking the treetops. Warriors scattered as the creature roared and threw itself to the ground, right next to where Zad caught and laid her queen.

The young archer across the river paled, his bow slackening and falling to his side.

"No." Kole pushed his way through the gathered warriors, snarling when he reached Zad, who stepped back as Kole took Este from him.

Crouched over her with blood coating the hand he pressed to her cheek, he murmured words we shouldn't have been permitted to hear. Removing the helmet, I looked away.

Nobody moved for the longest time, and then I called, "Someone send for Alahn. Now."

With a mighty roar, Rinny flapped into the air, branches rustling and leaves flying, snarling down at anyone standing too close to her queen.

Everyone looked at me with questioning eyes, and I felt my chest clench with sorrow as I watched the mated couple cling to one another in the bloodstained dirt. "Clear out," I said, my voice a rasp. "Lay down your arms and clear out."

Zad studied me with those amber eyes for two breathless heartbeats, then cupped his hands around his mouth, and bellowed, "Fight no more and disperse, or be captured and dealt with accordingly."

The healer came rushing out from the castle's side entrance, confusion upon his face as he took in the fleeing warriors. Many waded past him back into the keep while others made sure the Silver Court headed back the way they came.

"The queen," I said, walking over to Alahn. "Help her."

Old eyes drank me in, and he nodded once. "As you wish, my queen."

Zad and I watched from the broken bridge as the queen's furbane refused to be led down from the skies where she kept guard of her rider, and the healer struggled to help the silver queen.

I nodded to Melron, who then joined some of the wolves standing by, awaiting news of Este, unwilling to leave without their queen. After a moment of talking with them, their faces hard and grave, they came forward and did their best to remove Kole so that the healer could do his work.

The queen's side was covered in blood, a wound deep enough to show a glimpse of her ribs refusing to close.

Zad stood at my side as we both watched and waited.

And as the sun began to rise, the healer finally rose too, and said, "I've staunched it as much as possible." But the queen had long ago lost consciousness, half her face planted in the grass, eyes closed while Kole begged her to wake up. "Now it is up to her."

Reluctantly, Kole stood and whistled three times, calling the furbane down. It landed some feet away from them, large dark eyes like reflective glass orbs as they beheld the mess that was its queen.

"The queen should not travel," the healer said. "The iron's poison could spread."

"She would be safe here," I said, meaning it. "I would personally guard her."

"What?" Kole barked with a harsh laugh, brows low over simmering eyes. "Why?" Brushing his hand across his cheek and into his golden hair, he covered himself in smears of blood. "She brought war to your door."

Unsure how to say it, that I understood and would have done the same as his injured mate, I shifted and just stared at him.

Frowning deeper, Kole looked from me to Zad, then to Este. "She needs her people and her land."

Zad walked away then and gently collected the queen who'd tried to murder him as Kole climbed onto her beast and held out his arms.

With Este situated as best she could be, one of his hands around her and the other in the creature's feathered mane, Kole looked at Zad and nodded once before clicking his tongue.

Soon they were nothing but specks in the slow to color sky, and all that remained was a stain on the grass.

TWENTY-FIVE

Audra

WE LOST THREE WARRIORS DURING THE SHORT BATTLE led by Este.

"Quite fortunate," said Kash over breakfast the following evening, as though three people—two shifters and a faerie archer—dying wasn't so bad.

He hadn't noticed the rising of my brows, too busy stuffing curled bread into a little bowl of butter and into his mouth while he reached for some tea.

Zad was nowhere to be seen, supposedly out visiting some wounded wolves in the city and villages.

"How many wounded?" I'd asked. Unsure if I could stomach the raisin-loaded oatmeal before me, I merely dragged my spoon through it.

"We cannot be sure until Zad returns, as many of them shifted to heal. We're expecting quite a few."

The silence that'd followed had my teeth grinding together. "I don't know why I couldn't have gone with him."

"He did not ask?"

"More like he did not wait until I was even awake," I'd muttered. I'd checked his room after waking and found no sign of him, his scent faded in the halls. I'd arrived for breakfast, and Melron had informed me that he and Dace had left.

Shaking off the annoyance, I steered Van back over the river, my heels digging into his sides. We glided lower, and I inspected every leafy fern, arrow-pocked tree, and even the water for anyone who might've been left behind.

I knew I needn't have bothered and many Fae were unaccustomed to such things as collecting and mourning their dead, but I couldn't shake the habit of responsibility.

Finding nothing save for the odd weapon and a bloodied rock and tree, we flew back toward the keep, and I returned Van to his stall. He wasn't fond of his neighbors, and I couldn't say the wild things were fond of him, often scenting the air as though he were something far too foreign to belong here.

I wondered how many creatures thought the same of me and if I should care if they did.

It mattered not, so I would not.

The swishing of grass behind me entered my ears like a warm song, Temika's footsteps slowing as she met me outside the stables. "Where have you been?" Collecting herself, she added, "My queen."

"Vanamar needed company," I said, gazing back into the dark to find his eyes upon me. Smiling, I turned away and swept across the ankle-deep grass, marching uphill toward the castle.

The breeze carried a salty mist from the violent river at our side, and I inhaled deeply, wondering how I'd fallen for a land as murderous as many of its occupants. Perhaps the odd energy that warmed my cool blood, the unavoidable pull toward the forest and the skies and all its many creatures, made it so I couldn't fight it.

I wasn't sure what else this land would have me do for it or what capabilities it might bestow on me. Kash said it differed from ruler to ruler, and that over time, we would see what the fates wanted from me.

I didn't mind waiting when I was still allowing myself to grow used to all I'd already been gifted. The sight, the hearing, the musical notes and messages carried to me upon the wind—nearly every evening, I woke hearing, tasting, or scenting something new. As though I'd always had the knowledge tucked somewhere deep inside me, lying dormant, I knew what it was without needing to ask.

Uncertain if I'd have the same lifespan as the Fae, who'd been known to live for thousands of years, I couldn't be sure how long this reign of mine might last, nor what I could accomplish during it. But I was grateful I seemed to tire less easily, so I'd be sure to make the most of it.

"The ball," Temika said as she caught up with me, bobbing at my side.

"I haven't forgotten."

To rid the tension of Este's... visit, Temika and Kash had agreed upon a ball to celebrate the return of a High Queen and the lands' health.

It'd been four nights since Este and her army had left and taken to the hills and seas, and so I doubted she'd return so soon—if at all. Other than a message from her court delivering news that she lives and that Kole had not left her bedside, we knew nothing else.

"I have readied your gown," Temika informed me as we crossed the repaired bridge. "It awaits you in your rooms."

"Thank you," I said, unable to forget how the faeries loathed lack of manners, even after Ryle's demise. We waded through the foyer to the stairs. "What of the..."

Zad and some warriors fell into the doorway of the keep, laughing as they removed their fighting leathers and weapons, sweat droplets spraying.

Temika eyed them disapprovingly. "Ahem."

They all stilled then bowed, Zad's eyes finding mine for breath-catching seconds as he at last lowered. "Excuse us, my queen," Melron said. "We had an unexpected, uh... altercation with a bord just beyond the falls."

A brow rose, and I tilted my head. "Unexpected?"

Melron pursed his lips, Nerro thumping his back from behind and jostling him forward. "W-we went hunting."

Temika rolled her eyes, muttering, "Males."

"Hunting," I said, looking at Zad for clarification. He offered nothing but cool indifference, every feature honed into utter stillness. "Zadicus, I trust you're not killing endangered species for sport."

"They're pests," a warrior spoke up with a hint of outrage. "They ruin crops and fencing, and some have even killed villagers and townsfolk."

Zadicus continued to stare, and growing uncomfortable, I was about to look away when, finally, he nodded once.

"My queen, please," Temika said, moving for me with fluttering fingers. "We are running out of time to prepare you."

Reluctantly, I climbed the steps, Zad's gaze melting into my spine.

"The fates have truly blessed you." Temika stood back, eyeing my glimmering charcoal gown. Stepping forward, she fussed with the flowing skirts, the moon bouncing off the silk to reflect in her deep green eyes.

The bodice was made entirely from rose petals, their magic binds humming against my skin as they melded to my breasts and hips with every breath. "How will I get out of it?"

Temika giggled, tilting her head as she rose. "You merely take it off."

I frowned but followed her to the door, the breeze dancing through the windows to rustle my curled hair, throwing half of it back over my shoulder.

The queens had arrived within the hour it took me to ready myself, the moon now a full heavy light above the castle. Howls intermingled with the whine of birds and laughter floating up the stairs from the ballroom on the second floor.

Temika had been exuberant with glee when I'd requested we hold tonight's gathering inside the large, dust-laden room rather than the throne room. "Oh, it will be so pleased to be of use again."

And I'd have raised my brows, thinking it absurd that a room had feelings, if I now didn't know better. For they did, and the throne room had seen enough of this land and its occupants in the many years gone by. Its sagging weight could be felt like an old gnarled tree, pressing into my skin each time I visited.

"It's tired," Kash had explained to me over breakfast, watching me study the warrior lined walls, the dull light bouncing from their armor absorbed by the mosaic floors. "Too much bloodshed will do that to anyone."

After staring up through the exposed ceiling, I'd felt it almost sigh in response when I asked, "What of the ballroom?"

Said room was aglow with bone-hewn chandeliers dripping candlelight over the occupants of the gigantic space. Chairs, wooden and curved and sprayed in a silvery gray that sparkled, sat between four large rose-choked columns and in the corners of the room.

Queen Mortaine sat perched on one, her plum hair gathered into an intricately braided crown and her vine-wrapped gown slithering over her skin as she laughed at one of her courtiers.

"It is the full moon," Kash said, handing me a goblet of wine from a passing pixie's tray.

The male's blue lips tilted, and he bowed as we walked deeper into the room. It was unlike the welcome I'd receive during a function back in the Moon Kingdom—patrons remaining seated and in conversation, only some bowing and curtseying when they saw me arrive.

I found I liked the lack of fuss more than I'd ever thought I would.

"Some of the warriors are incapable of fighting the shift," Kash explained. "So they are—"

"Absent," I finished for him and stopped by the wall to take in one of the recently dusted paintings of the countryside—little huts and cottages sprinkled amongst rolling hills, dotted with wheat and spider-shaped trees. Inside the trees, if you peered closely, little orbs of light could be seen floating in the windows of homes high in the branches.

"Indeed. Some of the young ones"—Kash sipped his wine, dark eyes skirting the room when I turned to him—"they've yet to learn how to fight the impulse."

"I don't care."

He looked at me with his eyes narrowing. "Ryle would have one of their limbs if they failed to show to an important event. Full moon or no, they belong to this court."

"Why?" I asked, thinking they ought to loathe royalty rather than serve them.

"Why?" Kash repeated, brows now drawn tight.

Glancing across the room, I withheld a groan at the sight of my cousin, Adran, dancing and smirking down at a female wolf I recognized. He'd likely tricked the staff into letting him out of his room once more.

"It is how it has always been since any one of us can remember. Their fealty to the courts spans thousands of generations." His voice lowered, a note of warning within. "To try to change that would not please them. It would only offend them."

I pondered why that could be and thought maybe with the dangers of lupine genetics, they had need for structure, order, and something to defend and fight for.

To think of them without that…

A knowing look from Kash, and I half rolled my eyes. "Exactly," he said.

I brushed a hand down the petals over my stomach, knowing it wouldn't quell the trembling there as I felt Zadicus enter the ballroom. "You stated yourself that some cannot control it." Kash sighed, but I went on with a pointed look at him. "So you agree such punishments need to at least be less… gruesome."

Dace arrived, walking over to greet us with a bow. "Queen, everyone is now here. May we lock the doors?"

"Leave them open," I said, and Dace blinked but nodded and turned back to let the guards downstairs know.

The crowds parted, but my eyes were already fixed upon where he stood. And though I could sense his awareness of my attention, Zadicus didn't turn from the werewolves he was conversing with.

"Cousin," Adran called, smiling so hard I hardly recognized him. Perhaps he was heavily intoxicated. Either way, he was not himself. "This is Moyra, and we are in love!"

The female just laughed and dragged him out the doors, where they stumbled into one another in the hall, and then began to kiss.

We watched them go. "We were supposed to punish him." I exhaled roughly. "Again."

Kash snorted. "He'll find enough of that on his own."

True, I thought. Over the rim of my goblet, I watched Zad adjust the sleeves of his long black jacket, the magnificent arch of his wings visible yet still above his shoulders. The silver threading on his white ruffled tunic caught the light and threw it into the group of creatures that wandered over to him.

Our eyes met, locked for unblinking seconds that made my hands slacken, my heartbeat slowing so I could try to hear his. I couldn't, the reverberations and echoes throughout the castle mingling too loudly with the thud of my heart.

Long lashes dipped, and he looked away, stepping into the waiting group with a well-practiced smile.

"Darkness squash me," Kash muttered into his drink. "You two irritate the fuck out of me."

I smirked as he meandered over to Mortaine, who greeted him with a sultry, crimson smile. Before I could cross the room to the male who insisted on torturing me, a birdsong trill hit my ears.

"High Queen," the silken voice sang, and Queen Hydrah rounded me with a tight-lipped smile. Her white wings drew my eye, sheer in the middle and thickening into matching white feathers as they climbed up into sharp peaks. She noticed me staring. "Marvelous, aren't they? Indeed, it does not seem fair that not all of us in power are blessed with them."

I gave her my own tight smile in response. "Thank you for attending."

"But of course," she crooned, a long thread of tightly woven black hair falling forward to cover a dark eye. She seemed content to let it be as she took a step closer, her scent of berry-stained soil splashing over me. "I wonder if the land might grace you with another blessing." Her thick lashes bobbed as she assessed me. "The sensations during playtime"—her voice lowered suggestively—"unparalleled, if you know what I mean."

My teeth appeared as my smile broadened. "I'm sure," I said, locking that information away for later. "Though I'm quite fine without a pair of my own."

"You have wrangled one of the winged beasts, I suppose," the queen said, eyes never leaving me as she sipped from her tankard. "Just like Este, that troublesome traitor." Though her words were filled with venom, her eyes shone with mischief. "Not to mention, a winged prince. So you've likely little need of your own."

"I hear Queen Este heals," I offered.

"She should be dead." She laughed coldly. "I adore her, truly, I do." Sighing, she drained her tankard and dropped it behind her on the floor, where a passing warrior almost tripped over it. "But I was most aggrieved to hear about the stunt she pulled." Hydrah tutted. "Storming the heart of this land as though she had the right."

The wolf shot a dark look our way before realizing who we were, then wisely picked up the tankard and kept moving.

I knew false concern when I heard it, yet I forced my expression into cool neutrality. "It would seem she was blinded by love."

Hydrah rolled her eyes. "There's a reason our kind does not love like those in the mortal realms, why we sometimes kill our mates rather than suffer the indignity and horror of losing our hearts and minds." Licking her lips, she said, "Survival, my dear queen."

I could not argue with that and felt eyes burning upon me from the center of the room. "It is most understandable indeed." I finished my wine and turned to place the goblet on a chair at my back, hoping the queen would have floated away while doing so.

She had not. "I hope you'll visit us in the Bronze Court, my queen. There is so much I'd love to show you."

Her invite translated clearly into the threat it was; *you'd better visit us in the Bronze Court, and soon.*

"I find I am still trying to adjust to the Onyx Court, but as soon as I feel I am able, I would love nothing more," I purred, meaning it, for the glimpse I'd had of their land in the sky, as well as the rest of Beldine, had me itching to see what else laid waiting for me to explore.

With a pleased smile, Hydrah curtsied and turned away, swallowed by dancers as the violins and flutes gathered into a fast-paced tempo most could not ignore—especially Ryle's human ex-lovers who'd chosen to stay.

They were free to remain in their quarters and assist the castle staff or head into the city and find new lodgings, but they'd been warned that to misbehave or get themselves in danger would find them facing the same consequences every other creature was dealt—death. Either from their own mistakes or lack of knowledge, or from the warriors tasked with protecting the city streets, castle, and countryside.

I ignored the ancient crawling sensation that insisted on lulling me into movement, unable to shake the phantom sickness, that insidious terror from the time I was compelled to dance until my heart almost gave out. Looking at where I could still feel that burning gaze, my eyes connected with Zad's, Dace and members from other courts surrounding him.

As if he could tell, and he likely could, why I would not dance, he walked over.

Panic and relief and longing flooded me, my hands unsure what to do, curling and uncurling at my sides as I smiled.

Queen Mortaine took his arm, her laughing eyes directed at him as she said something that made him turn to her.

With a hollowing chest, I made my way to the doors before anyone else could stop me for more awkward conversation.

I'd almost reached the portrait of a long-ago High King at the end of the hall when I felt him at my back and spun around. He didn't stop. Zad took my hand in his, and we continued around the corner until we came upon two open doors.

We entered the second. The drapes were half-drawn, and a single feathered mattress sat upon a slim frame against the circular window.

"It's been days," I needlessly said. "I refuse to do this anymore. So if you've—"

"I know."

"You know?" I almost snapped, glancing up at his sharp profile. His hair was tied in its usual fashion at his nape, allowing shadows to float over the crooked ridge of his nose and those exposed curved ears. "Then why have you been avoiding me? We cannot keep dancing in circles..."

"I've been busy," he said, toneless as he closed the door behind him.

"Busy?" I climbed atop a rickety desk, the only other item of furniture in the small room, and watched the moonlight trace his every step as he slowly crossed the moss green rug.

"You could've died."

Stunned by the sharp words, I blinked. "I didn't."

"What if you had, *Audra?*" he growled, and I flinched. Voice softening, he repeated, "But what if you fucking had? You would've just left me, and without so much as warning me..."

I swallowed, more understanding dawning, then whispered, "I shouldn't have... I'm sorry."

Silence closed in, and slowly, his eyes roamed me as if checking I was actually here. I recognized the gleam in his burnished eyes before they darted to his boots, and he cleared his throat. "I'm ashamed."

Shocked again, my lips parted. I tried to hide it with a snide remark. "Well, this might just be a first."

He glared, and I smiled, but he went on, his eyes upon mine

beneath lowered brows. "I've been trying to figure out how to do this, being that I've gone and done exactly what you did to me."

I waited, frowning as I watched his high cheeks shift in torment, a hand tunneling into his hair with enough force to remove strands from the leather tie.

"I struck back," he finally said, low and swift. "I've failed you. I nearly failed this entire realm, but even though I shouldn't, I care more about all the ways I've let you down."

"Zadicus," I started, ready to reprimand him.

His raised hand stopped me, eyes dipping all over me, pinched at the corners. "I couldn't figure out how to apologize, how to make amends for not only that but also for my behavior. I... being here, Audra." He released a rough exhale. "It brings out that side of me, and I know that's not an excuse, but it's true, and you..."

At the sight of the sorrow in those gold eyes, I was certain my heart had paused.

"You are my heart, Audra. You carry mine. You carry it, and you wield the power to destroy it, and I've never feared anything as much as our time here has made me fear losing you. You could've died multiple fucking times, and I didn't know," he said, voice dropping to a low growl. "I just don't know what to do with something that formidable. It's—"

"Paralyzing," I ended for him, and his lips curled slightly.

A rough laugh hit the cooling air, his head shaking. "Melron, the other wolves, they dragged me on a hunt for they were sick of seeing me pace the halls and the gardens, muttering and attempting to conjure avenues that might hopefully lead me past all that has happened and back to you."

"I hate that you could not just come to me and say whatever you feel."

Zad's lips slid between his teeth. He released them, his eyes gentling on mine. "You deserve more than a fleeting handful of strung-together words. You deserve more than me—"

"Don't you dare even—"

"But." He cut me off with a feral grin that restarted my heart with a jolt. "You will have no one but me for as long as I shall live."

"And beyond that," I heard myself whisper.

Finally, within one breath and the next, he came to me, his hands parting my legs to fit himself between. "Forgive me," he rasped, forehead falling to mine, hands gliding up my bare arms to cup my face. "Forgive me, for I knew better, and I vow to do and be better."

"If you'll forgive me," I countered, absorbing his scent with my next inhale, sighing as it cooled some of the desperate heat inside me.

"Always," he said, our noses brushing. "I will always forgive you because there is nothing else, not for me, but also because you are a queen, and you acted as such. You didn't need to apologize, but I love you, and I thank you for doing what I so selfishly needed."

"Darkness," I breathed, gripping his rough cheek, tugging at my skirts with my free hand for my legs to bind around his waist. "I've missed you."

"I'm not done," he said, tone hard, but his eyes soft.

I waited for him to continue, biting back a smile.

"I was not only mad at you," he admitted. "I was furious with myself—for I knew—deep down, I *knew* what you would do. I knew you would outsmart anyone you had to and return home alive at any cost, and I was furious that I hadn't been able to give that to you. That instead, you did it yourself because I..." He blew out a warm breath, and my eyelashes fluttered as it met my mouth. "I couldn't keep up, couldn't keep my head and heart afloat, let alone on the same page with each new assault and fear. I failed you, and just know that has been almost unbearable, almost as unbearable as being without you."

My chest squeezed with empathy, with an understanding I hadn't fully grasped until now. The look in his eyes... I tipped up his chin, and declared, "You did nothing of the sort. And not once have I so much as thought that."

His shoulders and wings rose and fell with his next breath, and he nodded. His hand smoothed over mine on his face. "You might be of half-blood, but you are a true queen, Audra, the truest of them all. Beldine needs you, both continents need you, and I've been selfish in my quest to make you nothing but mine. I was wrong. I was a fool. I was drowning in love. And if you will have me, it would be an honor to stand by your side as you rule both realms as you are destined to."

"You are a fool," I whispered heatedly, "or else you'd have known my destiny has always been and will always be tied to you."

He cursed, hand delving into my hair as his mouth dove over mine, our lips fusing and parting with a ferocity that burned and renewed and would never be enough.

Zad pulled away, and I reached for him, needing more, but he wouldn't be coaxed. "And I..." He swallowed thickly. "I was rough with you"—he groaned when my tongue licked my teeth—"in your rooms. I was too rough. My words worse than poison. I'm sorry, so fucking sorry."

I nodded, holding his face to mine. "Don't be too sorry for that first part."

His eyes narrowed.

I grinned. "In fact, I think I might anger you some more just to bring that side of you out to play."

He raised a brow. "It has become quite clear that you enjoy sparring with me."

"More than I should." He smiled, but it waned, so I admitted, "but I like you like this more, and I need you, this you, so much more."

His lips parted, breath sailing out. "I do believe you might indeed love me after all."

"Until my dying breath and whatever comes after." My hold tightened, my lips grazing his. "You... you balance the scales. You make me better without robbing me of who I really am. And that is why my soul chose yours. That is why I let my heart do the same."

"Audra," he began, voice roughening when I reached between us to untuck his shirt. He cleared his throat, hands sliding up, fingers tight in my hair. "I don't deserve to, not yet—"

"You do. I liked it. I goaded you, and I should've said all this sooner, but even though you're the safest place I've found, the only place I want to be, you still terrify me."

He blinked. "I scare you?" I nodded, my lip taken by my teeth. He plucked it free with his thumb, a roguish grin setting fire to his eyes. "And what do you do when you're scared, my queen?"

I grinned in kind, then bit his thumb. "I fight."

He stared, then leaned forward to kiss me. "I'd ask you to stop, but I fear even if you did, it would never cease. This nagging need to make sure you're mine." A fluttering sigh fled me, and with his lips against mine, he purred, "You're the only place I want to be, too. No more visitors."

"Never," I promised, and our mouths joined in earnest, our hands tugging clothing out of the way so that our bodies could, too.

He swallowed every delighted breath, fingers sliding up my thighs to find me ready and desperate for him, and our tongues clashed with his throaty groan. "Starving, aren't you?"

"I'm about to fucking perish." I bit his lip and brought his hips forward with my legs. "Please."

That glint in his eyes and the matching smile almost had me combusting before his length found me. I watched his gaze darken with a hunger so base, so wicked that his every feature slackened and remolded into sharp determination as he slowly entered my body.

His nostrils flared. My head fell back. He caught it before it hit the wall, leaning forward to sink his teeth into my neck. I moaned.

He didn't suck but gently pierced the skin, his tongue lovingly lapping at the small punctures as he sank all the way inside me and cursed. "Never again," he insisted, rough against my skin, his grip cementing his vow. "Fight me, loathe me, curse my very existence, but never again will we go this long without each other."

"Never," I agreed when his head lifted, and his mouth found mine.

The slight tang of blood hit my tongue, and when I moaned once more, he snapped. His hips reared back before jutting forward with enough force to send the desk into the wall behind us, over and over.

I barely heard it, barely noticed anything outside of the firm hand in my hair, the other crushing the petals of my gown as he gripped my breast. I was shattering within what felt like a handful of erratic heartbeats. My thighs and body squeezed him as if I could wring out and absorb everything he made me feel to capture this burning euphoria forevermore.

"That's it," he urged, the rumble scraping down my throat with his husky laugh. "Show me just how much you've missed me."

My eyelids drooped, a sharp cry escaping. He clasped the back of my head, those feverish eyes never leaving mine as he continued to burn my body from the inside out.

Only when our lips met, shivers shaking my every limb, did he let go with a roar, his body stilling and jerking as his head tilted back to the root-strewn ceiling.

Still trembling, my fingers climbed to his throat, tracing each ridge, the light mist of sweat, the exposed Adam's apple, then rose to his lips when his head dropped. Melting eyes drank me in as even softer lips pressed against my fingers. "Mouth," he said, hoarse.

"So lazy," I teased, my chest still rising and falling in harsh bursts. "Come and get it."

Smirking like the predator he was, always had been, my stomach jumped as he leaned down and grasped my chin. With a gentleness that threatened to break me anew, he kissed me—long, caressing presses—and murmured, "My perfect storm."

Far sooner than I'd have liked, we left the room, and I asked, "What are you doing? Many more surfaces and beds await us."

"And I'd much rather find myself inside you on all of them." His hand tensed around mine, but he didn't slow his pace. "But we cannot ignore duty, the evening will soon be over, and we also cannot ignore the fact that you no longer wish to enjoy one of the finest gifts given to our kind."

"Meaning?" I said, though I already knew.

I just wanted him to hurry up and do what he did next as he swung me into the ballroom, then tugged me back into his chest in a flash, his smile crooked. "Music."

Breathless with joy, with everything that he was, I could only stare with my chest swelling to the point of pain.

The mischief left his eyes, his features softening as he murmured, "May I have this dance?"

In answer, I splayed my hands over his chest, and slowly, they crawled over his shoulders. His eyes shuttered as they brushed feathers and met behind his neck.

If there were eyes upon us, I didn't notice, unwilling to remove my own, my every sense, from the male holding me impossibly close to him. So close, I could see nothing but the tiny hairs drifting from his cheek to his throat, and when I turned my head, glossy black wings.

Carefully, I shifted to touch them, felt Zad flinch then shiver in response, and paused.

"Go ahead," he whispered, the delicious warmth of his lips and breath floating upon the side of my forehead.

Emboldened by the throaty purr vibrating inside his throat, I stroked the dense light-absorbing feathers and found them softer than I ever could've dreamed. "They're beautiful."

He hummed, arms squeezing me to him. "Not as beautiful as you."

I ignored the temptation to roll my eyes, smiling as feathers rustled, jolting when I reached lower and felt their stems. "You're welcome."

He huffed with silent laughter, then groaned. "Fine. Thank you."

"That wasn't so hard, was it?" I taunted, retracting my fingers and moving my head back to gaze up at him.

A raised brow greeted me, and then everything turned to shadows and muted sound and light as those giant wings unfolded and rose. They wrapped around me, cocooning us and drenching me in that intoxicating scent of his. "I'd forgotten how useful they can be," he murmured, leaning down when I leaned up for our lips to join.

Smiling against his mouth, I said, "I'm sure."

As he grinned, his eyes flashed. Teeth snapped at my bottom lip, stealing it before his tongue sought entry, and we held one another with such force that I barely felt my feet moving around the room.

Pulling away, Zad sighed. "Never, not once, did I think I'd return here."

"Would you prefer Rosinthe?"

He gave me a bland look. "Not unless it contains you."

I hummed. "At times, it will." My teeth sank into my lip when he nodded and smoothed his hand up my back, those impossibly soft feathers ghosting over my arms. With my heart thudding so hard that Zad studied me with narrowing eyes, I blurted before I lost the courage, "So you will marry me. For shadows cannot exist without the sun."

"Audra." He stilled, breath rushing from him, and we stopped moving. "You do not need—"

"I know. I want to. I want to be bound to you in every way possible." His eyes glistened, his wings drooping a little as my eyes did the same. "You are not my lord or my prince, but my king, always, and so I must make a husband out of you." My heart quivered but didn't beat as I failed to breathe, and whispered, "Please, do me the honor of making it official."

With a stillness that blistered, he searched my eyes as if trying to determine whether I was being sincere—that I truly wanted this.

Leaning into him, I held his gaze, hoping he could see and feel that I'd never wanted anything more.

"Okay," he finally rasped with a shaken smile, and I felt his happiness wash over me, over all of us, as butterflies sailed in through every window of the room, and clapping ensued. Stunned, I watched them fly above our heads in every color, dipping and swaying and leaving trails of glimmering dust in their wake.

Then my chin was tilted back down, and Zad's head lowered until his nose skimmed mine. His voice firmed, his wings dropped, exposing us for all to see. "Okay, my queen." Our lips sealed with our accepted fates, and as we clung to one another and the ballroom exploded with applause and merriment, they didn't dare part.

I was ready to ensure they never would again.

EPILOGUE

Though many things had changed for Raiden, Zadicus, myself, and many others, tradition would not.

Back in Rosinthe, Inkerbine, the annual celebration of peace and love, had arrived once more.

Gold and Silver ribbons fluttered from maypoles, the two villages either side of the large clearing empty, for most everyone in the land was in attendance. The light afternoon rain had covered the vendor carts, gowns and hair of every shade, and the darkening horizon in a glittering sheen.

Zadicus's wings shifted as we approached the back of the podium, nearing Raiden and his advisor, Patts.

As the High Queen of Beldine, Raiden could do nothing but be glad for a continued peace among us and both continents. Besides, with Eline and his babe at his side, it would appear any lingering resentment he'd felt from Ryle's deception and our annulment had faded.

Last Inkerbine, we announced a united continent. This Inkerbine, we were to stress that it would remain so, but no longer under the contract of marriage.

One meeting was mercifully all it'd taken, and it was my guess that with Eline being close to giving birth, Raiden had made it in haste—amenable while still remaining stubborn, but impatient to get the paperwork underway and return home.

"Tell me," Raiden drawled now, fire dancing in his palm as he lit a torch by his advisor that someone had missed. It vanished when his hand closed, and he swung a baneful smile at Zad. "How does one even fuck with those giant things upon their back?"

"In the air," I said coolly and tucked my arm within Zad's, "and at great... length."

The Sun Kingdom's king tightened his jaw as Zadicus brimmed with tension beside me.

I should've known he wouldn't be able to resist, and I bit my lips when he snarled, "How does one fuck with a face like that?"

"Ask your wife," Raiden said, his mouth loosening into a megawatt grin. "She knows exactly—"

Eline trudged over and smacked him in the arm. "Must you? You rotten pig."

Raiden cursed, turning to whisper sickening words into her ear before taking Rosemary, their babe, from her.

Zad was still trying and failing to hold back his laughter when Eline surprised us both and drew me into her arms.

It took a moment for me to hug her back, but I did. "She's beautiful."

"She gave me a glimpse of death and several stitches," Eline returned, standing back and grasping my arms. That feline smile of hers slipped into something warm and genuine. "Thank you."

I blinked, and Zad chuckled, pulling me close. "She means to say you're welcome, but her tongue is probably frozen to the roof of her mouth."

I made to shove him, but he predicted it and smacked a kiss atop my forehead as Eline adjusted her red gown and then stole her fussing daughter from Raiden.

We waited while Eline and Raiden moved beyond us into one of the tents to feed Rosemary, Patts muttering with Mintale about the squabbling farmers along the border who were up in arms about the new roads there being used for trade.

"In the air?" Zad murmured, Landen giving him a short nod as he rounded the trees. "You really thought he deserved to know that?"

He and Dace had checked the podium as well as the crowds for any unusual scents or creatures. One of the many things my time in Beldine had taught me was that nothing was ever as it seemed, and it paid to keep all senses open and accessible, especially while in a position of power.

Many had likely heard of my new title in a land across the Whispering Sea, and many were probably not pleased about it—to say the least.

They could feel and think whatever they desired. As long as I had what I wanted, everything I needed, I would endure whatever else came my way and give it no room to cause misery.

"He could very well guess at it, anyway. It was that or let him goad you into another annoying battle of snide and grunting remarks." Rechecking my near black gown with its daring, twisting corset of thorns, I said, "No, thank you."

"*He's* annoying," Zad said, stiffening as the king and his consort, Eline, left the tent and waded back over. "Like an insect that cannot be squashed."

"Oh, stop it." Wrapping my hand around his, we headed for the stairs and up onto the podium.

A round of applause greeted us, faces and colors and scents blurring into one another from the tips of our noses to the trees on either side of us, and all the way into the slow-rolling valley.

"Welcome to Inkerbine," I greeted before Raiden could beat me to it. Waiting for the crowds to settle somewhat, I hovered over the megaphone before continuing, "Though a lot has changed since we last gathered here, some things have not." Zad's hand was a steady weight at the small of my back. "Inkerbine has been and always will be a celebration of peace, love, and unity, and together, King Raiden and myself will ensure that as a whole, this continent will adhere to those principles and more all year round."

More applause sounded as I took a step back and into Zad's side, allowing Raiden to move forward to the megaphone. He plucked at his cloak, waiting, then said in a playful tone, "You might have heard we have a faerie queen in our midst."

Save for some shifting, absolute silence rippled at that, and

Raiden chuckled. "Fear not, for she has surely saved every single one of your souls from more bloodshed and inconceivable loss by ridding our neighboring continent of their corrupt ruler." He cleared his throat, and Eline's lips pulled into a small smile when Raiden gestured for me to join them. "Come forward, Audra."

Reluctantly, Zad's hand slowly released me, but I grabbed it and brought him toward the megaphone with me.

Raiden grinned. "Seeing as she failed to properly introduce herself, it is my great honor to present to you your queen of the Moon Kingdom and the new High Queen of Beldine." Belatedly, he tacked on with much less zeal and volume, "And her husband, the Moon Kingdom's new king and the High King of Beldine, Zadicus."

I could've both killed and hugged him.

"Power," Raiden mused, almost as if to himself. The audience grew quiet at that word, crickets and the sizzling of meat upon vendor carts the only sounds. "For so many years, we've grown to fear, admire, respect, loathe, or covet it. I was one who coveted it, and I must admit, a part of me still longs for it even though I was born with more than anyone would need."

Zad's form turned rock solid against me, his hand banding tight at my hip.

"I know," Raiden said, that mischievous lilt to his words. "Greed is a battle so many of us have fought. Some have lost themselves to it, and I'm relieved to say that although I was almost one of them, I indeed found a way to win against it. How?" He hummed in mock thought, then stated with a severity that shocked even me, "Well, I've learned there are some things power and greed cannot grant us, for the most precious jewels are often found in the aftermath of unnecessary bloodshed and in necessary change. In times of peace and heightened love."

Our audience, our people, roared with approval.

Raiden waited for the clapping to die down before looking at his wife. Eline moved closer to take his hand, Rosemary letting out a shriek of irritation.

Taking the babe from her arms, I tucked her close as her chubby hands reached for my hair and tugged. "I think you're right, king." I smiled at the babe, her huge green eyes, and whispered, "Perhaps your father isn't always stupid, is he?"

Eline coughed to hide a laugh as Raiden swung his narrowed gaze our way, his lips pinched.

"What?" I laughed too as Rosemary blew spit bubbles and grabbed at my lips.

Looking from her to me, Raiden shook his head. "Nothing."

And there we stood—former enemies, lovers, heartbreakers—to face the occupants of this realm and portray a unified front. One that, even if not the norm, felt right and so much more genuine this time.

A true merging.

"And, of course, I saved the best for last." Raiden returned to the megaphone and lifted Eline's hand into the air. "Allow me to introduce my oldest and greatest love, my new wife, the Sun Kingdom's new queen, Eline."

I looked down at the babe in my arms when her eyes widened from the revelry, willing her to remain calm, letting her know all was okay.

All was just as it should be.

"Welcome to Inkerbine," Eline called into the megaphone when Raiden moved to light the torches on either side of the stage. "Eat, drink, dance, and celebrate your neighbors—welcome your new friends and your brighter futures."

Silver and gold sparks flew toward the sky. Cheering shook the earth beneath the podium we stood upon, and Rosemary squawked and threw her arms out to Zad, who gaped at her, some people on the grass below us laughing.

Smirking, I passed her over and watched as he held her tiny body in his huge arms against his chest, her long lashes beating as she gazed up at him.

Zad's puzzled expression soon melted into gentle affection,

and when he looked at me with a heat in his eyes that spelled trouble, I shot him a glare and directed him and Raiden's spawn down the steps.

TEN SUMMERS LATER

"Who hit you?" I said, ready to throw them in the dungeon or string them up in the market square.

Pane giggled, uncaring that my tone hinted at someone meeting their end. At seven summers of age, he was already so much like his father that he never did. "Hali."

With the hem of her nightgown between her teeth, Halina paused, the nightgown falling as she shrank to her knees on her bed. "I'm sorry, Mama, but he deserved it." Her voice stayed firm, her eyes blue fire as she acted worried when we both knew she was not. "Truly, he did."

Sighing, I kissed Pane's forehead and tugged his bedding up to his chin. Then I rose and placed my hands before me, holding them and my daughter's gaze as I waded over to her bed.

"Reason?" I demanded.

"He said I was as ugly as a pile of soiled snow."

I refrained from rolling my eyes and shot a bland look at Pane over my shoulder. He'd wisely turned on his side, feigning sleep.

"So I did what you told me to do and stood up for myself."

"You hit him," I said. "With what?"

"With my hairbrush." Our eyes stayed locked as I waited. "Twice."

I waited some more.

"And I might have kicked him where the wind doesn't blow."

Darkness murder me or bring me wine.

"You do remember what I told you, do you not?" I arched an eyebrow. She might have only been four summers old, but she was more intelligent than anyone besides her father and I gave her credit for. With the exception of Mintale, who was notorious for stealing both younglings away to help him with *special castle duties* that always turned into tea parties, magic shows, and sparring matches with wooden swords.

"Because despite what your brother says, you are beautiful, but you are also smart." With her russet-colored hair and those eyes, she was bound to give us and many a creature a world of heartache. I gave her a look that had her eyes bulging. "I expect you to remember that."

"Yes, Mama," she mumbled. "Then I shall only hit him once next time."

I blinked. "You will come to your father or me before doing any such thing."

"But you said..."

"That you should defend yourself? Most certainly, and with anyone else, you should." Grumbling, I muttered, "Funny that you can remember that."

"Huh?"

"*Excuse* me, *pardon* me," I said, exasperated, then lowered to sit on her bed and tug her nightgown free of her teeth once more. "Hali, words, someone else's opinion of you, only matter if you let them, remember that."

"So," she said, scrunching up her little nose as she grabbed my hand to toy with the onyx ring her father had slid onto my finger during our private ceremony over ten summers ago. "I *can* hurt people as long as they're not Pane?"

"If necessary, then of course."

Zad cursed from the doorway, and I heard him shift.

"How much?"

I gestured for her to lie down and stood. "It depends on what they do, I suppose."

Zad coughed. "I think that's enough for tonight."

Biting back a laugh, I couldn't kill my smile as he finally

entered the room. "You can quit avoiding the responsibility of disciplining your offspring now." I patted his chest. "Crisis solved."

"Thank the fates," Zad drawled with mock relief, and his spawn giggled, not seeing the way he reached down to quickly pinch my ass before moving to their beds.

"Come now, it's time for rest."

Hali ducked under his wing as soon as he lowered to her bed, pulling it out and over herself.

"Darkness," Zad said with feigned confusion. "Wherever did she go?"

Pane laughed. "Don't act silly when we know you're not, Papa. We are too old."

"Papa will always be silly," Hali said, popping her head between Zad's arm and his side, then giggling when he caught her.

Zad pulled her onto his lap, and his smile sobered. "Sleep time, little princess."

She sighed, slinging her arms around his neck. "Kiss first."

He gave her three, then rolled her onto the bed where he gave her another before tucking her in. "No more hitting."

"But Mama says—"

Zad must have worn a look that silenced her, then turned to Pane.

He crossed to our son's bed and crouched down beside it, sweeping his fingers across his forehead, shifting dark brown hair from his amber eyes. "Are you sorry?"

Pane nodded. "I told her so after the first time she blood—" He swallowed at the rising of Zad's brows. "After she whacked me."

Zad stared at him for a moment. "You said so to stop her from retaliating, but did you mean it?"

"Not then," he admitted. "But she already knows she's not ugly."

Hali harrumphed. Zad shushed her and finished talking quietly with Pane.

"Papa," Hali yawned when Zad pressed a kiss to Pane's head

before rising to his full, shadow scattering height. "When do we go back home? Temika promised she'd have some log cakes."

Home.

We spent more time in Beldine than in the Moon Kingdom, though we did try to make sure we were in both places long enough to see to every matter that needed our attention before leaving.

I knew it would be tedious, some weeks busier than any we'd had before, but I'd never expected to love it. To enjoy dividing my time between the two places I'd come to love.

Zadicus had handed over the running of his estate to Emmiline, but we made sure to spend a few nights there each time we returned to Rosinthe.

"No, she promised me," Pane said, his little gray wings rustling the blankets.

"Did not," Hali snapped, who had no wings of her own—for which I was thankful. Darkness only knew what trouble she'd have found herself in otherwise.

"Enough," I said in an iced tone, and they both stilled. "Sleep, or I shall force you to watch me eat every piece of cake when we return while you eat nothing but vegetables."

Zad snorted, placing books back on their shelves and blowing out the few lit candles.

Both younglings, mercifully, promised they'd behave as Zad bid them both good night.

Their nursemaid, a friend of Berron's, nodded to us out in the hall before he entered their room to watch over them.

Unnecessary, most probably, but with temperaments that saw them both squabbling more than they got along, and fledgling abilities making themselves known when their tempers got heated, I thought it best to take every precaution possible.

Not to mention the fact that running two kingdoms meant I needed some damned sleep. And time to unwind with my husband beforehand if I should be so lucky.

Tonight, it seemed, I would be, as Zad pushed me into the

wall around the corner and pressed his mouth over mine. "You're going to turn our daughter into a spitfire."

"Darling," I purred, dragging my lips over his jaw to nip the lobe of his arched ear, "I hate to disappoint you, but a spitfire she already is."

His hands squeezed my hips, roaming up to cup my breasts. "She could never disappoint me."

I sought his lips, and he gave them to me. "She's just like me." Only, she'd been blessed with a loving, doting father. Not a cruel, unfeeling monster who would scare her into compliance like my own had with me.

Zad laughed. "This fact is not lost on anyone who has met her, and that"—he framed my face in his large, calloused hands—"is precisely why she could never be anything other than perfect."

Releasing a sharp breath, I climbed him, and he caught me with an ease that spoke of many summers, many winters, many springs, many triumphs and downfalls—all of them together.

For there had been many an unexpected conflict with he and I, and within our two colliding worlds, but we never gave in to any of it.

We took a breath, we took our time, and we figured it out.

Wading up the stairs and down the hall to our rooms, he didn't remove his mouth from mine, the doors opening silently and closing just the same.

He stripped me of my robe, and I tugged at his tunic until he tore it off, kicking his boots and pants aside as quick as lightning.

Upon the bed, he crawled over me, his fingers brushing over my legs. They parted more and more, the higher his touch climbed. He bypassed my mound to land on the faintest of scars from where our second child had been cut from my womb after perishing mere weeks before she was due.

A ritual of his I didn't dare take from him. Instead, I quit breathing, as I always did, when his mouth lowered for his lips to worship the mark that soon wouldn't be visible.

I hadn't yet decided if I wanted it to leave, but I did know it didn't matter—that he would forever know where it had been, and I would, too.

All our lives, we were taught to expect the death of a babe at some point, and therefore not to mourn what shouldn't have been.

I couldn't and didn't accept that, and it'd taken years for the pain to lessen. Even after Halina had arrived screaming and darkness-bent on turning everyone's worlds upside down, and years later, it still scorched me anew to think of the what-ifs.

And so I'd said I wouldn't do it again. I'd vowed not to after losing our first daughter, and Zad, though I knew he'd rather we try again, had only wished me happiness and agreed.

Then we'd discovered I was expecting once more.

We'd fought, oh, how I'd screamed, begging him to tell me why he'd do such a thing when he'd known I could not bear it again. He'd insisted he hadn't meant to, hadn't known he'd spilled himself inside me intending to create life.

I'd believed him. He could not lie, after all, but even so, we'd walked on eggshells for months until Halina arrived, and for months after as we waited to see if she'd thrive or weaken.

She'd thrived all right.

In his grief, Zad had unknowingly impregnated me—the longing for what we could not get back, could not have, unable to be suppressed.

It no longer mattered. What mattered was that we'd survived and that we'd learned through every jagged, breaking piece of our hearts that we could go on to survive anything.

When his teeth grazed my nipple, I purred, my back arching and my hands reaching for the satin skin of his arms, feeling the bulging muscle beneath as he leaned over me to give me his mouth.

He could read my intention, yet he didn't protest when I pushed at his chest and rolled to his back. With his wings kissing the nightstands, my work of art, my heart and soul, my demise and my future, laid his worshipping hands upon my hips, and awaited my next move.

I rose onto my knees, ready to impale myself on the twitching member beneath me, when a gleam lit those eyes, and I was lifted into the air.

My hands smacked against the wood of the headboard, my eyelids fluttering as my knees came to rest either side of his head and his eager tongue met my center.

A deep-throated groan accompanied the next swipe, and I mewled, desperate for more but shivering from the slow torture. Back and forth, he licked and sucked, his grip on my hips growing firmer as I came closer to erupting.

Then with a sudden swiftness that made my nails score into the wood, he flicked me apart, and I came with a silent scream. I was still unraveling when he lifted me down his body and slid me onto his waiting cock.

Shaking, I fell forward, and his fingers brushed the hair from my face before he tipped my chin to watch me with hooded eyes.

The fire crackled, the candles in the sconces guttering as a harsh wind shook the glass of the windows.

"I love you," I declared to his chest and kissed his sweltering skin.

"Every time you say those words, it still feels like the first time." Grabbing the back of my head, he said with silken roughness, "I'll never tire of hearing them, nor take them for granted."

I swallowed, knowing he spoke the truth. "Then you are as wise as you are handsome."

He grinned, a creature of immense strength holding back as I rose and began to rock over him. "You say them more as each summer passes." His nostrils widened when his eyes darted to where we'd joined, then back to mine. "Have you noticed?"

Stilling my hips, I held back a moan, feeling so deliciously full as I breathed into the crisp yet charged air between us, "You've changed me in ways I'm still getting to know, but"—my teeth scraped over my bottom lip—"my sneaky, heart-stealing king..." I heard his breathing slow as I said gently, "I find I do not mind."

He sat up, sinking impossibly deeper inside me, so much of him pressing on every place I needed him that it stole my breath and quickened my heartbeat.

That wicked smile grew, and he smoothed my hair over my shoulders, wings tucking around us. His hand came to lay over my breast, over the thundering beat of my heart, and I swore it expanded, trying to reach his palm. "Because you're mine."

Total darkness encompassed us, soft feathers rubbing at my shoulders and arms. It was my favorite type of darkness, where nothing but us existed. The heady scent of him was everywhere, inescapable, and his eyes so bright I couldn't look away.

My nail met his chin, lifting it for my nose to skim his. "For all eternity."

With our breaths colliding, his hand drifting to roam up my back and into my hair, he whispered my favorite vow, "Eternally my queen."

Want to be the first to know about new fantasy and contemporary romance books?

Make sure you've signed up for Ella's newsletter and follow on Instagram!

www.instagram.com/ellafieldsauthor

Enjoy The Stray Prince? You might also enjoy Bloodstained Beauty...

Fresh out of college and headed straight for my dream job, I didn't think things could get any better.
Then I met my dream man.

In an instant, my happy ever after had begun.
The life I'd stumbled into was beautiful, and the man I loved was perfect.
But perfection comes at a cost,
and I'd slumbered through all the alarms.

Then I met my nightmare.
The man whose bright eyes held untamed darkness.
The man who disarmed me with his peculiar behavior.
The man whose cold, merciless hands shook me awake.
In an instant, questions started to dismantle my happy ever after.

But whoever said the truth would set you free was wrong.
It wasn't going to repair the cracks in my naive heart.
It wasn't going to caress my face with comforting hands and reassure me it was all just a dream.
No, the truth shoved me down a rabbit hole, and I landed in the lair of a real-life monster.

STAY IN TOUCH!

Facebook page
facebook.com/authorellafields

Website
www.ellafields.net

ALSO BY ELLA FIELDS

STANDALONES:

Bloodstained Beauty
Serenading Heartbreak
Frayed Silk
Cyanide
Corrode
Evil Love
A King So Cold

MAGNOLIA COVE:

Kiss and Break Up
Forever and Never
Hearts and Thorns

GRAY SPRINGS UNIVERSITY:

Suddenly Forbidden
Bittersweet Always
Pretty Venom

Printed in Great Britain
by Amazon